Sign up for our newsletter to hear
about new and upcoming releases.

www.ylva-publishing.com

The
LIGHT
of the
WORLD

A NOVEL

ELLEN SIMPSON

For Ann and Harriet
Grandmothers, extraordinaire.

Acknowledgements

Back when I first wrote this story in November of 2013, I never intended to publish it. I was too afraid of having written something so original and so big by my standards. So I'd like to thank everyone who encouraged me and was interested in reading the story as it went through its many permutations: Fran, Elissa, Angela, Chloé, Deb, and most especially, Alex.

Also, to the comment crowd: You are my second, third, and fourth pair of eyes, catching me in my contradictions. Thank you for all your feedback.

I'd like to thank my editor, Gill McKnight, and the folks who wrote in all the lovely feedback on snippets of the story that I uploaded to my blog. Special thanks go to the whole Ylva creative team as well, for asking me along on this journey and waiting until I was ready to say yes.

I'd like to thank my family for understanding when I didn't call for weeks at a time. They were the ones who listened to my fears and hopes and dreams about this story.

And for Kody: I couldn't have done it without you.

Prologue

A BANGING ABOVE HER HEAD WOKE Wren from her fitful sleep. She sat up, heart hammering in her chest. Her head tilted low, chin tucked in tight, as she ducked under the exposed joist above. Her breath came in short, shallow gasps.

They'd found her.

Wren rolled away from the cast iron hinges of the trapdoor overhead. She gathered herself and her blanket into a small ball as far away from the sound as she could. Blood pounded in her ears. Above, the ruckus continued. Wren wrapped her arms around her knees and tried to steady her breathing. There was no time, and no escape. She had to hope they would not find this place or else it would all have been for naught.

The crawl space was lit by narrow streams of light from the kitchen above. They cut through the gloom and riddled it with patches of bright yellow. Wren inhaled and exhaled slowly, forcing herself to stay calm. The rough wood of the wall dug into her back and the pain kept her grounded.

There were seekers at the door. Seekers that must not find her. Wren clutched her heavy pendant to her chest and wove her fingers around the points of the red-orange gem. It was warm to the touch, warmer than it should have been given her interrupted sleep. She let the sharp points dig into her palm because the pain focused her terrified mind.

It was the only comfort Wren dared allow herself. The warmth of the gem was enough to steady even the most frayed of nerves. It was all she had to keep her safe, and it would keep her safe on faith alone.

She forced herself to be as still as death. The weight of the entire world pressed down upon her. She felt it through the thin blanket she'd wrapped around herself. She pulled the blanket over her head even though she knew it would be no use. She was as far away from the trapdoor above as she could possibly get. It didn't matter. If the seekers thought to look into the space—if they found the door—the pendant would do little to protect her. She couldn't get out of this crawl space.

If she kept breathing, it would be all right. The seekers would not find her and belief would keep her safe. She had to believe that salvation would come. The words of the prayer were on her lips and she exhaled a long, slow breath. If she said the words, the men above would sense the power. If she spoke at all, they'd hear her. They would catch scent of her fear and come running, looking to gut her for the key she guarded.

It would be no use, but she whispered the words of prayer like a soul desperate for salvation. They felt stiff and uncomfortable on her lips. The pendant was the only thing that would keep her safe now.

The floor above creaked ominously.

She should have known better than to trust the kind-faced woman who'd ushered her into the cellar. Her smile had been so concerned, eating up her story about a steady with a temper. Wren had fibbed, said he was looking for her and she needed a place to hide. The woman had left Wren with a threadbare blanket, a cup of soup, and a kind word. Yet she had sold Wren out just the same as everyone else.

One glimpse of the Light of the World and all the goodness in her was gone.

Muffled voices filtered down through the floor. Wren peeked out from underneath the blanket. Small clouds of dust puffed out of the cracks where light shone through from the kitchen above. Wren had picked this house because they had seemed like her type of people: good Irish folk. They should not have been able to recognize her burden for what it was.

"Looking for this here girl," the voice above said. It was crass and uneducated, which made Wren let out a quiet sigh of relief. Maybe they would be too dumb to think to check for a hidden door. Her fingers shook as she clung to the pendant. She'd be good, she swore to herself, she would not allow herself another dalliance. She would stay hidden and safe, and the secret would remain unknown.

There was more scraping and Wren tensed. They'd found the door. The pendant cut into her skin as she felt her palm grow wet. She did not move. She did not react. She stayed perfectly still. Her lips pressed into a thin line as she let the gem dig deeper into her flesh.

"As I told ye," growled the woman who'd been so kind to Wren earlier. The trapdoor was yanked open and the cellar flooded with light. Wren's breath ceased altogether. "There's nothin' down that cellar save some ol' sacks an' some potatoes, 'onestly."

"Still gotta check, Missus," the gruff-voiced man who had spoken before replied. He peered down into the emptiness, blinking owlishly. His eyes met Wren's though the loose knit of the blanket, and she renewed her desperate plea for protection.

The light of the world must be kept safe at any cost. Even if it meant her own life. She learned that mantra before she learned her own name. This was her purpose, her life. There was no other. If this was where it ended, where she died, so be it.

Protect me... Wren prayed. Her hand was shaking as she gripped the pendant. *Protect this place.*

"What'd I tell ya?" Wren's host demanded. Their voices were so loud.

The man sat back on his knees, one hand still resting on the trapdoor. Wren didn't know how he'd found it. It was so carefully hidden beneath a rug and a good layer of dirt that she'd missed it herself, the first time. "I don't..." He stared hard at Wren's still form and the blanket that covered her from head to toe. "I coulda sworn I 'eard somethin'."

Her host stepped forward and pushed the man's hand away from the trapdoor. It fell back into place with a clatter and a shower of dust. Wren felt as though she was choking on the clogging air. She let out the breath she'd been holding in a long, slow sigh. The light of the world had saved her. It had protected her and hidden her from those who sought to snuff out the light.

The man's footsteps above faded away. Wren lay there, ears straining, listening for any possible sound. Would he come back? The question brought with it another swell of anxiety. She had to get to the safe haven. There she could become someone else. They wouldn't know her name, or what she'd done to get away from them. There would be no evidence of the life she'd destroyed to escape the clutches of those who sought her out. The Light of the World had to be protected. It was her duty as a guardian never to allow it or herself to become compromised again.

Her heart ached as she sat in the darkness underneath the kind woman's kitchen. She hated what she'd had to do to keep herself safe. It wasn't fair to anyone, most of all to *her*.

4

There was no fixing it now. The deed was done and the letter left in their secret place where it would be found eventually—and maybe, one day, Wren would be forgiven.

Curling into herself, Wren fought back tears of relief and regret. They had not found her. The Light of the World had kept her safe. She hated it, hated the task and the duty that came with it. She hated that she had to leave it all behind. Everything she'd worked for, everything she'd *built*. She'd shattered *everything* into a million pieces, too preoccupied with duty and her obligation to care about the crumbling life she left behind. There was nothing she could do to change her fate.

Tears started to roll down her cheeks. Wren let out a dry, wretched sob. She had a long way to go before she'd be safe again, and a broken heart to carry.

Part One

Flashlights under Manhattan

Chapter 1

The Girl at the Funeral

MRS. MARY OGLESBY KESSLER'S FUNERAL was a well-attended affair, despite the woman's less than charming personality during her life. Neighbors and relatives filed into the outdoor venue behind the funeral home, standing underneath wide tents for shelter from the bright summer sunlight. They tugged at their ties and pulled off somber sweaters and suit jackets to show shirtsleeves, dressing down in a way that Mrs. Kessler would have glared at disapprovingly, had she been able to.

In life, her son and nephew lamented to the gathered masses, she was not always the easiest person to know. She'd survived two world wars and the Great Depression, they said. She'd lived far longer than any of her peers, dying only after one hundred and five long years on this Earth. She was off to join her husband Harry, gone these last thirty-five years. Maybe now, the minister mused in his brief eulogy, she'd finally be happy.

Sitting at the rear of the tent in an uncomfortable folding chair that dug painfully into her lower back, Eva Kessler crossed her arms across her chest. With every passing moment, she was increasingly aware of the scowl deepening on her face. Her annoyance grew with every comment by the minister that dismissed her grandmother's staunch denouncement of the existence of a higher power. Her grandmother had not been like that at all. She was a woman whose views of the world were so deeply founded in realism that she would have been hopping mad at this tribute to her memory.

The worst part of this ordeal was that Eva was the only person who seemed to care that her grandmother would not have approved of any of this. The entire event barely seemed to be about her grandmother at all. Rather, it was about people attempting to make themselves feel better for the fact that Mrs. Kessler was one hundred and five when she died and rarely had visitors other than Eva and occasionally Eva's parents.

Eva tugged at the sleeves of her uncomfortable black dress that she'd pulled from the back of her closet that morning, hoping by all that was holy that it wasn't part of a Halloween costume she'd bought before she'd dropped out of school. It was cut low enough to draw curious looks from her creepy second cousin Charlie and a scowl from his entirely-too-provocatively-dressed for a funeral date, despite her attempt to cover up with a cardigan. The drawback was that the funeral was outdoors under a canvas tent and it was close to eighty-five degrees in the shade. She was hot and uncomfortable as she listened to people who obviously didn't know Mary Kessler as anything other than a passing name in their Rolodexes talk about her as if she were the light of their lives, and it was making Eva crankier by the minute.

Tucking a stray lock of wispy brown hair behind her ear, Eva glanced back to see her mother standing next to her father with a comforting hand on his shoulder. He wasn't taking this well and had retreated outside to cry unseen. Feeling guilty, Eva looked away. His emotional devastation over his mother's death was jarring. She'd seen him like this only once before, and that was when she'd come to in a hospital room, her wrist stitched up and her family all around her. At least her grandmother was there on that day, but now they were all alone, heartbroken and grief-stricken.

Eva's heart broke all over again on hearing the wet, miserable sobs coming from her father.

Death was supposed to come; Eva had grown up knowing that. Now her father had a second void in his heart to match the one where his father had once been. Even though her grandfather had died long before Eva was born, Eva had always suspected that her grandmother had carried the same sort of wound, and that was what made her so hard and difficult at times.

Mary Kessler hadn't been an easy woman to love. She'd been caustic and cruel. She had a tongue that could peel paint with a sharp word, and a temper that was easy to heat and slow to cool. Eva had only truly come to know her when she was still attending classes in the city and would spend her afternoons crammed onto a corner of her grandmother's sofa, sipping lemonade and studying.

"Why you bother reading those books is beyond me," her grandmother groused when Eva pulled out a textbook she'd been assigned. She was up to her eyeballs in post–Civil War politics and the growth of the New York City political machine. "It's not like I'm a primary source or anything…"

"Grandma, you're ancient," Eva joked. "But I doubt you're that old."

Her grandmother picked up the crossword, muttering about ungrateful children, and all the sacrifices of her youth, and being far too old to handle such sass. Eva rolled her eyes and went back to studying.

All that had changed on that dark day two years ago. Eva had lost her control then, lost herself in her spiraling thoughts. The whirlpools and eddies had drawn her under until she'd swum so far down she'd forgotten how to surface. "You're a coward, trying to bow out before your time," her grandmother told her as she leaned over Eva's hospital bed. "Only an idiot tries to run away from their problems like that."

Eva's stomach ached with guilt and her mind buzzed with all the drugs they'd made her take. She bit back words that weren't suitable to say in front of an old woman. She bit back two decades of unhappiness that she'd never been able to feed into anything other than her own despair. She bit back accusations of her grandmother's struggle with the same thought patterns and repetitive spirals of misery. She buried everything behind a slow, forced smile. "I know."

The corners of Eva's eyes stung in the heat of the mid-morning sun. She dabbed at them gently with the sleeve of her cardigan. How much longer could she sit here and listen to people talk about the woman they felt obligated to mourn? Finally, the service itself was showing signs of wrapping up. Soon, they'd go off by themselves to the cemetery and it would truly be over. At least they'd gotten the wake out of the way already. Eva was sure that now it, too, would annoy her.

Slipping silently from her chair, Eva took off her cardigan and tied it around her waist as she headed past her parents toward the funeral home. Her fingers brushed against her dad's arm as she passed and he flashed her a watery smile from behind his fogged glasses before turning his attention back to the minister's closing remarks.

She crunched her way up to the funeral home's back door and pulled it open with a great deal of effort. She was assaulted with a welcome blast of frigid air inside the small lobby.

Eva pushed open the door to the bathroom, grateful that all the stalls were empty. She stared at her reflection in the mirror. She looked sweaty and uncomfortable, and her mascara had run. Bending forward, Eva flipped on the water. Her silver bracelets jangled loudly over the tinny sound of mournful music that played from some hidden speaker.

She trailed her fingers through the lukewarm stream, getting them wet enough to dab at her mascara without messing up the rest of her makeup. Her hair frizzed out of the French braid she'd pulled it into that morning and now framed her head like a wispy halo. Eva wet her fingers again and tried to smooth it flat, tucking the errant strands under bobby pins and back into the braid that was coiled around her head.

"Brown hair is a sign that you're meant for more than your looks. I would know," her grandmother told her when she was fifteen. Eva had complained when puberty changed her hair from being perfectly straight to the wavy monstrosity that she spent too much time trying to tame. "If you'd been blonde," her grandmother continued, "I would have worried about your morals."

"But Gran, you can't just say that blondes have bad morals!" Eva protested. She had been raised not to judge and her grandmother was constantly used as a model of what not to be. Her grandmother carried a great burden of loss. Her husband and brothers were dead, and she had only one son and one granddaughter. Her family line was ending with Eva. There were times, when Eva was at her lowest, that she caught herself thinking of how Mary had carried on despite everything. She never spoke of her losses, unabashed and unafraid to carry on despite them. It was only through others that Eva had learned about them at all.

"Well, in my experience, they do," her grandmother huffed in response.

Eva had never asked her what exactly she'd meant by that. Instead, she'd gone back to whatever she'd been doing before her grandmother's comment had thrown her for a loop.

Now Eva found herself taking in the scattering of freckles over her nose peeking through the makeup that she'd already sweat through. Under the harsh, industrial lights of the bathroom, Eva could see the lighter streaks in her hair from a summer spent out of doors wandering the streets of the city. It looked strange, almost out of place, as if she'd put the highlights in purposefully in an attempt to be someone else, or as if she were masking the truth of herself behind a socially acceptable veneer.

Eva puffed out her cheeks and scowled into the mirror. She looked like hell, she decided, poking at her cheeks and blinking her green eyes furiously to try to clear them before the tears came again.

She could not handle the people out there who had scarcely known her grandmother. They only pretended that they had. They weren't the type of people who would understand the woman who had sat Eva down after she had to drop out of college and demanded to know what she wanted to do with her life. Eva had been very careful never to tell her grandmother about her struggles to find a job worth doing with no degree, but her grandmother had seen it anyway. "You need to try harder," Mary insisted when they were alone. "The world isn't all misery and heartbreak."

"It feels like it is," Eva replied.

The sound of running water in the sink calmed her. Eva stuck her hands under the stream, pushing the tap as cold as it would go. She shuddered as the water hit her wrists and began to cool her. The service would be over soon, and then they'd leave for the cemetery to bury the one person who'd ever really understood her.

Tears prickled at the corners of her eyes and Eva sniffed loudly. She shut off the water and resolved to avoid thinking of the loss. Her grandmother wouldn't have wanted that. And besides, it wasn't as though Eva didn't have other things to think about. Her creepy cousin had a new flavor of the week, which was intriguing and a little sad. Maybe she'd spend the rest of the reception reflecting on how he was able to get the hottest chicks around despite being a total weirdo.

Eva steeled herself. She could handle this, she knew that she could. She shook herself before turning away and heading back out into the oppressive late-summer heat.

The service was over and her father was talking to Eva's mother and her uncle Nate. He was technically her father's cousin, but she'd always called him uncle. He and her father had been raised like brothers. Eva slid quietly in beside them, hoping that her absence had gone unnoticed by anyone other than her parents.

"Eva!" Nate boomed in a voice that was far too loud for the somber affair. He was a large, round man who was the complete physical opposite of Eva's willowy, beanpole father. Eva took after her father, but with her mother's shorter stature. People liked to joke that she was a carbon copy of her grandmother, back in the day. "How are you holding up, sweetie?" Nate asked.

Eva shrugged, looking away to cover another swell of tears. "I'm a little mad that Mr. McKay made the jokes he did. Gran didn't believe in heaven or god. I understand that it makes people feel better, but I don't think Gran would've liked it very much."

Nate smiled sadly and nodded. "You're probably right." Eva's lips twitched upwards into a weak smile and he added in an undertone, "She'd have had a fit. Aunt Mary was an old battle axe, that's for sure. It's such a shame she's gone."

"It really is." Her head ached from crying for what felt like days now. The temperature wasn't helping much at all to quell the headache. It was all she could do to be here and be supportive of her father and the rest of her family. "I'm going to miss her."

Sometimes, Eva caught herself wondering if who she appeared to be in public was just a mask, like the one her grandmother had worn for years to cover her own misery and self-pity.

There were so many people at this funeral whom Eva didn't recognize. They were an odd bunch of mourners: old and young, a hodge-podge of people whose lives her grandmother had touched. There was the family connection, as expected, but also several little old ladies who must have known Mary in their youth. Then there were the young people who delivered her mail and her Meals on Wheels when Eva wasn't staying with her. In Eva's mind, these people had no place here. This was mourning for family, not for strangers.

She stood, making small talk with her cousins and the few people she did recognize. There were the ladies who lived downstairs from her grandmother's tiny apartment, the old guy she'd always stolen newspapers from, the guy who owned the corner grocery store since the '80s and had watched Eva grow up. Mr. Bertelli, if Eva remembered correctly. Mostly she just remembered him as "mustache" because he had one of the most impressive she'd ever seen.

"What are you doing with your life now?" Mr. Bertelli asked her as he scratched at his collar. His beard was already growing in and the morning was not half gone. Eva remembered being utterly fascinated by his mustache when she was a child. Now it just looked to her as if someone had shoved a black feather duster under his nose. "I heard you'd left school?"

It was the question Eva never had an answer for because she was doing nothing right now. She was sitting in her tiny shared apartment, dodging multiple roommates she didn't particularly like, and applying for jobs while watching the precious months that her student loans were in deferment tick away down to zero. Apparently, getting sick and spending months under watch was not enough to earn you a more lengthy deferment period on loans that hadn't even bought a complete college education.

"I'm still in the market, yeah." She looked anywhere but his face. Her cheeks burned with shame. "Haven't really found much at all."

"Mrs. Kessler said you were thinking about majoring in history before leaving." At Eva's nod, he continued, "It is not the best, is it?"

Eva shook her head. "No," she confessed. "Not without more school, it isn't."

He clapped her on the shoulder, "Well, should you ever need something to do, I am in need of help to mind the counter." The smile that he beamed down at Eva was wide and genuine, despite the somber occasion. "Think about it."

"I will, Mr. Bertelli," Eva promised. She felt uncomfortable with the offer, which would only set her up for days of increased subway fares and long, transfer-filled commutes. He wandered away and Eva watched him go. The humidity was rising and it made the very idea of moving around and being social horrible, especially when all she wanted to do was to sit and think about her grandmother. She fiddled with a tendril of hair that she still could not, for the life of her, get to stay in place.

From where she stood, Eva could see a woman who looked to be around her own age sitting in the corner. She was staring down at the program in her lap. The woman's fingers played with a pendant that hung around her neck, and a sense of melancholy came over Eva as she watched her. She broke her gaze away, not wanting to get caught staring at a stranger. A chill ran up her spine and her eyes flicked back to the young woman, who sat with her eyes downcast and a shy blush warming her cheeks. What was it about her? Eva didn't know her and could not guess how the woman might have known her grandmother. The older gentleman who sat down beside her and placed a comforting hand on her arm didn't seem to know the woman, either.

Eva's father's voice cut through the quiet lull of conversation and Eva turned her attention back to her own family. Her dad had his arm around her mom's shoulders and Uncle Nate stood beside him with his wife Lisa. Eva's nose wrinkled as Charlie sidled up beside Nate holding hands with the girl he'd brought with him.

Grief was a strange thing, Eva reasoned, picking her way through the sea of folding chairs over to the small cluster of her immediate family. She would never even consider bringing a date to a funeral. It just seemed tacky.

"Hey, Eva." Charlie leaned toward her as she drew level with the group. His date gave Eva a dirty look and Eva puffed out her cheeks, scowling at the girl's too-bright and too-short skirt. This wasn't a wedding, it was a funeral, and a little respect was expected. "Whatcha doin' all by yourself over there?" Charlie asked.

"I was talking to Mr. Bertelli," Eva answered. She felt testy, ready to snap at any moment. The heat inside this god-awful tent was making her sweat and she shifted uncomfortably from foot to foot. "He was a good friend of Gran's."

Charlie nodded. "He really was." Tilting his head back and staring up at the roof of the tent, he barreled on, "After Grandpa died, I always wondered if there wasn't something going on there…"

"Charlie!" Aunt Lisa admonished, grabbing his shoulder and spinning him around to face her. He was a good deal taller than his mother, but she had the scary you-done-messed-up-son tone down to perfection. He looked appropriately chastised as she pulled him away, and her voice dropped to low and dangerous tones that Eva couldn't make out over the din in the tent.

Eva flinched and cast a sympathetic glance over to his date. "He's a bit of an ass," she explained in an undertone. "Sorry."

"And you are?" the date asked, speaking for the first time. Her nasal voice was higher than Eva would have expected and unpleasant, too.

"Oh, Eva Kessler," She offered her hand and didn't particularly care that it was probably clammy to the touch. This girl's attitude completely deserved it. "Mary was my grandmother, and Charlie's my second cousin." She glanced over at Charlie's mother, who was still chewing him out for being an insensitive prick. She didn't envy him. "How do you know Charlie?"

"We met at school," the girl replied. She seemed a little bit encouraged that Eva and Charlie were related. "I'm Ainsley. Ainsley Carter."

"Nice to meet you." Her smile was tight with false politeness. She couldn't stand people who judged so quickly and came to the totally wrong conclusion. It wasn't fair to anyone, and this girl didn't belong here. Her grandmother would have hated her. She was very blonde, after all.

"I think we have to go soon," Eva's father said, and the gathered cluster of their family's attention turned to him, almost as one. The burial itself was supposed to be a small, family affair. Eva scratched at her upper arm and wondered if Ainsley would be included in the family since she'd come with Charlie. She hoped that she wouldn't. It didn't feel right for another of Charlie's flavors of the week to be included in such a personal moment. Eva didn't want her there.

She'd been wrong to hope, Eva realized, as they trooped to the car. Ainsley was following Charlie and the rest of his family with a strange expression on her face as she rested a hand in what was apparently supposed to be a comforting manner on Charlie's arm.

Eva glared at them both, but neither looked in her direction. Annoyed, she glanced over her shoulder one more time at the tent. The sun was now high in the sky and there was little cloud cover to protect the tent or its occupants from the harsh rays that beat down upon it. In the doorway, the girl Eva hadn't recognized stood staring out at the hearse from behind large black sunglasses. She had a dark green cloche hat pulled down low over her eyes, and her hair, from what Eva could see of it, was the color of straw in autumn.

"Who the hell is that?" Eva muttered. It was useless, though. No matter how hard Eva tried to place the girl, she could not recall ever meeting her. With a frustrated sigh, she turned away and deposited herself in the back seat of her father's rented sedan.

"Who, honey?" her mother asked, turning to look at Eva with concern.

"The girl in the doorway." She pointed.

Her mother stared at the woman for a long moment before shrugging. "No idea. Maybe she's a friend of Charlie's?"

Charlie was a handful of years older than Eva, and she always hated that he was presented as the shining star of the family when Eva was definitely the smarter of the two. But Charlie didn't suffer from the "family funk," as Uncle Nate put it. He wasn't touched by the family plague of sadness. Instead, he was the guy who had all of his shit together, so much so that it didn't stink at all. "I don't know," Eva said. She pushed it from her mind as her father clambered into the car and cranked the air conditioning to maximum. They pulled out of the cul-de-sac and she lost sight of the girl.

Mary Kessler's will bore very specific instructions about where she was to be buried. The cemetery had been selected and the plot had been bought and paid for before Eva was born. If the date on the sale contract attached to the will was accurate, the plot was paid for even before her father had shipped off to Vietnam some four decades ago.

They were on the quiet, rural end of Long Island, far outside the city that Mary had called home her whole life. Away from the bustle of New York that sprawled out onto its west end, this place was a sedate oasis awash in greenery.

Farms and wineries flew by the car windows, pulling Eva back into the hazy place between memory and dream. The world drifted and colors blurred together into a wash of blue skies and green orchards as leaves stretched like fingers toward the blank canvas of her mind. Eva lost herself in these moments, caught up in the plummeting feeling of being undeserving of all the beauty in the world. All her life Eva had run from the feeling, pushing it away and burying it deep inside. If she ignored it, it would go away, she reasoned.

It wouldn't. She'd learned that lesson the hard way—a razor sinking into her skin and blood. *Christ.* There'd been so much blood. Her grandmother always urged her to embrace the emotions she felt and to never shy away from the depth of her feelings. Eva couldn't do that. She couldn't lay herself bare for the whole world to see. She did not want to end up like Mary: a miserable shell of an old woman all alone in the world.

The car jerked forward as the suspension dipped. Eva's father let out a startled sound from the back of his throat, and turned the wheel sharply. "Sorry about that. Didn't see that—"

"Drop off?" Eva suggested mildly.

"More like a cliff," her mother groused. She reached over and touched his leg. "Be careful, dear, it's a rental."

21

"Yeah, yeah. That's why you buy insurance." Eva's father laughed. The sound echoed, harsh and biting. It was too gregarious and too falsely cheerful to be how he really felt. Eva was used to the putting on of airs just to get by. She understood it more intimately than her father's fake, guffawing laughter.

Eva turned to the window, her forehead bouncing against the warm glass as they headed down the dusty dirt road that led to the cemetery. The road felt, and looked, as if it belonged upstate rather than on the island. Eva wasn't used to being jostled around so much in cars. Beautiful splashes of green swam together against the tears still pricking at the corners of her eyes. She couldn't get this much green in her day-to-day life. Her tiny apartment and too many roommates were so far removed from it that she felt as though she had ventured to an alien landscape, far from the busy concrete jungle of the city.

Living away from her parents' home was her single act of self-assertion following everything that had happened. She didn't want to retreat to the safety of her parents' home, and her doctors had agreed. Eva needed structure and something to do that wasn't wallowing. She'd been trying for months now to find a job, but she had never graduated. There weren't a lot of jobs available for people like her.

The cemetery was off a connector road, nestled by the ruins of a farmhouse. The roof had partially collapsed, giving it the sunken look of a building that was eating itself alive. The car jostled over some train tracks and a plume of dust rose behind them. The house was obscured by the dust until all that was left was the memory. Eva's father turned the car toward a cluster of trees that grew up like a beacon beside the grassy fields that surrounded them.

"Must be aerating these this year." Her father spoke as if he knew anything about farming. "No idea why your grandmother wanted to be buried here of all places." He glanced at Eva's mother. "It's not like anyone's buried here, I don't think."

"Your dad's in Arlington, right?" her mother asked.

"Uh-huh. I know that their marriage wasn't the best, but to not want to be buried with Dad… I really don't understand why she wouldn't have wanted that."

Eva shifted a little in her seat and tilted her head back against the headrest. Why had her grandmother wanted to be buried in this anonymous cemetery in the middle of nowhere? It didn't make any sense.

"Maybe this is about before she met Grandpa, you know?" Her voice shook, just speaking the thought. She did not want to disrespect the dead. Her grandmother had so rarely talked about the time before she had children. It wasn't taboo, it was just never mentioned. When Eva had pressed, her grandmother had always just said that the light had gone out of her world and that she had no reason to carry on after that. She'd gotten married after the war because it was the thing to do.

Her father was quiet for a moment, his face set in profile and his jaw tight. His Adam's apple bobbed. Eva wondered what he was thinking. "Maybe when we get back to the apartment we can start to look for an explanation for that," he said. "I'm sure that there is one. Papers or the like." There was a resigned tone in his voice of a son who knew nothing of his mother's secrets. Eva's grandmother had kept them as well as Eva had kept her own.

"Really, Dan? You think that a woman as private as your mom is going to just have stuff lying around that would explain away all her deepest, darkest secrets?" Eva's mother gave a good-natured laugh.

"Well, she better have left something. The woman was a damn mystery."

23

Eva's mother pushed his arm playfully. "I thought we weren't supposed to speak ill of the dead."

"Yeah, Dad," Eva agreed. She enjoyed ribbing her father just as much as her mother did because he walked right into these sorts of situations with all the grace of a bumbling professor. "Gran'll come back and haunt your ass if you insult her on today of all days."

Laughing, Eva's father pulled the car into a grassed-over parking lot and set the car into park. "Don't I know it?" He smiled fondly at the two of them.

It was cooler here. The cemetery was old; the graves were marked with dates that went back more than one hundred years. Eva bent down and brushed dirt off a grave marked "Monroe." Her fingers dug at the moss that had grown into the R.

A bobwhite called in the distance. The mournful cry filled the cemetery. It echoed like a gunshot, and in that moment even the cicadas fell silent. The hair on the back of Eva's neck prickled as a stiff breeze whipped through the lush greenery around her. The bit of moss in her hand fell to the ground. The bobwhite called again.

"Why here?" Eva murmured. She straightened and fell into step beside Charlie and Ainsley. She glanced over and offered an unsympathetic smile as Ainsley's heels sank into the soft lawn.

The spot that her grandmother had picked out was under a tree and far to the back of the small cemetery. It stood in shadow, but the light hit it in such a way that there was one place that was bathed in light. Eva could see Mary's grave marker, flat and silent, illuminated as if under stage lighting. A pool of sunlight amidst the shade.

In her pocket was a Loonie from a trip Eva had taken to Montreal and Quebec City in middle school. Her grandmother had been far too old to chaperone, but she'd sent along all her coins from her own trip to Canada many years before, as well as a note that told Eva not to talk to any strange Canadian men or women. She insisted that they were after nothing but her virtue. Eva had been all of fourteen at the time and had found the note hilarious. She still had it, tucked into a journal she'd kept during high school. It promised a smile—always.

As the pastor said his final words and they said their goodbyes, Eva stood in that pool of light and turned the Loonie over and over in her hand. The Queen's face on one side, the loon on the other. A dollar, a ticket into the world of the dead.

As they left, Eva flipped the coin expertly into the small hole where the urn that held all that was left of her grandmother had been placed. It clattered against the blown glass before falling silent amidst the flowers and dirt.

She walked away, her head held high. She couldn't look at her aunt and uncle, or her stupid, insensitive cousin and his date. Her eyes stung as she looked out over the cemetery, and the bright green of the vegetation twisted into a blur of tears tinged with summer.

Chapter 2

Slow Drive

UNSHAVEN AND BLEARY-EYED, EVA'S FATHER clutched a cup of coffee to his chest. He stared blankly forward as if lost in thought, his fingers curling on Eva's mother's knee. "You know," he said, "sometimes I feel like I never really knew my mom."

Traffic was a snarl at this hour, and the hour-long drive back into New York was already stretching well into its second hour. Eva stared down at her own cup of gas station coffee and picked at the fraying hole in the knee of her jeans. It was cooler this morning; rain had rolled in overnight and with it had come a more comfortable temperature. It was sure to still be hot in the city, but Eva thought that anything would be better than the heat of yesterday.

"Why do you say that?" Eva asked. Her mother was glaring at the line of brake lights and stopped cars that filled the road ahead. Her expression was stormy in the rearview mirror, but she hadn't objected to the conversation. Usually traffic like this called for absolute silence. Eva's mom couldn't concentrate otherwise. "She was your mom, after all."

This was a regular conversation in Eva's family. Eva didn't anticipate that her dad's response was going to be any different than before. There were questions about her grandmother and her grandmother's life that no one could answer. She was a strange and enigmatic woman at the best of times, and grouchy and bitingly sarcastic for the rest. There was a sadness that she carried with her like a great albatross around her neck. She never answered Eva's questions about her past even though she had grown up during the Roaring Twenties and had survived the Great Depression and the Second World War.

"I don't really remember them," her grandmother confessed. It wasn't too long after they brought Eva back from the hospital. She was sitting next to her grandmother in her rickety old bed, hands cupped around a mug so large that it must originally have been intended for beer. Her grandmother had been sick for a week over what Eva had almost done. Eva was sleeping on the couch in her grandmother's living room to make sure that her condition didn't get any worse. "It's almost like there is this terrible cloud that had descended over my memories and turned them all to ash," her grandmother told her. "I remember the major events—the Crash, FDR, Hitler invading Poland, Pearl Harbor—but I could not tell you what I was doing during that time."

"Why?" Eva asked. She curled forward and leaned against her grandmother's thin body then, burrowing deeper under the blanket against the chill that had settled over the apartment. "Was your life really that boring?" She hated that she couldn't hide her skepticism. It was obvious to Eva's entire family that their matriarch had a great deal more than just a passing memory of such events. She chose not to recall them, or to deny her presence during them, and even as a young child, Eva had been determined to know *why*.

Her grandmother huffed, folded her arms across her frail, aged chest and looked insulted. "It was hardly boring, darling.

It's just that sometimes you forget things. Especially at my age." She looked away from Eva then, out the window where rain pounded against the glass. Her expression darkened. "Sometimes you want to forget the things you remember."

Eva had never mentioned that conversation to anyone, and she wasn't about to mention it now. It didn't have any bearing on the current conversation. She and her grandmother had been far closer than her grandmother had been to Eva's father or her nephews. There was a shared history between them and a shared understanding of the cast of demons that danced mercilessly in the shadows of Eva's dreams. Her grandmother had them too, Eva was sure of it. The knowing looks and comforting smiles made that very clear to her when she woke up sobbing in the middle of the night to find her grandmother sitting beside her bed.

She held her tongue, not wanting to voice her thoughts. Eva hated keeping secrets. She'd grown good at it over the course of her life, but she hated the deception and the little lies that had to be told to keep the secrets safe. Her grandmother's secrets were kept by the dead now. The only way to discover the truth was for them to be shared beyond the grave.

Her father's shoulders rose to his ears in an elaborate shrug. Eva turned away and rested her chin on the palm of her hand. Was keeping that conversation to herself really the right thing to do? Would it help him heal and move on? Was it worth it to betray the confidence she'd kept? She hated omitting details, which was no better than lying outright.

Is this the sort of lie you want to tell?

Outside the window, a long line of concrete noise shields were covered in creeping ivy. The effect was beautiful, a great hulking monument to modernization and the long fingers of suburban sprawl. A small, sad smile crept across Eva's lips.

Even the walls had secrets, covered in the lush, reclaiming force of Mother Nature.

"I don't know," her father said. His voice was so quiet that Eva could barely hear it over the rumble of the car. Her father was not a quiet man by nature. He was quick with a joke and always laughed easily. Now his voice sounded lost amid the road noise and the steady sound of Eva's breathing. "She was just so... I don't know, unhappy all the time. Sometimes she'd spend days staring off into space, and she'd talk about the light of the world as though it meant something to anyone other than her."

Eva chewed on her lip for a moment before she sipped her cold coffee tentatively. It tasted bitter as she swallowed, and she frowned deeply at the taste. She hadn't put in enough sugar. *Gross.* "Maybe she was just depressed," she suggested.

It was a simple explanation to a situation steeped in stigma. Eva had grown up with the illness and had embraced it as a part of herself long ago. For many people older than her twenty-two years, however, it was a source of deep shame and something never to be discussed publicly. Eva's father almost never spoke of his own struggles with depression, and her mother never made much of an effort to understand. She just nodded, asked Eva if her medication was still working, and went about her day pretending it didn't exist.

Until Eva lost control one day, and they had all been forced to confront the real cost of ignoring such an illness. That day they called her a coward and demanded to know why she hadn't asked for help. Eva thought the reason was obvious, especially in their reaction to what she'd done. They'd demanded to know how she could be so selfish, not once bothering to ask why she felt her world was slowly spiraling out of control.

Eva shook herself free from memories of her failure. The car was moving again, slowly, but it was moving. They would be back in the city soon.

Her mother laughed. It was a short, derisive bark. "Oh, she *certainly* was depressed. No one could possibly be that negative without some depression coming into the equation."

Eva bit her lip so hard it bled in an effort to stop an angry retort.

"Let's not speak ill of the dead, Claire," Eva's father said quickly. He probably sensed disaster. This was an old argument they'd had many times. Eva didn't know if she and her parents would ever see eye to eye on the subject of coping with mental illness. Her parents believed that any depression her grandmother struggled with stemmed from her grandfather's death. It could not be that simple. Eva had always sensed that her grandmother regarded her husband as nothing more than an inconvenient necessity of life. The sadness her grandmother struggled with was there long before Eva's father was born. Of that, at least, Eva was certain.

Silence filled the car again. Eva sat back and drank more of her disgusting coffee. She was starting to feel carsick. The conversation wasn't helping. This was the sort of argument that Eva hated. There was no point in guessing. Her grandmother was dead, and they'd never know.

"I think there's something more to it than simple depression."

Eva's stomach turned. Her mother, of course, would not leave well enough alone. Eva wished she would let it go. There was no point in continuing to talk about this. They couldn't find out anything more because the subject of the discussion was dead and burned and buried in the ground.

No one interjected, so Eva's mother continued to speak. Her voice was sharp and biting over the sound of the road outside. "Come on, Dan, do you think that she married your dad for any reason other than convenience? We both know that they hated each other's guts."

Eva's father sucked in a harsh breath. Turning to stare out the window, Eva gritted her teeth. She would not rise to the bait. She would not. She could not. She did not want to have this argument.

"Once we get back to her place, we're going to find something to explain why she was such a miserable pill of a woman. Mark my words we will." It wasn't a secret that Eva's mother didn't care for her mother-in-law. They were constantly at odds during Eva's childhood, and doubly so after that day, when Eva became the object of a contest of wills.

On today of all days. We don't need this right now.

Despite the harsh way her mother had said it, the comment had made her think. There was something more to the story. Eva was sure of it. She braced herself for a fight between her parents, not sure if one was to come.

The silence stretched on.

She tossed every little tidbit her grandmother had ever told her around in her head as they inched their way back to Brooklyn and her grandmother's apartment. There were so many little comments that had to have meaning, such as not liking blondes when Eva showed her a picture of a fair-haired boy she liked. Or, after Eva's first breakup with her high school girlfriend, when Mary warned her not to invest too much time in loving women because they were fickle.

Eva wondered if this was her grandmother trying to tell her something about herself, but as soon as she finished one rant about loving women, she would start in on the men. There seemed to be no end to the comments. There had to be something else beyond the obvious answer that her grandmother was simply difficult to get along with.

Eva leaned forward and set her coffee into the cup holder. She brushed her father's arm with her fingers before she slumped back into her seat and he turned to smile at her. His eyes were crinkled and kind and his shock of graying hair caught the light and haloed him. Evidently, he was happy that she hadn't started the fight her mother so obviously wanted.

It was getting easier not to take the bait. Eva's mind was preoccupied with what her mother had not said. Something that she could not quite recall was shifting just below the surface. Her mind felt slow and weak as she fumbled through her thoughts. The straws she grasped at didn't fit her mental image of her grandmother. They were lies, a veneer on a crumbling foundation.

All her life, Eva could not shake the feeling that her grandmother wasn't always there, and that she was caught up in a bad memory of which she could never be free. Her father had grown up never truly understanding his mother, and had watched his own daughter grow closer to her than he had ever been. Eva owed it to her father to try to find some explanation for her grandmother's depression. All Eva wanted was for there to be another reason, something encouraging that would give her some hope for her own future.

She shook her head. It wasn't right for her to think that there should be another explanation. She was evidence enough that sometimes people simply couldn't help themselves. It was just a lurking, unpleasant feeling that Eva could never shake. Her grandmother saw something, once upon a time, and it had completely changed her. Eva wasn't sure if it was a great lost love or some horrible trauma. Her grandmother had lived through nearly two decades of unpleasantness before she'd gotten married after World War II.

"I was an old maid then," she told Eva. "No one wanted to marry a girl who was on the wrong side of thirty. Your Grandpa offered me an agreeable match."

"You say agreeable like you didn't love him, Gran." Eva was eleven, sullen and stubborn. Always determined to get the last word. "I thought you had to love someone to get married to them."

Her grandmother threw back her head and laughed. "That's true, Eva darling, but not everyone makes good choices." Her expression, and Eva remembered it clearly to this day, went dark then. Her face became unreadable and caught on a miserable grimace of a smile. "Not everyone has a choice in the end," she said. "Your Grandpa would have loved you, sweetie. You're a lot like him."

"I want to be more like you, Gran!" Eva stuck her lip out petulantly. "Your life is so much cooler than Grandpa's."

"You say that now, Eva..." Her grandmother shook her head. "Soon you'll find out I'm just a tired old husk of a woman whose world was ripped out from under her nose when she was scarcely old enough to realize it."

Eva had spent what felt like half her life trying to understand the great mystery that was Mary Kessler. The cryptic recollections and one-off comments only deepened Eva's confusion. Now that her grandmother was gone, Eva wondered if there was something left lying about in her grandmother's apartment that might hold the key to this mystery.

Her mind preoccupied, Eva leaned against the window and watched the slow-moving traffic. She soon dozed off as the gentle lull of the car moving through stop-and-go traffic made her eyelids heavy and sleep come easily.

The hole was deep, so deep that she could not climb out of it. Eva's fingers scrambled against the slime-covered walls of her prison, but could find nothing to grab onto. Everything smelled like decay, the constant and steady drip of water long forgotten and left to fester. Moss grew in brilliant patches of violent, electric green. It surrounded her, making the walls seem as though they were closing in around her. Fear gripped her like a vice.

She ran down a narrow passageway. Blue-green sludge got in her hair. Eva swiped at where it fell cold and wet against her forehead. She raised a shaking hand to touch the dampness and her fingers came away streaked black. She stepped into a large, dark room with high walls. Light played across them, dancing in beautiful, indescribable patterns. It was the most beautiful thing she had ever seen. A myriad of glowing geometric shapes swam like tropical fish against a stark black background.

Except that when she looked closer, the background was also moving. It was a living thing. Gooseflesh rose on the back of Eva's arms and a shiver ran through her body.

A girl was in the room with her. A girl she felt she knew.

"Who are you?" Her voice was lost in the darkness. "Who are you?"

The girl turned and her face was a blank mask of skin stretched over bone. A hollow rattled where her mouth should be, sucking in a long, slow breath.

Chapter 3

Buried, Not Forgotten

EVA AWOKE WITH A GASP. Her entire body shuddered as she surged forward, her fingers reaching for something that wasn't there. Her head pounded and her vision was still blurry with sleep. Sitting back, she rubbed at her eyes and blinked to see her father looking at her from the passenger's seat.

"Musta been some dream," he said wryly.

"It was... something," Eva replied. The disquiet feeling would not leave her. She reached for her coffee, only to find that it was cold. She drank it anyway, wanting to pull herself closer to wakefulness. The black pit and the dancing colors would not leave her mind. The memory of the girl's rattling breath made the hair on the back of her neck spike upwards. The car was hot, but the skin on Eva's arms was covered in goosebumps.

Blinking sleepily in the hazy mid-morning sunlight, Eva let out a yawn. New York stretched up above her in all directions. She exhaled and tilted her head back to gaze at the buildings, feeling far more relaxed than she had in the wide-open spaces of Eastern Long Island. There were people everywhere, and faint patches of blue sky could be seen above the buildings as they made their way through her grandmother's old neighborhood. A grin tugged at Eva's lips. She was home.

Ten minutes later, Eva was staring up at the brick building where her grandmother lived for close to thirty years. They parked in the tiny and absurdly expensive lot across the street, and her mother argued with the lot attendant that they should be allowed a cheaper rate because they were technically residents.

"No resident parking pass, no deal," the attendant said in a thick Brooklyn accent. "Take it up with the super."

There was drool on the window and Eva rubbed at it with her sleeve. She didn't want her parents to have to wash the car before returning it to the rental lot. It was just one more thing to remember to do, and they already had their work cut out for them.

After a few seconds, Eva was satisfied that the smear was gone. Already the memory of the dream was fading. She grabbed her purse and slung it over her shoulder. Her mother was gathering things from the back seat opposite her, a few notepads and a camera. She had a harassed look on her face, and the crow's-feet at the corners of her eyes seemed like deep lines cut in by years of worry. Her hair, nearly the same shade as Eva's, was frizzing in the morning humidity.

"Do we have a game plan for this?" Eva asked. Her voice was still thick with sleep. She knew that she must look like hell because she was sweaty from her nap in the too-hot car. She was sun-and-sleep-warmed, and in a good mood despite the smell of hot garbage that assaulted her nose as soon as she opened the car door.

"I figured we'd make one once we got up there," her mother replied. She held up a notepad with a triumphant smile. Eva bit back a groan. Lists were her mother's favorite thing, and Eva hated that level of meticulous planning. "Nate and Lisa have both said that aside from what was already left to them in your grandmother's will, they're not really interested in anything up there. It's all ours to process."

Eva sighed. The absolute last thing she felt like doing was spending days and days working in close proximity with her mother processing her grandmother's things. They were sure to come to blows before it was over. Eva couldn't imagine that her mother would be particularly compassionate about some of the things her grandmother had kept over the years.

"Goody. *Processing*."

"Yup, processing. There's close to four decades of junk crammed into that apartment. It's gonna be an undertaking," her mother said. "Maybe we should have ordered a Dumpster..."

The thought of throwing away her grandmother's things was horrifying to Eva. She knew it was inevitable, because they couldn't save everything, but Eva had hoped that they could say goodbye first. She tried to put on a brave face. *Put your best foot forward. Don't let her get to you.*

Eva stood in the middle of the parking lot and stared up at the six-story brick building that Eva's grandmother had called home for so many years. Crumbling at the corners, it was a former sweatshop turned into apartments during the first period of gentrification of this area some twenty years ago. Apartments were selling and renting for obscene amounts of money these days. A great deal of her father's inheritance was wrapped up in this apartment, but she didn't want him to sell it.

Eva loved this neighborhood. The apartment was bought and paid for long before the property values had skyrocketed in recent years. Her grandmother had been an institution in the neighborhood for so long that Eva felt that they couldn't have just anyone fill the void she'd left behind.

Looking up at the building, Eva felt the sharp sting of loss at her chest. Nothing was ever going to be the same again. The sense of finality in this moment threatened to overwhelm her, and it filled her with a with a strange sense of foreboding, that she couldn't shake.

"Come on," her father said when there was a gap in the traffic.

Still, Eva reasoned as they dashed across the street in the wake of a speeding cab, *Gran was a bit of a hoarder. There's a lot of work that has to go into this place before we can even consider putting it on the market.*

Eva hoped that it would take a little while to get the apartment all sorted out. She didn't want to say goodbye to this neighborhood just yet. She had so many good, positive memories associated with this place. They were the sort that she thought back to when she found herself wallowing in the melancholy that she sometimes could not shake. To leave her grandmother's home for good seemed like a final farewell, and Eva certainly wasn't ready for that yet.

They climbed the stairs to the fourth floor slowly, pausing to greet the new first-floor residents who were kids fresh out of college, and Mrs. Sandley on the second floor. She was a shut-in and was very sad that she did not have the means to bring herself to Mary's funeral. Eva's father lingered to speak to the old woman and help her back into her apartment with his usual politeness and distant charm.

"We should keep going," Eva's mother said. "He'll be along after he gets her settled." She nudged Eva on the shoulder as she rose on her tiptoes to peer curiously into Mrs. Sandley's apartment. The room was as much of a time capsule as Eva's grandmother's apartment upstairs was, overflowing with antiques and full of reminders of days long past. Her father was settling Mrs. Sandley back on her couch and offering to make her some tea to tide her over until the Meals on Wheels "boy" delivered her lunch at eleven-thirty.

Eva wasn't even sure that her father had ever met Mrs. Sandley before. He came here so infrequently that it seemed impossible that he would know her. He preferred to keep his distance from his mother's home, and instead would invite her to lunch in Manhattan or to come up to Connecticut on the weekends if she was willing to take the train. Both her parents said the apartment was full of bad memories. Her mother went so far as to say that there was a black feeling in the place, as if it were an inescapable pit.

Eva wasn't like her parents. This building had the sort of charm Eva adored about some of the older buildings in the city, all narrow staircases and windows that didn't open properly. The staircase was like something out of a Hitchcock movie, and she could just picture some beautiful silver-screen actress descending the stairs with ominous music in her wake. How anyone could find it unsettling was beyond Eva, but even she could not shake the uncomfortable feeling that had come over her since they'd arrived.

The door to her grandmother's apartment swung open silently. The breath left Eva's body, and her stomach twisted with an ache unlike anything she had ever felt before. The oppressive, flowery smell of her grandmother's favorite perfume was everywhere. It leaked into Eva's senses and threatened to overwhelm her. She raised shaking fingers to cover her lips and swallowed down tears and the desperate feeling of loss. She was a trespasser in a tomb, someone who should not dare take a step forward, and then another, until she was standing in the middle of her grandmother's cluttered living room.

Her mother had no such qualms. No reverence or respect for the dead. Upon entering the room, she went straight to the window and threw open the drapes. She coughed quietly in the dust as she tied them back. The little air conditioning unit that was held up by sheer force of will whined as Eva's mother cranked it on to its maximum setting and stepped back, surveying the room.

Eva was trapped in the middle of the floor and unsure of how to go about getting started going through everything— the entirety of her grandmother's *life*—so that the apartment could be sold. It was a feeling that ate at Eva, paralyzing her and making her linger in the middle of the room where she knew that she would not disturb any memories. There used to be a rule in this apartment that you took your shoes off at the door. There was still a line of her grandmother's shoes in the hall, which ranged from comfortable walking shoes to a pair of low heels that Eva couldn't help but imagine her grandmother scowling at. Eva bent and unlaced one battered Converse All Star with shaky hands, resting her foot against her knee as she did so.

"What are you doing?" her mother asked. She turned, setting her notepad down on the coffee table that held a stack of old *National Geographic* magazines and a few newspapers. There was an odd look on her face as Eva tugged off her first shoe and moved on to the next one.

"Taking off my shoes," Eva explained. "Gran... Gran liked it when I did that."

Her mother's round face, which had been pulled tight into an expression of confusion, seemed to slacken into one of understanding. She stepped forward and put a hand on Eva's shoulder. They were the same height, and the gesture was intimate for Eva, who was unused to physical contact from her mother. It was her dad who was the affectionate one. Her mother was more distant and less overt with her affection. Eva remembered the last time her mother had touched her like this, and that had been a dark day, too.

"Oh, Eva," her mother said. "Take them off if you must, but leave your socks on. I know that it got hard for your grandmother to move around toward the end. There's no telling what might be growing on the floor."

Huffing angrily, Eva stepped backward and away from her mother's touch. Her grandmother had been dead and buried for one day. *One day.* She didn't know why she expected her mother to be any better. It was a joke to think that she would be, given the way she'd spoken in the car. Eva didn't understand how her mother could be so cruel when the memory of her grandmother lying dead in a hospital bed was still fresh in everyone's memories.

Her mother was like that, though, so it was silly for Eva to expect any better from her. She was always making assumptions about how people lived their lives and kept their homes. Eva hated that there was even a doubt that her grandmother's life wasn't vibrant until the very end. She'd died peacefully in her sleep with her family around her.

Eva had been there.

"It's fine," she said quietly.

She glanced toward the small hallway that led to the storage closet. "Should I go get some trash bags or something?"

The apartment, her grandmother's last sanctuary, was clean, and her mother was stupid to say otherwise. *Christ, I sound like an immature teenager.*

Eva shook her head and set her shoes beside her grandmother's. She knew she had to stop letting her mother rile her up so easily, even if she was getting a lot better at not showing it.

"I figured that today we'd spend some time going through stuff, maybe collect some clothes to take to the homeless shelter and the Salvation Army..." Eva shook her head violently at the suggestion and her mother tilted her head to one side, confusion drifting across her face. "Why not them? They do good work."

Eva shrugged, fiddling with the braid that she'd wrestled her hair into that morning. It was starting to come undone. Eva stared at it in her hand for a moment as annoyance prickled at the back of her neck. This was exactly the sort of conversation she did not want to have with her mother. Getting into something like this would only make things worse.

She remembered being very small and walking by the haggard and cold-looking men ringing bells outside of Macy's. It was one of her first times into Manhattan with just her grandmother, and she was awed by everything. The city was alight with the magic of the coming Christmas holiday. The man rang his bell beside his little red pot and Eva begged her grandmother for change to put into the bucket.

"You shouldn't give to them," her grandmother said roughly, pulling Eva away from the man with his ringing bell.

"Why not?" She was five and didn't know when to leave well enough alone. They paused before a homeless man who was hunched over a subway grate and wrapped in a blanket. Mary handed him two dollars and pressed two quarters into Eva's hand.

"Give them to him," her grandmother said. "He is someone who is actually in need." The man stared up at them for a long time, smiling with bright white teeth and thanking her in a rough voice that only came after a long pause. It was as though he'd forgotten how to speak. Eva pressed the two quarters into his gloved hand. "You will seek," he whispered. "You got the look."

"She won't seek," her grandmother replied curtly. "Nor should you."

He smiled toothily at them again as Eva's grandmother pulled her away down the street to stare into the lavishly decorated Macy's windows.

"Why can't we give the money to the men with the bells? They don't say weird things—"

"Because sometimes people aren't as good as they say they are," her grandmother explained. She was clutching Eva's hand tightly in her own. Eva remembered glancing over her shoulder as the homeless man raised his dark head skyward and started to sing the saddest song that Eva had ever heard.

That was the first time that her grandmother had told her about the light of the world. The homeless man off Sixth Avenue had sung an ode to that very same light her grandmother insisted had gone out in her own life. The light she could never find again. His voice was pure and golden above the din of the city. He'd sung it for two dollars and two quarters.

Later that night they sat on the couch drinking hot cocoa and looking at her grandmother's little fake Christmas tree. "Why did that man sing that song?" Eva asked. She tilted her mug from side to side, making absolutely sure that she got all the marshmallows to the middle so that they'd melt and add a layer of creamy, delicious foam to the top of her drink. Her grandmother had been quiet the entire train ride back to Brooklyn, lost in her own thoughts. Eva remembered being annoyed at her, and had chattered non-stop in an effort to get her to engage. "It wasn't even a Christmas song."

Eva's grandmother was quiet for a long time after that, staring at the Christmas tree lights. Her face was a landscape of late eighties wrinkles and her posture was ramrod straight.

Sighing, her grandmother wiped away Eva's cocoa mustache. "He sang that song because he is a seeker of the light. He has been touched by it, he's seen it, he knows what it can do, and he's sore afraid."

"Like the shepherds when the angels told them about Jesus?" Eva asked. It was close to Christmas, after all, and even if they weren't a very religious family, the story was on Eva's mind.

"There's a lot of truth in that moment in the story," her grandmother agreed. "His light has gone out. He saw it once, it touched him, and then someone reached out and snuffed it away into blackness. It is a cruel fate, sweetie. You should never seek out the light of the world."

Eva sipped her cocoa, her eyes wide. "Why not? What's the light of the world?"

"I have no heart to teach it to you. That can only be the path of mourning."

Shaking herself, Eva blinked hard and focused her attention back on her mother. She had forgotten that conversation, amid the myriad others she'd had with her grandmother since. Her mind was racing with half-remembered conversations about the light of the world. Maybe that was the key to all this.

"Sorry," she said quietly. "When I was really little, Gran told me not to give to them because they aren't as good as they say they are."

"Because of how they treat the gays?" Eva winced. "Your Gran wasn't gay, why would she care?"

She shouldn't have said anything at all. *Stupid, stupid...*

The urge to fight back overwhelmed her and Eva looked her mother straight in the eye. "Maybe she was taking a stand, Mom, for something she believed in. Something that *meant* something to her."

She couldn't believe her mother sometimes. There were certain things that just weren't *said* and certainly were not implied. Her grandmother had always been one of those people, a good sort of person who would stick her neck out there for something that she truly believed in. What did it matter if her grandmother was or wasn't something? She cared enough to take a stand and to tell Eva that it wasn't right. *Why can't Mom see that?*

She stormed off down the hallway toward the supply closet to at least collect some trash bags and buy a few moments to herself to calm down. Her mother huffed quietly and reached for her notepad once more. Eva wasn't sure who she'd put this round to, but she did not want to go another until her dad emerged from Mrs. Sandley's apartment. It wasn't unreasonable to want to respect her grandmother's wishes and views in the distribution of her things, Eva thought. Her dad would see it that way.

There were times when Eva felt she was the only one who appreciated her grandmother for who she was. Eva embraced the good and the bad in her, the deep sadness and the mysterious ghosts that haunted her past. Eva knew those ghosts well because she was haunted by her own demons. Her mother didn't get it, and she never had. Throughout Eva's childhood, she had made no secret about how much she hated that her mother-in-law would have days where she was so sad she couldn't get out of bed. She hated it when she saw Eva having the same sorts of days.

Eva's dad did understand. He struggled with himself, but Eva always assumed that he stayed away because of the bad memories he had of growing up in the shadow of a woman as mercurial as his mother.

The hallway was dimly lit. A pale glow of yellow light illuminated the room, throwing everything into washed-out relief. Eva had always hated it as a child. It seemed to curl in around itself and create a dark void where there should have been bright white light. The entire apartment was off of this one corridor that dead-ended in the closet where Eva was heading.

Eva's grandmother had stored many things in the hall closet: Christmas presents and secret snacks, door hangings and cleaning supplies. It was the cleaning supplies that Eva was after now. The last time she'd been in there was before her grandmother had gotten sick. They had gathered up a great deal of clothing to be donated to the local women's shelter. "I have too many clothes," Mary had explained from where she held court in the comfortable and worn easy chair by the window, "and I want you to help me give them to people who actually will wear them."

Eva helped her without complaint, loading up the grocery cart three times and walking the trash bags full of donations down to the women's shelter some three blocks over. It was not long after her hospitalization, when her mother wasn't speaking to her and her father couldn't look at her without tears in his eyes. When Eva made the decision to drop out of college after spending almost a semester away, Eva's grandmother had not cared.

"You focus on learning how to get better," she said. She offered Eva things to do so that she wasn't stuck in her head. "Try a stunt like that again before I'm dead and in the ground, and I'll do it myself, Eva. You're too good to lose."

"I'll try, Gran," Eva promised.

Now, though, with the apartment devoid of the life it had housed for decades, Eva did not know where to start. She yanked open the closet door.

Slung over the back of the door was a plastic and nylon shoe rack that probably dated back to the '70s. Stuffed into one of the shoe holders was a roll of drawstring trash bags. Eva pulled them out of the stiff plastic and shoved them into her back pocket before reaching up to pull on the light switch cord that dangled from the ceiling.

As a child, Eva had always stayed toward the front of this closet. She'd been worried about monsters. Now, she was curious about what lay beyond the storage rack that was filled with household supplies and bed sheets. She had never been back there.

A chill shot up Eva's spine. The biting, anxious feeling of desperately having to pee and of knowing that she was where she should not be ate at her stomach. She shoved the feeling away. There was no one left to judge her now.

Eva stepped into the dim space beyond the storage rack. She was just barely able to make out the murky shapes of boxes and what looked like an old-fashioned desk shoved against the back wall underneath a leaning tower of encyclopedias. The air was thick with dust.

From the living room, Eva could hear her mother and father talking. He must have finally arrived. Eva wondered if her mother was going to say anything to him about Eva's outburst, but the conversation soon dissolved into the quiet sounds of papers being sifted around.

This was a huge undertaking and all three of them knew it, but it was something that had to be done. The property value for this particular building was through the roof right now. Eva wasn't stupid. Despite her emotional attachment to the place, she knew it had to be sold. She'd pretended she hadn't heard her father on the phone with a real estate broker inquiring as to what he was going to do with the property now that his mother was gone. People wanted this property. People would pay a *lot* of money to get it.

Maneuvering one foot carefully around a mop and bucket, Eva twisted her body so that she was she was parallel to the wall and could slip past the rickety-looking storage rack. It rattled as Eva wiggled past it, but thankfully did not tip over. Eva didn't want to think about what her mother would say if she got herself trapped in the closet by a piece of cheap IKEA shelving.

Behind the storage rack was a small space where Eva could stand. The light here was very dim, so she pulled out her cell phone and turned on its flashlight app.

This space had not been touched in years. A coating of dust more than a quarter-inch thick in places covered everything. Eva's nose twitched and she sneezed as she pressed herself flat against the wall so that she wouldn't disturb anything. An odd feeling came over her as she rubbed at her nose. She was uncomfortable, on edge.

Under the bright white light from her phone, Eva was able to see a small stack of shoe boxes next to the desk. They were piled up about waist high and were labeled with faded black letters on yellowing masking tape. The dates were *ancient*, far older than any story Eva had ever heard her grandmother tell.

Nudging a broken-looking vacuum cleaner out of the way, Eva inched forward and reached for the first box. The cardboard was so dusty it was almost slippery under her hands. Eva clamped her phone between her teeth so she could have both hands free. The box was heavy. She pulled it around and balanced it on the storage rack.

Pulling her phone from her mouth, she set it on the shelf above, pushing aside old aerosol cans to make space. She would throw them into a trash bag once she was finished checking out the boxes.

On the brittle, yellow masking tape label, a date was written in her grandmother's precise script. Eva stared down at it, chewing on her lip. It was strange to see something so old, and to hold it in her hands and know that it probably hadn't been touched for thirty or maybe even forty years. To touch something so old seemed almost to violate it. The date on the masking tape was seventy years ago, almost to the day. It seemed like a breach of some unspoken trust between Eva and her grandmother to touch these boxes, but Eva was curious and her grandmother was dead. She could look.

Eva bent and blew some of the dust off the top of the box. It was dated 1935–1940, which was before Eva's grandmother had met her grandfather. This was when Mary was in her late twenties, in the midst of the Great Depression and a buildup to a world war. This was a piece of history, *her* history. Eva's heart was racing. She was about to see it for the first time.

She wanted to call her father in and have him watch as she opened the box, but the words died in her throat as she pulled the top off to find two jumbled clusters of yellowed paper envelopes that had clearly once been tied together with ribbons. There was a leather-bound journal tucked into the bottom that looked suspiciously like the notebooks that Eva's grandmother had given her for Christmas every year since she turned seventeen. Underneath the two stacks of envelopes was a thicker envelope that Eva could tell contained photographs. The storage rack creaked as she tried to find a more comfortable position where she could get better light.

"Shit," she muttered. The box nearly slipped out of her hands and the light from her phone wavered. She turned and nearly tripped over the vacuum's hose as she grabbed another one of the shoe boxes and pressed the top back onto the one she'd just opened. Holding the stack of boxes against her stomach, Eva reached into her back pocket and carefully pulled out a trash bag. She shook it out and shoved her phone into her other pocket. One by one, each of the gross, old aerosol cans was thrown into the bag, and soon Eva had a space wide enough to relocate the boxes to the storage rack.

She pushed the trash bag through the space she'd created and it fell to the floor with a clatter, the bag spilling open and the cans rolling out into the hallway.

From the living room, Eva's mother called, "Everything okay?"

Eva coughed a little bit on the dust that had risen as the bag had tumbled to the floor. "Yeah!" she shouted back. "I found the trash bags and some other stuff. I figured that I'd throw out all the cleaning supplies that are older than me while I was back here."

"Good job, kid." Her father stood at the end of the hallway with a stack of books in his hands. "Bring out those bags when you're done. Your mom wants to do the entry closet today at least."

Eva gave a mock salute, and he grinned back at her. "Will do."

When her father was out of sight once more, Eva pushed the stack of shoe boxes that she was holding onto the storage rack's shelf and turned to collect the rest of them. There were five in total, dating back to 1923, when Eva's grandmother would have been thirteen years old. Eva had no idea why she would have kept her correspondence and letters from that long ago, but she apparently had, and Eva wanted to have a look at them. She stacked. She stacked the boxes on the storage rack so she could get at them easily from the other side and brushed as much dust off herself as she could before contemplating the narrow gap she'd have to wiggle through once more.

In the hallway, the bag that she'd filled up was lying open and some of the aerosol cans had fallen out. She bent and shoved them back in, then picked up the bag and slung it over her shoulder. After a moment's contemplation, she reached out and grabbed one of the shoe boxes as well. The faded masking tape dated it to 1925–1926, and it scratched against Eva's side as she tucked it under her arm. Her entire body was streaked with long gray lines of dust, like skeletal fingers that had reached out to hold her in the darkness behind the storage rack.

"Gross," she muttered. She left the door open and the light on. There was a mop in there, as well as all the non-expired cleaning supplies. Eva wasn't sure that they'd get to the cleaning stage today, but she wanted to at least pretend that she'd made an effort to be helpful.

In the bright, natural light of the living room, Eva was finally able to see that the shoe box was not the old, gray cardboard shape as it had appeared to be in the closet, but rather it appeared to be made out of some sort of archival material. The writing on the masking tape label was faded, but the box itself looked almost as if it were brand new. It wasn't like the others, held together with tape and sheer force of will. *Why is this one different? What's so special about it?* She deposited the trash bags and shoe box on the coffee table, lost in thought.

"What do you have there?" Her father peered curiously from where he was looking through a stack of tax returns.

"I'm not really sure," Eva replied. She brushed as much dust off herself as she could before settling down on the couch and pulling the box toward her. "I found this way in the back of the storage closet. It doesn't look like it's been touched since Gran moved in. The one I opened in the closet looked like it had old letters and pictures in it."

Eva's dad leaned forward and Eva carefully pulled the top off the box and set it down on the coffee table.

The inside of this box was different than the one that she'd opened in the closet. There were journals in here, little leather-bound notebooks stacked in three perfect rows, four deep. Eva figured that there was one for each month of the year between 1925 and 1926. She reached forward and picked up the first journal, and her father went back to his perusal of the tax returns.

"Don't you want to look?" She peered up at him, her bangs falling into her eyes.

Her father glanced at her sideways and shrugged. He shifted from his position at the other end of the couch. "Honestly, Eva, this is more important right now. I gotta figure out if I need to file anything for your grandmother." When she blew her bangs out of her eyes and made a noise like an irritated horse, he laughed and brushed them off her forehead. "You know that I want to read them too, Eva, but this has to come first."

Eva smiled at him, holding up the journal between her thumb and curled forefinger. "I'll give you a full trip report, how about that?"

He nodded. "Sounds good, sweetie."

She sank back into the couch that still smelled like the jasmine soap her grandmother favored. There was another scent there too, of the expensive perfume she wore only when she went out of the house. Cloaked in a sense-memory of her grandmother, Eva opened the diary and frowned. This one was dated September 1, and that wasn't what she needed. She leaned forward and picked up the journal from the stack opposite. Her grandmother must have been going through some sort of a journal-writing kick because the entry for January 2 was nearly seven pages long. It was no wonder that she'd had to keep a separate journal for each month.

Eva curled back on the couch, propped the book open against her knees, and started to read.

Chapter 4

Mary

January 1, 1925

The first of the year always brings about the most interesting changes. The whirlwind of 1924 has wound down to the slow creep of ice across the river. Change happens slowly when it is so cold that the wind steals your breath away. I envy the bears that sleep through the worst of the winter. Oh, what I wouldn't give to not have to venture out into the cold.

Got back from home today. Trip fine, long, train was clogged with people.

Mother gave me this diary to record my innermost thoughts, as though I am a girl of ten or eleven, and not living away from home. She thinks that it will help me to become a more actualized person, someone who will be suitable for marriage in a few years. I hadn't the heart to tell her that a girl working at my age is enough to put most suitors off entirely.

They need the money, though. David and Ovid are growing bigger by the day, and two younger brothers are enough to chase a self-sufficient girl from the house. It isn't as though father helps much these days. He thinks he's found the cure for the terrible memories he has of the war in the bottom of a bottle, but it's just snake water. Mother thinks that I didn't see it, but when I left on Christmas Day she was crying. They had no gifts for each other, this diary for me, oranges from Florida for the boys, and hours in church for all of us.

David and Ovid are too young to remember what it was like before father went away to war. I remember how he used to be, and I miss the man he left behind in France terribly. He's shell-shocked, and nothing seems to help anymore. Mother is beside herself. The man that returned from the war is not my father. Mother says I must be careful because father will not say that he is hurting.

I may be a girl alone in the city, but I've found safe lodgings and the work is steady. There is no need for her to worry so much, or if there was she could ask me to come back home. The work is all I can ask for. Mrs. Talbot, my landlady, is on good terms with my mother, which affords me some comfort away from home. I am not the only young typist working in the city, and with Mrs. Talbot's recommendation, I'm swimming in temporary typing assignments.

The latest is a very important attorney—Mr. R.M. Perkins. He is working on a large caseload and wants to hire me for more than just the temporary typist position I took in the fall. Some would think him an odd bird, walking around the court house with me following him like a lost chick, but that could not be further from the truth. He is very much the consummate Victorian gentleman. A bit dated, but a wonderful person. I started just before Christmas and he gave me a five-dollar bonus despite my having worked there only a few weeks. I was honored.

He told me he had three big cases coming up that he might use me for if I could continue to keep up. I thought it was awfully presumptuous of him, but what was I to say? The man gave me more than enough money to pay rent for the next month and a half, just for doing good work.

Mother says he wants something more from me. I don't think so. He has a wife, after all, and I'm not that sort of girl.

Eva smiled. Her grandmother, even as a young girl, had always been very pragmatic. Her writing was intense but heartfelt. She was dedicated to making the most out of the gift her family had given her.

"Anything interesting?" Her father asked.

"Eh," Eva shrugged. "Did you know your grandpa was terribly shell-shocked?"

Her father nodded. "My dad, too. Both of 'em had pretty bad PTSD from the wars they fought in. Mom never really talked about that time in her life."

"She didn't talk about her life *at all*." Eva's mother's voice was marked by years of annoyance. "The woman survived a century by being locked up tighter than Fort Knox about literally everything that didn't directly relate to the conversation at hand."

"Yeah," Eva had to agree. "I remember David and Ovid, her brothers, but I can't ever remember her talking about her parents, or the person she worked for back then."

"Well, life will do that to you." Her father went back to his stack of papers.

Eva wasn't ready to accept that. "But then why keep this record? Why leave it where it was sure to be found when she died? I know that she didn't like to talk about it, but then why not destroy the diaries so that we'd never get to see her at sixteen?"

When her parents said nothing, Eva knew she had a point. Her grandmother would not have kept these if they weren't meant for something more than a memory. Somewhere in these twelve little books, there was an answer to a question Eva did not even know how to ask.

She couldn't wait to find out more.

January 5, 1925
The weather turned better overnight. The snow is still drifting from the storms over the Christmas holiday, but it has started to

harden into the crunchy sort that melts during the day and becomes a slippery death trap overnight.

It was warm today. Warm enough that I was able to spend a few minutes outside, chatting with Elsie Goodrich as she smoked her way through three cigarettes. She's got shaky hands for a smoke eater, and seems to crave the hooch that Doris March makes in her closet as much as she does the smoke she eats.

I like Elsie. She's a lot like me—sent away because her father came back from the war a broken man. She smokes too much and drinks enough of that awful alcohol they serve in speakeasies that she's going to end up blind. There was a horrible article in the newspaper that I took from Mrs. Talbot's pile of firewood. Two people went blind drinking wood-grain alcohol. They're not sure the poor souls are going to live.

Elsie is always speaking of things as though they have no meaning beyond the off-handedness of her comments. She says that they're holding up as martyrs the people who've died drinking the swill in some of the gin joints in town, and if the two who went blind die, I'm sure they'll be included in that number. Elsie has a knack for dramatics and rather poetic language when she's waxing on about something doomed.

I didn't have the heart to tell her that I fancied myself anti-prohibition as well. Anything that can kill you isn't worth dying for.

Elsie is like so many other girls I know. She is a handful of years older than me and working as a teacher at one of the elementary schools set up for Yiddish-speaking children whose parents want them to learn English. She's Jewish enough that she can pass in that community while still being three generations American and naturalized. They don't like her in acceptable society and they don't care for her within the Yiddish community. She is ostracized no matter where she goes. I cannot imagine that: being a pariah among your own people.

Elsie isn't bothered by it. She tells me not to worry. She just lets it roll off her shoulders like water into a mill. It doesn't matter, she says, because it's the part she must play. Someday no one will care if she's a Jew or Irish or a Chinaman. She says that times are changing. I do worry about her. She puts on a brave face, but it can't be pleasant, getting the bum's rush no matter where you try to be yourself. I could never do something like that.

The strangest thing happened on my way home today. We were just passing from underground back above and I was struck. It was as if I had plunged my entire body into an icy bath, my body shivering violently in the cold. The train was quite warm, and the other passengers looked at me strangely as I tried to calm my shaking body.

A powerful feeling came over me then, like a piece of me had settled into place, a part of me I didn't know was missing. I have not been able to stop thinking about the moment; it consumes me, twisting about my consciousness and swallowing me whole.

I fear I am to dream of that moment. I dread it.

Eva read the diary for what felt like hours. She curled back into the couch while her parents moved around the apartment. They spoke in low voices to each other, but left her alone. Eva was grateful that she wasn't pulled away to start cleaning again. Her parents were giving her space.

She looked up when her father dumped a stack of papers on the far end of the couch and began to page through them. "Ow." She shifted to get the papers off her legs.

"Ow, yourself. I know that you need a minute, but I could really use some help with these, E." He held out a stack of papers.

Eva tucked a receipt into the diary. "Sure," she said. She didn't really want to leave her grandmother's story, but this was more important. They had only a limited time to do this. "What are we lookin' for?"

"Anything having to do with taxes from 1995 on," her father answered.

Eva nodded, and bent her head down to get looking.

The diaries soon were buried under a pile of found tax forms. It wasn't until lunchtime that Eva found herself with a spare few minutes to turn her attention back to them. The need to keep reading, to delve into her grandmother's hidden past, was overwhelming. She felt guilty, and had to fight down the urge to disappear into the bathroom with the diary and continue to read.

She got her chance when her parents left to make photocopies and pick up sandwiches for lunch, and a little thrill of excitement shot down her spine as her father made a shooing gesture on his way out the door. "Yes, yes, go back to your book. We'll bring you back a kebab or something."

"You're the best, Dad." Eva blew a kiss at him. She turned to see that the couch was completely overtaken by the papers they hadn't needed to photocopy. She surveyed the mess and groaned. "Great."

Her grandmother's favorite armchair was thankfully devoid of clutter. Eva settled down, curled into the worn upholstery, and began to read.

January 10, 1925

I met the most wonderful person today. I was on my way into Manhattan. I'd taken the subway as I was running late and had to get over the bridge to Canal Street in order to collect some things for Mr. Perkins from the office, before meeting him at the courthouse to take transcription of grand jury testimony. He doesn't trust the court stenographers, you see. I think they seem like perfectly nice boys, if a bit threatened by a woman who's every bit as good at taking dictation as they are.

While I was on the subway, I found myself sitting next to a most interesting young woman who had her nose buried in what I soon discovered to be an H.G. Wells novel. I was truly delighted, as I love Mr. Wells' novels myself. I spoke to her as we rattled over the Manhattan Bridge, and she was very willing to discuss the novel at length. She, like me, had read that particular novel more than once.

We spoke for so long that I nearly missed my stop. It has been quite a long time since I've been so engrossed with another person that I utterly lost track of time. She was ever so gallant, helping me off the train and smiling this mysterious little smile, like she was laughing at some private joke. She inquired as to my lodgings, telling me that she would love to discuss the novel and Wells' other works. If I was available, she added with a wink.

I was taken aback. That behavior is somewhat expected from men, but girls who are dressed well and are clearly educated don't behave that way. When a girl acts as a gentleman would, it feels oddly intimate, like the same sort of private joke that had her all smiles before. I stood there, flustered, and she let out a quiet giggle. Apparently a fella had tried it on her earlier in the week.

I asked if it had worked. I was still too thrown to say much else.

She laughed. It was only when the hearty guffaws had finished that she clapped me on the shoulder and assured me that it would never work.

I don't know why, but this bolstered my confidence. She was so very forward, not like Elsie or any of the other girls that live at Mrs. Talbot's, but in that way that makes you feel uncomfortable, a nervous feeling in your stomach. It was almost as though what we were doing was wrong.

She told me, her entire body caught up with an exuberance, that she would love to talk more about the books. I replied that there was a delicious Italian bakery near Mrs. Talbot's, and that the cream cakes were a dream. The train whistle blew and she dipped her head, promising to call on me soon, but reminding me of the coming snow.

Wren is fantastic with her literary analysis. She found Age of Innocence to be a stunning book, but she went on to voice an opinion I had not dared speak aloud. A woman winning such a prestigious prize is something to be proud of, but the book was so dreadfully dull.

I know that friendships are hard to come by. I know that there is not much in the way of time for them in a life such as mine, yet this feels utterly organic and natural. I am intrigued by Wren. I want to know more about her and I want her to tell me her story. I've told her some of mine and shown her the one photograph I have of all my family together. The one taken before father went off to a war. David and I are very young in it, and we look truly happy. Things were easier then.

Wren got very quiet after that, staring off into space and picking at the fringe of the blanket. "All I have left is duty, I can no longer see my parents." I did not understand, were they dead? Wren shook her head and looked away from me. "Someday, I may tell you, Mary." She got up to leave then, her expression distant and just a little sad. She asked if she could call on me again, and I told her that she could.

I truly hope that she does come around again. She's so invigorating to talk to and I have so missed good conversation in my life. All I can see when I look at her is that she seems grasped in the throes of melancholy and I do not understand why. Maybe in time she will tell me. I certainly hope so.

Chapter 5

A Forgotten Memory

It was cathartic to read her grandmother's words. They were a far-off and forgotten memory of a girl who had grown into the woman Eva had loved so much. They were hauntingly familiar, pulling Eva into recollections of the day-to-day life of a girl with hopes and dreams so similar to the ones Eva kept tightly guarded inside her heart. She had friendships, a family, a life, and a career, all at such a young age.

A hollow, uncomfortable feeling settled in Eva's chest as she turned the pages of the diary. She was older than Mary was when she wrote these entries, and yet she had done absolutely nothing with her life. The only great step she'd ever taken was deciding to move away from home. She had to get away from her mother's inability to recognize that Eva's struggles with mental illness were not a negative reflection on her ability to parent or her worth as a person.

Her grandmother was all of sixteen when she'd written these words. She was *sixteen* and her life was already more cohesive than Eva's had ever been. She had a purpose: she was working to help her family, and someday she wanted to go to college. There were days that Eva could not get out of bed when she curled up in a ball against the battered, brittle feeling that came over her and made it impossible to move.

Eva had always thought that her grandmother experienced the same struggles with depression that she and her father dealt with on a daily basis. It was such an obvious explanation of the long, morose periods her grandmother would go through sometimes. Reading these diary entries proved that that was not the case. Mary was a vibrant, thriving girl at sixteen, when Eva was just starting to truly struggle with mental illness. Her father had told her that it manifested for him even younger, at fourteen, just as he was starting to hit puberty. If Mary struggled as Eva had, there wasn't much indication of it in her diary thus far. Perhaps it would be further on, buried deeper in the pages of these little volumes? Eva was sure, if there was proof, this was where she would find it.

Turning the next page, Eva stared at the January 13 entry and exhaled quietly. So what had happened, then? Did her grandmother's depression manifest later in life? Was she just under so much pressure that she was soldiering gallantly on and not mentioning her mood? A friendship was just blossoming in the past few pages. Mary did not seem burdened by Eva's propensity for introspection, which was a trait she thought she and her grandmother had in common.

So much of what Eva thought was true about her grandmother's teenage and young adult life did not slot easily into place. There was no miracle answer. There was no skeleton in her closet as there was in Eva's, no failure and no heartache. There was just a girl making her way in the world at a very young age.

Eva wondered what had changed. She wasn't the sentimental sort, but she did hang on to things long after their time. These diaries were so carefully preserved, whereas so many of the other documents Eva had found in the shoe boxes were jumbled together. There was obviously care invested in making sure that they were kept safe and free from the aging that the documents and photos in the other shoe boxes experienced.

Why? What was so important about when you were sixteen that you had to squirrel it away in that awful closet and never speak of it? Eva could not recall her grandmother talking about these people. The mysterious Wren, or Elsie the Jewish school teacher, even Eva's great-uncles and great-grandparents were figures that Eva hardly knew beyond their names. Her father never talked about them, and her grandmother had certainly never mentioned them. *Why did you hide this part of your story away from the world, Gran?*

"Eva."

Eva looked up from the diary to see her mother pulling a trash bag from the roll set on the coffee table. She was sweaty and harassed-looking, the crow's feet at the corners of her eyes deep and striking against the pale skin of her cheeks. Eva's skin was much darker than her mother's Greek complexion. "Yeah?" she asked.

"Lunch is in the kitchen." Her mother gestured towards the shoe box on the table. "Are we keeping those?" She raised her eyebrows and shook the trash bag suggestively.

Panic rising, Eva shut the book with a snap. "I, um…" Eva trailed off, leaned forward, and deposited the diary on top of the stack inside the shoe box. She shoved the lid onto the box and looked up at her mother. "Yeah, they're journals from when Gran was really young, like sixteen. I want to see what's in them. I wonder why she kept 'em."

"Ah, the mysterious past that is never to be spoken of under pain of crotchety ramblings." Her mother appeared resigned. Her expression was that of a woman who felt out of place sorting the clutter of her mother-in-law's life. She let out a deep breath and moved away. "Read up on it later, go eat and then come back and help me." Her tone was curt and annoyed.

Eva winced. She was slacking, and her parents really did need her help, even if her mother was being awfully unfriendly about things.

The sun was shining brightly through the windows and Eva knew that it was probably unbearably hot outside. This was the sort of day that she'd go to the park or maybe scrounge up the train fare to take her bike down to Brighton Beach to go swimming and ride along the road by the shore. She wasn't used to being stuck indoors. Moving out had afforded her the freedom to do whatever she wanted, even if it forced her to resort to odd jobs she found on Craigslist for any sort of income.

Her mother was an avid gardener, and in weather like this she would go outside and enjoy the fruits of her hard labor. Neither of them wanted to be cooped up inside the stuffy apartment with each other and a whole slew of unpleasant memories. Eva bit her lip and looked back at the shoe box, knowing that she shouldn't have gotten sucked in while they were taking a break and annoyed at her mother for not pulling her away sooner. The quicker they got through this, the better.

Eva wolfed down her sandwich, watching her mother bustle through the apartment from the kitchen. There was an odd sort of precision to how her mother moved, collecting things and putting them into the trash bag. Each object was carefully inspected before a decision was made, and Eva felt herself start to relax, just a little bit.

She finished quickly and dumped her sandwich wrapper into the kitchen trash. Stepping back into the cluttered living room, Eva bent to pick up the shoe box.

"Put the box with your things. We need to clean out the front closet today, if nothing else." Her mother had drifted back over to the door of the entryway closet and was now staring at the piles of shoes she'd already pulled out as though they were going to bite her. A frown pulled at her face.

Eva gathered the box and set it with her purse and shoes by the door. There wasn't much hope of slipping away to read more now, anyway. Her mother was determined to get something done with the apartment today beyond her father's discovery of a collection of tax forms and his disappearing to go speak to the building super.

Reaching around her mother, Eva pulled open the closet door and looked inside. She stepped back, feeling overwhelmed. Even without the shoes and some of the coats, it was still a mess. Her eyes slid around the apartment. Her grandmother had so many beautiful things—rugs from all over the world, dishes that had come back from two World Wars and then Korea and Vietnam. There were figurines carefully arranged and books in the three languages her grandmother spoke lining the far wall of the living room. She had no television, only an old radio and a CD player to fill the silence while she was alone.

Eva smiled, thinking of her grandmother's reaction to the gift of the CD player. Eva had been fifteen years old. It had been for a birthday, Eva thought, or maybe Christmas, she couldn't remember. Her memory of that time was a haze of self-loathing.

She supposed it could have been either, though. Her grandmother was born in early December and as the years went on, the family had tended to combine her birthday and Christmas into one celebration. Eva had suggested the CD player to her family, and they'd all pitched in to help find the perfect model that would combine user friendliness with decent sound quality. Even her cousin Charlie had helped, using his high school's media lab to digitize and burn CDs of many of her grandmother's old 45s and 78s. He spent hours doing it, complaining to Eva about it when she helped him make up CD cases.

They all sat around Eva's parents' living room, scraps of sparkly wrapping paper at their feet and far too much stocking candy munched on as the last of the gifts were opened. Eva's grandmother had always liked to wait until last, when she'd have the most attention for her gift. She'd told Eva, rather conspiratorially, that she would orchestrate circumstances to end up with all eyes on her. She liked to feel important in her old age.

When Eva thought about it, she really was. She'd lived far longer than her brothers or their wives. Mary Kessler was a force, and they all bore with her. She was their matriarch for better or for worse.

Eva remembered that her grandmother had been quiet for a long time when they gave her the CD player. She sat and stared at it while they all waited with bated breath for her to unleash the torrent of words they knew she was just barely holding back behind her old, wrinkled lips. Eventually, after the minutes stretched by and Eva could see her father hastily whispering with her mother about returns, her grandmother turned to Charlie. "Is this why you wanted all my old records?"

"Yeah." He was contemplating a peppermint patty and nearly crushed it between startled fingers. "I made them into CDs for you, so you'd still have them and be able to listen to them on that."

"Well," Eva's grandmother replied, looking for all the world as though she did not know what to say. "That was very sweet of all of you. One of you is going to have to show me how this works before I leave because otherwise it's going to sit in a box and I'll keep listening to my 45s just to spite you all."

Eva remembered a lot of laughing after that. She laughed again, stepping back into the living room to see that her father had returned from his conversation with the super. He had a Glen Miller record in his hands and was fiddling with the dials on the CD player.

"This will come as no shock to either of you, but I can't figure out how to work this thing." He stood back and crossed his arms over his chest.

Letting out an amused little huff, Eva crossed the room in three quick steps. She took the LP from her father's hands and set it aside, then bent down to find the corresponding CD on the shelf below. It took a moment of squinting before she found it, but she let out a triumphant little breath and tugged the CD from the shelf.

A folded piece of paper fell from the shelf as Eva handed her dad the CD. She picked it up, curious. It was yellowed and creased, folded and unfolded many times over. Inside was a small photograph, no more than two by three inches, of a girl. There was no inscription on the back.

"What's that?" Eva's dad asked.

"Picture." Eva flipped the picture back over and stared at the girl's face. There was something familiar about her, and Eva could have sworn she'd seen that face before. "She looks familiar. A cousin, maybe?"

Her dad peered at the picture for a moment before shrugging. "Don't recognize her. Put it with that box of diaries. Maybe Nate knows who she is."

Eva moved to do so, unable to shake the lingering feeling that her uncle would not know who the girl was, either. Her father turned back to the bookshelves. Most of them were marked with flags indicating what was to be donated and what was for anyone who wanted it. Eva had helped her grandmother do that *years* ago, back when she'd had a health scare at the age of ninety-seven. The first real "oh my god you're *old*, Gran" moment had come in the form of what the doctors thought was a mild stroke, and Mary had spent much of the summer recovering and napping on the couch while Eva went through the large book collection she'd amassed over the years and helped her to mark what she wanted to do with them.

Death was on Mary's mind then, as it had been on Eva's. She spent the entire exercise thinking about how little what she was doing mattered. She was trapped somewhere between misery and the sinking knowledge that no one except her grandmother—who wouldn't be long behind her anyway—would miss her if she were gone. Eva shook herself. It didn't do to dwell on those memories. That was one of the first things they taught her in recovery, and Eva strove to be better than that girl who could not find a way out of her head. She was better than that girl.

She tucked the photograph into the box.

It was such a shame that her grandmother's entire life had come down to a series of flags and things shoved hastily into trash bags marked with Sharpie. Eva stretched, her fingers knitting together high above her head as her spine cracked loudly.

"Careful there, Eva," her dad joked. "If you crack your back too much, it'll stay all contorted."

"Sure, Dad." Eva took the trash bag that her mother held out to her and pulled a marker from her pocket. Her mother trailed half a step behind her and together they stood before the front closet.

"You ready to tackle the rest of this?" Eva asked.

"Not at all," her mother answered.

There really wasn't much left inside. Another shoe rack, this one metal, hung from the back of the door. Eva went rummaging for a screwdriver to remove it. Pair by pair, the remainder of Eva's grandmother's shoes were loaded into a trash bag marked "donate." The rack itself was jammed awkwardly with Eva's bag of expired cleaning products by the door. Once that was done, all that was left were her grandmother's coats and the vacuum cleaner shoved into a far corner. They pulled the vacuum out and left it in the middle of the living room because they would need it later in their cleaning adventure. On a shelf above the rack of coats was a reusable grocery bag full of winter hats and a few honest-to-god hatboxes that made Eva's mother laugh. She stood on her tiptoes and pulled them down one by one, and Eva opened each and modeled the ridiculous hats they contained. It set her mother laughing and had her father chuckling before long. Laughter was a cure-all when nothing else seemed to work in their family, and the silly hats were enough to send them all into peals of laughter.

———⊸०⊂∞०∘⊂———

It took three long days for Eva and her parents to work their way through the bedroom, most of the living room, and the bathroom. Eva divided her time between reading the diaries whenever she could.

Her body ached, but it was the precious seconds she was able to snatch away from the cleaning effort that Eva lived for. She read greedily, swallowing the words her grandmother wrote about Wren, her daily life, and the ridiculously snowy winter. She had never known her grandmother was such a talented writer.

Eva read late into the night, curled up under a thin sheet on the couch in her grandmother's stuffy living room. She didn't go home because her parents wanted someone to be in the apartment in case there were problems. Eva was fine with the plan. It gave her time to read in the evenings, and her grandmother's diaries gave her a lot to think about.

Wren was a central character to them. If it hadn't been 1925, Eva would have thought that her grandmother totally had the hots for her new friend. Wren seemed to dominate the entries Mary made following their meeting. Eva sighed and stared up at the water-stained ceiling. There was no way. Her grandmother wasn't *gay*. She certainly didn't spend her teenage years crushing on girls.

But could she have liked *this* girl? Eva wasn't about to go about labeling someone who couldn't choose a label for herself. She hated it when people did that with historical figures. Still, the implication was there, and Eva wasn't sure *what* to think about this revelation. Or potential revelation. Whatever it was.

She sighed, pulling the sheet up over her despite the heat, and turned back to the diary.

She was reading now because her mother hadn't particularly appreciated the first time she had disappeared under the guise of getting lunch from Mr. Bertelli's grocery on the corner and had been drawn into a week-long period later in January where her grandmother waxed on, almost poetically, about how truly wonderful and beautiful Wren was. She returned more than an hour later with sandwiches, but it had done little to assuage her mother's ire. At least she had an excuse when her mother demanded to know where Eva got off disappearing like that when they needed *help*.

"Mr. Bertelli offered me a job," Eva explained. She sat her parents down at the tiny kitchen table and passed out the sandwiches she'd bought. It was easy to talk when they were crammed into this room, away from the chaos of a half-packed-up apartment. She did not get pulled away into memory as easily. "I wasn't sure what to say and it turned into a..." She wrinkled her nose and trailed off, searching for the right word. "Thing."

"How so?"

"Well, I got drawn into a conversation with him after I put in the sandwich order," Eva said. This was true. It just so happened that she had sat on a bench reading for twenty minutes before this. "He wanted to know more about my availability and if I liked his store."

"When did he offer?" her mother asked.

"At the funeral. I wasn't really in a mental state to give him an answer then."

"That's smart of you, E." Her father reached over and patted her hand where it rested on the table. "Did you tell him anything yet?"

"I haven't. We don't live here, we're selling this place, and it takes forty minutes on the train to get back home." Eva took a bite of her sandwich. "Besides, I'm still not sure if I want to go back to school next semester—"

"Oh, I wish you would," her mother interjected.

Eva felt disappointment well up within her. She had hoped she could casually float the idea without her mother saying anything.

"Now Claire—" her father started.

"No, she should. Not having a degree is only going to hurt you, Eva."

"I couldn't hack it in college, Mom," Eva shot back. "Remember that time I tried to kill myself because I couldn't handle it?"

Her father hung his head, and Eva felt a flush of shame rise to her cheeks. It was a low blow and one she shouldn't have sunk to, but there was a reason Eva did not graduate from college. Her mother refused to admit that sending Eva into a powder-keg of stress and pressure had done nothing for her already fragile mental state.

"I wish you wouldn't do that." Her mother sounded exhausted, but Eva was done having this argument.

"If I don't talk about it, how are we going to get better as a family?" Eva asked. "We need to talk about stuff like this, Mom."

"You shouldn't turn Mr. Bertelli down," her father interjected. Both Eva and her mother turned and stared at him. He put up his hands, placating. "I don't wanna have that argument again, Eva. Save it for later, for therapy."

Eva looked down at her half-eaten sandwich. She suddenly wasn't hungry. "Okay."

"I talked to your grandmother's lawyer today and he wanted me to come in and talk about some probate details. It could be that we're not able to sell this place as quickly as we thought we might be able to."

"So what does that mean?" Eva asked.

Her father shrugged, picking up his sandwich. "Keep your options open, for now. This place still needs a lot of work before we'll be ready to sell it."

They left Eva alone in the apartment later that evening lost in her thoughts, reading her grandmother's diaries and trying to make sense of everything.

The warm glow of the lamp on the end table bathed her in yellow light as the air conditioner whined quietly in the background. Early tomorrow morning, her parents would be back with a U-Haul to cart away the last of the furniture that they were giving away and the donations to Goodwill and the local women's shelter. She had to go to sleep soon because she had to make an early start, but her mind would not stop racing.

She was alone now in this place that held so many memories for her, for her parents, and for her grandmother's ghost. They had systematically stripped it of its identity, removing all aspects of her grandmother from the space and leaving only furniture and items that needed to be appraised before they could be sold. The apartment felt empty and seemed to echo; the sound of Eva's turning the pages in her grandmother's diaries reverberated through the bare living room.

She was obsessing, she knew, and fixating on these diaries. They had to be important. What had her grandmother kept them for? Sentimentality was never her grandmother's style. Eva knew that better than anyone. She was the sentimental one of the two of them, and her grandmother had spent entirely too much time telling Eva to cull her past.

Her grandmother had taken care to protect these particular memories when the other boxes of letters and photos were kept in a chaotic mess. Her grandmother had kept them for almost ninety years through what Eva guessed were five major moves around the country when her father was a kid before finally coming back to Brooklyn.

"What are you hiding, Gran?" Eva asked herself in a hoarse whisper. She'd been trying to avoid breathing in all the dust that had been lifted into the air since they'd started their cleaning and removal venture earlier that week, but it hadn't worked very well. Eva wasn't sure if it was the stress or the dust, but she felt a cold developing in her aching lower back and the rawness of her throat as her sinuses drained. She had tea with honey from a jar so ancient she'd had to boil it just to get the contents softened up enough to use. The tea wasn't really easing the tightness in her throat.

Eva let the diary rest against her chest as she shifted on the uncomfortable couch. She wasn't sure what to make of her grandmother's fascination with Wren, and wanted to know more about Mary's life back then. Turning, she pushed herself up onto one elbow and set the little book on the end table that was doubling as her nightstand. She grabbed her phone, turned off the light, and settled back down.

Darkness filled the apartment and Eva felt herself start to relax. She had never had problems sleeping in this place beyond the expected backache in the morning. It didn't have the creepy vibe that some of her friends' grandparents' houses had, it just seemed warm and welcoming. The only ghosts here were memories, the kind that Eva did not want to forget.

Eva pulled up her phone's Internet browser and typed into the search bar the last name of the woman who'd run her grandmother's boarding house. She tried to narrow it down as specifically as she could, searching for Talbot + Brooklyn, NY + boarding house + women's suffrage. The name was common, so Eva wasn't sure it would be that easy.

The first few links were garbage, but about halfway down the results page was a link to an academic website that appeared to be run by a local amateur historian in his spare time. It talked about the boarding house Mrs. Talbot ran and how it was unique in its time because it allowed women to come and go freely without placing them under strict rules the way that many all-women establishments tended to during those times. *Context is everything.*

Eva read on greedily, her thumb flipping along the screen. She scrolled through interesting tidbits about Brooklyn at the time when the boarding house was active until she found the author's name and an address toward the bottom of the page.

There was a bookstore not fifteen blocks away that was run by the guy who'd made this site. She'd have to check it out, and maybe show him the diaries. He might be able to use them for some sort of research, or at least help Eva to learn more about her grandmother's daily life. Eva clicked her phone off and set it on the arm of the couch behind her head. She curled onto her side and settled into sleep. That could be tomorrow's project.

⸺∘◦⦅⦆◦∘⸺

January 25, 1925

Wren brought the paper around this morning so I didn't have to borrow it from Judith, the girl upstairs who writes a ladies' column in the Star. She's always so unpleasant when I ask her if I can read it, calling me a mooch and complaining about how I earn better pay than she does for doing a fraction of the job. She gets it free from her job every day. I don't understand why she's so grouchy about it. She acts as though no one ever gives her anything for free yet she shows her gams to every man who seems to be at all interested, and she definitely gets the looks that would have Mrs. Talbot in fits if she ever knew.

We have strict rules here. Mrs. Talbot doesn't keep a curfew, and she doesn't seem to put much stock in the Victorian beliefs of my parent's generation, but she does expect a level of respectability that Judith certainly doesn't bring to the house. Elsie and I think it's only a matter of time before she's kicked out. She's out, disappeared off to some speakeasy drinking bathtub gin and dancing the night away like she's a character in one of Mr. Fitzgerald's stories.

If you ask Elsie, she's far too much of a bore to be of any fun at a place such as that. She says I'm too young to go out and assess the situation for myself, though. So I am stuck at home most nights, reading stolen newspapers or books and wishing that Wren would come to visit me.

It is lovely when Wren does come. She's never told me in so many words what she does for work, but I get the sense that it's very important. Mrs. Talbot lets us use the kitchen to make coffee and we sit around the table discussing the society gossip pages and Wren's latest literary conquest. This time it is The Constant Nymph by a Brit named Margaret Kennedy and it isn't getting a lot of play in the papers here because it's too controversial. Wren says she found it quite on a lark when speaking to a bookseller and inquiring if someone else's novel had come in yet. A happy coincidence if I do say so myself. She's promised to let me read it when she's done with it.

We stayed inside all evening, despite the day being far warmer and blessedly snow-free for the first time in days. Wren doesn't seem to particularly care for being out in public. I've invited her down to the bakery or the bookseller's at the end of the block, but she always turns me down. The few moments I was able to have her in the harsh, biting wind were magical. She sparkled, glowed even, in the sunlight and I had no words for how beautiful she was in that moment.

As soon as it came, though, it faded away into nothingness. A crowd of stern-faced men walked by us then, and Wren went silent and distant. She seems almost skittish around other people or in large crowds, like a frightened lamb. I didn't notice it on the train when I met her, but I am almost certain that she was reading to calm her nerves. Her fingers tangled up in something around her neck as she pressed herself against the wall that overlooked the river. I asked what her cross looked like when the men had passed and we were alone again. I gestured to her necklace when she did not follow my question. Wren looked at me, sadness in her sharp green eyes, and shook her head. She said she wore no cross, and refused to speak any more about it.

It bothers me that she cannot open up to me about this. Our friendship is still in its infancy. Maybe this is knowledge that comes with time. I wonder what could have befallen Wren to make her so scared to be around people.

Perhaps in time, she will tell me more about her reasons for doing many of the queer things that she does.

Chapter 6
The Proposal

EVA'S PHONE RANG AT EIGHT-THIRTY the next morning. She glowered at the picture of her father smiling brightly on the screen before finally sliding her finger across to answer with a sleepy grunt. She hadn't slept well, and it was too early for her thoughts to come together in any sort of coherent fashion.

"Hey E, you awake?" His voice sounded bright and hopeful, almost like a puppy. Eva made what she hoped was an affirmative noise and rolled over onto her back. A spring dug painfully into her lower back and she shifted, her hips jerking upwards and her legs getting even more tangled in the sheet. The couch groaned under her and Eva kicked free.

"Sort of." She sounded as if she were underwater. Her head hurt. She needed to take her medicine. Eva sat up, happy to get away from the evil spring of pokey-back pain. "What's up?"

"I just got out of the meeting with your grandmother's lawyer," her father explained. He sounded breathless, as if he were walking quickly. Judging by the ambient noise in the background, he was probably somewhere in Midtown. "I'm heading over there. I thought maybe we could get bagels and I could tell you about the meeting."

Eva rubbed a sleepy hand over her face, catching a smear of drool and some early-morning eye gook. *Gross.* "Is mom still coming?" She wasn't awake enough to make plans yet. She needed coffee and her meds. Then, maybe, she could be human again.

"Not today, hon," her father answered. His heavy breathing stopped and the noise around him grew louder as the conversation lulled. Eva was about to ask why, when her father continued, "She's got to set up her classroom today, and this meeting was the only way I got out of helping with the third clean-up project in as many weeks."

"Slacker." Eva slumped back onto the couch. Her mother's school would be starting up soon, and Eva was trying to pretend she wasn't looking forward to it. Her mother being busy after a long summer of being home would be good for the entire family. Lord knew Eva needed a break from her mother's adamant denial of her daily struggle with depression. "Okay… so you're… you're taking the subway, right?"

"Yeah, it should be like twenty minutes or so. Start getting ready," he said teasingly. "Wouldn't want to catch you halfway through your process."

Eva scowled. He really did know her too well because it would take her far longer than a mere twenty minutes to be ready to face the day with so little sleep on the uncomfortable couch. "I'm about to go down into the station, so I'm gonna lose you, but I'll shoot you a text or something when I get to 25th Street so you can be sure to have pants on."

"Dad, it was *one time*," Eva protested. Once, he had walked in on her fixing her hair in her underwear and hadn't let her live it down since. If she were a boy, it wouldn't have been an issue, but fathers were weird about their daughters, and Eva's father was no exception to that rule.

"Uh-huh," he answered, his tone highly skeptical. "I didn't raise you to be a nudist, kid."

"Dad!" Eva shrieked into the phone.

He laughed and hung up, leaving Eva sitting in the silent apartment. She got up and headed to the bathroom, where she showered quickly and did not linger in front of the mirror getting ready.

She squirmed into a pair of cut-off jean shorts that she'd shoved into her backpack two days ago when she'd returned to her apartment to get some more clothes and to say hello to her roommates. Her parents were paying her rent for the month, and she really hated that all her roommates had to know about their doing that. They were all right, but she had no space to breathe at all in her tiny apartment. Staying here was a much-needed break from *people* even if it did come with long hours spent with her mother.

Eva checked her phone. The weather app said it was going to be close to ninety degrees today, which meant that it would probably be closer to one hundred in the stairwell and on the street. Her dad probably wanted to walk places with her today, or lug heavy furniture down the narrow stairs. Eva wasn't about to sweat her butt off for his sake.

She was just lacing up shoes when there was a quiet knock on the door followed by the sound of keys jingling. A moment later, the deadbolt turned and the door cracked open. Her father stuck his head around the door, one hand covering his eyes. "Everyone decent in here?"

"No, Dad," Eva replied in a deadpan voice. "I'm showing a scandalous amount of ankle." She finished tying her shoe and got to her feet.

He pulled his hand from his eyes and tugged at his collar. He was wearing a tie and carrying a suit jacket over one arm, and he'd rolled up his shirtsleeves to combat the heat that already gripped the borough. "Thank *god* for air conditioning," he said, pushing the door shut with a dramatic sigh and leaning against it, pretending to be breathless and parched.

Eva rolled her eyes, tucking her phone into her purse and fishing out her sunglasses. She perched them on top of her still-damp hair and smiled slyly at her father. If he was going to tease, she could tease back.

"It's hot out?" she asked mildly. "Maybe you shouldn't have worn a wool suit."

"Scorcher," her father answered. "And don't you start on the suit thing. You know very well that it isn't my choice, but I have to pretend to be professional. Sometimes." Eva watched with a carefully affected disinterest as he deposited his jacket over the back of her grandmother's favorite armchair. He tugged his tie off completely and shoved it into the pocket of his jacket after rolling it into a neat ball. "But yes, it is grossly hot out." He shook his head. "And the city smells like hot garbage and piss."

"Par for the course, then," Eva answered. She grinned at him. "How was the meeting?"

He gestured toward the door and Eva nodded. "It didn't go quite how I'd wanted it to, E," he explained as he locked the door behind them. The staircase was hot and stuffy. It felt as if they'd just walked into an attic, and as they descended, their feet made the floorboards groan as they hurried down. "Mom's lawyer is a great guy, but I don't think he saw this coming, or if he did he totally failed to mention it before now."

"What do you mean?" Eva asked.

Outside it was cooler, but not by much. A gentle breeze blew at Eva's damp hair and sent a shiver through her.

"It's a lot more complex than your mom and I initially thought." He pointed up the block. "Do you want to get a bagel?"

"Sure."

"Awesome, I'm starved. Anyway, because I'm Mom's only living heir, the estate's got to go through probate for a while—at least three months—in order to establish that there aren't any other judgments or liens against her estate."

"Gran paid all her bills though." Eva kicked a rock and watched it skid off the sidewalk and crash into a parked car's hubcap.

"She didn't pay the hospital bill after she died, and we've got to wait on them to bill her insurance and then for her insurance to bill us before we can do anything at all. The lawyer doesn't think it'll take more than six months, but with New York property law? Anything's possible."

"I see."

She felt like a child. She had no idea death came with so much attached to it. Things she wouldn't even have thought of a month ago.

"On top of that, there's settling the estate tax."

"Gran wasn't wealthy."

"Uncle Sam will get his due." Her father shook his head. "He always does. They'll settle the hospital bills and any other debt Mom has in probate and *then* we can sell the apartment."

They turned the corner and cut across the street. Traffic was light between the morning and lunch rush.

"It could be more than a year, judging by what I've been told by the lawyers." Eva's father let out a quiet groan. They skirted around the small cluster of tables that were jumbled out in front of the bagel shop. People, perhaps students, sat outside with iced coffee dewing in Mason jars. If she strained her ears, Eva could hear them tapping away on their expensive laptops under the shade of bright red and yellow umbrellas.

"Really?" Eva pulled the door open and was immediately hit with the warm, salty aroma of freshly baked bread. There was a hint of onion in the air, and Eva smiled, the onion bagels were still warm. They were her favorite. "That's terrible."

Eva's father tapped his chin thoughtfully. "It'd be terrible if the property had to remain vacant, but since Mr. Bertelli's offered you a job, why don't you stay there? We can come by on the weekends and give the place a fresh coat of paint and redo the kitchen floor, but this way there'd be someone in it, and you'd be living rent-free so you could actually start to save money." He flashed her a wry grin. "Provided, of course, that you think about going back to school, which it sounds like you were doing anyway... so—"

Eva's eyes widened and she turned to stare openly at her father. "Are you serious?" she squeaked. She was trying not to shriek with joy in the middle of the crowded shop, but it was a close thing. She was practically vibrating with excitement and her face felt as if it were about to split in two, she was smiling so broadly.

He grinned at her. "Yeah. Mom's lawyer said that it's better if the property is occupied anyway, and the property taxes for the year are already paid. This would only be until probably April of next year..."

Eva flung her arms around her father, hugging him tightly in spite of the fact that they were both hot and sweaty "It doesn't matter, it's perfect. Thanks, Dad!"

The awkward hug was cut short when the guy behind the counter cleared his throat loudly. They sprang apart and Eva hurriedly placed her order before turning to her dad. "Do you want coffee?"

"Iced, please," he answered.

They moved down to pay for their orders. A few people were ahead of them. Eva chewed her lip, thinking about her grandmother's diaries and the extra time that living in the apartment would give her to read them and try to make sense of the *why* of them.

"Hey, Dad."

"Yeah?"

"Did Gran ever talk about the diaries I found? Or what she did when she was sixteen and clerking for that lawyer?" Eva wondered if maybe it was just that she'd never asked the right questions, and that was why her grandmother had never told her about her young working years.

"I can't remember her ever talking about her childhood beyond her father being shell-shocked from World War I. Why?"

"The journals are from that year." Eva stepped aside so her father could pass the guy at the register a twenty. "I can't get over how different she is."

"How so?" her father asked. He accepted his change with a harassed smile that showed all the lines in his face. Eva was again reminded that he was so much older than many of her friends' parents. Two generations of having children later in life meant that Eva's family was exceptionally long-lived. Her grandmother had been absolutely ancient, creeping her way past the century mark with little fanfare, and her dad was well on his way to doing the same. He was graying around the temples and starting to look his age.

"Well, she just... There was always something about Gran, this great shadow of loss. From what you've told me, it was there in your childhood as well. When she wrote these diaries, it isn't there. Like, at all."

"Maybe it happened after they were written. That's most of her lifetime, E."

"You know as well as I do that that isn't how it works. She was basically an adult, and there's nothing that indicates she had it too."

"Maybe she was just better at hiding it," Eva's father suggested as they collected their bagels and Mason jars of iced coffee and slowly maneuvered their way to an empty indoor table. Eva wasn't going back outside until she had to. "She did live through an awful lot, your grandmother."

"Maybe." Eva shook her head. "The other boxes that I found were all cheap, you know, actual shoe boxes, but this one was different. It was one of those photo archival boxes that they used to sell back in the '80s. I think that they're acid-free or something like that, to preserve what's inside. I think that whatever it was happened in the year contained in those diaries."

"What year?" Eva's dad asked suddenly, his lips pursed together as though he were remembering something vitally important.

"Uh… 1925."

"She was just a kid then… Not that she ever spoke about her childhood." He sipped his coffee. "I remember she said once that was the year that the light had gone out for her."

The bagel was cooling in its basket in front of her, and Eva picked it up, contemplating it before taking a bite and enjoying the warm flavor of hot, crispy bread mixed with cool cream cheese. This place knew how to do a bagel— nothing fancy and certainly not too much cream cheese.

"The light?" Eva asked. She was trying to keep her voice down, as the people in the next table over were looking at them with interest. Eva supposed that it was a curious sort of a conversation.

Her dad shrugged, and when he spoke his voice was quieter as well. "She always called it the light of the world, but I never asked what it actually meant."

Eva chewed her bagel and wondered if maybe the answer was hidden in the pages of the diaries she had yet to read.

Chapter 7

The Grocery

TIME, OVER THE NEXT FEW weeks, twisted and mutated, alternating between inching forward and racing so quickly that Eva could scarcely keep up. Her mind fell into a haze, drifting, full of half-remembered stories and the words of a sixteen-year-old girl. Her grandmother's apartment stood empty save for Eva's memories.

In the late afternoon, the apartment filled with sunlight, but there was a kind of sadness in the light that Eva could not explain. It clung to the faded wallpaper with desperate fingers of sun that could never gain purchase. Instead it shifted, lingering on the lists of little repairs that had to be done in the upcoming weeks.

Eva spent the week leading up to Labor Day weekend frantically trying to find someone to sublease her apartment at the last minute. Thankfully, with colleges starting up once more, there was a huge influx of people who needed cheap places to live and had no time at all to shop around. After her ad had been up on Craigslist for less than three hours, Eva found a guy who looked to be a good fit. Two days later, she found out that he got on well with her roommates and was willing to let her borrow his battered pickup truck to transport her meager possessions to her new place of residence.

It was *weird* for Eva to load up the truck with her things and leave her forwarding address at the post office. It was a very adult move in a life that had, up until this point, been largely spent attempting to run away from her problems. There was a finality to moving away from her peers to be by herself that set Eva's heart racing. Could she do it? Would she be able to be alone without falling back into old habits? She liked to think that she was better than those old, tired thoughts, but she felt as though they were to be a constant throughout her life.

It's just a matter of "adulting," Eva told herself on Friday as she walked into Mr. Bertelli's shop. She was mostly settled into her grandmother's apartment now, her things lining the shelves where her grandmother's lifetime collection of kitsch and knickknacks had once been. Her books were in the bookshelves, her records on the turntable.

Yet there were signs of her grandmother everywhere. They didn't pack up the china or the kitchen, and the back closet where Eva found her grandmother's diaries was still largely untouched. It was a time capsule to a world Eva didn't think her father was quite ready to unpack.

Mr. Bertelli was overjoyed when Eva pushed open the door to his shop and slipped inside. He beamed at her, his dark eyes crinkling at the corners and his expression jubilant. "Eva!" he boomed. "I did not think you would be coming back!"

Eva stood by a rack of produce, feeling awkward. Now that she was here, asking seemed an impossible task. Her hands were heavy at her sides and she reached out to start tugging at the husk of a coconut. "It's good to be back," she started. It was clumsy. Eva's cheeks burned with the shame of not knowing what to say.

A long, pregnant silence filled the little grocery.

Mr. Bertelli stepped out from behind the counter. His apron was perfectly straight and tied in a neat bow at his hip. He wasn't that much taller than Eva, and he came up to her and held out his hand. She gave him her hand and he squeezed it gently, a kind smile drifting across his face. "You need to pick up dinner for your parents, right?"

Eva shook her head. "Actually, Mr. Bertelli, I'm here to see if that job you offered me is still available. My family can't sell Gran's apartment right away, so I'm going to stay there so that someone's at least living in the space. I was wondering—"

"If you could work here part time?" Mr. Bertelli pulled Eva into a one-armed hug. He smelled like spices and homemade bread. "That will depend on how good your Italian is."

"Awful."

"Ach, you'll learn." Mr. Bertelli gestured toward the back office. "Go have a seat in there and I'll tell you what the job entails."

Eva lingered while Mr. Bertelli locked the door and flipped the sign to indicate that the store was closed. Her breath caught in her chest, surprised that he would close up shop just to speak to her. She sat down in his cluttered office and started fiddling with her nails. She felt unworthy of such a sacrifice from a small business owner, especially if she were to be working there only part time.

Mr. Bertelli bustled in after her and paused, catching the look on her face. "Don't worry about the door. Most of my customers come later in the day, anyway." He crossed the room in three long strides and sat down behind his desk. "Now, Eva. Tell me more about why you want this job."

Launching into the explanation of the probate court and how long it was probably going to take to settle her grandmother's estate, Eva started to relax. It was easy speaking to someone who had cared for her grandmother as much as she had, especially when it came to griping about the refurbishment of the apartment. Mr. Bertelli used to hand-deliver groceries when it was too cold for Eva's grandmother to go out. He knew the place well and asked inquisitive, if politely removed, questions about how the fixing up was going.

She wanted this job because she'd never really had one that she thought could make a difference. Mr. Bertelli's store had been there, on the same corner, for generations. It had taken the brunt of anti-Italian sentiment during World War II and still its doors stayed open. Working here was like stepping back in time, and Mr. Bertelli had a wealth of information on the old neighborhood before it started to shift and change into something out of a TV show where everyone looked the same and no one seemed to struggle.

Mr. Bertelli leaned back in his chair and stroked his mustache. "You will learn quickly, I think," he said. His smile was kind. "Not just the Italian, but rather the flow of this place."

"Flow?"

He made an affirmative noise. "This place has a pace to it that is very different than what is outside, no? Outside it is always rushing around, no time to breathe. The people who shop here, they are timeless. They remember what it was like before, and I think you're that speed too."

"I guess so…" She wasn't so sure. If anything, she felt as though she was a colossal screwup who was still wallowing in loss and heartbreak. She missed her grandmother desperately. "Mostly I just think I'm the speed of failure."

"Well, with that attitude—" Mr. Bertelli shook his head. "Youth of today, I swear."

"I dropped out of college, Mr. Bertelli. I have no degree or skills. I've been living off my parents' and grandmother's charity for the past three years."

"Yes, but you had a reason for needing that break, no?" Beneath his heavy eyebrows, his eyes were warm. She thought she read pity in them, and she hated it. She didn't want his pity. "It is nothing to be ashamed of, not being able to cope. Some of the people who come here keep the old ways and they'd see it as a sin, but I know how these things go. Your grandmother made a point of making sure that I knew. You're safe here, if you'd like the job."

Eva swallowed. She never knew her grandmother protected her from the talk of the neighborhood. She'd never known that they even *knew*. Her parents, mostly her mother, had insisted on telling no one except those who needed to know. That number was small, a mere handful in the larger scheme of things. Color rose in her cheeks as she realized Mr. Bertelli knew.

She did not want to be the family secret. "My troubles are my own."

"Anyone with that sort of trouble needs a support network." Mr. Bertelli held his hand out across the desk. "So how about it?"

Eva shook his hand. "Sure."

It was a done deal then. Mr. Bertelli rummaged around in his desk and pulled out tax forms and took down her information. He had Eva count back change for him and showed her how to work the cash register for an elderly couple who smiled at Eva as though she were utterly charming while she muddled her way through it. She only stayed an hour, but she left feeling exhilarated.

She could not remember the last time she felt this way about something like this, and she spent the walk home thinking about the proposed shifts she would work as well as how best to ask Mr. Bertelli if he had any memory of the old times before the neighborhood changed. He was in his seventies, a great deal younger than her grandmother, but he was as much a fixture around here as she had been. Eva kicked at a rock. She wanted to know what he had to share about her grandmother, but it didn't seem right to ask. Her stomach sank just thinking about trying to figure out the right words to say to him.

There was no way to make it not sound bizarre. She shook her head, turning up her grandmother's street and stepping around a dog walker. *Hey Mr. Bertelli, I know I haven't been working for you long, and that you probably had a thing for my Gran, but do you think you could help me figure out this mystery about what happened her best friend from when she was sixteen?* She was embarrassed just thinking about the conversation.

He was doing her this huge, massive, wonderful favor in letting her have this job. Eva felt that grilling him over some cryptic things that her grandmother used to say, let alone what she wrote about in her teenage diaries, was a bad idea. He'd only just hired her, and even if he'd known her for most of her life, it felt like overstepping.

Eva swung the bag in her hands. Inside was the apron that Mr. Bertelli had given her while he was explaining his expectations and the shifts Eva would be working.

"We are open Tuesday through Saturday," Mr. Bertelli explained with a grin. His mustache trembled in an almost alarming way as he spoke and Eva tried very hard not to laugh as he continued, obviously mistaking her smile for enthusiasm. "Although, I assume that you are one of the godless youth of America; so, if I were to open for limited Sunday hours, you would be willing to man the shop alone?"

He wiggled his eyebrows, which set his mustache off once more. Eva bit the inside of her cheek hard. "You can have a half day on Saturday as well if you did that."

It was a pretty decent offer, one that would allow her a great deal more time in the weekend evenings to work on restoring the apartment with her parents. Eva was more interested in the side project of reading through and figuring out her grandmother's diaries, but she knew better than to prioritize it until the apartment was fully fixed up. She made a promise to her parents about it. And even if the circular thoughts that her depression tended to trap her in didn't allow for much else, Eva truly wanted to help fix up the apartment as best she could.

She agreed to the hours and asked when she should come in for her first day. Mr. Bertelli was impressed with her ability on the register; he'd said as much as she rang up a handful of customers. The afternoon was growing late now, and tomorrow the grocery would be closed for the holiday weekend.

He replied with a bright smile to match her own, as if he too, was exhilarated by the prospect of her working for him. "It is probably best if you come in on Tuesday morning after the holiday." He gestured toward the mostly empty store. "Everyone is done with their shopping now, and will be eating leftovers until at least Thursday. It will be slower, and the people will be more forgiving if you make mistakes."

She keyed in the code to get into the apartment building and headed up the stairs, exhausted. The sun was just starting to set, casting warm orange light into the stairwell as she climbed higher. Mr. Bertelli would not be able to pay her very much, but it didn't matter. She just needed to support herself long enough to prove to herself and her parents that she could provide for her own needs.

The weight of the responsibility settled onto her shoulders comfortably, and for the first time in a very long time, she felt hopeful. This was a chance, a start of something new, something that she had done entirely for herself. It was paved on the path of sadness, as were so many things in her life, but there was a light at the end of the tunnel. She could scarcely recall the last time she'd felt this way, and the feeling made her stomach turn with anxiety at the unknown.

The apartment was cool compared to the unventilated stairs. Eva kicked off her shoes and crossed the room to the couch. She set her bag from Mr. Bertelli's on the table and flopped down. All the pressure of talking to Mr. Bertelli, and the anxiety of having to ask for something she could not bring herself to feel that she deserved, came crashing down upon her. She wrapped her arms around a throw pillow and inhaled the scent of her grandmother's perfume. This relaxed her to the point where she could start to use the techniques she was taught to quiet her mind.

In and out. Breathe.

Sleep came easily.

The well was dry when she fell down it. She tripped head over foot and tumbled headfirst into a black pit of despair. Muck, black and slimy, covered the walls and Eva's nails raked through it as she tried to gain a handhold so she could pull herself away from the inevitable spiral of the nightmare.

A solitary figure, seemingly made out of muck and grime, emerged from the shadows. Her presence came in a flash of light from on high. It formed her where there was only black ooze before. She stood with her hands clasped behind her back. Her breath rattled in her chest—in and out, in and out. She had no face.

"You're a seeker. You're looking for the light of the world."

Eva's fingers dug deeper into the wall until blood and grime mixed together.

She turned, her gory fingers pressing into the spaces where the faceless girl should have had eyes. The mire on Eva's hands smeared the empty sockets, filling them with blood and decay.

"I do not seek the light of the world." Eva's voice was forceful. The dreams could tell her again and again that she must find the light. That it would fix her. But Eva knew better. There was no fixing her. The dreams were tricks to make her want something that she could never have. "I am not the kind of broken that any drug, or god, or dream can cure—"

The faceless girl leaned forward and pressed damp fingertips to Eva's still-protesting mouth. Eva breathed in the taste of dirty lake water mixed with the coppery taste of blood. "Wake up," the girl said. "You are out of cycle."

"Out of cycle?"

"Only finding The Light of the World will make the truth known."

Eva woke up panting, tears streaming down her cheeks. Her mouth tasted like blood. She spat into her palm. She must have bitten her tongue during the dream.

She had much more vivid dreams now, and assumed that they were a part of her grieving process. The girl with no face was just another representation of all the things she felt but could not articulate. The well was the depression itself. It couldn't be more complicated than that. It was easy to explain away horrible nightmares, but harder to stop them.

The clock on the wall read nine-thirty and the sun was starting to peak through the blinds. Eva sat up and rubbed at her eyes. She had not meant to sleep so long.

Chapter 8

A Gamble

It was early when Eva's father arrived that weekend, but she could not have been happier to see him and his toolbox, and the brand-new mattress he lugged up the stairs with her help. This was the first time she'd ever had a mattress that she'd picked out. And she needed to stop sleeping on her grandmother's lumpy, uncomfortable couch.

They were in the bedroom, setting up her mattress on her grandmother's old metal bed frame. They had spent the better part of the morning tightening the screws and blasting the whole thing with WD-40 to make sure that it didn't squeak. The bed had always squeaked when her grandmother had lived here, and she was either too deaf to notice or simply past the point of caring enough to do anything about it. Eva, however, was a light sleeper and was having none of that.

They had tossed her grandmother's mattress out of the one window in the apartment that overlooked the Dumpster in the alley behind the apartment building. Eva's dad had taken one look at the tag on it, seen a date in the early '80s, and winced before announcing that there was no chance of salvaging it and that donating it would be a crime against lower backs and spines everywhere. Throwing the mattress from a window was oddly satisfying for both of them.

Eva's father fiddled with the new mattress, making sure it was straight. He gave the bed frame a good, hard shove. It rattled against the wall but it did not squeak. Eva let out a quiet, satisfied sigh and stepped back.

"Probate court takes forever and a day, especially in New York, so you're safe for a good while. Mr. Bertelli's giving you something to do, so it's perfect, Eva."

Over the course of the week, Eva's father went to see Mary's lawyers on three separate occasions. Probate court sounded as though it was *beyond* a hassle. The lawyers were attempting to hurry along the hospital where Mary had spent her final days. They were moving at a glacial pace when it came to billing, and no one was sure how much Medicare would cover once the bill did come. This bill—Mary Kessler's last outstanding debt—would determine whether or not the apartment had to be sold. Mary had enough in savings to cover the cost of her funeral and burial, and they hoped that there was enough to pay the hospital as well. Until that bill came, Eva's living situation was all the more tenuous.

She hated hearing about the ins and outs of the probate court proceedings. It felt as if it were disgracing her grandmother's memory somehow, all the talk of splitting up funds and selling the apartment to cover debt and inheritance. Eva didn't think that a monetary value could be put on Mary Kessler's life, but her father and her grandmother's lawyers were certainly trying. After each update from her well-meaning father, the well of sadness within Eva seemed to deepen a little more. It was wrong and unjust, and she wanted to be better than wallowing in the loss, but she couldn't shake it. She tried to tell her father, but the words wouldn't come out right. They were sticky and clogged in her throat, twisting into hurtful and unpleasant things she didn't mean. Things that made the feelings she wasn't able to talk about seem childish.

Her father understood, or at least she thought he did. On Sunday morning, after she told him the news about her position at Mr. Bertelli's grocery, he took her hand and smiled. "I'm really sorry that I sort of left you in the lurch," he said. Eva looked down at her feet. "I haven't really given you much support because I've been so busy settling your Gran's estate. It's just the ugly part of dying." He reached out and squeezed her shoulder. "Don't worry."

There were times that Eva thought her father was the only person who understood her as a complete person. Even her grandmother had her moments of looking at Eva as though she were a puzzle meant to be solved. Her father never looked at her that way, and he always seemed to know exactly what to say to calm the spiraling thoughts in her head before they got out of control. She might have related more to her grandmother on a personal level, but only her father could assuage her doubts with a kind word. Sometimes that was all Eva needed.

Later that night, when her father had left for home, Eva finally allowed herself to think about the implications of everything that had happened since her grandmother's death. This was the opportunity that she had been looking for, a chance to start over again with a job and purpose in life. She could figure out if she wanted to go back to college, or if she had some sort of a future working for Mr. Bertelli. She had a chance to help her parents say goodbye to her grandmother. She had a chance to get to *know* her grandmother better than she ever had in life. The possibilities were overwhelming.

Guilt welled up in Eva. She had to stop thinking about her grandmother as some grand puzzle to be solved. The story was so fascinating, and the players intriguing to the point where Eva wasn't sure she wanted to stop. She had to know what happened to Wren and why her grandmother had taken such care to preserve these memories. She knew, even before her discovery of the diaries, that there had always been something that had gone unsaid. It was a deep and old wound that Eva was desperate to understand. The pieces to that puzzle were carefully scattered in a story written in her grandmother's own hand.

But then why do I keep dreaming about the light of the world? The phrase was just one that her grandmother had used. No one else in her family seemed to know anything about what it meant. It felt stuck in her head, like a cog in her inner workings that she couldn't stop turning. This was the problem, she got *fixated* on things and she couldn't let them go. *But why am I fixated on the light of the world?* Perhaps there was some importance in that phrase, concept, whatever it was. Perhaps she just hadn't realized it yet.

Maybe in solving the mystery, I'll be able to give Gran some sort of posthumous closure on whatever was making her keep these diaries. That thought alone was enough to keep her looking for answers.

Eva sat cross-legged on the couch. She curled her toes into the soft fabric of her favorite flannel pajamas, distractedly picking at some lint on the fraying knee. On the table was a to-do list that she'd written out with her father. It was headed by his promise to get the electricity and water transferred into her name first thing in the morning so that she could start to build a credit history. The "January Diary," as she'd taken to calling it, and a steaming mug of tea sat next to the list. Outside, it was still unbearably hot and certainly too warm for tea, but Eva was a creature of habit and she enjoyed her tea before she went to bed regardless of the temperature outside. The low hum of the air conditioner would help to put her to sleep.

Scrawled out on a second page of legal paper was the start of a list of names and places that she'd found in her grandmother's diary entries. She figured that at some point she'd drag out her busted old laptop and start to search for their names on the Internet. Maybe she would get lucky and she'd find someone who was still alive who remembered Mary Oglesby and Wren. Maybe there was some sort of public record.

Eva was growing increasingly irritated with her grandmother's cryptic sixteen-year-old self. Mary still had yet to write out Wren's full name, while other people were always referred to by their first names. She liked the nickname, but attempting to figure out what it was short for had presented Eva with too many options for her liking.

It created a sense of mystery around the identity of Wren. She wanted to know who this woman was. There was a connection between the two girls that Eva recognized as one she'd experienced herself a few times in high school. Close, intense friendships, especially ones that formed quickly like this, were the hallmarks of lifelong friendships. Or more.

Now *that* was a weird thought.

All the insinuations and rumors that skirted the edges of Eva's childhood memories of her grandmother came roaring back to her. Eva shook her head. Her grandmother was just taken with this girl who offered her friendship when she really didn't have any before. The girls at Mrs. Talbot's seemed catty and Mary had written about how she couldn't relate to them easily. This was a manifestation of that need for companionship, it had to be.

Eva wasn't going to read into things. She was not inclined to make assumptions about things like potential lady crushes out of the blue like the rest of the people in her family.

She leaned forward and picked up the pen, adding her great uncles' names to the list. They'd both been dead for years, but maybe searching online for them would turn up some sort of connection or lead. As she worked through the entries she had already read, she kept coming back to the website that she'd found a few nights before. The webmaster might be able to help her track down the names and places in the diaries.

Eva scribbled down the name R.M. Perkins, the attorney for whom her grandmother had worked, and sat back on the couch. There was a sense of dread that came with asking for help, a fear that she would never be seen as good enough if she relied on others for assistance. She knew it was foolish, but that was the problem of her illness even though she tried not to let it rule her day-to-day life. It flared up when she had to ask for help with things that she thought she should be able to manage on her own.

If she contacted anyone, it would make this all very real. All of this would no longer be a game of speculation in her head, but rather a reality that she would have to discuss with others.

Eva had grown up during the Internet age; she'd had friends who'd had good and bad experiences meeting people on the Internet. She wasn't sure if the man behind the website would want to help her or turn out to be a total creep.

Eva sighed. She was using her parents' scare tactics when it came to the Internet. She wasn't afraid of meeting people online. Her fears had nothing to do with that. The knot of anxiety in the pit of her stomach tightened when she thought about what this man's help might uncover.

Whatever her grandmother had buried might be better staying buried. What if it was something scandalous? Eva wasn't sure that there was subtext there, but what if her grandmother had loved another girl? What if she asked for help and that was the answer that they found? How would her parents react to that bombshell? Would they care?

Their easy acceptance of Eva's interest in girls as well as boys made her assume it wouldn't be an issue now, but she couldn't be sure. *Maybe it would absolutely shatter Dad's world.* Eva wasn't sure how to even begin to broach the topic with her father. Were these old stories about a sixteen-year-old girl better left forgotten? Did she want to go airing what essentially amounted to family secrets to a complete stranger?

Eva puffed out her cheeks and glanced down at her watch. It was too late to try calling the bookshop and it was a holiday weekend so the shop owner, a Mr. Theodore Schultz, probably wasn't around.

Asking for help was the worst option, but it was also a necessity if she wanted to push on. She needed someone who'd grown up here and had *lived* in the neighborhood for many years to parse out the changes that had happened over time. She was not sure if this bookseller was the answer, but he was as good a place as any to start.

At college, Eva considered studying history. She had an interest in the law and had thought a lot about the possibility of writing about historical events. She'd never gotten beyond the core courses before she'd withdrawn, and the classes she had taken were focused on periods of history before her grandmother's time. She felt utterly mystified by some of the historical references her grandmother made.

In a way, reading about her grandmother's grand adventure living alone in the city at sixteen made Eva feel awful. She was twenty-two and hadn't decided what she wanted to do with her life. Sometimes Eva felt as though she still hadn't decided if she wanted to live it yet.

Eva reached for her phone. She was feeling utterly overwhelmed again by the completely indefinable mass of the "the future" pressing down around her, and didn't want to think about it anymore. It would only make her feel sadder. Half buried under the legal pad, her phone blinked with a new notification. Her dad had texted to tell her that he'd gotten home okay. Eva flicked her thumb across the screen, navigating to her email app.

Late last night, during a fit of pique over her inability to find anything more in her grandmother's documents relating to Wren, Eva had looked up the contact information for Mr. Schultz. She stared at a blank email for a long time before typing out his email address, fat-fingering the keys a few times and having to go back to correct herself more than once. Tongue caught between her teeth, Eva began to type. It was slow going, with a lot of muttering about the autocorrect, but soon a message began to take shape.

Mr. Schultz,

My name is Eva Kessler. I found your email address on your website about mid-1920s local historical landmarks while searching for Mrs. Talbot's boarding house. My grandmother, Mary Kessler (you might have known her, she was out and about in the neighborhood quite often until she passed away last month), was a resident of that boarding house in 1925. Your website was very helpful. I'm looking to try to track down some of her old friends and colleagues and I need some help doing that. I don't have a clue where to start. Would you be interested in assisting?

My grandmother wasn't much for sharing her past, and when asked she always spoke about the light of the world going out. I was wondering, as you appear to be something of an expert on the time period when she first started using that term, if you could spare any insight into the time when she was living at the boarding house. I want to find out if any of her friends from that era are still alive, as I mentioned before. This is something of a family mystery, since my grandmother was so tight-lipped about her youth.

I'm not sure if you are open tomorrow as it is Labor Day, but please let me know if you are.

Thank you,
Eva Kessler

Eva read the email a few times over to make sure that it made sense and that she hadn't fallen victim to autocorrect's changing her words around. On more than on occasion, Eva had made an ass of herself doing that. She felt an anxiety about her writing that she could never calm.

She set her phone down on the table and leaned back against the couch. She nursed her tea and stared at her largely incomplete list of names. Maybe Mr. Schultz would have some old pictures or something that he could show her—and maybe they'd be able to figure out who Wren was.

———◦◦◦———

That night she did not dream. After the unwelcome visits from the faceless girl, a dreamless sleep was a godsend. Eva woke up to find a blinking notification on her phone. Still half asleep, she stared at it for a moment before her brain registered what it was. She had an email back from Mr. Schultz.

Her mind felt hazy, she'd yet to take her meds. She rolled over and reached for the pill bottle, half-buried in her purse. She popped it open and dry swallowed the little blue pill. It went down rough, and she had to pull herself up and wander into the kitchen to get a drink of water before she was able to sit down and read the email.

As her brain woke up and the pill took its hold, Eva's mind settled and her ability to concentrate returned. She swiped her thumb over the screen and opened her email app. The email was short and to the point, and she was momentarily taken aback by its brusque tone. If Mr. Schultz was a no-nonsense type, it might make this process easier.

Eva,

We are, in fact, open today from 10-7. The shop is usually busy on the weekends. If you were to stop by in the mid-morning there's usually a bit of a lull before the lunchtime crowd starts to arrive when we would be able to speak.

Did your grandmother leave behind any papers or documentation? The Light of the World is not a commonly discussed cultural phenomenon. If she did leave any, would you mind bringing them with you when you come?

Thank you for taking the time to not only find me, but email me as well,

Theo Schultz

Eva stared at the email for a long time, reading it over and over, before opening up a new email to reply. There was something weirdly *pushy* about the way that Mr. Schultz was asking for documents that she didn't like. Also, she had mentioned the light of the world very much in passing and she wasn't interested in trying to solve that mystery. Not yet, at any rate. She wanted to know more about who Wren was, maybe track down a name.

Mr. Schultz,

I was more hoping that you could point me in the right direction regarding some of the names in my grandmother's papers, actually. The light of the world, as far as I can tell, was just an expression she used. I'm not entirely sure that I'm comfortable sharing the diaries with a complete stranger, as they're really personal.

I'll definitely come down sometime before noon.

Thanks,
Eva Kessler

By the time Eva was ready to leave the cool sanctuary of the apartment, the sun was already beating down outside and the temperature was skyrocketing toward the nineties. These were the worst days of summer, the tail end and last hurrah. Eva dressed for the day, tugging on a T-shirt from a concert that had cut-off sleeves and a braided neckline she'd done herself. Shorts were a necessity, but she had walking to do, so she wore her battered All Stars instead of sandals. She paused in front of the bathroom mirror to tug her hair into a messy bun, pinning her bangs off her face with a few ancient-looking bobby pins of her grandmother's that had been overlooked when they were cleaning the bathroom earlier in the week.

Just as she was gathering her things, her phone chimed in her pocket. Another email.

Eva,

I am something of an expert on the phenomenon of the Light of the World, which is why I asked about it when you emailed me initially. Again, I'll state that it is not the sort of concept that a person simply mentions in passing, which is why I would like to see your grandmother's papers if at all possible.

I understand though, that this could be hard for you, but urge you to bring them with you when you come.

Looking forward to meeting you,

Theo Schultz

Eva left the apartment and immediately regretted her choice to wear a dark-colored shirt. Even with cut-off sleeves, it was far too hot to wear anything other than light colors today. She hurried over to the shady side of the streets because she could already feel her body temperature starting to rise. The last thing she wanted to do was show up to speak to Mr. Schultz looking as if she'd just run five miles.

After reading Mr. Schultz's email, Eva wasn't sure that she wanted to bring the diaries with her. She ended up deciding to just bring the January diary and leave the rest behind. If Mr. Schultz turned out to not be a total weirdo, she'd consider letting him see the rest of the diaries.

She tucked the journal into her pocket. After walking for two blocks, Eva wondered if she should have put the diary into some sort of a heat-resistant bag. Would the heat damage it?

This is why I need Theo Schultz's help. She had no idea how to properly handle documents that were so old, or what sort of protection they would need in order to be transported around in a hot Brooklyn morning. Feeling a little helpless, Eva quickened her pace. *Fall can't come soon enough.*

Chapter 9

Schultz's Booksellers & Antiquities

THE BOOKSTORE WAS OFF A side street that fed into a busy intersection, and Eva nearly walked right past the nondescript storefront. It was only by sheer chance that she glanced upward to see a small, faded black sign with chipped gold lettering indicating that this was a bookshop that dealt in rare books and antiquities.

In the storefront window was a display of recent best sellers, propped up and arranged on a piece of fabric that had once been red. It was sun-bleached and faded, making the whole display look shabby. Eva wondered if it was done for the aesthetic, to appeal to the hipsters who were slowly invading the neighborhood. She shrugged. It wasn't her place to judge what a worthwhile display was, anyway. She pushed the door open.

Inside, it was cool and dark, and it took a moment before Eva's eyes adjusted to the gloom and the brightly colored spots at the corners of her eyes disappeared. Every available surface in the bookshop was crammed with books. Long shelves ran perpendicular to the doorway, falling back into darkness. They were marked with hand-drawn signs on cheap poster paper that were decorated with swirls and a creative flair that made Eva smile. They were *definitely* trying to appeal to the hipster demographic.

Across from the entrance was a counter space and a low children's bookshelf displaying picture books that Eva remembered from when she was a kid. A boy was sitting in one of the two armchairs that were arranged at the front of the shop, reading one of the thicker *Harry Potter* books. He glanced at Eva as she stepped inside before going back to his book.

Behind the counter, a bored-looking guy of indeterminate ethnicity leaned on one elbow as he flipped through something on his phone. His skin was deeply tanned and his hair was locked into strands of medium thickness. He was toying with one that had fallen loose from the band holding his dreads behind his head.

When the door snapped shut behind her, the bells affixed to the door handle jangled. He looked up. He was not-quite-shaven and had a defined square chin and intriguingly bright eyes that glinted greenish-gold in the sunlight. "Can I help you?" he asked. His accent said he was a local.

Eva squinted. He had a name tag pinned to his faded and slightly moth-eaten V-neck shirt that read "Al." She smiled and approached the counter. He grinned back at her. His smile was crooked and charming.

"I'm looking for Mr. Schultz." Her purse swung down and thumped against her thigh. "He should be expecting me; I emailed him this morning... Eva Kessler?"

Al's brow furrowed as if trying to recall. After a moment he nodded. "He's out the back with Liv." Stepping around the counter, he jerked one tan thumb toward the blackness at the back of the store. He was lanky and a *lot* taller than Eva. "Wouldn't stop talking about your email earlier."

Eva flushed, feeling sweaty and embarrassed that she hadn't bothered to make sure that they knew she was coming. She had not thought to email back after reading Mr. Schultz's final reply, but instead chose to hurry though her morning ablutions and out the door. She'd woken up late, it was a holiday weekend, and she'd had to hurry to meet him at the time that he'd suggested. "Uh, he did?"

"Yeah." Al shrugged. "No idea why, though." He gestured with his chin toward the back of the store. There was a door back there, half-hidden in gloom and stacks upon stacks of books. "They're just through the door there. Knock, you might save Dad from one of Liv's tirades."

Who is Liv? Eva guessed another staff member of the bookshop, but she'd been wrong before. She supposed she'd find out. "Mr. Schultz is your father?" She was curious. Should she be trying to make a better impression on this guy? Eva worried at the inside of her lip, trying not to bite it and look out of her depth or anxious.

He made an affirmative noise before slinking back behind the counter in his low-riding jeans and worn-out shirt. "I take it we might be seeing more of you?" He picked up a pencil and tapped it on a folded-up newspaper on the counter that Eva hadn't noticed before. He clicked his phone back on and consulted the screen before writing a word into the puzzle. He'd been cheating at the crossword! She gave a little mock-horrified gasp. He grinned sheepishly at her. "I was stuck."

"I'm sure," Eva said stiffly. She wasn't able to keep the smile from her face, though. She was brought up in a family where cheating at the crossword was on the same level as having sex in a church—it simply was not done. It was a great affront to the crossword gods that Al was a dirty cheater. "Your dad sounded pretty keen to see some of my grandmother's old papers," she said, patting her pocket, "so we'll see."

"Well, cool." Al gave a mock-salute and went back to his crossword. He paused, the back of his chewed-on pencil halfway to his mouth, and met Eva's eyes once more, winking. "Be seeing you around then."

Her cheeks burning, Eva hurried away down the first line of bookshelves she came upon. She did not like it when guys flirted with her, even if the banter was easy and to be expected. Al seemed nice enough, though, and that was what made it difficult to forget his charming smile.

She pushed him from her thoughts. She was here to get help puzzling out her grandmother's diaries and maybe figure out what the heck the light of the world was, not to flirt with cute shop boys.

The aisle was clogged with books stacked on the floor and two or sometimes three deep on sagging shelves. The door at the back of the shop was clear of them, but just barely. Eva had to move carefully so as not to upset any unstable towers of books. She knocked on the door, anxiously raising a hand to pat her hair into something resembling order.

She knew that she looked flustered; a combination of the heat and Al's easy smile had done her in. She sucked in a deep breath, struggling mightily to school her expression into something politely neutral. It was a lesson she'd learned while in recovery—how to pretend that she wasn't feeling anything at all.

Today though, it was a losing battle. She just wanted to look as if she hadn't been eyeballing Mr. Schultz's son and sweating like a pig on the way over, but it was hopeless.

The bookshop's cool interior provided a welcome respite from the heat. She loved bookshops, especially ones like this. She liked the wide-open spaces of the big commercial stores as well, but stores like this, with their twisting aisles and reading nooks hidden at the dead ends, were Eva's one true love. She could spend hours here, surrounded by the words of the living and the dead, lingering, learning. She wanted to spend an eternity here. She could see herself easily spending her entire working life in a place like this. She'd be *good* at it. The only problem was that most bookshops wanted even their *clerks* to have a college degree. It was another possibility that had to be dismissed due to circumstances.

Caught up in a daydream of a settled future working in a bookstore, Eva nearly missed the sound of a chair scraping against the floor beyond the closed door. She exhaled quickly, anxiously shifted from foot to foot. She'd never been good with nerves. Her ears strained to catch the low murmur of voices. The discussion sounded heated but amicable, like casual banter between two friends.

Eva waited, hand half-raised to knock again. The door was flung open and a short, round man with greying curls and the most impressive set of eyebrows that Eva had ever seen stood in the doorway. Those eyebrows easily gave Mr. Bertelli's mustache a run for its money. Eva hid her smile behind her hand.

"Can I help you?" He shoved his round wire-framed glasses up his nose with his thumb. His voice sounded as though it was trying to be cultured, but there was a hint of something underneath that Eva recognized well, an accent that could only be from here, or maybe over in Red Hook. He was a local, and therefore exactly who she needed.

"Hi." She tucked her purse under her arm and stuck out her left hand. She was humming with anxiety, but the smile on her face was genuine. She could only assume this man was Mr. Schultz. He looked a bit like Al, especially about the nose and eyes. "Eva Kessler. We spoke via email?"

His eyebrows drew together for a minute, just as Al's had, before realization dawned. "Ah," he said. He reached out awkwardly with his right hand to shake hers, then switched to his left to take Eva's and shake it firmly. Eva was used to that. Being left-handed made everything slightly off for her when it came to meeting people, she always forgot and proffered the wrong hand. Her grip simply wasn't as firm in her right hand. Her father swore by a firm handshake, and Eva wasn't about to disregard his advice in favor of right-handed culture. "Theo Schultz. I'm glad you came, I got a little worried when you didn't email me back again."

"Yeah, sorry about that." He held the door open for her to step into the room. "I woke up late and saw your response." She shrugged, giving just a little indication of how terribly awkward she felt. "I hurried over so I wouldn't miss your quiet period."

"It's no trouble." He waved her off. There was a small smile playing at his lips. "I was just very interested in what you'd found. It's not every day that someone emails me out of the blue asking about something as specific as The Light of the World."

Eva opened her mouth, wanting to protest that she really wanted his help with her grandmother's diaries rather than with the light of the world, at least at first. She was sure the answers to all her questions lay within the pages of those diaries. She wasn't sure the light of the world would be as interesting to her. She swallowed the words and tried to meet his smile with one of her own. There would come a time to temper his expectations.

He led her into a workshop that was lit by two large skylights. A wide workbench dominated the room and was covered with papers, books, and rolls of maps and blueprints. In the far corner was a smaller desk with a computer and scanner.

A young woman sat at the computer. She had a bored look on her face, one finger toying distractedly with a chain around her neck as she clicked through the online edition of the *New York Times*. Eva was struck by her, taken by her casual grace as she lounged in the desk chair.

"Liv," Mr. Schultz called to her.

Eva's stomach flip-flopped. She felt she knew this woman but could not place her. Where had she seen her before?

Liv uncurled from the chair and stepped closer. She had an almost predatory look about her slate-blue eyes. She was wearing jeans and a sleeveless button-down collared shirt that looked as though it had seen better days, but there was an elegance about her that set Eva's teeth on edge. Her hair was pulled back into a bun. She hadn't bothered to pin back the blond hair that spilled loose to frame her face.

"This is Eva Kessler," Mr. Schultz continued his introduction. "She's the one who emailed me about The Light of the World of all things, can you believe that?"

Liv held out her hand and Eva took it awkwardly with her right, shaking it weakly. She looked up to find herself on the receiving end of a dimpled and crooked smile that made Liv's eyes seem far warmer and friendlier than before. "Olivia Currance. It's nice to meet you."

"Eva Kessler. You too." She faltered. Liv had not let go. Her hand was very warm.

Eva felt scrutinized, as if she were being carefully assessed as Liv's gaze raked over her face. "Um..." she started again, slowly pulling her hand back from Olivia's tight grip. "Is it all right to call you Liv?"

"Most everyone does." Liv jammed her hands into her back pockets, spinning on her heel toward Mr. Schultz. There was a small rectangular carton pressed against the fabric of her back pocket. Cigarettes, Eva guessed. "I'm going to go out front for a bit, is that okay?"

"It's a filthy habit," Mr. Schultz replied. He made a shooing gesture all the same. He had the distracted air of an absent-minded professor, but there was a sharpness about him that made Eva feel that she should be on the defensive. It wasn't so much that he was frightening, but rather that he was *intense*. Eva, a few years removed from her failed attempt at college, had forgotten how unnerving intensity could be.

Eva tried to hide her nervous smile by busying herself with her purse. She wasn't entirely sure how best to venture into this conversation. She could think of a million questions.

Mr. Schultz regarded her for a long moment, his eyebrows drawing together into a single bushy line. The door closed behind Liv's retreating back and Eva swallowed her nervousness. She supposed that Mr. Schultz wanted to talk about The Light of the World, given how excited he was by her mentioning it. That seemed like a good enough place to start. It gave Eva some leeway to temper his expectations and also to gauge how he would react to a potential deep friendship developing in the pages of her grandmother's diaries.

"Do you know what The Light of the World is? My Gran talked about it all the time, but never really explained what it was."

There was a pregnant pause and a pensive expression slipped over Mr. Schultz's face. Eva wondered if he were, trying to pick out exactly what he would or would not say. When he spoke, his tone had a heavy feel to it and seemed to fill the entire room. "The Light of the World is one of those strange cultural phenomena that scholars spend their entire lives studying."

Turning on his heel, his shoe scuffing on the rough wooden floor of the workshop, he crossed to a bookshelf and pulled down a thick volume. When he stepped closer, Eva realized it wasn't a book, but rather a folio. Mr. Schultz opened it with a practiced flick of his wrist and pulled out a journal that was not dissimilar to her grandmother's diaries. He thumbed his way to a marked page and began to read: "As far as this researcher can determine, the concept of The Light of the World is something of a spiritual representation of love to some, but an actual physical manifestation has never been proven. There are stories that crop up about once a decade or so that seem to indicate that there could be a physical being connected to this concept. It is this researcher's opinion that the likelihood of the light of the world existing in the present day is slim; however, such an individual certainly could have existed in the past."

"So, it's an idea?" Eva raised an eyebrow. She was so sure that it had to have been something else, something *more* than that. Her grandmother wouldn't have fixated on it so much if it hadn't been important. An idea wasn't enough, Eva thought, to shift a person so drastically. It couldn't be.

Mr. Schultz snapped the journal shut and shrugged broadly, and Eva could see a little bit of Al's slouched shoulders in his demeanor. Al was so much skinnier than his father. His mother must be tall, Eva guessed. Al was tall and dark-skinned, while Mr. Schultz was as white as they came. "As far as anyone can tell, the light of the world is a myth. I take it your grandmother talked about it a good bit? Was she an immigrant?"

Eva shook her head. "No, she was born here in the city in 1909. Her parents were immigrants, but they were both Catholic as far as I've been told. My family's pretty agnostic now. The light of the world was just something she talked about a few times in the diaries, and a lot later in life. I was more interested in discussing the Talbot boarding house, actually. There are a few names in here." She reached into her pocket and pulled out the January diary. "I wanted to see if you could help me track them down."

Schultz nodded, stepping forward with eager eyes. Eva understood his interest. The journals were the sort of thing that she, too, would read greedily. They were full of fascinating detail of a time and a place so different from today. She bit her lip and sighed, tucking the diary into her purse. "She talked about the light of the world as something that she'd lost, but she never said exactly what it was."

"Perhaps it was her way of talking about something else?" Mr. Schultz suggested mildly. "Those were very different times."

Eva frowned. "I don't think so," she explained. "My grandmother was a hard woman, but I loved her all the same, but there was always this great sense of loss that followed her around. It wasn't for my grandfather, or for my great-uncles who died long ago. No, this loss was deeper than that—an older, festering wound. My father asked her when he was a kid why she was sad all the time, and she told him that it was because the light of the world had gone out. I think that she saved these diaries because she wanted to tell someone about what had happened to her, but she either forgot about them, or found that she couldn't do it."

"If I could have a look..." Mr. Schultz did not sound eager now, just respectful. Eva grabbed the diary back out of her purse. She held it out to him and he took it, staring down at the looping cursive of her grandmother's handwriting.

There was a long pause while he read. Eva shifted from foot to foot, feeling awkward. Mr. Schultz turned a page and squinted, his lips moving silently as he read something and then repeated it back to himself. His eyes were racing across the page now. "There are more of these?" Eva nodded. "And what makes you think that she saved them for any particular reason?" he asked.

Eva leaned against the table. "The box they were in, along with a few others, was jammed in the back of her storage closet under a ton of dust. This was in the only one that looked as though it had been carefully packed. It's an old scrapbooking box, probably from decades ago now, and it's acid free. That means, to me at least, that she probably was keen to preserve whatever was kept inside." She sighed, turning to face Mr. Schultz once more. "It isn't so much that there could be an easy explanation to all of this, it's just that I feel that there's *more* to it. There has to be. It's too simple otherwise, and I can't accept that. My grandmother wasn't a simple woman."

"And if the light of the world truly was a person, would that change things?" Mr. Schultz suggested. There was a strange hint of eagerness in his voice that caused Eva to look at him sharply.

"Probably," Eva admitted, "because it would mean that she'd lost the love of her life or something equally tragic."

Mr. Schultz handed Eva back the journal and turned to the wall of bookshelves. "Well," he announced, resting his hands on his hips, "why don't we look into it and see if we can't find something to give you some closure?"

It was late when Eva found herself drawn back into her grandmother's world. Her tea was steaming on the coffee table. The night was warm, and the blanket that Eva pulled over her knees was more for comfort than warmth. She leaned back and started to read.

April 3, 1925

The drizzle of this morning let up to a sky the color of a robin's egg. I was only able to work a half day today as Mr. Perkins was in a closed deposition with the state's attorney and I was not allowed into the room.

I'm concerned about him. This is the second time in as many weeks that he's told me to go home early so that he may speak with someone privately. It is as though he does not wish for me to know what is going on.

Wren says he's working for someone, she won't tell me who, but that he's working for someone who might get him killed. I have no idea how she knows, but her conviction was so sincere that I was inclined to believe her. Wren knows things like this. She looks at people as if she can see straight through them. She took one look at Mr. Perkins when she came to meet me after my unexpected half-day today (we were just to meet for lunch) and understood exactly what was happening.

Wren's ability to do this is so infuriating! She laughs it off and says my cheeks are admirable when they're puffed out and flushed with anger.

I don't understand her. She is a mystery, quick to smile, quick to hurt, and quick to heal. She gets into arguments with Mrs. Talbot about women's suffrage and rights; she reads voraciously and seems to have money even though she does not work. Mrs. Talbot says she's a bad influence, but I won't stop seeing her. She is my only true friend.

We went to the park today. Everything is in bloom, and after taking the crammed uptown train, it was a welcome reprieve to walk among the flowering trees. There is a kind of magic in spring that is still clinging to winter's chill—flowers against a cold background, beauty in death. Wren says I'm particularly morose today.

In the shadow of a tree, she took my hand and I felt my heart swell within me. Her cheeks were flushed a warm pink in the cool afternoon. Her hand was warm.

She did not let go until we left the park.

Eva's tea was stone cold by the time she stopped reading and rereading the entry. She swallowed a mouthful with a wince and went to heat up her mug in the microwave. Her mind was reeling from what she'd just read. Maybe her suspicion of a lady crush wasn't that far off. Maybe this deep friendship was progressing to something different?

She couldn't wrap her head around what that might *mean* for her family. This changed everything. It wasn't just a mystery now, but a family secret that her grandmother had buried in the back of her closet.

"Closet." Eva gave a derisive snort of laughter. "Of course, Gran. Of course." Her tea warmed up, she went back to her spot on the couch and continued to read.

May 30, 1925

It is too hot. Wren and I were up on the roof earlier, until Judith came and chased us down. She said we were being too loud, but I doubt it. We weren't even talking, just enjoying the breezes that swirl around up there. Wren brought a book of poetry, but she wasn't reading it. She likes to do that, give dramatic readings when she has a captive audience of one.

Judith does not like Wren. She never has, and it isn't on account of the newspapers, as far as I can tell. Wren won't be open with me about what she does for work, so I can't tell Judith how Wren is a seamstress, or a teacher, or a clerk at the post office, I think Judith gets upset. She doesn't like not knowing things, filthy gossip that she is.

It was odd to see Wren actually fight with her, though. Wren got right up in her face, all flashing anger and clenched fists. Her hair was flying every which way, wisps of it flying straight up in the breezes we so wanted to catch. She told Judith exactly where to take her complaints and her nosy nature. I've never been prouder of anyone in my life.

Wren is a lifesaver. She is the only one who understands how worried I am for Mr. Perkins now that he's spending more time than ever in those closed-door meetings. He keeps muttering under his breath about having to find something. Something that will "save her," whatever that means. He won't elaborate when I ask him and I've decided I like my job too much to push it. Lord knows I don't want the bum's rush out of that job. Not yet at any rate.

Sometimes I catch myself thinking about what it might be like to have a little house somewhere. Maybe out in California, or perhaps Chicago, though I hear the winters are dreadful. I wonder if I would ask Wren to come with me, and if she'd come at all. I wonder if she's the sort of person who will ever settle down.

Judith demanded the same thing, and Wren just about decked her. I was shocked, and she did not apologize before storming out. Her hand was clenched around something at her neck, the cross I think she wears.

I wonder if she means to cloister herself once she's lived a little. She has no future, she tells me. I don't believe her.

We ended up sipping some of Elizabeth from upstairs's hooch on my bed, our feet knocking together, lamenting Judith and her bad temper. It wasn't a bad night, just odd. I've been having a lot of those recently.

Chapter 10

Olivia

EVA STARTED AT MR. BERTELLI'S shop that Tuesday with little fanfare. The work was dull, but the company was good. Mr. Bertelli had a bunch of funny stories about her grandmother that he seemed more than willing to share. Eva was grateful that he did not need prompting to relate a story about this or that, always with a wealth of detail that she could never quite recreate in her recollections of her grandmother.

The first two days she worked were slow, and she spent the hours between one and three each day after her cleaning and stocking tasks were completed leaning against the counter and reading her grandmother's diaries. The progress she made was slow. Her grandmother's handwriting was cramped and at times difficult to read. Each entry required several re-reads to pull names and places out to add to Eva's ever-growing list.

Mary was an interesting and compelling narrator. She told stories from the depth of her heart and short experience, revealing what it was like to be so young and so burdened. Eva shared bits of the diaries with Mr. Bertelli when he asked what she was reading on Thursday afternoon.

"She sounds like she was a really interesting teenager, Eva." Mr. Bertelli wiped his hands on his apron before turning back to the side of beef he was cutting up in preparation for the weekend. "As do her friends." He paused, one hand on the counter. "In the morning, I'm going to show you how to make sausage."

As a lover of food, and yet utterly negligent about remembering to eat, Eva perked up. "Awesome."

He smiled at her from under his mustache. "In this neighborhood, you have no idea how much of a relief it is to hear you say that."

Chuckling, Eva turned back to the book. She was fascinated with the dynamic that was developing between Mary and Wren. It felt so genuine and organic, the sort of friendship that a person could spend her whole life looking for. Eva wished for friendships like that, but her inability to look outside of her own head made it impossible. She felt trapped by the pull of sadness in her heart, and she had locked herself away when she was a child for fear that it would affect others.

That was before she'd been diagnosed and before her mother had gone into full-scale denial about the whole thing. Sometimes, Eva thought that she was somehow stunted by how little time she'd spent with others as a child. She had always been the weird, friendless kid in school.

A bell jingled and Eva looked up. A woman wearing large sunglasses and a loose linen shirt was standing in the door. Her hair was tucked up under a hat and she looked almost as if she were trying to disguise herself. Eva tucked her bookmark into the diary and set it aside. She swallowed down the nervousness that came with meeting strangers. "Welcome to Bertelli's Grocery," she said. "Can I help you find anything?"

The woman at the door pushed her sunglasses up. "Hey, Eva."

Eva felt a smile tugging at the corners of her lips. "Hey, Liv." A little thrill shot through her. Liv had come to see her at work. Cool, collected Olivia, had come to see her at work! She felt honored and a little flattered that Liv had bothered to find out where she worked. She'd left her contact information with Mr. Schultz in case he had any questions for her before she went in to see him again, but she hadn't expected to see anyone from the bookstore at Mr. Bertelli's.

Behind the meat counter, Mr. Bertelli whacked at a troublesome joint with his cleaver. Remembering herself, Eva straightened up. "What can I help you with?"

Liv approached the counter and Eva was able to see why she was as covered up as she was. Already little patches of redness on her ears and neck caused by the blazing sun were showing on her skin. *She must burn easily. That must suck.*

Eva had gone to the bookshop the previous evening, but Liv hadn't been there. Theo had convinced her that it was okay to leave her grandmother's diaries with him. Eva still wasn't sure if she trusted that he had her best interests at heart, but he was very persuasive and after some reflection, she didn't see the harm in letting him read them.

"I just wanted to drop by to see what you were up to tonight," Liv said. "It's Al's night to close the shop so I'm free if you'd like to get a drink."

Eva blinked. "A drink? Like drink, drink?"

Liv frowned, furrowing her brow. "Are you not twenty-one?"

"Oh, I am... I just... I don't really ever do that with friends." Eva winced. *Mostly because I don't have any.*

"Perfect time to start, then. I'll come collect you after work. I know a good place."

Eva floundered. "Is this like a—I mean, I'd be fine with that but, like, I hardly know you and maybe..." She trailed off, embarrassed.

"I just wanted to hear some more about your grandmother, Eva." Liv reached forward and touched her shoulder across the counter. "I don't want to make you feel uncomfortable."

"I wasn't."

"Good, then five it is." Liv paused, her warm fingers pressing into Eva's skin. "See you then." And with that she was gone, sweeping from the shop in flurry of pressed white fabric and blue jeans.

"Bye..." Eva looked down at her hands and felt a flush blossoming across her face. That girl was going to be a problem.

Behind the meat counter, Mr. Bertelli started to laugh. He leaned on the glass display case, still wearing his bloody gloves, the cleaver loosely clutched in one hand. "I think she might not have anticipated your reacting that way, Eva."

"Thanks, Mr. Bertelli," Eva grumbled. She looked up and met his eyes. "I just don't ever really do that."

"Let her take you out. It's what grown-ups do with each other after a long work day."

"Uh-huh." Eva knew he was right, but she didn't want to admit that a lesson in how to be an adult was really not what she wanted from him.

⸺∘≪✦≫∘⸺

True to her word, Liv returned just as Eva was walking out the door.

"Hey."

Eva froze. Liv was right behind her. Her layers were gone now that the sun had lost some of its intensity. She wore cut-off shorts and the same white linen shirt from before.

Eva smiled slowly, nervousness leaking into her posture. She didn't know what this meant, or was supposed to mean. "Hey," she replied.

"You ready to go?"

Nodding, Eva fell into step beside Liv. "Where are we going?"

"This place I know, just a few blocks over." She turned to meet Eva's gaze. Her eyes were warm and bright, not harshly closed off as they had been on their first meeting. "One of those coffee shop/bar double features."

"Ah." Eva looked down at her feet. Her shoes were disgusting after she had spent all day helping Mr. Bertelli stock shelves and clean out the meat display. She needed to buy shoes just for work. "I've never been to one of those."

"Really?" Liv bumped her side. "You're post-college age, Eva. How did you never make it out to a place like this?"

"I just *didn't*." She didn't look up. She hated this moment that always came when she was least prepared for it. The brutal, unpleasant feeling in the pit of her stomach when she felt compelled to *tell* someone why she didn't finish school. There was this societal expectation that she share what she studied. It was all the small talk people Eva's age engaged in, or at least it felt that way to Eva. She knew that there was no way around it, especially in situations like this.

It wasn't that it was any of Liv's business, or that their relationship would change at all if she knew, but rather it was the understanding that there was always a loss of respect that went along with such a revelation. Eva didn't want another person thinking she was a coward.

The limited interaction that Eva had with Liv up until this point seemed to suggest she was a good person who would understand what Eva was trying to tell her—if, of course, Eva should want to tell her the truth. A big part of Eva did want to tell her and see what happened. Not everyone was going to react the way her mother had, right?

Liv shifted beside Eva. She was tense, the muscles in her neck tight. "Look," she said. "I don't mean to—"

Fuck it.

Eva cut her off. "I never graduated."

"You didn't?" Liv stopped walking.

"No. I dropped out the spring semester of my sophomore year." Eva sighed. She was committed now. She might as well see it through. She twisted her wrist and tugged the watchband on her right wrist loose. The scar was still there, milky white against her tanned skin. It was a testament to her still being alive and it was a constant reminder of her foolish decision. "I did this instead." Eva raised her gaze to meet Liv's. She would not be ashamed, she would *not*. "I couldn't stay there after that."

Liv sucked on her lower lip. She stood there in the middle of the sidewalk, her fingers twisting around the leather strap of her purse. "Did you, um… get treatment?"

Eva nodded.

"And are you better?"

"You don't get better from something like that. You just get better at coping." Eva turned and started walking. She had no idea where they were going, but stopping did not seem like the right option.

They walked in silence for a few blocks, stepping around joggers and dog walkers. A street performer was drumming on an upturned bucket, but Eva barely heard him. Her attention was caught up in her confession and in how Liv had reacted. It wasn't like people to just take what she said at face value. Usually they would start to look at her differently. Time would tell if Liv was the same as the rest of them.

"Did you just do one?" Liv's question came out of the blue.

"I didn't have time to get to the other before I passed out."

"Oh." Liv went quiet again. "Can you drink?"

"Yeah."

"Okay. Good."

"I'm not, like, broken or whatever. I take medication, I get sad sometimes, and sometimes it's worse than just *sad*. I obsess about little details to avoid dealing with the bigger picture." Eva followed Liv down a side street. The coffee shop was in a basement, but it had large windows that were opened wide onto a little courtyard with a few spindly stools. Eva nearly tripped over an old paint can filled with cigarette butts.

At the door, Liv paused as her fingers closed around the handle. "I know a lot of people like you, Eva." She turned her head to look over her shoulder and smile at Eva. A dimple was showing at her cheek. "I wasn't judging. I just wanted to make sure I understood."

"And do you?" Eva asked.

"I do." Liv replied. She tugged the door open and gestured for Eva to head inside. "After you."

"Thanks."

Inside, it was cool and in the fading afternoon light, the far reaches of the shop had fallen into shadow. Eva liked it immediately. The place had a very homey vibe to it that made her feel welcome. The walls were painted a very light gray that looked almost blue in the low lighting. The bar was set against the back end of the shop and a tiny kitchen was tucked behind a half-closed black curtain. A few comfortable-looking couches lined the walls. Eva approached the bar and surveyed the tap list. She felt lost.

She was about to ask for help from the bartender when Liv stepped up behind her and put her hand on Eva's shoulder. "Let me get you one. Go grab the table by the window."

"You sure?"

"Yeah."

Eva retreated at Liv's firm nod. She took a seat by the window and waited for Liv to come back with two glasses of amber liquid. She set one in front of Eva. "If you're not much for this sort of thing, this will be the easiest one they have on tap for you. It's a golden lager." At Eva's blank look Liv gave a dimpled smile. "A summer beer."

"Oh!" Eva perked up. She liked those sorts of beers. They weren't bitter or too sweet. "So, perfect for a day like today?"

Liv leaned forward on her elbows. "Yeah."

Eva took a sip, frowning at the alcoholic taste before the back-end citrus flavor hit her tongue. "That is good."

"Isn't it?" Liv took a sip of her own beer. "So, Eva, now that you've told me about a demon from your past, would you like to share any more?"

Laughing, Eva grinned. "Why don't I just tell you about my Gran, okay?"

"Sounds good."

Eva sipped her beer. "Her name was Mary Oglesby. She married my grandfather in '42 or '43, whenever he came home from the war. She was born in 1909. The diaries I found are from when she was sixteen, in 1925."

"And she just passed?" Liv ran a hand through her hair. "*Christ,* she was ancient."

"She was very stubborn," Eva agreed, "even about staying alive. My dad likes to joke that she was trying to outlive him."

"Does he, um, suffer from what you have, too?"

"Depression?" Liv nodded. "Yeah, he does. My Gran mighta had it too. We can't really be sure. She never was diagnosed or anything like that. She just seemed to be haunted by this old loss—and in the diaries she hasn't experienced it yet. I keep thinking that she must have saved them for a reason, and not just the whole light of the world thing that I told Mr. Schultz about."

"Do you think that what happened to her is documented in the diaries? Theo's still working his way through them, won't let me read 'em."

With an apologetic wince, Eva picked up her beer once more. "I'm sorry he's monopolizing them."

"It's fine, really." Liv inspected her nails. The polish was chipped in places. "It isn't every day someone comes in asking about a phenomenon like the light of the world. He's just being thorough."

"I'm really more interested in finding out about what happened in 1925 that made these diaries so important," Eva confessed. She didn't want to talk about the dreams she kept having about the light of the world. She didn't want to worry anyone with what were pretty obviously run-of-the-mill stress dreams. "But knowing what the heck she meant by the light of the world would be cool, too."

Taking a long pull on her beer, Liv smiled almost sadly at Eva. She licked at the corner of her mouth, her pink tongue flitting out and filling Eva's vision to the point of distraction. She could not look away, and the color rose on her cheeks. "Be careful what you wish for, Eva. Some historical stones are better left unturned." She leaned across the table and patted Eva's hand gently. "Even if they're really fun to try to figure out," she added with a grin that made Eva's heart flutter in her chest.

This girl was *definitely* going to be a problem.

Later that night, still a little buzzed and awash with the memory of Liv's pleasant smile, Eva turned her attention back to her grandmother's diaries. She was working her

way through June now, and was surprised to discover her
grandmother on a date of her own—a date with Wren.

June 14, 1925

Today it was unbearably hot outside. Wren spent much of the
morning asking and eventually convinced me to go with her to
Ebbets Field and watch the Robins play. She was confused when I
called them that, though, and would not stop ribbing me for it later
on in the grandstand. In my heart of hearts I know that these are
Uncle Robbie's boys and it simply is not polite to call them anything
but who they are. Dodgers they may be on paper, but they are the
Robins in all of Brooklyn's hearts. Wren should know that. She's
from here, too.

Despite the ribbing and running commentary from Wren, the
game was lovely. Terribly exciting, too. Dazzy Vance pitched well and
the Robins won a 12-3 decision over the Reds of Cincinnati.

It was strange to be out with Wren like that, as if we hadn't a
care in the world. Ever since we met, it's been a pattern of meeting
behind closed doors and out of the public eye. We have our moments
out of doors, naturally. Not like this, though.

Wren seemed to enjoy the clandestine nature of our meetings up
to this point (or at least that is what she says, but I'm not sure that
she's entirely solid on what the word clandestine means. Honestly,
we spend half our time with Elsie and Mrs. Talbot. That is hardly
a secret.). I do not think that she particularly liked the screaming
crowd of our neighbors from all over Brooklyn shouting out cheers
for Dazzy and the boys, but she was the one who suggested going
and I was not about to pass up a chance to go see the Robins when I
didn't have to pay for the ticket.

It felt like the sort of outing one would go on with a steady, what
we did today. I cannot shake the feeling that that was what it was
meant to be, for Wren seemed preoccupied the entire game, not truly
paying attention to the dizzying performance that the Robins were

putting on for the adoring crowd. Her hand kept touching mine, curling against the skin there and refusing to let go despite the heat of the day.

Afterwards, we walked around Crown Heights. I asked her why she had wanted to come out like this. It wasn't like her to want to be so brazen about things. She was quiet for a long time after that. Quiet and stoic. Everything she is not usually.

We are brazen about things, even if whatever it is between us has no name. She acts like a fella, holds my hand in public, lets me walk on her arm. She's cut her hair short with the fashion and styles it like a boy's sometimes. I want to know why she does this, why she hides herself away when she should be giving herself to the world. The world deserves to know her. She shouldn't feel like she has to hide.

Wren said that she wanted to give me something that I would enjoy, a gift of sorts. A happy memory, she called it. Again I asked why; people do not do kind things for me just for the sake of friendship. They always want something from you. Father told me that time and time again. You must protect yourself against their designs if you want to get anywhere in this world, he said. I wonder if he protected himself.

Wren doesn't want anything from me that I would not willingly give her anyway. She is my closest friend, my confidante, and the person I trust most. I do not mind the playacting, but sometimes I wonder what the purpose is. She treats me the way a fella would treat his lady, even though we aren't steadies. Girls don't do that sort of thing.

Today, Wren was different. She brought me out of Crown Heights and bundled me onto a train that took us into the heart of Manhattan. I felt like I was being shanghaied and said as much, but Wren just laughed it off and told me not to worry. I find myself so caught up in her that I forget myself. She is overwhelming with her mere presence and I have to remember to keep my head straight or else she'll vanish like a figment of my imagination and leave me in nothingness, trapped in the middle of the city.

She said she wanted to show me something and pulled me along through the crowded station. I was still dressed for the ball game and looked out of place among the well-dressed folk of Midtown. Wren had the loveliest flush of pink to her freckled cheeks after we'd left, and it had only grown deeper as we traveled into the city. She took my hand then, standing in the middle of Pennsylvania Station, and pulled me through a door that I had never seen before.

I cannot explain what she showed me in words because there are no words that could ever do such beauty justice. At first, all I saw was blackness. Wren pulled me deep into the darkness, so far down that I could hear the subway making its journey above us. How she'd found this place I have no idea, and I was terrified we would be discovered trespassing.

Wren told me not to worry, that everyone who might discover us was out at church or watching the Yanks play in the later game. She spoke in the hushed, reverent voice that my mother uses when she's speaking in church. It calmed me until I asked where we were. We were somewhere under the station, she wasn't sure which side, maybe Seventh Avenue.

There is a room far beneath the city that holds three doors that open up into paths of light. Upon the wall is painted a plume of flames that rises up into the darkness and chases away the shadows.

Wren pulled me inside the space, her fingers clutching mine. She gestured up at the ceiling with a wide sweep of her arm. This is her sanctuary, she explained. It is apparently the only place in the city where she feels safe.

And I did not think to ask her why then, as her hand was in my own and the darkness didn't seem so black.

Chapter 11

The Hidden Room

THE MYSTERY ONLY SEEMED TO deepen as Eva read further in her grandmother's journals. She had a few theories as to what the relationship was between Mary and Wren, but she kept them to herself as she read. She almost felt afraid to voice them for fear of what might happen if they were spoken out loud.

What if her grandmother had been in love with Wren? What if she had fallen in love with this girl and it had destroyed her?

The questions kept piling up, each one more unsettling than the next. She turned the pages eagerly, heading into late June in search of the entry that *had* to be the key to all of this. The city was gripped in a heat wave in the diaries, and her grandmother was falling in love. It struck Eva as odd that her grandmother, in six months of very detailed diary entries, had never once explained who Wren was. She was a close friend, obviously, and Eva was pretty sure her Gran was crushing on her something fierce. And then there was the *date*. Eva wasn't sure what to make of that. And Wren was a mystery. Eva knew next to nothing about her, except that she seemed nervous in crowds, and that she had freckles across her nose and long blonde hair. It wasn't much to go on.

It was lunch time, and Eva was in the back room of Mr. Bertelli's shop. She was bored, killing time since she had already finished her soup and tiny salad made from the dregs at the bottom of the pre-made mixed greens bag she'd bought a few days before. She was going to have to get groceries soon, there was no food in the apartment. She'd eaten through most of what was still edible in her grandmother's pantry already.

"A room under Penn Station with three doors, huh?" Taking the pen that she'd been chewing on, she wrote down the location on the list that she'd tucked into the front cover of the diary.

She was settling into a routine. Every morning, she woke up and sometimes caught herself expecting to hear her grandmother banging around in the apartment's small kitchen, putting the kettle on and making breakfast. Mornings were the worst for Eva because before she took her medication, everything seemed so much louder. The visceral feelings of loss and longing for her grandmother's presence were enough to set her curling into a ball and sobbing. She had to struggle to find the motivation to get up sometimes, to make herself take the pills that would quiet everything down to the point where she felt that she could function again.

It was troubling that she was still struggling with this, and that she couldn't bring herself to let her grandmother's memory go. Liv told her that everyone grieved in a different way when they had drinks together two weeks ago. Perhaps this was just a part of her process.

She didn't mention it to her parents when they called to check in. They were thrilled that the job at Mr. Bertelli's was working out so well for Eva, and happy that she was able to find a group of friends who seemed interested in helping her get more meaning out of the diaries. She didn't mention the light of the world to her father again. Mr. Schultz, who insisted on being called Theo, was fixated on it enough for Eva. She didn't need her parents' deciding to get involved as well.

This was her life now, at least until the apartment was sold. She did the same things every day. And no matter how interesting it was to spend time with Theo and Liv and occasionally Al, when he wasn't busy with his graduate classes in photography, her life had fallen into the humdrum of adulthood she used to rail against when she was in high school.

It showed how little she knew back then.

Eva found that she liked ease of it. Routine was simple, and it was predictable. There was something about it that kept her feeling sane, with none of the spontaneity that had thrown her so much in college. She liked this new set of events that had come to rule her daily life. Eva liked steadiness because it was less likely to surprise her. Her grandmother had been steady, right up until the moment that she'd passed away.

Grief was a strange thing. It twisted into her subconscious and festered there. It was as if a part of her were missing, and it was a deep and aching wound. She couldn't stomach the loss. There were reminders of her grandmother everywhere in the apartment. Even when she was trying to focus on other things at work, Mr. Bertelli would share a humorous story that cut into Eva unexpectedly. She had to find a better way of coping with the loss.

Perhaps she was, by obsessing over her grandmother and her relationship with Wren. Perhaps she could find Wren, or her grave, or her children, or *something*. Perhaps she could track down someone who would be able to tell her what her grandmother meant when she'd told Eva time and time again that the light of her world had gone out.

Once her salad was done and the Tupperware was rinsed out, the afternoon passed quickly for Eva. There was a delivery, and she spent the better part of the afternoon carefully checking bunches of bananas for spiders before Mr. Bertelli shooed her out the door at four-thirty on the dot. "Have a good night," he called after her, holding the door open with one broad palm for a tiny old woman wearing a kerchief over her stark white hair.

It had cooled off significantly over the past two weeks since that scorching-hot Labor Day when she'd gone to meet Theo for the first time. Walking down the shady side of the street, Eva was almost cold. She jammed her hands into the pockets of her jeans, balling them into fists and hunching her shoulders against the stiff breeze that whipped up the street.

Her bag thumped against her leg, and the wind caught her apron and almost tugged it clean away from where she'd tucked it into her bag. It was getting darker earlier now, which meant that Eva couldn't linger in the back room of the bookshop for as long as she might want to without risking the ire of her parents, should they ever discover what she was up to.

Her mother would lose her mind if she knew that Eva was out much past eight o'clock. Eva made a point of calling them at ten or so every night and saying that she'd turned all three of the locks and put the chain on and that no one was getting into the apartment through the front door. It was a little passive aggressive and immature, she knew. She had lived in the city for a year now with no problems, but her mother still insisted on speaking to her as though she were a child when it came to safety.

Perhaps she was just afraid of what Eva might do when left alone, which was ironic as this whole plan of Eva living in her grandmother's apartment was, according to Eva's father, her mother's idea.

In Eva's search for the answers locked inside her grandmother's diaries, Theo had turned into a valuable resource. He knew *everyone* in the neighborhood, and had some dealings with Eva's grandmother later in her life. He was grumpy and unpleasant, but he was able to produce information out of nowhere that was both pertinent and useful to their continued search.

He and Al ran the bookshop as a father-son team with Al handling most of the customer interaction. Liv was there to help out while she looked for a subject for a master's thesis in women's history. They were an odd little trio, but Eva could not be more grateful for them.

Al was all kinds of charming distraction, even if he was not really interested in the diaries at all. Liv was a flat-out enigma to Eva. She couldn't get a read on her. One moment Liv would seem absolutely fascinated by the diaries and the next she'd appear to be overcome with a melancholy that gripped her whole body.

Eva knew that melancholy well. It plagued her too, but Liv never said anything about living with depression. Eva would sit in the back room of the bookshop and watch the transformation come over Liv. She would disappear outside, chain-smoking on the bookshop's front stoop and scowling up at the sky where it was visible between the buildings across the street.

There was a bleakness about Liv when she looked up at the skyline. "I'm sorry," she said when Eva followed her out one night. "I just need a moment sometimes."

"Are you okay?"

"I'm fine, Eva." Liv exhaled smoke from her nose. "It's just a silly thing. I feel so bad for her."

Eva tilted her head to one side, leaning against the sun-warmed brick next to Liv. "You do?"

"She was in love with her best friend. It's tragic."

"That sounds like something Al would say." Eva shook her head. Al had taken a peek at a few of the entries that they were focusing on and announced that there was some seriously lesbian crushing going on. "But I think you're right."

"Does that bother you, that your grandmother might have loved someone other than your grandfather?"

Eva shook her head. "Not really. He died before I was born, but everyone says that she just about tolerated his presence. Everyone in the family thinks she did it because that was what was done."

Liv put her cigarette to her lips. "I wonder."

It was that same melancholy that Eva felt if she thought too long and hard about her grandmother, but there was no personal connection. Liv was great with the other parts of their research into the life and times of Mary Oglesby. She'd found an old list of residents of Mrs. Talbot's boarding house with the help of Kelvin Stanton, who worked at the Brooklyn Historical Society, and a few late nights down in the archives, herself.

She'd returned on the third night with a coffee from the bakery up the block clutched in one hand and a photocopied list written in nearly indecipherable handwriting in the other. Liv presented the list to Al and Eva. She'd done it with a flourish, pointing to one name in particular.

"I found her." Her tone was triumphant. There was Eva's grandmother, plain as day. Liv went on to produce more documents from the folio in her bag. Mrs. Talbot's personal account of her residents showed that Mary paid her rent on time and that the only complaints that were ever fielded by Mrs. Talbot about her revolved around her penchant for stealing the newspaper after a girl named Judith who lived a floor above her was done with it.

"My Gran did that until she died." Eva laughed when Liv had leaned in close to read the photocopied ledger over Eva's shoulder. Liv smelled like cigarettes and summer, honeysuckle with a smoky overtones that reminded Eva of the times when she and her parents had gone camping in western Connecticut when she was very young. It drove Eva almost to distraction to be that close to Liv, who had absolutely no respect for Eva's personal space, situating herself so that Eva couldn't escape without some rather awkward brush pass. It was clearly flirting. *Clearly.*

"I remember when I was a kid," Eva said, and found herself staring into Liv's intense gaze, only inches away. "Old Mr. Sorrenson would get into these insane arguments with her because she'd get up super early and steal the crossword page out of his copy of the *Times* every morning."

"And what did your grandmother say about that?" Liv was leaning forward, her hair hanging in perfectly straight lines down her back and spilling over her shoulders like a river of yellow silk. She tapped her fingers on her chin and shifted her weight to the other elbow as she asked Eva the question. Eva couldn't look away from Liv's fingers. Her breath caught in her chest, watching how they played subconsciously with her lower lip as she read.

"She told him to prove it."

They both laughed and Eva was able to push away the distracting thoughts of Liv's lips.

They were a strange little band of historians. They were a hodgepodge of people with different approaches to life who did not match at all. Even between Al and Theo, there were stark differences. Al, according to Theo's grumblings, took after his mother rather than Theo. Liv was the unifying force between them, keeping everyone on task and on track, never wavering in her pursuit of the *research*. They were perfect, really, and Eva was growing comfortable and content within the space that they'd created for her.

It had been a long time since Eva had friends like this.

The friendship spilled out of the research project and into the sphere of Eva's life that she'd thought she was going to have to manage on her own. Her parents were happy that she was working at Mr. Bertelli's shop, and they were happier still to hear that Eva had managed to rope Al and Liv into helping her peel off the wallpaper in the apartment hallway. It was the first step in the restoration project that Eva promised her parents she would start on, once she got settled into her new routine.

It was fun stripping down the wallpaper armed with putty knives and wet sponges that Al found in the basement of the bookshop. They spent an afternoon listening to Eva's grandmother's old 45s and revealing a battered-looking wall beneath the yellowing wallpaper. It was a wall that should never be allowed to see the light of day again, they decided, so Al promised to come back the next weekend and help Eva plaster it smooth.

"I had to do the same thing in my bedroom when I was a kid," he explained as he shoved bits of wallpaper into a trash bag. "My mom wasn't exactly handy and my dad, well, you know how he is."

Liv laughed. "He's a walking disaster."

"But in a good way," Eva assured Al.

Eva liked Al; he was quiet and took pictures with his phone constantly, trying to capture the beauty he saw in everyday life. He'd shown her a few of his pictures, the ones that were still on his phone. After some needling, Eva convinced Al to give her his Instagram username, only to find that she was not the only one who was just a little bit smitten with his beautiful photos. She paged through comments from girls who didn't seem to realize that Al wasn't particularly interested in having them fawning all over his photographs. He replied to critiques and other artists mostly, and also to Eva. It gave her a small feeling of triumph whenever she got a notification on her phone. Perhaps she was being immature for liking that. Perhaps she was just grateful that Al was her friend and paid attention to her. It was really that she was happy someone cared about what she had to say enough to respond to it.

The bookshop was empty when Eva pushed the door open. It was just after five o'clock. Al was sitting on a stool behind the counter where his laptop was set up and a digital SLR was plugged into it with a carefully coiled USB cord. His knees were scrunched up against the counter as he typed away, looking like a dreadlocked and annoyed frog.

"Get any good shots today?" She walked across the front of the store to lean over the counter and look at his screen upside down from above. She couldn't tell what he'd taken a picture of from that angle; it just looked like a bunch of blurred lines and squiggles.

Al shook his head. "This is the worst assignment." He groaned and it reverberated around the bookshop. He ran a hand over his face, his eyes narrowing as he wiggled his finger over the laptop's track pad and made an adjustment to the color saturation of the image. "How the hell do you photograph light?"

"No idea." Eva shrugged.

"I get it on a fundamental level, and like, technically, but that isn't what the assignment is about. I swear, either the professor is trying to see how stupid we are or wants us to take advantage of the late-summer shadows to get some interesting black and white shots." Al tugged at his hair, clearly frustrated. "I just don't know."

Eva tilted her head to one side. *Light...* She tapped her bag and grinned at him, an idea starting to form. "Maybe we can find this place my Gran described in her diary. Apparently there's this place that she was taken to—a room where there are three doors that open up onto paths of light. My Gran was usually pretty awesome at describing things, but she said that she couldn't find the words. Apparently it's absolutely beautiful."

He inclined his head and scratched at his sideburn for a moment, sighing dramatically before tipping his laptop closed. "Anything's better than this shit. Where is it?"

"Under Penn Station."

Al groaned again, this time long and drawn out. "Like they're going to let a guy who looks like me anywhere near the inner workings of a place that busy." He shook his head, adding in an undertone, "Racist-ass cops."

"Maybe your professor could pull some strings?" She had no idea where the place was, only that it was under the station somewhere and that it probably was not on the Seventh Avenue side, which probably meant that it was either under The Garden or close to it.

"If you can actually prove it exists, sure." Al shrugged his shoulders in a resigned way. He smiled tiredly at Eva before turning his attention back to his camera. "Until then I'm applying rainbow pastel filters to see if I can salvage something good enough for class."

"I'll try." Leaving him to his task, Eva drifted toward the back of the store. Theo had told her that she had free access to his resources if he wasn't around, but she still felt a little uncomfortable coming into his space unannounced. She knocked quietly and she heard Theo's voice call, "Come in!"

Eva pushed the door open to see Theo, his glasses half-falling off his nose, staring down at an old map. He was wearing white archival gloves that looked to be about three sizes too small for his thick hands and was barking out observations to Liv, who was sitting at the computer taking notes.

"Hey, Eva," he said, straightening up and pushing his glasses up his nose with his thumb. "Is it that late already?"

Eva shrugged. Liv turned her wrist over to look at her watch face and visibly winced. Her hair fell into her eyes as she entered the save command and stood, stretching her arms high above her head. A pale sliver of her stomach showed as her shirt rode up and bunched around her shoulders. Unable to look away, Eva swallowed. Her mouth was suddenly dry.

"I'm afraid so," she said as firmly as she could, tearing her eyes away from Liv, who was now bending over to stretch and, oh yes, she wasn't even thinking about looking at that, oh no. "I found a passage that I think you might be interested in. I'd be curious if what's described is still in existence."

Eva produced the sealed Ziploc bag into which she'd put the journal in case it rained. "I marked the pages where it's mentioned. Wren took her to this place after a baseball game. She called the Dodgers the Robins, which was all kinds of hilarious."

"Well, they were called that when Robinson was skipper," Theo muttered, and Eva couldn't help but wonder if he was at all bitter about the fact that the Dodgers were playing in L.A. and not in Brooklyn anymore. Now they were stuck with the Mets and that was just terrible.

Theo read quickly, using his archival gloves to flip through the pages, while Eva glanced over to see Liv straightening up and tucking something on a chain back under her shirt. She flushed, knowing Liv had caught her looking, and she busied herself with pulling out her own notes.

"I went back after I read that and tried to pull as much location information as I could out of the diary." Eva brushed her frizzing bangs away from her eyes and tucked them behind her ear.

Her spindly handwriting covered the notepaper that Liv plucked from her fingers. Liv read it quickly, and turned on one booted foot and headed to the shelves where they kept Theo's rather eclectic collection of old maps.

"Get the subway map, too," Theo called as he absently rolled up the map he'd been reading earlier. He slid it into an archival tube that looked so bulky that Eva wondered if it were bulletproof. "A room full of light underneath Manhattan, huh?"

Liv spread the first map down over the table. It was obviously a copy. Liv left the other map off to the side and brushed against Eva as she set the notepaper on top of it. She traced her finger down Seventh Avenue.

"Is there any chance this was destroyed when The Garden or the subway was being built?" She tapped her finger over the large space that Eva knew currently housed Madison Square Garden.

Theo tugged off his gloves. "I don't think so. Mrs. Kessler was very specific about saying that she was underneath the subway..." He passed the journal over to Liv, who took it gingerly and frowned.

Eva watched her read, following the lines of her face as she took in her grandmother's words. There was a pained look in her eyes that made Eva's brow furrow, but then Liv leaned down and tapped the Sixth Avenue subway station. "They would have come out here," she said quietly. "And then probably walked up a block to the station, before circling to wherever the doorway was." She set the journal down and sighed. "Wish she'd been more descriptive though. It's not a lot to go on and they're not going to let anyone down there to look around without some kind of proof."

"What about having Al ask his professor? That could probably get a pass if we provided compelling evidence..." Eva suggested tentatively. "Since he's doing a photo assignment on light and all."

"Crap, if you ask me," Theo grumbled. "He should be studying anthropology or history."

In the few short weeks that Eva had known Theo and Al, she'd started to catch on to the friction between father and son regarding Al's academic pursuit of photography, as well as Theo's hatred of Al's fairly lucrative side business as a wedding photographer. Theo seemed to think that Al should be studying the same things for which he himself had a passion, which made Eva smile. Her mom was the exact same way.

Liv frowned and her eyes flashed with that steely quality that made her seem both warm and cold at the same time. "He could get us in the door, though. Afterwards it wouldn't be too hard to go down as far as we possibly can..."

"A kid that looks like him probably isn't going to get a pass for something like that from MTA or Amtrak, though." Theo made an annoyed sound at the back of his throat to punctuate his gripe, running a hand through his hair. "Why was his mother so beautiful and charming?"

Eva and Liv exchanged a look and then hastily looked away from each other before they burst out into giggles. Theo's love for his departed wife was a beautiful thing, even if he was very direct about how much he had cared for her.

"Well, we could try it, right?" Liv suggested, and Eva nodded vigorously.

"I'll talk to him." Theo pulled his gloves back out of his pocket and reached for the topmost book from a stack at the corner of the table. He picked up the book and headed toward the door, which he opened expertly with his foot before bustling out into the storefront.

Liv's fingers trailed along the spine of the journal and she picked it up once more, offering it back to Eva. She smiled, their fingers brushing as Eva reached out to take it. "Your grandmother was an extraordinary woman, Eva." There was so much emotion buried in her voice that Eva's breath caught and she almost forgot that Liv's fingers were resting on her own, lingering and not pulling away.

They were warm, oh so warm, and Eva's heart was pounding. Liv was smiling at her, all dimples and terrible charm, and Eva wanted to say something to her but all the words she knew died in her throat.

She was so screwed.

Chapter 12

The Blue Web

Sunday afternoon, Eva hauled three buckets of painter's plaster up the four flights of stairs to the apartment with Al and Liv's help. Thankfully, Mr. Bertelli let her close up the shop at two o'clock rather than the usual three o'clock because business was slow. She needed the time to make sure, yet again, that her father was okay with their getting started on this project without him. He'd expressed some concerns that they might not do a good job restoring the apartment, but Eva was quick to try to put him at ease. She didn't want to have to redo anything once it was done.

Plaster was not the ideal choice for the job they were doing. The guy at the hardware supply store had suggested that they put drywall over the exposed wooden paneling. Eva hadn't thought that was such a good idea after looking at the wall. It was a going to be a monumental task.

She explained this to her parents and the guy at the hardware store. It was a gut feeling, and one she couldn't shake. She wondered if it was her grandmother's way of bossing her around from beyond the grave. The guy behind the counter had looked at her as if she were crazy, but listened to her concerns. Drywall would not really work with the building's aesthetic as all the charm was in the old-fashioned way everything was put together. After hearing her out, he'd simply nodded and directed her to the plaster.

All three of them were breathless by the time they reached the apartment. They collapsed into an exhausted heap on the couch.

Al looked around. "I like this place more now. Every time I come here you've taken out more and more of your grandmother's stuff. It's a lot less cluttered now."

"I'm getting better at throwing things away," Eva answered.

Liv said nothing. She leaned forward and picked up Eva's notepad. "Are you taking notes on everything you read?"

"Yeah." Eva rubbed at the back of her neck sheepishly. "Theo won't stop fixating on the light of the world, so I'm trying to find good reasons to draw his attention away from it."

"Good luck," Al snorted. "Dad's obsessed."

"Yeah." Eva sat back on the couch. "That's what makes me nervous."

Liv met her gaze for a moment before looking at the list. "I'll run some of these by Kelvin, see if we can't find some leads."

"Really?" Eva asked.

"Sure." Liv tugged the paper from the pad and folded it into her pocket. "I don't mind."

"Awesome." Eva got to her feet. "We should really get started if we want to be done sometime tonight."

Al pulled out his phone and they looked up a few videos on appropriate techniques for applying plaster. "This doesn't look too bad." He picked up the spatula and waved it to mimic the video.

"It isn't rocket science, Al." Liv smiled. She began setting up the lighting.

"I should set those up," Al said and pocketed his phone. He had brought over some clip lights he used when taking pictures.

"Afraid I'll break them?"

"Nah, just a little protective since they're expensive." He glanced over at Liv. "And they belong to my professor." The bright white bulbs were clipped to the backs of chairs and cast the hallway into stark relief.

"Understandable. Still rude." Liv laughed.

While Eva and Al sorted out the lights, Liv watched from afar, her arms folded and a roll of painter's tape on her wrist like a bizarre bracelet from the '80s.

When they finished positioning the clip lights, Al flipped on the overhead light. "That fixture is terrible." He scowled up at the yellow bulb. "You've got to get a new fixture up there." He flicked the light back off.

"Tell me about it," Eva replied. "My mom is going antiquing to try to find something better."

Her fingers touched the stripped walls with reverence. They'd sanded them down yesterday; Theo had quite the collection of unused power tools in the bookshop basement that he didn't know how to use, but Al certainly did.

Al shook his head, a broad grin cracking across his face. "You Connecticut types and your antiquing." He swept his arms around him majestically. "This is *Brooklyn*. We thrift here."

"Not everyone wants to be a hipster." Eva shoved at him playfully. He let out a yelp and hopped away on one foot. Eva giggled and turned to smile at Liv, who was lurking just at the end of the hallway. Liv rolled her eyes, but she was smiling. "Hey, can I have the tape? We have to cover the cracks."

"Why do you need to do that, exactly?" Liv tossed it over.

Eva pulled a strip of tape from the roll. "The guy at the hardware store told me that I should tape over the cracks so as not to create more in the plaster."

Al rummaged in one of the plastic bags from the hardware store. There were two more rolls of tape in there with the rest of the supplies Eva had bought. He tossed one roll to Liv and kept the other for himself. "Meet in the middle?" he asked Eva.

"Sure." Eva glanced over at Liv.

Liv nodded her agreement, rolling up the sleeves of her fraying flannel shirt and getting to work on the wall that she'd been leaning against.

They worked quickly and in relative silence. Al turned on the radio in the living room after practically cooing at Eva's grandmother's 45 collection. They paused for a few minutes to figure out how to hook the record player back up to the speakers.

The work went quickly once the music was playing. The wood they'd revealed underneath the wallpaper was a worn, dark brown. Eva wondered if it had been stained at some point to give it the dark finish that made the whole place seem so forbidding. The tape they were using was bright blue and soon there was a spider's web of blue across the dark wood that they spun themselves, hiding away the imperfections.

"Are you sure that this isn't going to fall off once we start to plaster it?" Al surveyed their work.

Eva looked up from where she was taping down empty garbage bags so that they wouldn't drip all over the floor. "Pretty sure." She had a piece of tape stuck to one finger and Liv pulled it off to tape down the far corner of the sheeting. Just being this close, and seeing the small, closed-off smile at her lips, sent Eva's stomach into knots.

Al sat down on one of the buckets of plaster and pulled his phone from his pocket. "My dad just texted me."

Liv stood close to Eva, so close that Eva couldn't decide whether to back away or move closer. "If you're done." Al rolled his eyes at them.

"Done?" Liv asked innocently. She backed away to secure the last trash bags. "Done with what?"

"Whatever that was!"

"Taping up bags?" Eva's brow furrowed.

"Oh, whatever." He made an annoyed noise.

"What did your dad want?" Liv pulled her phone out of her pocket. "He didn't text me."

"Weird." His shoulders slumped and Eva wondered what could possibly be the matter. He ran a hand through his hair, fiddling with the band he was using to hold it back. "Our request to get into those tunnels was denied. He says he's going to go into the city to try to speak to the station master, but not to expect anything. What a load of bull. Sorry, Eva, guess we can't have a grand adventure."

Eva let out a deep sigh. She should have known better than to expect anything from their request. Theo had told them not to get their hopes up when he submitted the paperwork. "Stuff like this comes in to the MTA all the time," he explained. "There's no way anything will come of it."

It was agreed that they would send in the paperwork anyway, just in case.

The apartment filled with silence. Disappointment surged within Eva. She slid down to sit on the floor. She didn't care that she was going to be covered in wet plaster streaks.

She had been so hopeful that the place Mary wrote about actually existed. She wanted to stand in the same place her grandmother and Wren had stood and to see what they had seen. Basically, she wanted to know if this was all just some story concocted by a sixteen-year-old girl. Maybe the room full of light meant something else. Maybe it was a euphemism. Maybe it was just a fantasy about a future that her grandmother could never have with Wren.

This was their clue, the only clue that seemed tangible. There were names upon names in the paperwork from Mrs. Talbot's boarding house, but they meant nothing in the long run.

"I'd really hoped that they would at least let us look."

Al stood at the end of the hallway. "Yeah. It's for a good cause."

An entirely selfish cause, Eva thought, but she wasn't about to argue.

They probably saw the request and dismissed it as narcissism and never looked back.

"What time is it?" Liv asked suddenly.

Al bent to his phone. "Five-thirty," he said.

Liv had pushed herself to her feet and was hurriedly unrolling the sleeves of her ratty button-up shirt. "We can finish this tomorrow." She spoke quickly and moved even faster, glancing over at Eva for agreement on the new plan. "Right?"

Eva nodded. Monday was her only day off, and she usually spent the day doing work on the apartment.

Liv gathered her things. "I have an idea," she explained, pulling on her coat. "Get your stuff."

"What do you mean, an idea?" Eva asked.

"Just trust me," Liv replied, bending to cuff her jeans.

They pulled on their jackets and shoes quickly. Eva barely had time to unplug all of Al's super-bright lights before Liv was hurrying them out the door. Her fingers lingered on Eva's back for just a second too long as they scooted out onto the landing. Al raised an eyebrow that only Eva glimpsed; he'd seen the touch. He didn't say anything, and Eva didn't either. It was an unspoken agreement to leave it alone.

Al's boots thumped loudly on the stairs. Eva's sneakers and Liv's flats pattered quietly along behind. As they stepped out into the crisp October evening, Liv began to explain her plan. "This is the busiest time of the day, right? So if we wanted to sneak in, now would be the time to do it."

"Do what?" Eva asked with a sick feeling. She knew what Liv was talking about doing.

Al's smile flashed wide and bright. "I like the way you think, Currance," he said.

"Thanks, Al." Liv started walking toward the subway station. "We need the cover of the crowd, right? All the tourists are leaving right about now and there's the commuter down to DC as well. We'll find a door or something and see if we can't break into the tunnels under the station."

Eva steps faltered. She didn't want to break the law to figure this out, and they'd already been denied the pass to have a look around. She glanced from Al, whose face was lit up with a mischievous smile, to Liv, who was grinning broadly.

Liv's eyes told another story, though. They were troubled, and Eva wondered why. Was she worried and just putting on a brave show? Why do this at all, then?

"I don't know…" Eva began, trailing off. Anxiety twisted like a knot in her gut. It seemed like a terrible idea. It couldn't end well. She shook her head and met their expectant gazes. She would not allow herself to become defeatist. Still, she had to voice her concern. It wasn't right not to. They had to think this through. "What if we get caught?"

Liv held out her arm to Eva. "Where's your sense of adventure, Eva?" She leaned in close. "It'll be worth it," she whispered, her breath hot on Eva's cheek. "I promise."

Still reluctant, Eva nodded and did not dare move because Liv was still pressed close against her side. "I suppose it could be fun."

Liv let out a whoop. Her eyes sparkled in the growing darkness. "This *will* be fun, I promise." Even so, her eyes were still worried.

Eva hoped this wouldn't end with their getting arrested.

Chapter 13

The Station

THERE WERE MANY THINGS ABOUT Liv that Eva found to be vexing and intriguing all at once. Her sense of spontaneity was something that Eva had picked up on as soon as they'd met.

In her head, Eva could hear her father telling her not to get caught up in the *whys* of people. Liv didn't seem to have any whys, just a lot of charm and charisma. Eva knew she was fighting a losing battle. Liv was different. Eva might be too wrapped up in trying to find the why of her grandmother to think about much else, but there was something about Liv that made it impossible for Eva to put Liv from her mind.

The more they delved into the diaries, the more convinced Eva became that there was something about Liv that was unique. She possessed an uncanny ability to discover information hidden in the pages. She picked out offhand, abbreviated messages, and twisted them around until she figured out what they might mean in a context that worked for the diary.

"I'm studying women's history," Liv told Eva late one night in Theo's back room. They were alone in the semi-darkness. "I want to tell stories that have never been told before."

Eva turned to smile at Liv then. "I think it's noble, what you want to do."

"You're very dedicated to solving a puzzle of your own, Eva." Liv's voice seemed like it was under water and distant. "That's noble, too."

"Someone has to figure out what happened to my Gran."

"I just hope that what we find won't hurt you in the end." Her fingers snaked out to touch Eva's for the briefest moment. "I'd hate to see you cry."

The scar on Eva's wrist burned then, white hot and marked by her bitter resentment over her lack of self-control. Liv had turned away and left her in the darkness of the workroom. Liv was a puzzle that she couldn't quite put together; the pieces never really seemed to fit.

The train to Penn Station rocked back and forth and as more and more people got on. Eva's thoughts drifted. She was thinking about the diary entry that had gotten her to this point. A room full of light far beneath the city sounded like something from an urban fantasy novel. It seemed as if it were put in there to give Theo a reason to keep on with his ridiculous quest to find the light of the world. Eva sighed. It all seemed so utterly improbable.

Theo had fixated on that entry as soon as he read it even though, to Eva's mind, her grandmother hadn't said it represented the light of the world in any way. She found it foolish for Theo to become so invested, especially because there was *no way* that they'd be allowed into any tunnels they found.

In a way, Eva felt protective of Wren's sanctuary. It was the place she had told Mary in confidence where she felt safe. It seemed almost like a violation to try to find it.

Eva had connected the dots and decided it was Wren, and not some strange metaphysical or magical artifact, who had broken her grandmother's heart.

She gave a little snort of laughter and Liv turned to look at her. "What?" she asked.

"I was just thinking of how my Gran was in lesbians with Wren and how it probably would have been called a deep friendship back then."

"Deep friendship, huh?" Al ducked his head down to be on their level. "You sure they weren't just BFFs?"

"Could have been that too," Eva giggled. "But we don't want to invalidate their feelings. Deep friendships were *full* of feelings."

Liv gave a little snort of laughter. "Deep friendships, *honestly.*"

Eva found the whole idea terribly romantic. Theo had several books on the 1920s buried in the bookshelves at the back of his workshop. Eva had read them greedily curled up in one of the battered old armchairs at the front of the store. She learned about Brooklyn at the time when her grandmother had lived in Mrs. Talbot's boarding house, and about how very different life had been for women back then.

Her grandmother had always been somewhat of a forward-thinker. It wasn't until Eva had started to read about the time period that she realized just how revolutionary her grandmother's working and living alone had truly been. Society expected her to get married and to have children. The times were changing, but not as quickly for poor families. Her grandmother had to work to support her family, and Eva could only assume that Wren did as well. Her grandmother never really wrote about what it was like to be a woman alone in that world. She lived in a relatively safe space but there must have been challenges. Eva wondered why her grandmother never really talked about them. Maybe that was why she seemed so infatuated with Wren—because Wren was a happy part of her life.

Liv's fingers curled around Eva's as they pulled into Penn Station. The hot, acrid smell of subway exhaust and warm garbage hit her hard in the face as she hurried off the platform and let Liv draw her away from the crush. Her grip was strong and Eva didn't want her to let go, not even when Al came to stand on Liv's other side.

"Should we hit up a drug store for some flashlights?" he asked in an undertone. "Or do we, like, even know where we're going?"

"To an extent, yeah."

Eva glanced at Liv, eyebrows raised.

"I was worried that we weren't going to get the pass." Liv unzipped her bag. Inside was a jumble of shiny silver-wrapped granola bars and some flashlights.

"So you thought we'd go anyway?" Eva asked, looking Liv in the eye.

Liv shrugged, raising her hand in a three fingered salute. "Always better to be prepared," she joked. "Scout's honor."

"You're doing it wrong," Al pointed out, adjusting her fingers so that they were in the correct position for a Boy Scout salute.

"And you were a Boy Scout, Horral? Guess we all have our secrets," Liv replied with a knowing grin. Eva winced at Al's full name. It was just *so* unfortunate.

"Come on." Liv's fingers tightened around Eva's. She was pulling her toward the far end of the platform. "We have to be careful," Liv muttered. She was scanning the walls carefully "There are doors everywhere that lead nowhere."

They stood at the very end of the platform and stared out into the darkness. Eva caught a glimpse of a rat crawling in the trash down by the tracks. She recoiled. "I hate rats."

Al let out a low whistle. "That one looks like it's the size of a cat!"

"Ugh." Liv turned. Her hand was sweaty. "Okay, we need to start looking for a door like that one." She pointed to a door Eva could barely pick out that was well concealed in the blackness. "These doors are part of the original construction." She reached into her bag and pulled out a flashlight. "See the numbers and the way the doors are built? That's in case the sewers ever flooded."

"So they built them like they should be on submarines?" Eva raised an eyebrow. "Liv, that sounds like bullshit."

"I'm serious, Eva. It was in the book that you didn't have time to look through the other day."

"It was?" Eva tilted her head to the side.

Al nodded in agreement. "It was." He tapped the side of his head. "Dad was talking about it non-stop. Seemed to think that that was our in."

"Doors are awesome." Liv shrugged.

Eva thought they were both insane. "Okay. So we have to find a door that looks like it belongs on a boat. Shouldn't be too hard."

It turned out *that* was the understatement of the year. Eva let out a low groan twenty minutes later, when the crush of people around the station had become worse. They had looked at countless doors and been stopped by two security guards and an off-duty cop for loitering. Al's camera proved invaluable, as did his student ID. He was doing a photography project, he told them, and would be done soon.

"I hate how they only card *me*." Al grumbled.

"Sorry, Al." Eva patted his arm sympathetically. "They can't help their prejudice."

"Yeah, especially when blondie over there is the real devious one." Al rubbed at the back of his neck. "This is hopeless. We're never going to find it before the crowd thins."

Liv seemed to be coming to the same conclusion. She was biting on her fingernail and staring up the platform at the cop who had just given Al a hard time. There was a pensive expression on her face. Her eyes narrowed as the cop glanced back at them. She reached out to grab Eva's hand.

"I think I know where we can get in." Eva could feel the cop's eyes following them as they hurried back the way they'd come. As they turned the corner, she saw him reach for his radio.

Eva's heart hammered in her chest. Had he seen them? Had he realized what they were up to? Was he calling for back up? "I think that cop's on to us."

"Don't worry about it." Liv led them on a circuitous path through the station, cutting up the stairs from the subway and over to the Long Island Rail Road tracks, until they stood before a door Eva could have sworn wasn't there a few minutes ago.

"Great," Al muttered. "Magical doors."

Liv shrugged. "Keeps with the theme."

Eva glared at the door, but it was just that: a door. Liv tugged on the handle. It swung open silently.

"Okay, now I know it's a magic door," Liv joked.

"How the fuck is that just, like, open?" Eva demanded. "That's a huge security risk."

Liv peered into the darkness. "Or someone's already down there."

Eva shook her head. "We shouldn't go, then. I don't want to get into trouble." She stared through the doorway. It opened to a metal staircase that led down into blackness. She swallowed. Ever since she was a child, the darkness had not been her friend. She blamed her grandmother's stories of the light chasing away all that was bad and evil in the world. An anxious feeling settled at the base of her stomach, and she felt as if she had to pee and throw up all at once.

A cop appeared at the end of the hallway, barely visible in the sea of people. "Shit," Eva muttered.

Al went pale. "Okay, Liv, we gotta go if we're gonna go."

"Uh-huh." Liv reached into her bag and clicked on a flashlight, handing it to Eva and then taking another for herself. She gave Al one and he started slowly down the stairs, his boots clanging on the metal steps as he descended into the darkness.

Eva followed, squinting into the gloom. Her eyes snapped open when Liv locked the door behind them with a loud click.

"Why did you do that?" Eva hissed, pulling free of Liv's hand. "Now we're stuck."

"Shush," Liv replied, pressing a finger to her lips. "Keep your voice down." Her own voice was a low hiss. "If that cop did see us, it'll take him a minute to find the keys and we'll have time to hide."

That didn't sound particularly promising. Eva looked toward the stairs. She could see the glow of Al's flashlight far below and decided if they'd gotten this far, she might as well go all the way down to the bottom. She took a deep breath of the warm, earthy air, and started down the stairs.

They seemed to go on forever. Eva started counting. She was at more than a hundred before she lost track of her count. Al's flashlight had all but disappeared and the only sound that Eva could hear was her own quiet breathing and the steady thump-thump-clang of their footsteps.

The stairs ended soon and they found themselves on a slope of rock and hard-packed earth. Eva shined her light down onto her mud-splattered shoes and let out a quiet whistle. They moved on, their footsteps echoing in the dark.

"How did you know where the door was?" Eva asked Liv in a hushed voice that reverberated off the walls and rattled about their heads.

Liv smiled, her cheekbones hollow in the light cast by their flashlights. "This is one of the access stairways to the tunnels that the power companies use. The fiber optics are down this far so that they won't get disrupted in the event of something like 9-11 happening again."

"Where the heck did the door come from, anyway? I swear it wasn't there before. How did we miss it?"

"I'm not sure." Liv replied. Her voice sounded far away. "I just saw it and tried the handle. There are only a few places it really could have been."

"And it opened just like that?"

Liv sighed, clearly a little annoyed. "Yes. That's what happened," she said. "I pulled the handle and it opened. I can't explain it."

A little thrill of worry shot up Eva's spine. The door had just appeared. That wasn't possible. *What the hell is this place?*

The slope became steeper and Eva could see the quiet pool of Al's flashlight in the distance ahead. Her pace quickened to keep up. Soon the corridor opened up into a chamber that appeared to be carved out of the very rock that formed the island of Manhattan. They came to a halt and rested. Liv drew up behind her, one hand resting comfortingly on Eva's back, and they both turned to Al, who had almost disappeared into the gloom but for the whites of his eyes and the yellow T-shirt he wore.

"Damn," he said quietly. The acoustics carried their voices much farther than Eva would have liked. "How the hell did you know this was here?"

Liv shrugged. "Your dad's got a map of all these tunnels."

"My dad has a map for everything." He pointed his flashlight off to their right and stared into the darkness. "How do we know which way to go?" he asked.

"Yeah, for real," Eva agreed. She was starting to get her bearings. They'd been moving eastwards, more or less, since they'd entered the tunnel, so they had to be under the sunken basement of The Garden. The tunnel stretched in both directions.

She glanced around and saw nothing to use as a landmark, but Liv was already striding forward. "I have a feeling it's this way."

"I have a feeling that she's got GPS," Al muttered. He allowed Eva to go ahead of him as they ventured deeper into the darkness.

Chapter 14

Under The Garden

THE DARKNESS WAS UNRELENTING. IT pressed at the edges of Eva's vision and nearly swallowed the steady beam of light coming from her flashlight. The claustrophobic feeling of the tunnel made her want to scream in the warm, humid air. She couldn't scream. They could be caught. Someone could find them and then they'd be in a whole mess of trouble. Eva clamped her hand over her mouth and tried to keep the sound in.

There was a sense of familiarity about this place. The dampness and the gloom felt suffocating to her. The fear that curled in the bottom of her stomach felt tangible. She could reach in, pull it out, and examine it. This was the black place where nightmares were made. They were fools for willingly trespassing here.

Ever since they'd started to walk away from the bottom of the stairs, Eva couldn't shake the feeling that they were being followed. This place reminded her too much of her dreams. The faceless girl could be lurking around every corner, waiting to reach out and press Eva's eyes from her face and into darkness.

They were being drawn in.

She knew that it was all in her head, but there were times when Al or Liv would pause to get a better look at the floor or the ceiling and in those moments, the echo of footsteps in the distance could be heard. Eva bit the inside of her cheek. She couldn't voice her fears. She didn't want the others to think she was afraid. Fear was contagious, and the last thing they needed to do was to panic.

"Do we really have a clue where we're going?" There was exasperation in Al's voice. He lifted his camera bag off one shoulder and settled it onto the other. Blinking owlishly in the dim glow of the flashlights, he rubbed at his shoulder. He turned, staring at the passage as his fingers dug into the muscle. "Like, at all?"

Eva glanced at Liv. She had been so keen to take on the role of leader earlier, but now she looked lost. Her eyes were darting around, and she seemed jumpier. Eva wondered if it was because it had been hours since she'd had a cigarette.

"I think I do. There are maps, I studied them." She shrugged.

"And you've got a photographic memory now?" Al asked.

"I never said that. Just that I—"

Eva stopped them. "I know there are far more important things to argue about right now, but does anyone else have the sense that we're being followed?"

Liv looked down at her feet. "I haven't heard anything."

Eva glared. Liv obviously had no idea where they were. If they got caught, it might actually mean jail time.

"It's because you're up at the front," Al replied.

Eva flicked her flashlight over the ground, taking in the jumble of footsteps. The diamond pattern of her sneakers, the tread of Al's boots, and the smooth outlines of Liv's flats were visible in the slightly damp and muddy ground. "Maybe it's an echo? Maybe it is just us."

Liv moved her gaze downward and scowled. "Maybe not." She gestured with her flashlight. There was another set of footprints, a man's footprints that led farther into the darkness.

"How likely is it that anyone else knows about this place?" Eva looked from Al to Liv to the footprints. They were an ill omen surrounded by a pool of yellow light. Someone else was down here with them and they were going to get caught.

Al poked his finger into the footprint. Eva was half expecting him to announce that it was fresh and that he had the scent, like an expert tracker from a nature documentary. "These are at least a day or two old." He indicated how the mud had started to dry at the edges. "Electrical worker, maybe." Al glanced around. "A lot of The Garden's lights are probably wired down in here."

They both stared at him. "What?"

"How the heck do you know that?" Eva demanded.

Pouting, Al pushed himself to his feet. "I was a Boy Scout, remember? There's totally a tracking merit badge."

"I don't think I'll ever get over that," Eva replied.

Beside her, Liv laughed before her expression shifted into a frown. "From what your dad said, these tunnels aren't used very often..." she trailed off and wiped her forehead with the back of her hand. It was getting warm.

"What would Theo know?" Eva frowned. She felt that she could not voice some of her suspicions about the bookseller. They didn't seem particularly appropriate at this moment, either. He was the one who'd told them they had no chance of getting down here, and yet here they were.

But what if he said that on purpose to keep us away? There was merit to the suspicion, but Theo was Al's dad and Liv's boss. If they weren't worried about him, she probably shouldn't be, either. She moved quickly to clarify her question when Al and Liv looked at her oddly. "I mean, what would Theo know about this sort of thing?"

Exchanging a long-suffering look with Liv, Al let out a slow breath. "I've learned that it is better to never, ever, underestimate what my father does and doesn't know. He's a failed academic, which means he'll do just about anything to prove he's smarter than you." He followed the path of the alien footsteps with the beam of his flashlight. "The only person who can give it as good as he does is Liv."

Liv's laugh was gentle and calming. She smiled serenely at Eva and gestured that they should start moving again. "I just fell in with him because he was curious about the same things I was." She started to walk again. "And he likes to argue with me."

Eva knew that well. She'd seen them go at it a few times over the proper handling of documents and what to buy from estate sales. Liv had an eye for rare books that rivaled Theo's, but Liv's tastes tended to be more on the practical side of things. She favored books that they would be able to sell, whereas Theo tended to favor those that interested him.

"But you win," Al pointed out. "You and dad are like oil and water, but you always can get him to see reason." Water was dripping somewhere. Plink. Plink. Plink. The hair on the back of Eva's neck rose and a shiver ran through her. "You win way more than you should against him. He's like, super intense, and you're all logic and he's all grumpy mutterings."

"Well, someone has to verbally spar with the poor man," Liv sniffed. She shifted forward, brushing against Eva. Her fingers tangled in Eva's free hand. Eva's breath caught in her throat. She glanced down at their joined fingers and a smile blossomed across her face. She could deal with this, she really could. She liked Liv and she liked holding hands. Liv seemed to chase away the darkness. She would keep them all safe. "Goodness knows *you* weren't going to do it." Liv's tone was derisive.

Al folded his arms across his chest. "I resent that," he groused. "I can argue with my dad perfectly well, thank you very much."

Eva giggled, leaning against Liv's shoulder and smiling brightly. "Sure you can, Al."

"I can!" The petulant tone was enough to make Eva roll her eyes. "I seriously can."

"Uh-huh." Liv leaned in close. "Don't worry about Theo, Eva, I've got him." The promise was a whisper at her ear. "Nothing bad is going to happen."

"You're awful sure of yourself." Eva turned. Liv was *right* there. Eva couldn't look away. Liv's fingers tightened their grip.

An exaggerated groan jolted them from their moment. "Oh my god, you two. Stop it." Al made a face.

Eva laughed. "Oh fair sir, lead the way then, and I shall stay as far away from you as I can with my lady knight."

"You are both awful and ridiculous."

The moment was ruined, but the promise of it remained. Eva's cheeks burned as she let Liv lead her farther into the darkness, where even their flashlights were snuffed out.

Al continued leading their charge. The path grew steeper with every step they took. Disaster scenarios played through Eva's mind—an abyss, the tunnel suddenly ending, and then stepping out into a void. She kept her gaze firmly on the beam of her flashlight as it bounced off the damp walls. Eva hoped they wouldn't end up in the river, or worse, the sewers.

Al was three steps ahead of her when he stopped short. His light shone off to one side and vanished into the crushing blackness. Eva drew level behind him and Liv peered around his shoulder, turning her own light to join his.

There was an opening in the wall. It was so small it looked like nothing more than a jagged slash in the rock face. Al pointed his flashlight at it, and the light seemed to be sucked into the crack.

Eva's heart pounded as she stared into the crevice. She had no idea how far they'd come, or how Al had managed to spot this in almost complete darkness. She clung to Liv's hand. "Are we going in there?" she asked.

"Come on," Al said. Liv seemed to agree and followed him. Eva allowed herself to be drawn after them into the narrow entryway.

It was a tight fit. Eva's shoulders scraped against the wall and Al had to stoop to avoid banging his head against the rock above. Somewhere in the distance, Eva could hear water dripping. If this meant that they were close to the sewers, they were going to turn around right now. She was not having that misadventure, not today.

They pressed forward. Her hand was sweaty against Liv's palm. She couldn't quite catch her breath. The air was warm this far underground, and moist with humidity that seemed to cling to everything. Eva's hair was frizzing, falling into her eyes and making it hard to see. Liv's hair, usually so straight, was doing something similar. There was a halo of unlocked fuzz around Al's head reflecting in the light like a divine glow above his head.

Their footsteps echoed in the large chamber into which they emerged. Liv let go of Eva's hand and stepped forward, her light pointing upward toward the ceiling. There was an awestruck look on her face. Her lips moved in silent words.

"There's no way," Eva breathed. "This place cannot exist." *This was a dream.* The cavern wasn't as dark as the tunnel had been. A single beam of light filtered down from far above. A crystal formation caught Liv's flashlight and refracted it down onto them.

"This is the place." Her voice was hushed, as though she were standing in a church. "If we were here during the day we'd know for sure. But I'm almost positive. This is the place." Al and Liv stayed silent. "Do you think this is it?" She sounded hesitant now, but the high ceiling and arching blackness around them had a heady effect on her. There was something almost terrifying about this place. She couldn't put it into words.

Liv nodded and turned her flashlight to the far wall. Eva followed the beam of light, but as the light hit the wall, her breath caught in her throat and her fingers rose hesitantly to cover her lips. "Oh my god..."

"Exactly."

Across the wall was one of the most beautiful graffiti displays that Eva had seen in her life. A swirling plume of light arched upward toward the ceiling and curled outward toward the far walls. It was truly stunning. Each line of color seemed to refract the light of the flashlights, glowing with a strange sort of radiance for which Eva had no term of reference. The colors seemed to dance as the light hit them.

Behind them a camera shutter clicked, and then it went quiet once more. Eva turned to see Al standing with his flashlight tucked under his chin, fiddling with his camera, a film canister held carefully between his teeth.

"I hadn't realized that you'd brought your manual camera." Eva turned to watch Al hurriedly remove the old film. Eva hadn't used a film camera since middle school, but Al was an expert. He moved with quick, sure actions, extracting the old film and tucking it into his pocket before popping the canister he held between his teeth open and letting the fresh film roll fall into his waiting palm. The flashlight tucked under his chin bobbed dangerously but it did not drop. He nimbly caught the film around the catch, snapped the back shut and started the auto-wind process.

"Yeah," Al answered, spitting out the film canister. "Wish I'd brought the digital now though, because I have only one roll of film left."

He raised the camera and adjusted the stop as Liv stared up at the wall before them. One of Liv's hands was playing with her necklace. Eva had wanted to ask her about it many times, but had never quite found the words to do so. She watched as Liv's lips moved silently, the fingers of her other hand moving to trace one arching plume of red-gold that seemed to glow against the darkness.

Liv was entranced, as was Eva, by the great mural on the wall. Their lights were not enough to do it justice. Eva wished that it was daytime and that the light could filter through and illuminate the wall, as it was so obviously meant to do.

Her grandmother had stood here, right here, holding hands with the girl she was starting to fall in love with. The idea of it set Eva's heart racing faster. She thought about the symmetry of the moment, her thoughts going a mile a minute. There was no Al snapping pictures back then, just Mary and Wren, two people who were flirting with something that should have been so much more than what her grandmother had eventually ended up with.

The Mary that Eva had come to know from the diaries would have been disgusted that she'd become a soldier's wife, sitting at home with a young child as he went off to war, and then another war, and then another one, again. She'd been alone all those years with only Eva's father to keep her company.

Eva turned her flashlight to the ground and took in the mix of sludge and silt. Their footprints were everywhere. But the other set they'd seen before was there too, pressing at the edges of the story their own feet told. Eva's flashlight tracked the strange footprints across the cavern. The light caught on something and she stepped forward. There was a deep groove cut in the mud where something appeared to have been dragged away from the wall.

This is it. The voice was like a whisper in the back of her mind. *This is the answer, it has to be. Everything that you've done up to this point has been to find this clue that will bring everything together and give this fool's errand meaning.*

She moved away from the others. The grooves that she'd found went all the way to the far wall. A little shiver ran through her. She moved quickly, squishing through the mud.

The far-side wall held deep scratches. It looked as though nails had been dragged along it. Big, scary nails. The kind from horror movies. Beside the scratches were embedded slivers of wood.

The smell of cedar was so strong that Eva's nose wrinkled and she sneezed. Rubbing at her nose, she moved closer. It was the remains of an old trunk. The red cedarwood on the inside prompted her allergies to act up. All around it were muddy pieces of clothing half buried in the muck.

This is it! Eva's triumphant whoop echoed through the chamber. "Hey Liv," she called. Liv's beam of light snapped over to her and bathed her in a warm yellow glow. "Come check this out."

Eva bent to examine the scraps of clothing. They were hand stitched, and the fabric felt old and scratchy under her fingers. Liv drew level with Eva, depositing her coat and bag on a dry patch of floor and aiming her light at the... "Is this a *girdle?*"

"I don't think so." Liv laughed. She reached for a lace glove beside the not-girdle. "It's a corset, maybe. But man, this is really old." Her voice was hushed. A train rumbled by, brakes screeching, above. There was an intermittent roaring that made Eva wonder if the Rangers were playing.

"Yeah," Eva agreed. There were no papers anywhere in the mess, just clothes and the shattered pieces of cedarwood. Eva picked up one of the larger splinters. Under closer inspection, she could see that the wood was pink on the inside. Her eyes widened.

"Look." She cradled her flashlight between her cheek and shoulder, holding up the piece of wood for Liv to see. "It's been snapped apart recently."

Liv ran a fingertip over the faded gray side of the wood. That was the side, Eva reasoned, that had been exposed to the elements and the pink had faded away. "Anything that's been down here a while would fade like this." She took the splinter from Eva and flipped it over and over in her hands. "And if it was just recently broken..." She frowned and Eva moved closer with her light. She cast Liv into shadows. The hollows of her cheeks and throat were tantalizing, and the gold of her necklace chain glinted from under the collar of her shirt, momentarily captivating Eva's attention. "Someone's been here." Liv straightened up and broke the spell. "And they've taken whatever was locked in that trunk."

"You really think so?"

"Yeah," Liv said. Her hand holding the splinter of wood was shaking. She gathered a few pieces of clothing and pushed them back into the trunk. Her light caught one dress that was stained the rusty brown color of dried blood.

Eva let out a slow, steadying breath. "Something bad happened here."

Liv made an affirmative noise.

"We should get out of here." Eva pushed herself upright. "If someone else is down here, they shouldn't find us."

Liv tucked the glove that she was holding into her back pocket. "We should go," she agreed. She bent and scooped up her jacket and bag. "Obviously, whatever was down here is gone. We need to regroup. Figure out what brought Wren and Mary to this place initially."

"You sure they didn't just want to make out?" Al called. He had dug a small hole in the mud and positioned his flashlight so it caught the wall and its strange luminescence. He was leaning back, his face half-hidden behind the camera. "Because, from what I've read, your Gran totally had the hots for that Wren chick, Eva."

"Hey, Man Ray," Liv called. "Wrap it up, we're gonna bail."

Eva's thoughts were racing. She was so glad that she wasn't the only one who saw the deep connection between Wren and her grandmother. Before she'd had to leave college, she had taken a women's studies class that had talked about what it was like to be queer in the '20s, and Theo's books had expanded upon that point somewhat, but it still wasn't talked about. Her grandmother never mentioned it outright. Eva wasn't even sure Mary knew what was happening when she went off with Wren into the city as if they were a couple. She'd even said that Wren played the gentleman to her lady.

Still, though, they wouldn't need to escape down to a place like this just for a moment alone; they could do that behind closed doors at Mrs. Talbot's boarding house and no one would be any the wiser. Eva shook her head.

"There's gotta be more to it than that. They had plenty of time to be alone." She trained her flashlight on the smashed trunk and then flicked it back to the wall with the mural painted upon it. "Maybe this trunk had something to do with it."

Liv shook her head. "There would have been notes, papers, something." She jerked her thumb toward the chest. "The cedar was picked deliberately because it would hold up down here. It would preserve the contents. There must have been something important in there." She wrinkled her nose, toeing the battered edge of the trunk with her shoe. "Not just clothes."

Eva wondered what was in store for her grandmother and Wren in the next few diaries that she'd just started to read. She, Theo, and Liv had focused on the earlier ones first, trying to establish a timeline to help pinpoint what exactly they were looking for within Mary's account of her life at sixteen. Theo was looking for references to the light of the world, while Eva and Liv were trying to figure out who Wren was. There was nothing in what they'd read to indicate that anything other than a single trip to this place had occurred.

Someone had gotten here first and had taken the precious clues that Eva had been hoping to find. Disappointment flooded through her. She'd gotten obsessed with the idea of finding out who Wren was, and now it seemed like a dead end. Her hands clenched into fists. They were so close to something huge and to run into a brick wall was devastating.

Eva's shoes squelched as she turned away. Liv was fingering her necklace again, her flashlight making a pool of light at her muddy feet. Her expression was dark, clouded by something that Eva could not describe.

The necklace intrigued Eva. There must be a great importance to it, and yet Liv, who usually was rather open about everything, kept it as good as concealed yet was drawn to it whenever she was thinking or stressed.

It has to be important to her. Maybe a family thing? Fuck it. Eva took a deep breath, intending to ask.

Al's light flashed in their direction and Eva was able to see the look on Liv's face. Pure anguish was written across it. Eva wondered if she'd hurt herself and was trying not to show it.

"Are you okay?" She kept her voice low so as not to draw Al's attention.

Liv started. Eva raised her light to point somewhere off to Liv's left. She wanted to be able to see Liv's face to know if she might be lying. "I'm fine." She pulled her lips into a strained smile. "It's just this place, you know? I felt like we were on the verge of actually *finding* something, and then there's nothing here but someone's memories all mixed up in the mud."

Eva put her arm around her. She getting used to Liv's constant presence, and starting to know the signs when she retreated into her quiet moments, such as chain-smoking on the bookshop's front stoop. Those were the moments when touch seemed to be what Liv needed more than anything. Maybe she was like Eva. Maybe she had moments when she just felt sad.

Liv curled into Eva. Her breath was warm on her neck, and they were close, so close to mirroring what Eva suspected had happened to Mary when she came down here for the first time. Liv's eyes were shining and her fingers were trailing a shaky pattern up Eva's arm.

"I won't give up if you won't," Eva said. Her lip jutted out stubbornly as her fingers slowly started to become slack, loosening her grip on her flashlight until it seemed as if it would slip from them at any second. Liv's fingers were touching her side now, moving slowly toward her hip. Eva let her eyes flutter shut, knowing what would come next.

Warmth blossomed across the pit of her stomach and Liv twisted into her, her hot breath on Eva's ear. "You never struck me as the quitting type," Liv whispered. Her lips brushed against the delicate gold loop in Eva's lobe. "And I am entirely serious," she added. "Should you be willing." And then she stepped out of Eva's arms.

Eva was flabbergasted to see a bemused smile on Liv's lips. Her dimples deepened in full effect. She thought this whole thing was funny, the... Eva let out a frustrated noise and scowled at Liv. She knew exactly what she was doing... the *tease*.

"I suppose this isn't really the place." She tried to sound casual.

Eva jammed her hand into her back pocket and turning to see that Al was lurking at the entrance. She wondered if Liv had backed off because Al was there and she didn't want to make him uncomfortable. Eva had awkwardly played the third wheel enough not to wish that role on Al.

Liv gave a grunt of affirmation and strolled over to Al. Eva followed half a step behind and soon the three of them were standing by in the crack in the wall where they'd come in. Al indicated two other ways into the cavern. "I want to try going through one of them and see where it comes out. That one slopes up, so maybe it comes out somewhere nearby."

Nervously, Eva shook her head. "Not until we definitely know where they go. You could end up in the river, or at some dead end and no one would ever find your body," she said, grinning at the last bit. They would come back, she knew, and they would explore this place further. But first, they had to go back to the surface, back to the real world and out of Wren's underground sanctuary. It didn't feel like a sanctuary. It was a dangerous place. They needed another look at Theo's maps to try to get a sense of where these tunnels went.

"As much as I would love to explore," Liv said, shaking out her coat and shrugging it over her shoulders, "I am inclined to agree with Eva. We have no idea what's down here."

Al scowled but it didn't translate into the rest of his body language. Eva figured that if he had really been a Boy Scout, then he knew better than any of them to be prepared. They needed a better game plan if they were going to go exploring.

There was still the added challenge of getting *out* and Eva was trying not to think too hard about that.

"Aw," Al said, fiddling with his camera bag strap. "You guys are no fun."

"There could be huge rats, Al," Eva said. "I don't want to mess with them unless I'm mentally prepared, and probably armed."

"We should get out of here," Liv said, glancing around. The same roaring sound that they'd been hearing ever since they'd arrived echoed louder and she instinctively stepped closer to Eva. "We can tell Theo what we found tomorrow, after we finish with the plaster at Eva's. Maybe he'll have some insight about what we should do next."

Eva nodded and Al made an affirmative noise, but there was so much that was left unsaid between the three of them. Obviously someone else knew about the underground cavern. Someone else could be searching for the light of the world, whatever it was. After seeing this place, Eva was feeling more and more inclined to believe that it was not an expression of either physical desire or a single person. It couldn't be. It was a shrine to the light, no matter what that was. They'd trespassed in its sanctuary, the one place where Wren had said she would always feel safe.

Part Two

The Unsent Letter

Chapter 15
Al & Eva

July 25, 1925

I had a dream last night about the room under the city. Wren was there, standing before the great wall of light, her hands raised up in supplication. It wasn't right. Everything was all wrong. She was screaming at the wall, begging it to stay closed. It wasn't time, she said over and over again, it was too soon.

The wall erupted then, and blackness oozed from its center. It engulfed Wren and consumed her. Her screams—oh, her screams were terrible. I was rooted to the spot, I could not move, I could not breathe. Wren was dying before me and I couldn't do anything at all.

I woke up screaming. Judith was banging on my door and I barely had time to put on a robe before she and Mrs. Talbot burst into the room. They were frantic. I'd been screaming, crying and sobbing for what felt like hours. I'd awoken Judith and she'd run for Mrs. Talbot.

I could not keep my composure, even though Judith makes me so angry sometimes. I did not want to show the weakness of being scared of a nightmare to her, not when she already thought so little of me. She gathered me up in her arms, though, without saying a word, and held me while Mrs. Talbot checked the room over and made sure that the window was closed and locked. The room was so hot and stuffy.

Judith held me like a mother would her child while I cried myself to sleep.

Unable to wrench herself away from the diaries until close to ten o'clock, Eva ended up spending most of the remainder of Monday morning scrubbing mud from her poor shoes. It took her almost an hour to make them look clean again. Then she placed them in the sunny front window of her apartment so that they'd dry faster.

She hoped they would be dry by tomorrow when she had to go back to work. Her mother constantly harped on her about proper arch support, but Eva was fairly flat-footed and the shoes were comfortable. The old ladies who came into the store, Eva thought, got something of a kick out of them. She was a young, fresh face to them, and they were endlessly curious about her. So much so that she was grateful for the day off. She was sick of having every aspect of herself picked at by people who had no business even noticing such things. Even if it was only for few hours, the reprieve was worth it.

The jeans that she'd been wearing the night before had gotten off relatively easy compared to her poor shoes. Eva hung them up in the bathroom after she'd washed them out in the kitchen sink. She would take them down the street to the laundromat with her work clothes after they finished the plaster in the hallway and save herself a trip.

Al came over with two sealed containers of soup that afternoon. Theo had made it the day before. He'd been cooking while they had their misadventure under the city. Al held out the bag as if it were his ticket to get into the apartment. "I come bearing gifts," he announced. "My dad was worried that you weren't eating."

"That's, um, nice of him," Eva answered. She stepped away from the door.

In the bag with the soup was a thick loaf of brown bread. "That smells *divine.*" Eva poked it curiously.

Al toed off his shoes. "My dad made the bread this morning. It's something of a secret family recipe." He followed Eva back into the kitchen. "You should eat some of it now. It's better when it's fresh."

"Well, I haven't eaten dinner yet. You ready to eat now?"

"Sure."

Eva took down two bowls and a sauce pan. She poured some of the soup into the pan and dug in a drawer for a bread knife.

"The recipe is an old one of my mom's. From home," Al said. Eva clicked the stove on and turned to face him.

"Where was home for her, exactly?" She had been looking for a way to ask Al about his absent mother since Theo had first mentioned her. Judging by Al's dark complexion, she obviously wasn't white. Eva didn't know how to ask about it, though. It didn't seem right to be nosy about the subject because Al and Theo didn't talk about it that much. That only made Eva even more curious about her, and where she'd come from.

"Her family was from Ethiopia," Al explained. He leaned around Eva and put the cover back on the container of soup. "They first tried to go to Israel but it wasn't really *for* them, you know? So they came here and two generations of mixed marriages later, here I am."

"Why didn't they like Israel?" Eva rummaged in a drawer for the limited number of spoons and bowls that remained in the apartment after her mother had swept through the previous weekend with yet another box for donation. She'd promised to get Eva some newer cutlery, but she hadn't been back to the City since. Eva was stuck with six mis-matched spoons, all but one of which were dirty. She moved over to the sink to wash a second one.

Al shrugged, his hair sticking out like a porcupine's quills. He was wearing it down today, and it played about his ears. "Politics, maybe? I'm not really sure, my grandmother never talked about it. Sort of like yours really, all tight-lipped an' shit about the past." He shook his head. "I think it was probably because they weren't up to the standard. They couldn't speak Hebrew or read much. Apparently that's important for finding work over there."

"That sucks." Eva shut off the tap and shook the excess water from the spoon.

"Yeah. The community here's really small, but it was a lot more willing to accept my family when they came. It means I'm here, right? No mandatory military service for me!" He pumped his fist in the air. "And I get to decide if I want to keep kosher or not. Bacon is way too delicious to have to give up."

"You're ridiculous."

"I keep it at Passover, though."

"Al, everyone keeps kosher for Passover, it's part of the holiday." Eva raised an eyebrow.

"Yeah, but not everyone gives up stuff for Lent, so, like, I'm sure some people don't." He rubbed at his chin. "My friends party for Mardi Gras and then promptly ignore the actual purpose of the holiday."

Eva shook her head and turned her attention back to the stove. Her family was never particularly religious; she'd never given up anything for a holiday before.

"So this is one of your mom's recipes?" She'd never asked what had happened to Al's mother and wasn't sure that she could without upsetting Al to some extent. It seemed like a recent wound for Theo, which probably meant that it was just as raw for Al. Liv had mentioned something in passing about very aggressive breast cancer, but Eva didn't have any of the details. She couldn't imagine what it would be like to lose her mother, even if they didn't get along. Al never talked about his mother, and Theo barely mentioned her. They talked about death all the time as they tried to sort through Eva's grandmother's diaries, but Al never once mentioned the loss of his own mother. The hurt that it took to keep that loss bottled up inside must have been unbearable.

Al nodded, leaning over and inhaling the fragrant steam that rose from the saucepan. "My grandmother was ostracized for marrying an Ashkenazi Jew from Flushing, but she tried to keep the culture alive and taught my mom, and I guess by extension me, everything she could remember about the Beta culture." He sighed, rubbing his hand over his forehead. "My family's really just a hot mess."

"At least you didn't have a grandmother who somehow had a falling out with her lesbian BFF and then was all emo about it until she died." Eva pulled the saucepan off the burner and flicked off the heat. She poured the soup into both the bowls. It smelled amazing, like cinnamon and curry mixed with a nutty undertone. "What's making it smell like nutmeg?"

"It ain't nutmeg," Al leaned forward, sniffing. "It's fenugreek." He nudged Eva with his shoulder. "Although, I gotta say she isn't the only one entering that market."

They ate in relative silence.

"Thanks for this," Eva said. "I know your dad worries, but I'm really okay."

"I think he just knows how it can be," Al replied. "He's a lot like you, Eva."

Eva didn't think she was anything like Theo. She nodded anyway, not wanting to offend Al. "I'm going to have to get this recipe from you sometime."

"Can't. Family secret." Al winked at her.

"Uh-huh."

"I mean it. If I told you, I'd have to kill you."

"You're unbelievable. It's freakishly delicious. I want to eat it all the time." Eva laughed.

"I'll tell my dad." Al got up and took both their bowls to the sink. While he was washing the dishes, Eva wandered into the living room and began to set up for their plastering adventure. Yesterday they'd done all the prep work, so now all they had to do was apply the plaster in small patches, step by step, along the walls. She was just about ready, her sleeves rolled up and the plastering float in her hand, when Al emerged from the kitchen, drying off his hands. "We ready?"

"Yeah." Eva held out a second float to Al.

As they worked, they talked about what they'd discovered the day before and if it would be worth it to tell Theo what they'd done. They both decided that if Liv hadn't told him already, then they weren't going to mention it, either. He was sure to blow a gasket. Theo was protective of his son, and of Liv as well. Eva was a stranger, but his impulse to feed her indicated that he must care. She didn't want to alienate one of the few people who'd been willing to help her try to decipher the hidden meanings in her grandmother's journals.

After they'd finished, Eva ducked into the shower. Afterwards, a towel wrapped around her head, she dug the June diary from her bag and carefully removed it from the Ziploc bag she kept it in. It was getting colder now, and she didn't want to be walking over to the bookshop with wet hair. She'd pushed a very plaster-covered Al toward the bathroom with a spare towel and a promise that she didn't care that he showered and used her stuff. She'd loaned him a shirt of her dad's that she sometimes slept in. Al had stared at it before shrugging and taking it into the bathroom with him.

Eva didn't mind this easy friendship, and she didn't mind Al in general. He was cute in a way that made her look twice, but she didn't feel with him the way that she did when Liv leaned in close or held her hand. Eva knew that she had it *bad* for Liv, but she didn't know how to talk to her about it. There had been moments, such as the teasing proposal from last night for instance. Okay, so it had been bad timing, but there was potential there. Eva wanted more from Liv, but she couldn't quite put her finger on just *how* she was supposed to behave when surrounded by two criminally attractive, flirtatious people.

She still wasn't quite sure if Al liked girls. Eva had a bit of a history of crushing on gay guys in high school, so she liked to think that she was pretty good at figuring out if a guy was gay or not. Al was a complete mystery; he didn't ping at all. He was just there, a good guy who was content to smile and flirt without ever trying to make it go further. Eva appreciated that.

Al would be easy. She could ask and he'd probably say yes. But that wasn't what she wanted. What she wanted was to have that moment Liv proposed. She wanted to taste the lips that had come so tantalizingly close to her own. It just felt natural. Their personalities fit too perfectly. There had to be something there.

Eva pulled the towel from her head and threw it over the back of her grandmother's favorite armchair. She'd hang it up when Al was done showering. She had to talk to Liv about what had almost happened down there. She'd started so many texts only to slowly delete the words one by one. There was no way to approach it that didn't make her feel that she was woefully out of her depth. She didn't know how to even begin the conversation. *What the hell am I going to do?*

The June journal rested against her knees and Eva opened it to the next entry after the one that had started them down this rabbit hole in the first place.

16 June 1925

Had court today, went into the city with Mr. P. and sat in the back taking notes for him. The case is exceptionally dull compared to some of the others he is only just now starting to tell me about, the ones that have him locked up for hours with the state's attorney. He's giving evidence against rum runners. It's all terribly exciting.

Unlike his current case, which is dull, dull, DULL. I found my mind drifting as I sat there. The chairs in the back of the courtrooms are uncomfortable, and by the end of the morning session, my legs ached to move around.

He let me go for lunch (thank goodness) and I found myself alone in the city, with a newspaper and the wedge of cheese and bread that Mrs. Talbot had told me to take with me when I told her that I would probably not be back home in time for the usual curfew. I'm so happy that Mrs. T understands the nature of the work that I do and allows me freedoms she restricts with some of the other girls.

Judith has been exceptionally nasty about this, accusing me of all sorts of untoward things when I come back late. She thinks I'm sleeping with Mr. P and that he's taking me out to gin joints after work for dancing. If she didn't fancy herself a vamp from the movies, I'd say she was jealous. She's after a man. Any man will do. I think she's just annoyed that I told her that I don't think anyone who frequents such an establishment would be the marrying type. She's just wasting her time.

I spent my lunch reading the paper (mostly for the baseball scores, I confess) and sitting on the courthouse steps thinking about the future. It's been weighing on my mind a lot these days, wondering what the future might hold.

Judith says that I should settle down, become a soldier's wife. My mother agrees with her and I hate it so. I don't want that. In my perfect world, I would die an old maid surrounded by books, and maybe Wren would be there too. I do not need a man to care for me or ensure my happiness. I can make my own destiny—

"Um, Eva?"

Eva started, and her eyes flew up from the diary to see Al with what she assumed to be his plaster-covered shirt under one arm and his towel in the other. She'd completely lost track of the time while reading. It looked as though Al had been standing there for more than a few minutes. She held up the diary. "Sorry, I was distracted."

"It's cool," Al replied. "Where do you want me to put this?" He held up the towel.

"Just hang it up in the bathroom," She glanced to her own towel. "Can you do mine too?"

"Sure." Al grabbed it and disappeared off into the bathroom. He reappeared pulling at his locks to make sure they were dry. "Why do you use men's body wash?"

"Because it smells good," Eva replied without missing a beat.

"Okay." They stared at each other for a minute before they both burst out laughing, and Al gestured to the diary. "Is there anything more in there about that cavern?"

Eva shook her head. "I went back before then, actually. Last night after you guys left, I found an entry talking about a bad dream. Right now she's on a rant about how she doesn't need a man."

"Yeah, 'cause she's a lesbian." That set them laughing again. Her Gran was so enamored with Wren that it wasn't even funny. Eva shook her head and closed the diary. It really wasn't funny, and yet it was.

"Did they even have those back then?" Al mused.

Eva shrugged. "I think so." She'd seen pictures in school of the usual women dressed as men, wearing boater hats and surrounded by flapper girls. She'd never really thought much about the other sort of queer women, the ones who would pass as "normal" to the everyday viewer, because not everyone was super butch and gung-ho about appearing that way. She grabbed her coat and put the journal carefully back into the plastic bag, which she tucked into her purse before slinging it over her shoulder.

"I still can't believe Liv ditched us," Eva said as she zipped her jacket. It wasn't really cold enough for hats and scarves yet, but it was starting to get there. October was unusually cold this year. The nights had turned crisp and the trees in the parks were starting to turn. "She did promise to help with this." Liv wasn't usually a flake and she seemed to enjoy spending time with them. It was odd.

Al shrugged, scratching at the back of his neck. "Dad said he needed her." He was still playing with his hair, which showed some signs of being wet. Eva hadn't bothered to ask him if he'd wanted a shower cap and she mentally kicked herself about it now. "Apparently he pulled some strings with that guy Kelvin from the Brooklyn Historical Society. Got permission to borrow some papers and he needed Liv to serve as a second pair of eyes."

Eva nodded. She couldn't even be mad because it was a perfectly legitimate reason to miss a let's-plaster-the-hallway party. Liv had a career and her livelihood to think about. Her weekend had already been freely given to Eva, only to be derailed by an adventure in the depths of the city. *And it was all for nothing.*

They had found nothing beneath the city, just a smashed chest. It seemed to indicate that someone else *had* been down there, but it could have just been a looter. The workman theory that Al had proposed—that someone *had* been down in the tunnels, someone who had an actual reason for being there—made more sense than the theory that someone else just happening to stumble into the same tunnel as them. Still, Eva couldn't shake the feeling of unease. She felt there had to be something more to this. That place was too unreal, too beautiful, to rest undiscovered for so many years. Eva frowned and glanced over at Al, who was fiddling with his jacket.

She could ask him what he thought, except she wasn't sure what she thought about it herself yet. Maybe it was better to give it time. Maybe she could talk to Liv about *that* at least.

"You'll bring the containers back when you're done with them, right?" Al ducked into the kitchen and emerged with his canvas grocery bag clutched in one hand. He bunched it into a ball and haphazardly shoved it into his shoulder bag.

Eva nodded. "Of course." Stealing old Tupperware that had clearly seen better days was the least of her concerns.

The walk downstairs and out onto the street was quiet because Eva was lost in her own thoughts and Al distractedly typed into his phone. She had to pull him out of the way of oncoming old ladies and dog walkers on more than one occasion. Eva let him do it, though, because she had enough to worry about.

Her grandmother had had a secret that appeared to be growing into a multi-faceted monster. There was so much that they didn't yet know. Eva was desperate to figure out who Wren was, and Theo was fixated on the light of the world. Eva still suspected it was a short, flowery way of referring to Wren, but she wasn't about to disagree with Theo's probably crazy theory that it was some sort of power source that is unique in its continued appearance across history. Her grandmother had never really been the type to embrace such things. Even when she was sixteen, there was little or no mention of god or religion in her diaries.

As they crossed the street and headed down the side road toward the bookshop, Eva sighed. She was starting to think that there had to be more to the story. The dream that her grandmother had described in her diary was so similar to Eva's own that it was almost uncanny. Wren was in that dream. Was Wren the girl with no face?

Nothing about this had been simple, from Liv's ambiguous friendship to Theo's obsessive theories to Al's easy smile and pleasant company.

There was no one up front in the bookshop when they arrived. Al headed to the counter, where he pulled his name tag from the jar of pens and rulers and pinned it to his chest.

"They're probably in the back," he said. "It's about to get busy in here though, evening rush and all, so I'm going to stay here. Tell me if you find anything good."

Eva waved distractedly and headed for Theo's workshop. Her footfalls were silent and, in the late-afternoon light, little clouds of dust rose up in her wake, rising into the air in almost perfect clouds. Theo really needed to get a vacuum back here.

The door to the workshop was half open, and there were several large archival boxes on the floor full of letters and papers, all sealed away in neat little plastic bags with neat handwritten labels on them.

Liv was sitting on the worktable, a pile of bags next to her and a clipboard balanced on her lap. She was wearing cropped jeans today and oxfords with bright pink and yellow zigzag-patterned socks showing at the ankles. Her oversized sweater was the same slate blue as her eyes and made her look absolutely adorable. Eva grinned shyly at her as she pushed the door shut behind herself. Liv watched her slip into the room, her elbow on her knee and her chin in her palm, and smiled back.

Eva *liked* it when Liv smiled at her. It made her feel warm inside, which was how she'd felt yesterday when Liv got so impossibly close. The urge to walk right up to Liv and kiss her on the mouth was so strong that Eva had to stop herself just inside the doorway and stay there until she felt that she was under control once more.

"What's all this, then?" she asked, unzipping her coat. She hung it and her bag up behind the door and stepped forward to examine one of the plastic storage bins on the floor by Liv's feet.

"This is the Talbot House collection," Liv explained, showing her some of the papers in her hand. "Theo's just left to collect the rest of it. It's boring mostly, and a whole lot of what we don't want."

Eva stepped forward and dangerously into Liv's personal space to peer at the manifest in her hand. "Do you think any of my Gran's stuff is in there?"

Liv shrugged. "I don't know," she replied. "Kelvin said that the list wasn't complete but that we were welcome to look over the whole collection. Apparently no one's asked to see them since a women's studies grad at NYU used them for her thesis." She blew her bangs out of her eyes and turned to meet Eva's gaze.

Feeling flustered, Eva took a step back and rocked on her heel, not quite meeting Liv's gaze. "Why do you guys care so much about this?" she asked. "I get that Theo's been studying the light of the world phenomenon for most of his life and my Gran's stuff is as tangible a lead as any, but it just seems like that isn't what this is about..."

Liv's face softened and she reached out, her fingers brushing against Eva's cheek as she smoothed the locks of hair that had flown free in her walk over. Eva's fingers scrambled for something to grasp, to fiddle with. She swallowed, feeling hot and anxious.

"We're doing this because this is what we do, Eva," Liv explained quietly. "Theo might want to prove a point to everyone, but this is what I love more than anything else in the world. I love history and puzzles, and you've given me both."

Eva looked up at Liv through her bangs. She was smiling that small smile that made Eva's stomach lurch forward and her breath come unevenly. Liv's fingers lingered on her cheek and she leaned into the touch, relishing how good it felt. She could stay like this forever, she knew that she could.

Time would never allow that, though.

Chapter 16

The Talbot Collection

THE FINAL BOX OF THE Talbot Collection arrived some three days after the rest. Eva eyed the smaller storage container and the messy pile of papers inside it with some trepidation. Something wasn't right about this. These documents were supposed to be protected and cataloged, not thrown in here in a jumbled mess.

Theo rummaged around in his bottom desk drawer for another pair of archival gloves. "You'll need to wear these." His voice was muffled by the drawer, his head nearly buried as he leaned down to dig deep into it. "No idea why Kelvin would—ah ha!"

"Why aren't they all sealed in bags like the others?" Eva accepted the gloves and pulled them on. The fingers were too long, flapping about like pieces of tape at the ends of her fingertips. Eva tugged, trying to force more of her fingers into the glove to no avail.

Theo glanced at the box on the table, pulling on his own gloves. "I don't know." His tone was forceful, so forceful that even Liv, across the room, looked up sharply.

Eva took half a step back and put her hands up. "Hey, I was only asking," she said. "No need to get all testy." She glanced over at Liv, but her attention had returned to the computer screen. Perhaps she had imagined Theo's reaction. Perhaps she was just on edge.

"I just took what Kelvin was willing to offer me." His tone was much more conversational and friendly than a moment ago. "Besides, there's a wealth of information here that will serve us both well."

Eva let out a slow breath. Maybe she was just imagining things.

"Now." He reached into the second box from the collection and deposited a stack of documents in archival sleeves before Eva. "We are looking, I think, for any mention of your grandmother in these documents. Afterwards we can narrow it down and maybe, just maybe, find some clue as to who Wren was."

When the papers arrived from the historical society, Theo's entire tone had changed. He had seemingly let go of his pursuit of the light of the world, at least superficially. He still talked about it, mostly to himself, but to Eva he was much more focused on Wren and discovering who she was.

Yesterday, while Eva and Liv were putting away some of the documents, Theo had started in on an impassioned rant about how it was just awful what happened to Eva's grandmother and wouldn't it be nice to have the full story there? He'd bustled out of the office and Eva nudged Liv. "What made him change his tune?"

Liv's lips drew down. "I'm not sure." She glanced at Eva. "Maybe he just realized that the light of the world isn't something he can find in the diaries of a sixteen-year-old girl?"

"Maybe." Eva wasn't so confident. The way Theo would look at her grandmother's diaries gave her an uneasy feeling. She'd caught him at it enough times to recognize the glint in his eye and the curl at his lips. He wanted something from them that Eva was not certain they could give him.

"The light of the world is a concept," Liv went on. She gathered papers neatly, stacking them in little rows and sorting them into an order that made sense only to her. "Theo knows this. He's latched onto your Gran because she's given him the first credible lead that he's had in years."

"But it isn't a lead. It's just a thing she used to say. Probably because she was talking about how much she loved Wren, and we don't know what happened to her." Eva ran a hand through her hair. A frustrated little groan escaped her lips.

It was easy to dismiss Theo's fixation on the light of the world now that they had something solid to look at that came exclusively from clues in the diaries. He was so forceful in his belief in there being truth behind the concept, however, that Eva wasn't entirely sure it would ever go away. His focus was on the mystery of Wren now, but something about the way he pawed through the papers and muttered about clues did not sit right with her.

Eva held the stack of papers to her chest and sighed. Theo had swept back into the room and collected a second pile for himself. She couldn't tear her gaze away from the greedy way he started to rifle through them. She was staring at Theo as he picked up a second pile for himself. It just didn't seem *right* for him to be so invested in the light of the world. That wasn't why anyone else was here, looking through these papers.

She wondered, maybe, if he felt discouraged. They were all trying to act like they were discouraged that they "hadn't been allowed down" to check out the underground room that Eva's grandmother had mentioned with such awe. Liv hadn't told Theo that they'd gone. The three of them agreed that it was probably for the best that he did not know what they'd done. They had no way of predicting how he would react, and all evidence pointed to a bad reaction. Eva did not want that kind of trouble for Al and Liv. She could leave, but they still had to work with him.

"I think if we dig a little deeper, we'll be able to figure out the connection between Wren and the light of the world, too." Theo said as he bustled between the bins, pulling out documents and setting them out in neat rows to be examined.

Eva's eyelids fluttered closed. *Here we go again.* Behind her, Liv coughed. Eva glanced over her shoulder and saw Liv rolling her eyes.

Eva sat down at the end of the table closest to Liv. She was typing away, busy with a special order for the bookshop. Eva set her paper pile down and didn't look at Theo. She was annoyed, and she felt it was justified. He had tempered his excitement over the light of the world over the past few days, but now it was back with a vengeance. This wasn't about him and his interests, but he would never see that. Eva came to him for help, but now it felt like she was the one doing all the helping.

While she had expected to deal with some quirks from asking a guy like Theo for help, she had not expected such a dogged pursuit of the light of the world from him. He wanted to know about it for his own personal gain, and Eva wanted absolutely nothing to do with that.

She drummed her fingers on the table. *What the hell am I gonna do?*

The steady tap-tap-tap of Liv's typing soothed her. Eva looked down at the first document in her pile. It was a grocery list dated 1923. Who ate that many beans? Eva made a face. "Do we have a bin set up for irrelevant stuff?"

Theo grunted and pointed to the storage bin in the middle of the table. "Put 'em in there," he said, not looking up.

"Okay."

The box was far enough away that Eva wasn't going to be able to simply discard the irrelevant documents into it as she read. She set the useless grocery list aside and started on the next one. This was a love letter, from a man named Jacob to a girl named Elsie. A note at the top indicated that Elsie had moved and left no forwarding address. Eva let out a little snort of laughter and set it aside as well.

The next one was a letter still in the envelope. This one looked more promising.

Shifting forward in her chair, Eva stared down at the date and then the address, trying to recall exactly what her grandmother had written about her correspondence with her parents in the diary. She could not recall the dates exactly, so she cracked open the archival bag and carefully slid the letter from its envelope.

The return address was in Calverton, New York. Eva frowned. That was the town where they'd buried her grandmother, the place with seemingly no connection to her family. Eva's heart pounded. This could be something. The postmark was September 15, 1925, but the name and address were smudged by water damage and impossible to read. Eva removed the letter from the envelope. It stuck to her gloves. She kept her movements careful and precise. She didn't want to give away her excitement. This could be a clue!

Her heart raced as she unfolded the letter. The penmanship was neat and flowing, like a school teacher's would be up on a chalkboard.

The letter was to a woman named Catherine. Eva's heart sank. Her grandmother had mentioned at least two women with that name who lived in Mrs. Talbot's house, Upstairs Catherine and Seamstress Catherine, and they didn't get along. Eva remembered laughing at those entries, but now all she felt was bitter disappointment, they were in this for the long haul. It had seemed so promising.

"Damn," she whispered. Still, she drew the letter close and read.

As the words drew her in, a ringing started in her ears.

Dearest Catherine,

It pains me greatly to have to write to tell you of your brother's passing. He was ill during the night and by morning the doctors said that there was no help. They were powerless to do anything for him save pray for his soul. I know that you cannot leave work for trivial matters such as your family, but I do wish that you would come home. Your mother misses you terribly and I find myself longing for your company as well.

You have a duty now that you must do, and the city is the only place where that task can be fulfilled, but your absence is marked by both of us now that you are no longer with us. Your actions are never in question, not even when you took on the mantle that we so feared you would. You have a greater purpose than your mother or I, and it is the will of a higher power that you do your duty to the fullest.

Your brother has gone with God now, and it is just your mother and I at home. We are but two people who sorely miss their now only child.

Grief is a scary thing, Catherine; you know this as well as I do. It drives us to do great things. Terrible things, but great things. It wracks at our consciousness and pulls us in a million different directions, for it is only in grief that we see our fears. We are but pawns in a much greater game, you more so than most. Please send word if you can return before the year is out. The trains are running smoothly now, and I am sure that if you were to save a few pennies, you would be able to return home.

I miss you so.
  Your loving Father

Eva felt hollow, almost brittle. She reread the letter, and the awful ringing in her ears only got worse. Was this how people communicated back then? A letter into the city to tell a poor girl that her brother had died? She shook her head, feeling the prick of tears at the corner of her eyes. That wasn't *fair*. How could anyone stomach getting a letter like that? How had Catherine been strong enough to read it?

There were smeared splotches on the corners of the pages. They were tearstains, Eva realized. Catherine had cried reading this letter.

A warm weight pressed against her back. Eva turned. Liv was leaning over her shoulder, reading the letter with narrowed, piercing eyes. "That is the saddest thing I've ever read," Liv said in a low voice.

"She cried." Eva indicated the places where the ink was stained and the paper was warped.

"I would have too." Liv's voice was a whisper in her ear.

Eva did not want to think about Liv crying. She was probably the type who cried beautifully, like in the movies.

She sighed. "Do you think this could be something?" Eva asked.

Liv pursed her lips. She hummed the affirmative. "Could be."

Eva stared down at the letter for a moment before her eyes drifted over to Theo. He was looking at them, his gaze open and dark, as if it were set to devour them both whole. Eva felt a shiver of fear run up her spine. *That isn't natural.*

But just as soon as it appeared, it vanished. Theo shook himself, as though he'd been out of his body. He went back to looking at the document in his hand as if nothing had happened.

Chapter 17

Catherine Monroe

IF SHE WAS REALLY HONEST with herself, Eva was grateful for a second pair of eyes on the letter. She had a deep-seated worry that she was going to read too much into things if she got too excited. Her grandmother's diary required a certain level of interpretation, but that was different. Eva knew her grandmother. And even though the girl in the diaries was far less touched by life experience, she was still the same person beneath all the sadness.

She was getting very good at reading between the lines with her grandmother's diaries. There was a lot that Mary said that she did not explicitly state in those diary entries. This letter seemed to have the same weight to it. It was far more than just tragic news. Still, Eva could not let go of the feeling that she was looking for something for the sake of wanting to find something.

Liv was still there, standing just behind her. Eva didn't trust herself to move. She wanted to lean back and let Liv press against her. Theo was still absorbed in his letter and didn't seem to be paying them any mind. Liv smelled of fresh air and the slightest whiff of cigarette smoke and coffee, like a café on a blustery morning.

"I think this might really be something." Liv's breath was warm in Eva's ear. Eva hummed, shifting in her seat, distracted by Liv's presence. "See how he talks about duty and a higher calling than her parents?" Liv tapped the page with a finger, careful to only graze it with her nail. "Wren talked about that same sense of obligation to Mary."

Eva nodded. The warmth at her back was gone. Liv had stepped away. Eva frowned and turned to see Liv collecting a notepad and pen from the desk. She pulled the computer chair over to sit next to Eva, their knees brushing against each other. Eva couldn't move.

She could never figure out how to behave around Liv. She sat there and watched, hands in her lap, as Liv copied down the letter in quick, precise handwriting that made Eva bemoan her own smeary left-handed scrawl. When Liv was finished, she reached for the archival bag and wrote down the catalog number. She then held it open for Eva to put the letter back.

"I thought we were sure that Wren wasn't living at the boarding house," Eva said when Liv wrote a big "Wren?" at the bottom of the page.

"I know, but it doesn't mean that she didn't leave the letter there or receive mail there. That happened all the time back then, especially if the..." Liv flipped the letter in its archival bag over and read the return address with narrowed eyes. Eva wondered what she could possibly have been thinking, but Liv was already off to the races, pushing back in her chair and scooting on its wheels over toward the computer.

"Careful!" Theo called, not looking up from his pile of papers.

Liv made a noncommittal noise, her feet arresting her movement. Eva slipped from her chair and went to stand behind Liv, who had pulled up Google Maps and was typing in the letter's return address. Eva watched as the website ticked away, her fingers circling the hard back of Liv's chair.

The thrill of the chase was with her now. She'd been carried along by Liv's enthusiasm, fully prepared to ride it for as long as she could. When the results came up, the scenery on the street view was eerily familiar. Eva stared.

"We buried my grandmother in that cemetery." She tapped the screen where the side road and vine-covered gate looked almost overgrown. "Must've been before they cut back the kudzu for the year."

Liv clicked back into map view and there it was. The small patch of green labeled "Bluff Cemetery" was on the far side of a little train track icon. The red flag was just a little way down the road.

"You did?" Liv turned to Eva, frowning in confusion. "I thought she was from here." She clicked back into street view and moved the map until they were back at the entrance to the cemetery. As Liv moved the cursor over, a wash of brown and grey swam into view. Eva stared at it, not really fully comprehending what she was seeing. It must have been winter when they took the second picture.

"Yeah, she insisted on it," Eva said. She leaned over Liv's shoulder to get a better look at the street view of the cemetery. It was full of dead leaves and trees with skeletal branches reaching toward the heavens, not the overgrown swath of green it had been at her grandmother's funeral. It was so strange to see it in a different season, all life gone from it. It looked almost haunted. "My dad didn't understand it; no one we know is even from Calverton."

"Weird."

"Totally."

"Maybe that's why the letter was there, though. Maybe your grandmother knew Catherine."

Eva shrugged. "She could have. There were two women named Catherine mentioned in the diaries. Maybe more. The name was common as dirt back then."

Liv made a humming noise and opened up another tab, pulling up the New York Historical Society's website and then logging into an area of it that Eva had never seen before. She clicked through a few pages almost too quickly for Eva to follow and arrived on a search page. She typed in the address from the letter and soon there were scans of old deeds and a few photographs filling the results tab. "It says here that this belonged to the Monroe family from about 1809 to 1934, when it was sold following the death of the only living heir of the property, a Catherine Monroe."

"1934?" Eva frowned. That was well outside their time frame.

Shifting against Eva's shoulder as she clicked through to the next document, Liv said nothing. Her eyes scanned the document quickly before she let out a low whistle. "Wow," she said, and leaned back to that Eva could read the article.

Eva's hand slowly rose to cover her mouth. The story of the death of the Monroe family's first son, in the trenches of France during World War I, opened with an optimistic tone. There were more children, the family would persevere. As she kept reading, the true tragedy became evident. Their second son died of an unknown cause, and then the family lost everything not long before the Crash in 1929. To make matters even worse, their daughter, Catherine, had disappeared in 1925 not long after the death of her brother, and was never seen again.

"She was seventeen when she disappeared..." Eva breathed. She frowned, scrolling back up to the top of the page. "And they didn't declare her dead until 1934? Why in the world?"

"It was harder to keep track of people without the Internet." Liv shrugged. "But she could be the Wren we're looking for."

"Wren is such a weird nickname for Catherine." Eva shook her head.

Catherine Monroe, who went by Wren to friends, has been officially declared dead after vanishing without a trace almost nine years prior to this date. The investigating parties are certain of Miss Monroe's death, citing that she has not been seen in nine years and there was little chance, at the time of her disappearance, that she left the area. The family has elected to place a marker in the family plot despite the fact that no body has ever been recovered. Authorities have declared her case closed, and after an exhaustive search have no choice but to rule that Miss Monroe may have died unknown in Brooklyn, where she lived and worked. Anyone with information regarding her disappearance or death is urged to come forward at this time.

Eva could scarcely believe what they were reading, or their stroke of good fortune. "No. Way." This *had* to be their girl. She went by *Wren*. Wren! The timing was right.

Wren Monroe had disappeared in the latter part of 1925, right around the time that Eva's grandmother's journal entries completely changed in tone. Eva hadn't read them fully yet, but she had skimmed them. She was shocked by how drastically the tone had changed in November and December of 1925. Wren had gone missing at the end of November. This would make it all make sense.

Eva let out a strange, strangled laugh. It just figured that their missing character, the one unknown entity in their search, would turn up in such an innocuous manner.

Liv grinned triumphantly. "Yeah. Way."

"This is her." Eva's confidence leaked into her tone. "It's gotta be. Everything fits."

Theo called from across the room, "What have you found?"

Eva turned and Liv peered around her, a smile plastered on her face. It didn't reach her eyes, though, and Eva felt a coldness radiating off her that felt like a deep loss. "I think we might have just identified our mysterious Wren." Her tone was the same as the look in her eyes, a little distant and measured. It was as though she didn't want to give anything away. She turned back to the computer and hit the print button.

Theo pushed himself to his feet, his chair scraping against the hardwood. Eva winced at the noise. Despite Liv's odd look, she could not keep the smile from her lips. She was practically vibrating with excitement because now something might finally happen. They had a *name*, and with it they could find out more. They could narrow their search. They could track down relatives!

Only, they couldn't.

There were no other Monroes. The line had ended after Wren disappeared. Still, there might be cousins. Eva wasn't giving up hope. And besides! They had a name!

She was practically hopping up and down as Liv handed Theo the transcribed letter and then the newspaper article that they'd found from 1934. He read them quickly, pushing his glasses up his nose and staring so intently that his already impressive eyebrows joined together into one long, bushy caterpillar across his forehead.

Watching Theo read, Eva could see a multitude of emotions crossing his face. His eyebrows scrunched into an even bigger caterpillar, before they relaxed, the lines in his face creasing upward into a genuine smile. "I can't believe it," he announced, and the excitement felt real. He handed Liv back the notepad and added, "I never thought we'd actually find out who she was so definitively."

"Me neither..." Liv replied. She shifted from foot to foot, holding the notepad against her chest, the white of it a stark contrast to her charcoal-gray sweater. "Well, it's impossible to be completely certain, as Eva's grandmother has passed, but it is a really strong suspicion."

Theo clapped Liv on the shoulder. "This is why you are my assistant," he explained. "And I am the expert. This is something! Far more of a something than we've had to go on in ages regarding the light of the world." He was positively beaming as he turned to Eva. "Do you realize what this means, Eva?"

She shook her head, still not quite following how they'd segued from probably figuring out who Wren was to talking about the light of the world again. It seemed to Eva that they were making an *extreme* leap in logic.

Liv's face seemed to close off entirely. She looked almost hesitant as Theo continued to speak, her lip caught between her teeth.

"If we know the girl's name, we might be able to track her through the city. We know that the room underneath Penn Station is one starting point." Eva and Liv exchanged a quick glance at that, but neither of them said anything. "But what if there are more clues within these documents? If we know more about who she was, we might be able to piece together why she disappeared and maybe take a guess at where she went."

Eva glanced between Theo and Liv, who was staring down at her shoes, her fingers playing with her necklace. "That's..." Eva started, her voice shaking slightly as she tried to figure out the proper tone to take with him. She could see how Liv had retreated. She didn't know if she should do the same. "That's really good, right?"

Theo bounced away and headed back to the pile of papers in their little archival bags on the table. "I want to go through as many of these as we can today. I have a good feeling about them." He spun on his heel, looking rather like an overly excited poodle, his greying curly hair and eyebrows flying every which way as he moved. "If we can find something on the light of the world, it'll be huge, trust me."

And that was the crux of the issue. It wasn't that Eva didn't trust him; it was more that he wanted different things than she did. The small aside at the end of the article came to mind. The family had been buried using some of the sale of the estate in the non-denominational cemetery up the road from where they lived. The same place where her grandmother had insisted on being buried.

As Theo turned his attention back to the pile of papers on the table, Eva glanced over to see Liv's fingers tangled up in the chain around her neck. Her eyes were worried and she had sucked her lower lip completely into her mouth, pressing it into a thin line that seemed to amplify the emotion that was starting to show on her face. Eva took half a step forward, toward Liv and away from the overly excited old man, but Liv shook her head and turned away. She would not look at Eva as she fiddled with the collar of her shirt and tucked the chain smoothly below it out of sight.

Again, a question about the necklace sprang into Eva's mind. First one, and then another, until they rattled around with no space for her to find the words to open her mouth and simply ask.

Probably just a nervous habit, she reasoned, turning back to the table. She had no idea where to start with her pile, so she set down the one letter that had been their biggest clue and sighed. Her shoulders slumped and she was about to hook her ankle around her chair to pull it in behind her to get back to work when Liv's voice cut through the silence that had descended.

"I'm going to go smoke." Liv scooped up her old battered army coat from where it lay over the back of the computer desk.

Eva didn't think twice before she headed for the door and grabbed her own coat, following Liv, dodging around Al and a customer he was helping.

It was freezing outside. The wind whipped up the street and Eva tugged her coat collar up for more protection. Liv had her back to the wind and was lighting a cigarette, her hand cupped around it. It took her more than one try before she managed to get it lit.

Eva watched as she sucked smoke into her lungs and tilted her head up to the sky, exhaling smoke and breath, a message upon the wind.

"You don't really want to find the light of the world, do you?" Eva asked. She jammed her hands into her pockets and stood hunched against the wind.

"I think some things should be left alone," Liv replied tersely. She took another pull on the cigarette and stared at Eva intently. "Think about it. Before, this it was all about solving your puzzle, now it's about his once more."

"If you don't like it, why do you work with him?" Eva asked.

"Because someone has to keep him from getting too far off track and usually I'm the one for the job," Liv explained. She shook her head, a rueful smile glancing across her features as her bangs blew down into her eyes. "And as much as I hate to admit it, telling your grandmother's story is far more interesting than chasing something that shouldn't exist."

Eva tilted her head to one side. "You really don't think it exists?"

"I never said it doesn't, I said it shouldn't. The light of the world has existed on the fringes of historical research for decades now," Liv took another pull on her cigarette and glanced up to see Eva's confused expression. She smiled, and seemed to decide to try to explain it a different way. "Why do you think Theo's so obsessed with finding it? He wants to prove to the academic community as a whole that they were wrong to laugh him out of grad school when he presented his thesis."

"So this is all about his glory?"

Liv shrugged. "It could be, and I don't like it." She glanced at Eva, her eyes crinkling at the corners and her smile slow and easy. "I think he could write a book about your grandmother and get just as much respect from the academic community, if not more."

She had a cigarette dangling from her lips, but Eva wanted to reach out to her, pull her in close, and kiss her for being so insightful and so kind. She was a good person, a true and honest one.

"Do you really think so?" Eva asked quietly, her voice almost lost on the wind.

"I do," Liv said firmly. She pulled her cigarette from her lips and raised her arm, and Eva didn't need telling twice. She scooted into the warmth of Liv's one-armed hug. "Your grandmother had a wonderful life, Eva. And if what happened to Catherine Monroe is what broke her, then it is up to the historians who have researched her story to tell the world about it."

Chapter 18

Belief

IT TOOK NEARLY A WEEK to sort through the remaining documents. Eva spent countless hours huddled in her sweater in the backroom of the bookshop, her eyes aching in the low light, sipping tea with Liv and Al. They scoured the documents for any further mention of Catherine Monroe while Theo started the laborious process of digging through countless old newspapers to see if he could find any articles about her disappearance.

It was slow, trying work. The writing on some of the documents was nearly illegible. It would sometimes take hours to decipher the contents only to discover that the document had very little to do with the query.

"This is hopeless," Al announced on the afternoon of their fifth day at it. "There's nothing here." He got to his feet and stretched his arms over his head, fingers spread wide. "I give up."

"We can't give up," Eva protested. There were papers strewn all around her, documents that meant little to their search but still might have some meaning. Liv was gathering a small stack of her own that she wanted to look at further.

"I know, but for me there's no point. Liv's got this crazy book idea—"

"It isn't crazy, Al." Liv looked up sharply. "Mrs. Talbot was a fascinating woman who did a great deal of work for the young women of the area. It seems a shame that outside of this room and the Brooklyn Historical Society, no one knows anything about her."

Al shrugged. "I suppose. I just think this is boring."

"It isn't boring." Eva met his eyes. "It's just a slog. Like most things that aren't fun are a slog."

The clock on the wall ticked. It was the only sound in the room, counting down the minutes until Theo would usher them off home when the hour grew too late to read any further. They were pulling long hours, trying to get the most out of their time with the documents. Theo was only able to secure a temporary loan.

The silence stretched on. Al shoved his hands into his pockets.

Eva felt defeated. They had a name and that was it. There was no other mention in any of the hundreds of documents that they had spent the past several days reading through. It felt like a hopeless pursuit.

Well, not entirely hopeless.

"Liv's book idea isn't really all that crazy, you know." Eva kept her voice deliberately mild. "She's definitely got enough primary sources here that the rest of the research would be a breeze."

An amused bark of laughter came from beside her, and Liv's hand rested gently on her shoulder. She leaned in, eyes shining with repressed laughter. "I am sitting right here, Eva. I can defend myself." Liv's voice was dry, carefully filtering any of the humor she found in the situation out into a neutral tone.

Eva's eyes narrowed. She was on to Liv's game. "Everyone needs a knight in shining armor, Liv, even you."

The hand on her shoulder squeezed gently, and Eva felt the breath leave her body. Her stomach was somewhere near the floor as Liv moved even closer, her eyes half closed and her lips twisting into that dimpled smile Eva found so charming. "That's very sweet of you." Her fingers brushed Eva's cheek.

Al coughed. Loudly. "I am also standing right here."

The warmth at Eva's shoulder was snatched away and Eva glared at Al. "So you are."

"You two are gross."

"We're adults, we cannot possibly be gross." Liv stuck her nose up in the air. "And if you don't want to help, that's fine, Al. I know this is boring."

He shook his head. "Nah, it's fine. Someone's gotta stay here and make sure you guys leave room for Jesus."

"You're Jewish." Eva wrinkled her nose. "And we don't need a chaperone."

Al deposited himself back into his chair with a thump. "It's an expression, Eva. And I doubt Kelvin would appreciate it if Dad returned his papers all wrinkled because you two decided to make googly eyes at each other."

"I'm surprised you're not offering to videotape it," Liv said.

"Ugh, that's even worse. You're like my sister, Olivia." He made a face. "Ew."

"Thank god for small favors," Liv replied. "Do you still have that accounting document? It might be interesting to look at the finances of the house. Maybe Catherine paid rent?"

"She shared a bed with my Gran, actually, when she did stay there." Eva pointed out. They both looked at her. Her cheeks colored. "Like, platonically. For sleep."

"Let's be honest here, Eva. How gay was your Gran?" Al wiggled his eyebrows suggestively.

Eva groaned. "I'm not about to assign her a label that she didn't choose herself."

"Why not?" Al asked.

"Think about it, Al."

"I mean, I get it, but it's so *obvious*." He frowned. "They were as into each other as you two and equally disinclined to talk about it."

"Look," Eva began, "there's nothing wrong with claiming that such-and-such historical figure was queer in today's understanding of the word, but I just get uncomfortable with the idea of it. I knew my Gran and I never knew about Wren. There was never another girl in her life, either. It was just this one moment in time. I wouldn't call her gay. If anything, I think her feelings for Wren deeply confused her. She wasn't raised in a time when queer women were visible at all and she certainly didn't identify with them. It doesn't make sense to give her a label like that."

There was a warm presence on her knee. Liv's hand was resting there, quietly reassuring.

"Huh," Al said. "I'd never really thought about it like that."

"I wanted to label her like crazy when I first stumbled into this mess, but it doesn't really make any sense to do it. Seeing the subtext and calling it gay or whatever is one thing," Eva agreed. "But it's another to make a logical leap and start saying so-and-so was one way when they don't understand the word the same way we do. We don't even know if she was attracted to men or just married my grandfather because that was what was expected. I mean, she said it, but who knows how she really felt. She could have just hated my Grandpa."

"Are you sure you never finished college?" Liv asked. "That was way more succinctly put than any of my women's studies professors ever said it."

Eva's cheeks burned. "I mean, I didn't. But I don't know, I guess I just don't like jumping to conclusions."

"Nothing wrong with that." Al leaned across the table. "Here are the accounts, Liv."

"Thanks." Liv's hand left Eva's thigh. "And you're right, Eva. We shouldn't do that."

Eva smiled. "Thanks for being so understanding about it, guys."

"I can still call them gross, right?"

"Oh definitely, they were disgustingly cute together. Totally gross." Beside her, Liv laughed and laughed.

———— ∘⚬⚭⚬∘ ————

Inky blackness pressed at the corners of Eva's vision. It was so thick she felt that she could reach out and grasp it. As if it were a solid thing that could consume her if she pressed on.

Turn back, her mind screamed, turn back, stay alive.

She was standing before a gate. It arched high overhead, so far up that Eva could not see its apex. In the center of it was a great seal, twisting and pulsating with darkness.

"This is the door to destruction."

The girl with no face had returned. She reached forward and grabbed Eva's head as Eva tried to twist away from her. Her fingers were like icicles, sticking to Eva's flesh and pulling at the skin hard enough to rip the flesh away.

"This is the door to the end of the world."

"Why am I here?" Eva tried to wrench her head away, but it was no use. The grip was too strong. It had her. It had her and it would not let her go. "What brought me here?"

"You seek the light of the world." The girl's face seemed to shift then, the face underneath the face warm and familiar. Liv's face. Why was Liv in her dream?

"Liv!" Eva screamed. "Liv, let me go!"

"You seek the light of the world," the girl with Liv's face said in a voice so unlike Liv's that it rattled Eva's bones. "This is what happens when you get too close, seeker."

Pain erupted across Eva's ribs, twisting against her racing heart. The blackness around them pooled in Eva's chest, blood seeping out and darkness seeping in—

Eva's eyes flew open.

Her alarm was going off.

———◦◦◦◦———

The nightly slog through the documents left Eva bleary-eyed and sleepy behind the counter of Mr. Bertelli's shop. They had managed to get through the bulk of the collection the night before and she was exhausted. The late nights were starting to take their toll. Eva knew she looked like she'd just rolled out of bed, but a job was a job and she was dedicated to being there on time, even if she was half-asleep.

The little old ladies, the grocery's most frequent customers, told her that it wasn't right for her to look so sleepy on the job. "Be a professional, dearie," one woman said after Eva counted back her change. "It's not hard."

"Have a good day," Eva replied through gritted teeth. She knew what she was doing was important, even if they did not.

In the early-morning lull, Eva found herself sucked once more into her grandmother's world, curling around the pages of the July 4 entry and the very feel of Roaring Twenties America.

July 4, 1925

Wren came by this afternoon with a basket full of food and invited me to come in to the city to have a picnic with her in Central Park. Despite all of her misgivings about Wren, Mrs. Talbot took one look into her basket and insisted on throwing in some wax-paper wrapped packets that we later discovered were freshly baked cookies. I think Wren is growing on her.

She's been so reluctant to trust Wren that this is a huge step forward for her. I think she fancies herself my mother in a strange way. I'm the youngest boarder here by at least two or three years and Mrs. Talbot spends entirely too much time looking after me. Wren has been a thorn in her side since January, but I think now, after showing that she's not trying to hustle me, Mrs. Talbot is starting to try to like her.

It isn't just anyone she gives cookies to.

How she finds the time to bake is completely beyond me. Mrs. Talbot is constantly busy with her temperance meetings and events. She's the one who does most of the work around the house, too. Wren almost burst out laughing the first time we saw her in trousers and a workman's shirt, hammering away at the water heater. She's an old maid, according to Wren. An old maid who sees all of us paying guests as her children.

I keep telling her to be nicer, especially if Mrs. Talbot is going to give us cookies. Wren just laughs and leans in closer and I completely forget what I was thinking about.

I am starting to feel hot in the face when I'm around her. What is she doing to me? How has she managed to wrap me so effortlessly around her finger and trap me in these feelings of unnaturalness? I have no name for how I feel about Wren. She has pulled open my ribs and settled herself right beside my heart, nestled in against my soul and I do not think I could ever carve her out.

Women do not love like this, this girlish love that feels like the first kiss at the end of a grand romance. I cannot feel this way, it isn't right or natural, and yet I cannot stay away. There are times when I feel so silly, playing the lady to her gentleman, but I cannot pull away when she offers me her arm. I want it, and she wants it. Although I would argue that she looks far better in a dress than I do. Especially the shorter ones that are fashionable today. Legs for days, that one.

I think Wren was in a charitable mood today. She told me bit about her family today. It's the most open she's ever been with me about this sort of thing. We sat together in the park and she told me of her brothers. The older one died during the war, near where my father served. I told her of my father, how he came back but was not the same. She got quiet then, and turned away. At least he came back, she said to me.

At least he did.

We are not perfect, Wren and I. I think that we have more differences than similarities and we're both scared to admit it. Wren spends half her time gone from my life. I don't know what she does and I can only hope that she is doing a just and moral trade; I'd hate to think of the alternative. I've read stories of loose women in the penny papers aplenty. I know how that goes.

What's almost worse is that she won't tell me where she goes when I ask. I keep seeing that room full of light beneath the city when I close my eyes and I hope that that is truly her sanctuary. There should be only darkness there, darkness on the edge of void, but it is full of all the light and goodness I see in her.

She seemed to be on the verge of telling me something today. She started so many times as we sat in the sun in the park, started and stopped. Started and stopped. The words must have tasted like sandpaper, going off of the face she made alone. She wanted to tell me, and I tried to listen, even if I could not hear anything.

Wren has a secret, I know she does. Even a simpleton could see it in the way she hides behind bravado. I want to know what she's keeping from the world.

How does one ask another to speak the darkest secret they hold? It must be dark, otherwise I'm sure she would tell me.

Wren comes to see me at night sometimes, long after Mrs. Talbot has turned off the lights. She looks so drawn then, and weary as if she's been running, and dirty as if she's been hiding. I let her wash by candlelight in my room and don't say anything at all when she sheds her clothes and crawls into bed beside me.

There are things, Wren tells me, that go bump in the night. They want the light, and she's trying to keep the light from them.

I have no idea what she means when she says that. I am scared for her, I truly am. A girl like her should not go out into the darkness like that; there are unsavory characters that are sure to be afoot.

But Wren promises me that she is protected no matter where she goes. I only hope that it is the truth, but I fear that one day she may not come back to me.

And I do not know what I will do when that day comes.

The love story between her grandmother and Wren was beautiful. Eva thought it had all the hallmarks of an epic romance, the sort that novels were written about. When she was younger, she loved those sorts of stories. There was a depth to them that captivated Eva. They drew her in and made her feel as though those experiences were her own. As she grew older, though, she found herself more and more caught up in the reality of situations.

Something was nagging Eva about Wren's story. They had no idea who she was other than a girl from rural Long Island whose family was long gone. Eva supposed that they knew Wren's secret. Her grandmother suspected that Wren wanted to tell her something, but so far there wasn't any indication in the diaries that she had entrusted it to Mary.

There was something lurking in the hazy details of that room beneath the city, at the edges of the diary entries and in Wren herself. Something had consumed the light of this seemingly wonderful girl. Something had pulled her away from a happy life and she was never seen again.

Eva kept going back to the diary entry she'd read weeks ago now about the night her grandmother woke up screaming. Chronologically it took place after the July 4 entry, but it carried the same feeling that Eva picked up on, time and time again, in the diaries. Something wasn't quite right with Wren. Something didn't make sense.

Mr. Bertelli's shop was deader than dead that morning. Eva had already straightened and prepped everything for the Tuesday rush. She was picking at the Sudoku at the back of the *Village Voice* when Al appeared with a grocery list and a rolling cart. Bored and maybe a little desperate for human interaction, Eva asked him to stick around.

"Is it always this dead on Sundays?"

"Yeah."

"I'm sorry."

"Don't be. Mr. Bertelli just started opening on Sundays. It's my only solo day. I'd rather it not be busy." Eva put up her hands. "I'm still learning the ropes."

Al hopped up on the counter. "It can't be that hard."

"There are spiders. On the bananas. Constantly." Eva poked him in the side. "Get off the counter."

"Fine," he said, drawing out the word. "Do you need any help with anything?"

"Not unless you want to mop out the back room." It was the one task Eva still had to do, but she had not started on it yet because she usually saved it for after she closed up shop for the afternoon.

He shoved his hands into his pockets. "I don't mind."

"Really?"

"Yeah. I haven't got anything better to do. Liv and Dad are at it again, anyway."

Eva made a face. "What now?" She led Al over to where the mop bucket and dump sink were tucked behind the door to the back room behind the freezers. "Don't tell me that he suggested Liv's book was a bad idea."

"Nah, nothing like that. Liv just thinks he needs to remember why we're working on this. I agree with her." He turned on the tap and Eva threw in a dissolvable soap packet. "He's too invested."

Eva bit her lip and looked away. "He is too invested," she agreed. "Almost scarily so."

"I can see that." Al swung the mop around the floor expertly as he spoke. Eva leaned against the doorway, a box of apples ready for the shelves pressed into her hip. He glanced up and met Eva's eyes with a curious look on his face and clarified, "Like, in his motivations for helping you?"

Eva bent, setting the box down on the floor. "It's a little weird, isn't it?" She tugged a box cutter from her apron pocket and carefully cut away the packing tape. "He's a guy who has so many other things he can do with his time, and yet he's choosing to help me." She started to unpack the box.

Al leaned on the mop, his chin resting on top of his hand. "You have given him a chance at his white whale, though, Eva." He smiled almost fondly. "You're the only person in my lifetime who has given him a solid, concrete lead to the light of the world beyond acknowledging that the cross-cultural concept exists."

The two apples in her hands felt as though they weighed a hundred pounds. Eva turned to stare at Al as he went back to his task. The floor gleamed in the sunlight that streamed in from the front of the room, the racks of olive oil and vinegar that Mr. Bertelli stored toward the front of the store casting golden and red shadows across it as he worked. "So he doesn't care?"

"About your grandmother? Probably not beyond the capacity of what her life experiences tell him about the light of the world," Al said dejectedly, scuffing at a stubborn patch of the floor with his toe. "It sucks, but he's spent his entire life being laughed out of research institutions because of his beliefs. You've given him a chance to find something more." Al shook his head, a rueful smile tugging up the corners of his mouth. "Shame we can't tell him about our adventure under the city."

"Tell me about it," she lamented.

The pictures he had taken that afternoon were gorgeous. The light of his flashlight just barely caught the edges of that beautiful mural. There was something almost sinister about the way the light hit the painting. It glinted dangerously with just the slightest hint of the underlying image. The photographs were stunning, and they captured the essence of the assignment that he'd hated so completely that his professor had begged him to allow them to be displayed at the school.

It was a terrible secret to keep from Theo, but they still had no idea who had been down there before them. Liv had suggested that they just let it lie for now, and Eva was inclined to agree with her. There was something haunted about Liv when she talked about that place. Eva knew, she understood it well. Her dreams had shifted after they came back from the tunnels. They were full of that cavernous room, only cast in shadow, and try as she might, Eva could not shake the nightmares.

That place had been a sanctuary for Wren, but from what, Eva did not know. Eva certainly didn't feel safe down there. Her hands moved of their own accord, arranging the apples onto the display and trying for a pyramid pattern.

"I wouldn't feel bad, though. He's still going to help you." Al went back to mopping. He was rocking back and forth on his feet, squeaking away as his boots moved on the wet floor. "Just, after his own ends."

Eva's shoulders slumped. She knew better than to expect anything more, and yet it hurt to hear it admitted so freely. Al was right to tell her. Liv was right to be concerned, too. All that Theo cared about was finding the light of the world.

"What happened to him, to make the light of the world, of all things, his white whale?"

Al jammed the mop back into the bucket and squeezed it out. He didn't look at Eva when he spoke, and Eva wondered if what he was telling her was some sort of a family shame. "He's never really told me how he found out about it. I think it was from when he was a kid. His grandmother's best friend was this old Irish lady, which was a huge deal back then, because that was back when people didn't interact with, well... people who were different from them." Al laughed a little. "My family loves to break down social barriers or something."

Eva grinned. "I suppose so."

"So this Irish lady told this story about this girl that she'd helped once. She said she was hiding from a bad boyfriend, you know? But then, like, the girl disappeared before her very eyes. She was there, in plain sight, but the boyfriend didn't see her. When she asked about it later, the girl said that was the power of the light of the world. And he asked her what it was, over and over again, until she died, and he still didn't have an answer. I don't think she ever knew."

"I guess he's just like me, then," Eva muttered. The dreams could get... intense.

Al stared at her blankly and Eva shook her head. That wasn't a detail for him to hear. "He gambled his entire academic future on it once he got to grad school. He wrote this paper that basically talked about all his theories about the light and all the research that he'd done. They laughed him out of the room where he was supposed to be defending his thesis."

Eva couldn't think of anything to say because she'd never felt shame like that. She could take one look at all that Theo had done, and his slightly crabby and unfriendly demeanor, and she could almost understand it. "Almost" being the key word there.

"So, if he's just like me, chasing after a secret from the past, then why obsess about the light?"

"I think it's because he thinks that it will somehow fix everything." Al wheeled the mop bucket over to the dump sink and tipped it over with one foot. "Stupid, I know, but it's what he really thinks."

Eva didn't understand how anyone could have that sort of a relationship with their parent. She loved both her mother and her father, despite her mother's constant push for her to be better than she was, and her father's god-awful jokes. She knew that there were times when Al and Theo's relationship wasn't the best, and she guessed that this might be one of those times. Al could see that his father had a white whale, and Theo refused to admit it.

She picked up an empty box and collapsed it flat so that she could load it into the recycling bin in the alley behind the shop. She left it by the back door so she could take it out when she locked up and left for the day. "Do you believe in it?" she asked as Al trailed behind her.

"In what?" Al asked.

"In the light of the world. In whatever power it's supposed to hold."

Al scratched his chin and allowed Eva to lead him back to the front of the store. He selected a basket and began to make his way down the aisles, selecting his supplies. He was somewhere over by the rice when he finally answered, half-shouting over the tops of the aisles. "I don't think I do," he explained. "I think that the light exists in some capacity, but not in the capacity that my father thinks it does. It's an expression for something else. In your grandmother's case, for that girl she fell in love with but was afraid to tell you about."

Eva fiddled with the checklist of things that she was supposed to do before she left Mr. Bertelli's shop. They were all done, even the "rainy day" option of mopping the back room. She slumped against the counter and fiddled with the fraying ribbon that still hung out of the end of her grandmother's July diary, an ancient bookmark. The back of the book popped open with a low creaking stretch of ancient leather. Eva squinted in the early afternoon sunlight to read the faded lines written in pencil there.

Sometimes I feel that we will disintegrate into fables, for we are not absolutes.

The handwriting was different from her grandmother's, more angular and with far less flourish. Eva read the words out loud and was startled when Al heaved his basket of food up onto the counter. She pushed the journal aside and started to ring him up.

"I think it's something," she said, ringing up a packet of Little Debbie cakes and wrinkling her nose at them. "I don't know if it's a power, but I think it's more than just a metaphor."

Al dug in his back pocket for his wallet. "Maybe it's both?"

"Maybe," Eva agreed. She totaled his order and helped him stack it into bags so that nothing would get crushed on the walk back to the bookshop.

They fell into a silence as Eva counted out the register's small change and Al waited outside while she locked up. Eva left a note for Mr. Bertelli saying that there had been only a handful of customers so she'd put out some stock and that he should have a good Monday.

Al offered Eva his arm as they walked toward the bookstore and Eva wasn't sure that she should take it. All she could think of was Liv's smiling face and her worried eyes as she read the papers that Theo had produced from god-knows-where. She leaned against him, protected against the cold, and tried not to think about how this could all come down to a choice once more.

She always made the wrong one.

Chapter 19

The Unsent Letter

ALL THAT REMAINED OF THE Talbot Collection was the final box.

Eva's mind drifted to it and the sorting task that awaited them at the bookshop. She picked up her pace and Al stretched his stride out beside her. This was the box that had arrived after the others and that was filled with documents that were not properly cataloged or preserved. Every time she and Liv had debated starting into it, something would distract them. Now, with the deadline to return everything looming, they had to get moving on sorting through the documents it contained.

The need was more pressing than Eva's unshakable desire to avoid the box entirely. There was something off-putting about the way that it was presented. Not what Eva would expect from a collection from the historical society. She shook her head.

"What?" Al asked.

"Nothing," Eva answered. "I'm just being paranoid."

This was not a new feeling. Eva's suspicions were starting to sound like one of the disaster scenarios she cooked up sometimes when she was feeling anxious about confronting her fears. It was her brain's way of handling the depression sometimes—pushing some little, inconsequential detail forward and not letting her forget it.

That was part of why she hadn't pressed the issue and had allowed the distractions to come as they had. She spent the better part of a week very pointedly ignoring the box sitting on Theo's desk. He kept it removed from the rest of the papers so as not to mix anything up. Already Liv's computer desk, the work table, and every other surface in the room was covered in documents from the Talbot collection.

After they'd discovered the name Catherine Monroe, Eva had moved on to going to through the July diary. The rest of the June diary had very little to add to what they already knew, even after a close reading and several re-reads. Mary had been working in the city, taking notes on a case and learning all kinds of things about the legal process.

It was so jarring to realize that her grandmother was only just coming up on seventeen at the end of the year and that she was seriously considering trying to attend a women's college or maybe even a university to get a degree in law. Eva wondered what had happened to make her change her mind about going to school. She had no idea how college had worked back then, and when she'd asked Theo, he'd only grunted in response that the process of acceptance was very different and very few women were actually allowed in.

"Mostly men," he'd added when he noticed that Eva was staring down at the address and details of Sarah Lawrence College that had been painstakingly copied down in Mary's handwriting. "It was hard for girls, especially from a working-class background, to afford university."

Eva shook her head. Theo was trying so hard to be nice about things, but it was just so transparent. He wanted something from Eva that Eva wasn't sure she could give him. She wasn't sure that she *wanted* him to have it even if she could give it.

"You okay? You're awful quiet." Al shifted his grocery bag from one hand to the other.

"Just thinking." Eva shook herself. They were nearly at the bookshop now and she would not allow herself to be so distracted. They had no choice but to handle those documents now, and she had to steel herself for the disappointment that was sure to follow. Their search had been fruitless up to this point; it was stupid to hope this last box would contain anything about Catherine Monroe.

The last box of papers was strewn open on the table when Eva and Al arrived at the bookshop. Liv and Theo were sitting at the far end of the table. Their heads were bent close, poring over Liv's legal pad and speaking rapidly in hushed voices. As soon as Eva stepped into the room, they looked up as one, both eyeing her with some trepidation.

Al waved to his father as he circled around the back of the bookshelves to the hidden staircase that led upstairs to the apartment he and his father shared, groceries in hand. "Hey guys. I got groceries."

"Oh good, groceries," Theo said. He brushed past Eva and clasped her warmly on the shoulder for a moment before disappearing up the stairs after Al. "Al, leave out the Little Debbies!"

She stared after Theo. Everything that Al had told her about his past was still rattling around in her head. She couldn't ask him about what Al had said, about the light of the world and the family history that was carefully hidden behind a veneer of academic interest. There was no point because he wouldn't be honest with her.

Eva shrugged off her coat and hung it on the rack behind the door with her bag. She left the door open. With both the Schultzes upstairs, if someone needed help with something in the shop, it would be up to Liv to assist.

Liv had sat back in her chair. She looked striking in cropped chinos that were riding up to reveal a new and exciting pair of brightly colored, zigzag-patterned socks. "Don't ask about the Little Debbies," she joked.

"Wasn't planning on it."

"Good. They're gross and he's addicted to them." Liv rolled her eyes skyward.

Smiling, Eva pulled up a chair next to her, nudging Liv with her knee as she settled in at the table. "Hi." She grinned shyly. It felt tight and unpleasant. She'd shown more teeth than she'd wanted. Feeling uncomfortable, Eva tugged off her floppy knit hat and tried to smooth her static-charged hair. It mostly just rose back up in the air as soon as her hands left it and she gave up with a dramatic sigh.

"Hey, yourself." Liv grinned back at her. Her hair was sticking straight up.

Eva felt like a big goof when she was this close to Liv. There was no concept of personal space between them. A genuine feeling of affection that Eva was not sure how to put into words settled at the pit of Eva's stomach and blossomed across her cheeks. She'd never had a friendship develop into an attraction like this before.

"Al was gone a while, did you rope him into helping you close up?" Liv asked. She picked up her legal pad and flipped it closed once more. On the first page was the letter that they'd found from Catherine Monroe's father. The other pages held notes for her book and references they'd found in the diaries that might help to illustrate life at the Talbot House.

Eva laughed. "A little. I think I had fifteen customers all day. Mostly people who needed breakfast stuff. The neighborhood's still getting used to the store being open on Sundays, I think. Al mopped the back room and we talked a little bit about his dad."

At the mention of Theo, Liv's entire demeanor changed. Her shoulders slumped forward and she glanced toward the door warily. Something was lurking at the corners of her eyes, and they darted back and forth from her notepad to the door and back again.

Eva reached out and rested her hand on Liv's knee to steady her. "Is, um, everything okay?"

A great battle was playing itself out in the way that Liv's sand-colored eyebrows drew down. She licked her dry lips. Her knee started to bounce under Eva's fingertips.

"I'm glad he told you," she said, tapping a pen on the legal pad in her lap.

Eva frowned. That could not have been what Liv wanted to say. They'd talked about Theo before, so this wasn't exactly new information. Well, maybe the details weren't all there, but it wasn't as though Eva didn't have at least a basic sketch of the story. She opened her mouth to reply, but Liv cut her off.

"You should know his motivations going forward with this." She fixed Eva with an earnest look that spoke volumes about the nature of what they were about to do. Liv glanced toward the door once more. Her leg stilled. "I called Kelvin, the guy at the Brooklyn Historical Society." Her voice was no more than a whisper. She was speaking quickly, her eyes fixed on the door, unblinking. "I wanted to ask why that last box wasn't properly cataloged or preserved. He'd never heard of it—the box."

"He hadn't?"

Liv shook her head. "Had no idea what I was talking about."

A strange ringing sound filled Eva's ears. The force of the realization hit her like a gut punch. She gaped at Liv. There was no way, it couldn't be true.

All the pieces seemed to slot into place, and her fears, the paranoia that she'd dismissed so effortlessly as a creation of her anxious mind came roaring back. Theo had told Al about his failure to procure permission to get them into the tunnels, but he had not told Liv, whom everyone joked he could not lie to. Theo knew things that he should not have known. Eva felt herself harden inside.

"These papers were in that trunk, weren't they?"

Liv didn't answer, staring at the notepad in her hands. Eva watched as her lips moved quickly but silently; it was a prayer and she knew the words well. "I don't know." She picked up the box. Only a few things were still in it, letters half-shoved into envelopes and a battered-looking book that might have been a journal. Everything smelled of ancient mustiness, with a faint scent that Eva would know anywhere. She sneezed. Cedar, as damning to her sinuses as the night was dark.

Everything was just thrown in, disrespected and discarded. Theo did not respect the dead.

"We have to get them out of here." Eva kept her voice at a whisper. She reached out and touched Liv's arm to show her that they could do this together. She had to understand that Eva would go with her if she didn't want to bring Theo into this anymore. "Al will understand if we leave, Liv. We need to look at these away from him."

Shaking her head, Liv set the box back down on the table. She arranged her notepad carefully as she closed the box. Eva tried to get her to stop, but she shrugged off Eva's hand. "No," she said, not looking at Eva. Her chin jutted out defiantly. "This is where I let him get close and hope to god he figures out on his own that it's better to stay away."

The truth fell like ash around them.

"You let him get close?" Eva was confused. She knew what Liv was implying, but that could not possibly be true.

Liv stood and paused, her lips pressed into a thin line. She seemed to come to her conclusion then. She leaned in and her lips brushed against Eva's so gently that Eva could have sworn it hadn't happened, except that heat instantly raced across her cheeks and across her chest. It was a simple gesture, but one that was so wholly unexpected that Eva didn't quite know what to do with it. She sat with her back ramrod straight as she tried to figure out how best to react to what Liv had just done.

"You'll understand in time," Liv promised. Her fingers brushed against Eva's cheek before she vanished into the gloom of the front of the bookstore, her coat under one arm.

Oh my god. Eva raised shaking fingers to her lips and stared out the open door into the shop after Liv. The bell at the door sounded, and soon the thumping of Al's boots could be heard on the stairs as he hurtled down them, eager to greet a customer. He stopped short in the doorway, realizing that no one had come in. His hand rested on the door frame.

"Liv go out to smoke?"

She pulled her fingers from her lips. Her cheeks were scarlet with embarrassment, and with shock. She shook her head. "She left."

She didn't know how to say what else had happened. She certainly couldn't say that Liv had dropped two huge information bombs onto her and kissed her before running off clad in brooding mystery. Al wouldn't understand anything but the last bit. She had to tell him, though, because it wasn't fair to leave him in the dark.

She slumped down in her chair. She had no idea how to tell Al that Theo had been down there in the cavern, that

Theo had smashed the trunk. Liv knew more than she was letting on.

Liv kissed me.

It didn't make sense. Why would it be Liv's choice to allow Theo time to get close to whatever was contained within that box? How could she know what was in there in the first place?

Why did she kiss me?

"Like, just up and bounced?" Al asked. "That's not really like her."

"I know," Eva replied.

She kissed me and she left me.

There was no use thinking about it anymore. Not until she could get Liv alone and make her explain. She stood up and reached for the box, without gloves and not really caring that she was touching these old documents without them. Her mind was on other things.

The first document she pulled out was a list of names, ones that she did not recognize from her grandmother's diaries. She stared down at the writing. It was similar to the line scratched in pencil at the back of the July diary. This was all in ink, beautiful calligraphy across a dirty, mud-streaked page.

Eva's fingers shook as she picked up one letter from among all the rest. It was sealed, but the address was unmistakable.

An unsent letter.

Addressed to her grandmother.

Eva sat down in a hurry and wondered if this was what Liv had seen and what had made her leave. But why run away from the answers?

Her hands were shaking, and the envelope felt so flimsy and insignificant. Al was still leaning against the doorway, looking confused. "Wait, shouldn't Dad be down here?" he asked.

Eva shook her head, the letter almost shaking in her palms. "This is addressed to my grandmother. It was never sent."

"Then open it," Al urged. "Pretty sure it's legal to open letters addressed to people who've passed, anyway."

Moving carefully so as not to disturb the contents, Eva slid a finger under the ancient seal on the back and felt it pull under her finger, splitting open easily as she moved her finger down the paper. There were several pages inside, and Eva pulled them out gingerly, unfurling them and setting them straight.

The writing was faded, but unmistakably the same as the writing had been on the back of her grandmother's diary.

November 15, 1925

Dearest Mary,

I do not know how to write this letter to you and have you understand the depths to which it wounds my soul to put pen to paper. I fear that I will never possess the courage to send it to you. I hope you will forgive me, one day.

I have told you more than once that what we have together is a love as great as all the ages. It is as forbidden as all the great stories of old. Yet I have had you in a way that would make most men weep for what they can never possess. You are my beauty, my star. You are everything and all that I have ever wanted in life.

Yet I know that I cannot have you.

I have told you of my duty and the task set before me. You are my one person, the one soul to whom I can divulge this knowledge. You were supposed to be forever.

The seekers have found me and I must flee this place. I do not know where I will go, or if I will live long enough to see my legacy passed on. All I know is that I must go, and you cannot come with me.

We were supposed to be forever, Mary. We were supposed to be the two that ended this cycle of living and dying. Nothing I was taught told me what to do in the event of falling in love. You've told me many times that that is something we cannot have. We do have it, though. We have it over and over again, as life could have passed us by in an instant, and I would look only at you.

You are my sun, my moon, my stars, and I must leave you broken and alone until the end of your days, for the light in your world truly will go out at my absence. I am certain of that.

Do not weep for me, Mary. I am just a passing shadow across the glorious plain of your life. You will stand someday atop the highest peak in the land, and you will shout my name to the wind, and maybe then I will find you once again.

Until then, know that the light is with you always. It will never go out, and I may never die.

Wren

"They found her and she had to run," Eva breathed. *Liv had to run.*

Al had crossed the room and she held out the letter to him with shaking hands. He took it gently and read it quickly, his brow furrowing as he scratched with one finger at the back of his head in between the locks of his hair.

"They found her and she had to run."

"Who are 'they'?" Al asked. His eyes flew over the letter and Eva watched as they grew wider and wider. "Dang, Eva."

He set the letter down. The whites of his eyes seemed to pop in the relative gloom of the workroom. Unable to help herself, she smiled. This was their answer, even though her heart felt as if it were being ripped into a million pieces.

Liv had known something about this from the start and yet she'd stayed with them for some reason, and led Al and Eva down into that cavern. Why did she do that?

Eva's head hurt at the implications.

The seekers—whoever they were—had come after Wren. She had a secret, and that secret had driven her away from Mary. She knew about the room full of light under the city, and it was supposed to keep her safe. That place had felt nothing like a sanctuary to Eva.

So, how was Wren connected to the light of the world? *Was she the light of the world?*

"I know," she replied. Her voice felt like sandpaper at her throat. All the secrets were slowly tumbling out. Eva couldn't contain them, and now Al knew as well. Secrets upon secrets, lies upon lies.

Theo was right all along—there was something more to her grandmother's story.

"We should show my dad, this is a huge break," Al said. His face fell, but then he added, "Look, I know what I told you is bad, but he'll want to know this. It's good for both of you. It gives a concrete reason why Wren disappeared from your Gran's life."

Eva nodded, staring down at the envelope in her hands. It felt thick, as though there was something else tucked inside. She flipped the envelope open and peered inside.

There was another folded sheet of paper. Eva tipped the envelope over and let it fall into her palm.

Al's boots thudded up the stairs, but the sound was far away, like a scene from under water.

Inside a tissue sleeve was a photograph of two girls who looked impossibly young. They were sitting side by side on a bench in what could only be Central Park. The taller of the two had light-colored hair, whereas the shorter and slightly younger-looking one could have been Eva if the photograph were not so old. She had brown hair cropped short and blowing in a breeze. It was combed absolutely straight, except for the corners that were flipping up, frizzing.

"Gran." Her voice was hushed, reverent.

They were dressed in short dresses and wore hats that cast their faces into shadow, but Eva recognized the little upturn in her grandmother's nose even here. She stared down at the photograph, drinking in the blonde hair, the high cheekbones and carefully painted lips of the girl who could only be Catherine Monroe. She was leaning against Mary with her arm around her shoulders, and their heads were inclined together in a pose that spoke of the intimacy of their relationship. It was a tender, beautiful moment captured forever.

A protective urge came over Eva. She stood and hurriedly crossed to the door, her fingers sliding the photograph back into its protective sleeve. She tucked the photograph into her jacket pocket. She didn't know why, but she didn't want Theo or Al to see it. Not just yet. Not before she showed it to Liv. Not before she decided *if* she wanted to show it to Liv.

"You found a letter?" Theo bustled into the room.

"Yeah," she said. "Come see!"

Theo didn't even bother to ask where Liv had gone. He pulled on his archival gloves and greedily began reading the letter. Eva could see the triumph grow across his face as he took in Wren's final goodbye. This would be his proof, now and forever, and Eva knew that she would never get that letter back.

"This is it, Eva." Theo's hands were shaking as he held the letter between them. His eyes were wide and so wild with excitement that Eva couldn't help but wince she watched him. She'd never seen a man come face to face with what had been called his white whale before. "This is the final piece to the puzzle."

He turned to Al, who shrugged. "Good for you, Dad," he offered. Eva could only guess at how times they'd been in this position in the past, Theo happily chattering that he'd found the secret he'd always been looking for, and Al indifferent by wayside.

Was it even the final piece to the puzzle? Eva wondered. There was so much more that they didn't yet know. What the purpose of the light of the world truly was seemed to hang in the balance. Was it the sort of thing where it was just there, a constant, a light that had shown the way to many over the years? The questions grew and grew, and the most important one still remained, etched upon the very fabric of Eva's being.

Why did Liv leave? Eva's thoughts were racing.

Theo pulled Liv's notes toward himself and made another notion. "This is Catherine Monroe's pronouncement, her one slip-up in all her cloak and dagger; this is the one thing that she messed up with. And this is going to give us our answer."

Theo sounded so triumphant that Eva felt her blood pressure spike. She folded her arms over her chest and glared at him from her position by the door. "It's a farewell letter that was never sent, not a confession."

Pointing at her with the back of his pen, Theo shook his head. "That is because it is both, but it is a confession first of all."

"I don't think it is." Eva's tone grew more insistent. She could not believe him. That letter was so sad, so horribly depressing, a love letter and goodbye, and he was treating it like a smoking gun! "These are the last words that we know that Catherine Monroe wrote, and it's a *goodbye*." She felt her hands start to clench into fists, feeling the very weight of all that her grandmother had suffered through coming back to stare her dead in the face. "If... If she'd received this letter, maybe things would be different."

Waving a hand dismissively, Theo went back to his notes. "That may be the case, Eva," he began, scribbling away, "but that's in the past. We can't change it now. All we can do is go forward and try to understand what it was that Catherine Monroe probably died for."

Eva wrapped her arms around herself and sighed. She should have known better than to trust him. He was clearly out only for himself now. He'd been bitten by the bug, and his pursuit of the light of the world wasn't going to end until he'd faced failure once more.

Defiantly, Eva shoved the diary back into her bag and grabbed her coat from the back of the door. "I'm going home." No one was looking at her, but she said it anyway. She turned on her heel and ignored Theo's calls for her to leave the diary behind so that he could compare it to the events described in the letter.

Just thinking about all the suffering her grandmother could have avoided if she had received that letter was making Eva's head spin. Tears pricked at the corners of her eyes. She could have had a chance at happiness. She *did* have a chance at happiness and someone had chased Wren away.

If her grandmother had been able to love Wren, would she have had children? Would she have brought Eva's father into the world? *Would I even be here?* It was a stupid, pointless exercise. The past was written. It couldn't be undone. Eva hated that. She wanted her grandmother to have had a chance for happiness more than anything. She didn't care that circumstances had made that impossible.

Eva swiped moodily at the tears. She was upset and the night was bitterly cold. The chill settled into her bones as she hurried across the street and uptown toward her grandmother's apartment.

She wanted Liv, she wanted Al, but most of all, she wanted to tell her grandmother *why*. Her grandmother was dead. She would never know the truth now.

The apartment was silent. It smelled of fresh plaster.

Eva pulled the carefully wrapped photograph from her pocket. Two people in love stared back at her in that charming '20s style. It was a memory of a time and place that had cut Mary so deeply that the wound festered for a lifetime.

Eva pulled the July diary from her bag and settled down into the couch. The tears fell freely now. Her grandmother had lost this girl, and no one could ever tell her where Wren had gone.

"Wren loved you," Eva said to the diary as she flipped to the right page. She sniffed. "She loved you and she wanted the entire world to see it."

July 25, 1925

Wren came to see me today bearing the most hilarious story about a gentleman who got thrown out of a Yanks game for trying to get Babe Ruth to sign his baseball. He was going to sell it to the highest bidder he could find, and had already placed the newspaper notice, Wren explained, and the bull had figured it out and had gotten word to the boys down at the ball field and he'd been given the bum's rush.

I don't know why this was so funny to me, but it was. A foolish man trying to make a buck has its moments of charm, I suppose.

We were sitting reading Judith's newspaper in my room when she told me all of this, prancing around the room excitedly and practically shaking with mirth. She'd heard the story from one of the ad girls she works with, apparently, who'd heard it from some gossipy vamp on the corner. It sounds like Wren's workplace is a total hen party.

This is the first time she's ever talked about her work. The first time she's opened up about that aspect of herself. You could have knocked me over with a feather I was so shocked by the honesty.

I told Wren what I thought of her workplace and she threw her head back and laughed some more, cackling madly as she proceeded to do impressions of every single one of the girls she works with.

Somewhere in the middle, she and I got very close together. I could look into her eyes and see the flecks of gold and green in them. She is so very pretty, even in the candle light of my bedroom long after dark.

Wren leaned in, as we were sitting next to each other, a smile on her face, and kissed me.

It was wet and had too many teeth and tongues involved for my liking, but it felt like nothing I'd ever felt before. And I wanted her to do it again. She seemed fearful, as I told her again and again that it was all right. She would not touch me again until after she crawled out the window to head down the fire escape ladder to the street below us. She touched my hand and my cheek then, and I would have begged her to touch me more, but the windows above and below us were open to catch the breeze and I didn't dare speak.

Chapter 20

The Guardian

BANG, *BANG, BANG.*

Eva pushed herself forward, scrambling away from the creeping darkness. Her feet sank into the mire. Her fingers clawed through the mud. The girl with no face was just behind her. Her pace was sedate, even, and calm despite Eva's frantic movements. Every time Eva looked over her shoulder, she was exactly the same distance away, never any nearer or farther.

Her lips burned with the memory of the kiss. It warmed her gut, twisting and settling between her legs. She wanted another.

"You are a seeker," the girl said in Liv's voice. It rattled in her throat like the wind caught on a loosely latched door. "You seek the light of the world."

Eva sank to her knees. "No, I don't! I want nothing to do with it!"

Bang. Bang. Bang.

The girl with no face now stood before her. Her expression was impassive. Liv's features slid into view on her face. Eva opened her mouth to scream, but no sound came out. She was on her knees before this powerful entity, supplicant and surrendered, half-buried in mud.

"You seek the light of the world."

"No." Eva sobbed the word. Fingers like ice caressed her cheek. "I don't want it. I've seen what it does."

Lips breathed death on Eva's cheek, on her lips. "Run," the creature said. "Run while you still can."

Bang, bang, bang.

Eva awoke with a start. Her sheets were twisted around her ankles and her heart was racing. A thin sheen of sweat covered her skin and it took a moment for her half-awake mind to realize that the sounds that filtered into the edges of her dreams were not part of the dream at all.

Someone was knocking on her door. Eva grunted and rolled over, trying to bundle herself back into the warmth of her covers. It was probably a salesperson. They'd go away eventually.

The panic of the moment before was gone. Exhaustion threatened to claim her once more, but the knocking grew more insistent.

"Go away," she muttered. It was just after seven in the morning. No one should be knocking this early. She couldn't think straight, her thoughts like a slog through molasses.

More knocking. Eva let out a frustrated groan, threw back her quilt and reached off the side of the bed for her pants.

Grumbling to herself and still half asleep, Eva pulled on as much clothing as she could. She was halfway into the living room before she was dressed. Her baggy sweats covered her feet and her oversized cardigan that she'd pulled over her sweaty chest was practically falling off one of her shoulders as she stumbled toward the door. It was too early to bother with a bra, so whoever it was would just have to deal. She tugged her cardigan shut and held it in place, squinting through the peephole on the door. It took a moment for her to find the sweet spot, but when she did, she let out a surprised squeak.

Liv was standing awkwardly in the hallway outside the door. Her hands were plunged into the pockets of her ratty army jacket and a thick gray scarf was wrapped tightly around her neck. She looked nervous and uncomfortable. Her hair hung limply around her face and it looked as though she'd been out in the rain.

"Hang on!" Eva pulled the chain from the door. She should have made an effort to put on clothes because she had no way of ducking out now to throw on a bra or even a T-shirt. She must look a fright, sweaty and breathless from her nightmare and still half asleep.

The chain rattled and Eva let it drop, undoing the locks one by one. Why on earth was Liv coming over here so early in the morning? Where had she disappeared to last night?

Eva pulled the door open and blinked sleepily at Liv, her fingers still resting on the doorknob. Her cardigan wasn't fully buttoned and the cold hit her exposed skin. Eva reached up and shakily pulled the sweater closed, holding it in place where the buttons wouldn't do the trick.

"Hey," Liv said, not pulling her hands from her pockets. She shifted from foot to foot. "May I come in?"

Eva inclined her head and stepped aside to allow Liv into the apartment. She wrapped her arms around herself once she'd closed the door and rubbed her scratchy cardigan over her arms to get warm. There was a thick chill in the air now that set Eva's teeth on edge.

"What's going on?" There were so many questions rattling around in her head that she wasn't entirely sure where to start.

Liv stood in the middle of the living room, still in her coat and shoes. In the dim, pre-dawn light, Eva saw that Liv's jeans and shoes were streaked with mud. Her hair had been soaked and was now stuck half frozen to her head. How had she gotten wet? It hadn't rained last night, had it? "Would you make some coffee?" she asked. Her voice sounded raspy with overuse and exhaustion. "I need it for this."

Need it for what? Eva frowned. The urgency in Liv's voice didn't brook much argument. Eva was still wooly headed with sleep and hadn't taken her meds yet. Liv looked as though she hadn't slept in days. Coffee would do them both good.

She crossed the living room and slipped into the kitchen. Liv trailed behind her like a shadow. Her face was a stony mask of indifference. Nothing betrayed what she was thinking.

The sun was just starting to break the horizon, and as its rays lit the gloomy kitchen, the ashy pallor of Liv's face grew more and more evident. Eva's breath caught, looking at her. Her hands fumbled for the coffee pot and she let out a quiet curse. Her cardigan had fallen open again. She turned away and hurriedly did up the buttons. It wasn't much, but at least she wasn't so exposed.

Liv's eyes bored into Eva when she glanced over her shoulder. She was staring unblinkingly ahead, not really looking at Eva but rather through her at nothing in the shadowy corner of the kitchen.

The coffee-making routine calmed Eva's anxious mind. She rinsed out the coffee pot and loaded it back onto the machine. She didn't bother grinding fresh beans because the noise would be too much at this early hour. She dug in the freezer for the bag of ground coffee her parents had brought her on her first weekend here.

Once the pot was set to brew, Eva turned her attention back to Liv. She looked disheveled and exhausted, her entire body drooping. This was not how Eva pictured Liv. This was not how Liv was supposed to be. She was the put-together, suave one. Gone was the woman who could lean down and brush a kiss to Eva's lips and vanish as though it meant nothing at all.

This was the first time since meeting her that Eva thought Liv looked small.

"Are you okay?" Urgency crept into Eva's voice as she asked. She tried to swallow it down, but it was an articulation of the nerves that wrestled in her stomach. Liv wasn't like this, and her nature didn't blend very well with silence. She had her bouts of melancholy and her sadness that seemed palpable at times, but it was not the sort of thing that drove her to muteness.

That was how Eva was supposed to be. That was how Eva had spent the past year learning *not* to be. It was only in recovery that she could finally see how detrimental her illness had been to her ability to feel human. The mark on her wrist burned at the memory.

"Not really." Liv shook her head and collapsed onto one of the kitchen chairs. She nudged a stack of mail out of the way and rested her head on her crossed arms on the table. Her entire posture radiated defeat.

Behind Eva, the coffee pot gurgled. Eva inclined her head to one side, ignoring it for the moment. "Do you want to talk about it?"

"I can't." There was a dark undercurrent to Liv's tone that made Eva wonder if this, too, was part of the secret that Liv was apparently so keen on keeping.

"Can't or won't?"

"It isn't safe for you to know."

"Then why come here?"

"I wanted to see you." Liv turned away. Some color had bloomed back into her cheeks. "Is that such a crime?"

The coffee pot gurgled. "No," Eva said, "it isn't." She reached for coffee mugs. "Don't see why it isn't safe for you to be honest," she added, mostly to herself. She pulled the sugar bag down as well.

Behind her, Liv chuckled. Eva turned. Liv was sitting up, and the sleeve of her jacket fell off her shoulder to reveal her equally muddied sweater beneath it. "You're not thinking about it right, then."

"Come again?"

"You're still thinking about this on a small scale, which, I can assure you, no one else is anymore." Liv sighed. Eva wanted the coffee to hurry up and brew so she could feel awake enough to process what Liv was saying. "Theo has guessed that Catherine Monroe was connected to the light of the world. Deeply connected. It's only a matter of time before he puts the rest of it together."

"The rest of what?"

"The mystery." Liv tugged at a lock of hair. "She was murdered for it, you know."

"How do you know?" Eva asked.

The coffee maker was making hissing noises and belching out steam with gusto now, and the smell of freshly brewed coffee filled the kitchen. Eva ignored it. She wanted to know the truth, and she wasn't going to back down until Liv told her what it all meant.

Liv looked down at her fingernails, flicking tiredly at some mud that was caked into the bed of her thumbnail. "Because it's what's going to happen to me if I'm not careful."

Eva stared at her. "What do you mean?"

"Seriously, Eva?" Liv's face was a wash of incredulity. "You haven't figured it out yet?"

There is a moment before any great realization when the pieces slot into place and everything goes from confusion to easy sense. Eva had encountered that moment before, on more than one occasion—the gentle slip of a blade into her skin, the moment she woke up in the hospital with her grandmother frowning down at her. These passing seconds could change a person, and could set into motion the events of a lifetime of choices. Eva had stood on that path, her future going off in two separate directions, and made a choice. Again and again, she made a choice. It was always the wrong one.

The choice was clearer now. Liv was holding out a brass ring and all Eva had to do was reach out and allow her mind to accept the impossible. The truth of Olivia Currance would come with it—the truth and the lie upon which all of this was built.

"Who are you?" Eva demanded. Something was there, the hazy, half-formed image of an idea that hadn't had time to come into its own. Liv wouldn't come out and say it, but she knew. She knew what had happened to Catherine Monroe. Eva rocked forward and blurted out the words. "Are you one of the people who want to find the light?"

"No." Liv's reply was so forceful, so above rebuke that Eva pulled back from her. Her feet tangled underneath her and she stumbled back against the counter. Liv looked up and her gaze was intense as it met Eva's for the first time all morning. "It is my duty to protect the light and that place beneath the city."

All the breath left Eva's lungs. All she could hear was the coffee maker reaching the end of its cycle. It was going to start beeping in a second. The ringing in her ears started then, the pieces of the puzzle rushing in along with the final ounces of water squeezing from the bottom of the coffee maker to percolate. She spun and jabbed at the off button before turning back to Liv. "You're going to have to explain just so I'm sure I've got it right."

With a shaky little laugh, Liv ran a hand through her hair. A small smile played at her lips. "I know. Could I have some of that coffee first?"

Eva awkwardly fumbled for the pot and poured two mugs before heading to the refrigerator for her half-empty bottle of milk. She set it and the second mug on the table. Her knees felt weak as the dawning realization weighed heavily on her shoulders. Eva curled back into the chair across from Liv, her knees drawn up against her chest, and cradled her mug.

Steam clouded her vision, making Liv look far away. It aged her, cast her in a milky glow that stripped her features of her youth. She seemed almost timeless, dirty and exhausted as she was. Liv made her coffee with milk and sugar, her movements quick and efficient; there was no wasted energy in any of them.

"It's my job to protect the light of the world." Liv sat back. Her expression was imperious; she looked like a queen on her throne. "Once, Catherine Monroe held my post. As have many others." Blowing at her coffee to cool it, Liv looked a picture of calm. If she picked up on Eva's confusion and agitation, she did not let on. Her features were impassive. They had to be to deliver such a bombshell. There was no deception in her. This was the truth.

Eva leaned forward. "What is it, then, the light of the world?"

"It is a belief, Eva. You know this."

"There's more to it than that."

Liv smiled. "Perhaps there is." She pulled her necklace out from beneath her shirt.

A little swell of triumph surged in Eva and a tremor ran down her spine. She'd been *right*. There was something about that necklace. Her breath caught. Liv held the necklace up to catch the weak light of dawn shining through the kitchen window.

A warm feeling rose in Eva. It curled around her icy chest and made her feel as if she were standing on the beach at mid-summer. All her worry and fear seemed to melt away into nothing but a gentle heat.

Leaning forward, Eva stared at the necklace. It was a star-shaped stone, with multiple points jutting out at sharp angles. They looked wicked, glinting in the light. "Can I touch it?"

Liv shook her head. "That probably isn't smart."

The sun peeked over the building across the street, the dawn now fully breaking. Sunlight streamed in through the kitchen window. That was when Eva saw it, saw the gem shift. At first she thought it was just the light reflecting off the stone, but as she moved closer, she saw that the gem itself was shifting. It pulsed and grew smaller before all the light within it turned to void. Then, in Liv's hand, it seemed to give a great push outward. It bent the sunlight. It sucked all the light from the room, plunging it back into semi-darkness.

"What—" Liv pressed a finger to Eva's lips. "Watch." She reached forward, her fingers curling around the star. She said something low, so low that Eva could not hear it, and the light caught up in the glowing gem twisted inside. Eva pushed back in her chair.

That wasn't possible.

"This only..." Eva swallowed, her chair scraping against the kitchen floor as she got to her feet. "This only happens in dreams."

"It is in dreams that this was made." Liv closed her hand around the gem and the room exploded in color. The light twisted within the gem, curling in and onto itself, settling and rising once more before it burst forth in an orange glow. Eva's jaw dropped in awe as the light warped and changed before her eyes, drawing in the darkness from the corners of the room.

It curled around Eva, wrapping her in warmth and pressing into her skin. She was flushed, exhilarated by the sensation. She felt as though nothing could ever go wrong again. For the first time since before she took her downward turn, her mind felt quiet and whole. Not chemically or even by external, superficial means. A bone-deep inner contentment that she hadn't felt in years. She felt *happy*.

"Who are you?" she asked again.

"I am the guardian of The Light of the World."

Chapter 21

Disappeared

THE CLOCK ON THE WALL ticked loudly. Once. Twice. Three times. Three beats of silence passed between them before Eva was able to open her mouth and formulate a response. She stared at Liv sitting calmly across the table from her. Her mind raced with disbelief.

"And Catherine Monroe?"

Liv sat back in her chair, cradling her coffee mug to her chest. Her expression became clouded. "She was a guardian at a time when it was far more dangerous to be one. It's only recently that it's become easier."

Eva groped for her chair. The light filled the room still, chasing away the shadows and engulfing them both in a safe, contented feeling. Yet there was something about that calming feeling that Eva could not shake, an unnaturalness that set her teeth on edge the longer it lasted. She felt ill at ease, just looking at the light for too long. There was something otherworldly about it. There was a pull at the pit of her stomach that felt uncomfortably like a relentless desire to possess that light and hold it to her forever. "How do you mean, it became easier?"

"The seekers were better organized then. The two world wars depleted their number. They were based in France."

Liv drained her coffee cup and set it down on the table. The necklace, its chain still wrapped around her fingers, caught the light. It was beautiful.

"This is what my grandmother saw... when Wren took her down to that room," Eva breathed, staring at it. It was like watching sunlight glisten off a lake in late summer at the last moment before the sun sank beneath the tree line.

Nodding, Liv tucked it under her shirt. Eva felt hollow at the loss of its warmth. "I'm sorry that I couldn't tell you before now." Her eyes were soft in the early-morning light. "There are so many things that I want to tell you but I never knew how to start."

"You're just like her," Eva said. "My grandmother described Wren the exact same way: trapped by melancholy and full of secrets."

"They are secrets that must be kept." Liv's eyes were downcast. "They're the sorts of things that will destroy people if they're let into the open."

Eva eyed the lump under Liv's shirt where the necklace lay. "I take it that this is one of those situations where the necklace is not a necklace?"

Liv chuckled and nodded. The smile that drifted across her lips was warm and open, despite the secrets she guarded. "Don't ask me to say any more. I don't think I can tell you much more than what I already have."

Liv got up and refilled her coffee cup. They sipped their coffee in silence for what felt like a long time, Eva lost in her thoughts and Liv slipping further and further into exhaustion.

Eva's grandmother loomed large in her mind, floating forward and beseeching Eva to try to understand, to try to see what it was that Liv was saying and yet not saying. Secrets upon secrets, lies upon lies. Her coffee burned her tongue and stung her throat as she swallowed—a hot reminder of all that she did not yet comprehend.

Setting her cup down, Eva knew that she could not keep silent. If she didn't press, Liv would shut down and never answer any questions. This was her golden opportunity. "Why do you work with Theo, then?"

"Because it's a good job that pays well," Liv said, sounding almost sheepish. "Honestly, I didn't even know about his obsession with the light until I'd been working for him nearly a year. We got drunk one night on good wine and he told me about his failure to earn an advanced degree in history. I was thinking of going back to school and I think he was trying to be encouraging, warning me of the dangers of chasing a white whale."

"Why stick around after you found out? He's after you, in one way or another. He's way too much of a bloodhound to not sniff out that necklace of yours eventually."

Liv blinked before realization seemed to dawn on her face. "My necklace?"

"Uh, the light of the world," Eva clarified, feeling sheepish. "Any mention of it and he jumps onto the scent."

"Sometimes the best hiding place is right under a guy's nose. Besides, I don't think he's any the wiser. Or at least, I didn't think he was until you came along." Liv set her coffee mug down and ran her hands through her hair once more, pulling out tangles and staring down at the floor. "You came in with your grandmother's diaries, your grandmother who knew what the light of the world was but had the good sense not to write down any details about it specifically. Wren was another story." She shook her head almost ruefully. "She was the key, and I fear that Theo might be slowly unraveling Wren's part of this mystery, at least."

Eva bit her lip. "I'm sorry," she offered, picking up her coffee once more. "I didn't mean to cause you any trouble."

"It would have come eventually. That's the fate of people like us. We are guardians, getting discovered is the last thing we want but always inevitably happens."

The silence that fell after she finished speaking seemed to stretch out into the kitchen, leaving Eva with more questions than answers. She fidgeted in her seat and tugged on her sweater, trying to pull her cardigan up and stop a cold draft from going down her back.

"Do you know what happened to Wren? Like, what really happened and not just speculation?"

"There were two others in between us, Eva. I only have fragmented memories from times before... The memories come with the necklace and the job, unfortunately. It sucks having to remember things that didn't happen to you." Liv sighed and sipped her coffee. Eva wanted to ask more, but Liv continued. "Wren went into hiding. The seekers found her. I know that much. I also know that she died down there, in her safe haven. Her body will never be found because there is no body to find. The seal took her, same as it takes all of us." She ran a mud-streaked hand through her hair, seemingly unbothered by the dirt. "No one is going to have any documentation of it, Eva. That isn't how people like Wren—people like me—die. And it isn't that I don't want to look into her life, because it is fascinating, I just don't want Theo to get too close again. I worry that he already has."

"The seal?"

"Don't ask me to explain that, Eva, please."

Biting her lip, Eva fell silent. She wanted to know more, and the urge to needle Liv until she received a satisfactory answer was strong. She knew better than to ask. Liv had never been so open, and it would be foolish to exploit this openness by asking questions now that Eva was sure Liv would answer in time.

"Theo can never find out about what that room hides. With the knowledge he has now, if he ever were to find his way back down there again... I don't know what would happen to him."

Eva hummed her agreement. "You don't think that he'd try something, like... to get the diaries or something?"

"Honestly, it remains to be seen what he will do," Liv replied.

Eva closed her eyes. The sun was rising now, and the kitchen was bathed in the same warm light that the necklace had pulled from darkness. Theo wouldn't hurt anyone; he wasn't that sort of person. The morning was gray above the little patch of sunlight that hit the window perfectly. Soon, it too, was gone. The day looked cold and rainy, bleak. The sort of weather one expects in autumn.

"Where did you go last night?" Eva asked. "You look like you got caught in the rain."

"I did." Liv sighed. "I was about. I had to think, rustle up a game plan."

Eva wondered where "about" was. She wondered where Liv had been when she'd realized that Theo was going to discover the truth about the light of the world no matter what she did to stop it. Had she gone back down to the room under the city? Was it a sanctuary for her, too?

Eva reasoned that it wasn't particularly prudent to ask. Liv had shared a great deal about what it was that she did. These were secrets that Eva should not know. Secrets that her grandmother had never told anyone. She'd taken them to her grave.

Theo was stumbling closer to the secrets. The diaries held clues that were carefully coded into the tragic love story of Mary and Wren. Tragedy awaited them, and Eva longed to change the outcome of the story.

"Should I hide them?" Eva gestured toward the living room. The diaries were still nestled in their box on the coffee table, with the July volume resting on top of the box.

Liv shook her head. "I don't think that will be necessary." Liv stood and took her coffee cup to the sink, then picked up the milk bottle and put it back in the refrigerator. She seemed to struggle to say something, her mouth opening several times with no sound coming out. Instead, she stood with her hand on the refrigerator handle.

"What should I do with this?" Eva gestured to the space between them. Her cheeks were burning. There was still that other matter, the gentle kiss pressed to her lips and Liv's sad smile. She wasn't touching that one, but with the knowledge of who Liv was, the final pieces to the puzzle of Catherine Monroe fell into place.

They knew what had happened to Catherine Monroe, and Liv had said all that she was willing to say on the matter.

Liv's shoulders slumped. "I think you should do whatever you want with it," she answered. "You've found out who your grandmother's mysterious Wren was and you've found out why she vanished from your grandmother's life. I don't know what else you can do. There's no family. None of us have family. We're supposed to cut all ties, let go of all worldly attachments. Wren didn't do that with her family."

Eva sighed. "What about the attachment Wren had to my grandmother?" *What about the attachment you have to me?*

Liv was silent. Her expression was clouded and unreadable. The question was on Eva's lips, threatening to bubble over.

You kissed me. Not the other way around. It can't just be me feeling this.

The question would not come freely. Eva swallowed it down and changed the subject. She'd promised she wouldn't ask any more questions, but it was better than the alternative.

She was so unsure of herself when it came to Liv that even discussing the fantastic and impossible seemed easier. "What is the light of the world, really? It's a necklace, but what does it *do?*"

"Do you know the story of the light?" Liv asked. She shrugged off her jacket.

Eva inclined her head to one side. "There are thousands of them..." she started, before looking sharply at the greenish-black slime that was tracing a strange veiny pattern down Liv's neck. "Hey, this can wait. Do you want to shower?"

Liv seemed to practically melt with relief, her shoulders drooping and her jacket dangling dangerously from one hand. "That would be *amazing,*" she practically groaned. "Don't think I won't tell you, Eva. But god, being clean after the night I've had." She leaned forward and pressed her lips to Eva's cheek. "Thank you."

Her cheek felt like it was on fire, a flush she could not quell. Eva smiled. This wasn't a one-sided thing. Liv was blushing right back at her.

Standing up, she put her empty cup into the sink beside Liv's and opened the cabinet underneath the sink. After a moment of rummaging, she found one of Mr. Bertelli's store's canvas grocery bags. "Put your dirty clothes in there," she said. "I'll loan you some clean ones."

<hr>

The words came more easily after Liv's shower. She sat on the corner of Eva's bed and told the story in bits and pieces, leaving out details where necessary, but not shrinking away from the general gist of it. Her idle fingers tugged at fraying corners of the quilt's stitching and she looked lost in one of Eva's dad's shirts slung over her shoulders. Baggy sweatpants that had once belonged to a high school boyfriend of Eva's practically fell off her hips.

"These aren't yours." Liv joked.

"Ex-boyfriend's," Eva explained.

"Wait. I thought you were..." Liv tilted her head to one side.

I thought you were gay. The word did not need to be spoken in order for Eva to know what was on Liv's mind.

Eva laughed. "Nah, I don't care one way or the other. Bi and all that."

"They're still huge. How big was the guy?"

"Big enough to be a colossal jerk when I got diagnosed." Eva shook her head. "But it doesn't matter." She curled up at the head of the bed, a pillow in her arms. "Tell your story."

"Oh, okay. Fine." Liv rolled her eyes. "Before there was light there was darkness." She looked uncomfortable, being cast as the storyteller, but she was trying, which Eva appreciated. She was quite sure that no one had ever asked Liv to tell this story before. She snuggled down under the covers, her cardigan bunching up around her ears as she leaned back and tried to soak in as much of this moment as possible. She imagined that her grandmother and Wren had a moment similar to this, and she wondered if she was somehow repeating the pattern.

"And into the darkness there came a light, you know, like in the Bible. Only no one knows where the light came from. Some people say that it's a fallen star, other say it is the tear of God himself, weeping at the darkness he created. Either way, it's something that's been around since the dawn of time in one way or another. I've always been more inclined to believe the fallen star mythos myself, because it almost seems plausible."

"Yeah," Eva agreed. "The overtly Judeo-Christian overtones get to be a little much otherwise. Plus, the light of the world could be Jesus."

"Only it really isn't. Perhaps once it was where those stories drew their origin from, but the light has always been just that, a light." Liv inclined her head and cracked a smile. "The light was a shining beacon that drove away all that was evil in the world. It was an act of mercy that the shadows were allowed to survive. Over time the shadows began to grow resentful of the darkness that they were cast into, and grew to hate the light and all that it stood for. The light of the world can chase the darkness from people's hearts and lock it away in a place like the vault where all other shadows were kept." Liv leaned back, staring up at the ceiling. "The problem is that the vault grew weak over time, and soon shadows began escaping the void."

Eva blinked. "So they were trapped there but the, um… the seal grew weak? The seal that ate Wren?"

"I wouldn't say it ate her. That's not how it works. But yeah, something along those lines. Once there was a whole order of people who worshiped the light and dedicated their entire lives to its preservation and the containment of the shadows. As the shadows started to rebel, they built a stronger seal to place over the void, using the power of the light of the world to trap the shadows and lock them away from humanity forever."

"Why would they want to lock away the shadows? Like, did they do something bad?"

Liv thought for a moment before responding. Eva watched the expression on her face shift from contemplative to amused, in seconds. "Well," she began, almost giggling. Her smile was dimpled and Eva could not look away. "They were all the darkness in the world. The initial breaking of the seal on the place where they were held was a story borrowed by the Greeks and then the Romans."

"Pandora's box?" Eva's eyes were wide at the revelation, but it made sense. Theo had said that the light had flirted with the edges of religious narrative since the stories had started being recorded.

"And the hope that remained was the light and its guardians." Liv looked down at her crossed legs, fingers splayed out across the warm colors of the quilt. "Over time the guardians have dwindled down to just one. That one's duty is to watch the vault and make sure that nothing ever threatens the seal that's been placed upon it."

"What would you do, should it be threatened?" Eva asked.

Liv pulled the necklace out from under her shirt and stared at it with a contemplative air. Eva couldn't help but feel very aware of the circumstances they found themselves in now, two people sitting on a bed with very little space between them. This wasn't the sort of thing that she could simply pass off as a quiet moment of revelation between two friends. This felt like so much more than that.

"Probably the same thing that Catherine Monroe did," Liv replied.

"Catherine Monroe's leaving absolutely devastated my grandmother." There was something that Liv hadn't read yet in the diaries that Eva had kept away from Theo and the others. She hadn't wanted to share the devastation and the anguish of the loss with them. She pushed herself out of the bed. "Hang on; I have to show you this."

She ducked out of the bedroom and hurried down the hall.

Eva reached under the September and October diaries for the volume that documented November. This one was far more worn than the others, and the edges were frayed as though it had been read and re-read many times over. Eva could picture her grandmother staring at the pages and wondering what went wrong.

This one diary was probably the reason her grandmother had kept all the rest. There were blotchy smears in the ink here and there, in the documents and small scraps of paper. Everything her grandmother remembered about Wren. Some of the information had been added later, and at the very end were updates from every November 20 for the nine years that Wren was missing before she was officially declared dead and a headstone was erected in the cemetery where Eva's grandmother would be buried eighty years later.

Liv was sitting on the edge of the bed with one of Eva's pillows in her lap. She leaned forward, her arms wrapped around it. Eva sat down next to her, their shoulders brushing, and handed her the diary. "This is when it stops. The December journal is about her search too, but she documented most of it in here. I think that this is the only reason that the police even investigated Wren's disappearance."

Taking the diary in both hands, Liv read the words that Eva had read the night before, probably committing them to memory in much the same way that Eva had found herself doing.

November 20, 1925

She is gone.

She vanished into the nothingness that is this city. There is no light now, only the darkness that she swore to always protect me against. It closes around me, pressing in at the edges of my vision like an electric light snuffed out. There is nothing here anymore. She has gone and has taken my heart with her.

I have spoken to everyone I believe her to have known, everyone who might have known her. No one seems to know anything about where she might have gone. The police are living up to their name, bull and terrible. They laughed at me when I told them that there was a girl missing, and said to check the whorehouses before coming back to see them. Wren is not like that at all. She had a job, she had friends, she had a family.

She had me.

I was not good enough, it seems. I was not enough.

She is gone and I do not know how I will ever feel right again.

Liv stared down at the open book before her, her eyes half closed and her body seeming to collapse as she rested the diary carefully on Eva's spare pillow. She looked as though she had come face to face with being cast into the same role as Catherine Monroe.

"She said in her unsent letter that the seekers were after her," Eva said after the silence had grown almost uncomfortable. Liv was still sitting, immobile, next to her.

Eva placed a hand tentatively on Liv's shoulder and was shocked when Liv flinched at her touch.

"The guardian can tell only one person of the light, before they lose all ability to speak of it," Liv said quietly. Her voice sounded hoarse, as though she were struggling not to cry. "I don't know if it's true or not, but this... Eva, she *hurt* your grandmother to keep her safe, to keep her away from the light of the world. She would have sent that letter, if she had been able to. The seekers made that impossible, Eva. The seekers took away her ability to speak the truth to anyone."

"Why would anyone willingly do that to someone they loved?" Eva felt like crying.

"I don't know," Liv replied. "I suppose it was the only way to keep Mary safe."

Throwing caution into the wind, Eva reached forward, twining her fingers around Liv's and letting their joined hands rest on Mary Oglesby's journal, on the tear-stained pages that told how love had gone from her life. Eva didn't know what she was offering. Maybe it was a promise, or maybe it was recognition of what Liv had just said. If the guardian could only tell one person, it meant that Eva was that person Liv deemed important enough to share her story with.

Somehow, staring at their two hands so tightly clasped on Mary's journal, Eva believed everything might be all right.

Part Three

The Light of the World

Chapter 22
A Lie of Omission

Eva didn't go to the bookstore for nearly a week. She begged off requests from Theo to come down, saying that she was buried in work on the apartment in the evenings. It was a lie, but it was one that Eva told easily. She couldn't stomach the idea of looking at Theo. The worry that he might see that she knew more than she was supposed to almost paralyzed her. It was better to stay away. She didn't know if she could lie to his face.

Al came by the apartment on Tuesday night and tried to apologize for what his father had said. The hollow feeling of knowing beyond all doubt that Theo did not care about her grandmother, and saw her as only a means to the ends of his own agenda, was enough to make Eva feel sick with unease.

There were no words for what he had done. She thought he should have come himself and not made a martyr out of his son. Al's apologies fell onto Eva's deaf ears. She had no interest in his apologies when he was just the messenger. Besides, Theo was trying to rationalize why he had decided to focus more on the light of the world now that they knew who Wren was.

All Eva wanted was help. She wanted closure for her grandmother and to understand what had happened to her when she was younger. She didn't want to get dragged into an increasingly supernatural mystery and a struggle between of good and evil.

Liv made it very clear that this was about good and evil. Catherine Monroe was the sole line of defense of the great seal that the mural in the cavern underneath Penn Station covered. She had been killed by that seal, sucked into the darkness where no human could survive, and another guardian had taken her place. That guardian, a boy named Lewis Marconi, also was killed by the seal. And then another, Ja'nae Christian. Now it was Liv who carried their burden, the same burden that guardians of the light had carried since time began.

Theo's ambition and what might happen to him should he get too close to this made her uneasy. Liv was very clear that those who seek the light of the world are enemies. They want to use its power for themselves, to let loose the shadows upon the world, and they are not to be trusted.

The truth bit at her, fearful and unpleasant. It gnawed at her stomach and made her turn Al away. "I'm sorry," she told him.

"Don't be," he replied. He was already halfway down the first flight of stairs, looking up at her. "I don't blame you for being upset."

"It isn't you," Eva explained.

"I know. This isn't the first time the light of the world has gotten in the way of things for me, Eva. I'm used to it."

Eva watched him go. It was cold outside the apartment, and a chill settled against her spine that she could not shake off. When the door on the ground floor closed behind Al with a sharp bang, Eva slipped back inside. She went to the box on the coffee table and counted out the twelve diaries. She trusted Al, but she could not get rid of the worry.

Her fingers caressed the smooth bindings of the journals. She was starting to doubt things that she knew to be real. The truth was so strange.

When Eva was younger, she used to imagine a world where magic and the supernatural fused together into a perception of reality that was very different from the world where she lived. She would get caught up on those fantasies, and the ease with which she slipped in and out of them was a comfort as she sank into funks. Magic wasn't real, though. She grew up to become a romantic, yes, but she knew how to keep herself grounded in reality.

Liv had thrown her for a loop. What she said seemed so probable, and yet improbable.

Magic didn't exist in this world, at least not in the manner in which Liv described. It was a complicated concept of good and evil, a fallen alien star come to earth to wreak havoc on the worldview of an entire species. Eva wasn't sure she could believe.

She was starting to think that she did not really have a choice in the matter. It was either she believed or she would fall victim to the same derision that had so plagued Theo. Eva was not a skeptic by nature. She wanted to believe in truth, and the light, and the good of people. There was no reason for Liv to lie to her, and what she had done with her necklace was astounding. No science that Eva could think of could explain that. It wasn't some trick of her mind, sinking her deeper into a funk she wouldn't be able to escape for weeks. This was real. This was true. Magic, the kind that Eva wanted to believe in as a child, did not exist in this world. And yet her grandmother's words were seared into her mind forever.

There were some things, it seemed, that were a magic all of their own. There was a darkness in things, and a lightness, too. The choice between the two extremes had destroyed her grandmother's life. She had lost someone for whom she cared deeply. She had lost her and she never knew what had happened to the girl she'd fallen in love with.

Eva's heart ached just thinking about it.

The death of Catherine Monroe hurt her grandmother. It left her deeply scarred for the rest of her long life. The letter that was never sent bore with it an uncomfortable legacy of a hurt that had never had a chance to heal. Eva couldn't help but wonder whether its delivery would have made her grandmother's miserable existence a little better. A goodbye like that was just as devastating as never knowing.

The light was passed on when the guardian was absorbed into the seal. Her grandmother had never known that, and Eva was grateful for it. To know the fate that had befallen her beloved and to live on for so many years was surely worse than anything else.

Every newspaper report on the disappearance of Catherine Monroe had said that her body was never found. Would knowing there were no remains make it any better?

Eva spent the week at work listlessly mulling over what Liv had told her about Catherine Monroe's death and the light of the world. It was November now, and the days were growing colder.

On Saturday, she begged off from working at the grocery store. Both her parents were in town and she wanted to spend the day with them. Her mother had found a good light fixture to replace the miserably dim hall light. They wanted to install it and Eva wanted to be there to help.

There was also the question of what else they needed to do to the apartment before the probate court hearing in January to officially start the proceedings for selling the apartment. Eva's father had figured out that there weren't a lot of outstanding debts in her grandmother's name. She owned the apartment outright and had for years, so except for the hospital bills, it should be a pretty straightforward case. The Veteran's Administration had covered most of the bills and what was left was easily payable from the bank account that had been willed to Eva's father.

Every time Eva thought about that looming court date, a sick feeling of dread settled into the pit of her stomach. She hated that she might be out of a place to live as early as the beginning of the year. She was not yet ready to let go of her grandmother, and leaving the apartment would force Eva to move on.

She wasn't about to tell her parents how she felt. They didn't really like or understand her need to delve into her grandmother's past as much as she had over the past few months. They were grateful for the free labor she was putting into the apartment, but Eva could tell that her mother, especially, wanted her back in school and away from the city.

"You're wallowing," her mother told her over the phone when they scheduled the visit. "You're letting your grief get the better of you and you're refusing to move on. Your Gran would not have wanted that."

Eva resisted the urge to roll her eyes, her mother never looked at the full picture. Eva had not had anything to say to that. She'd hung up the phone and curled into a ball on the couch, unmoving for hours. She wasn't wallowing in her own sadness or misery. It wasn't that simple. Depression wasn't some mental hump she could easily pull herself over. Things like this never were.

Her parents arrived a little after ten on Saturday morning. Her dad brought freshly brewed coffee that Eva didn't need but wasn't going to turn down. Her mother was carrying the light fixture. It looked absolutely awful, a big brass thing that would cast far more light than the yellowed glass of the current one.

"We brought bagels," her father announced.

It was strange to see her parents.

Eva hadn't seen them in close to a month, and it was weird to be around them. They were reminders of the life that she still lived but scarcely focused on. She was so caught up in the past that the little reminders of her present stood out like beacons in the night. She stood in the middle of the living room, watching as her parents moved around the space that Eva had come to think of as her own.

"You've done a lovely job," her mother said as she moved through the apartment, looking at the fresh plaster on the walls and the tile work that Eva and Liv had done in the bathroom. They'd spent most of Monday working on it, and Eva had asked as many questions as she could about the light of the world while they worked. Eva was not sure if the scrutiny her mother was giving it now was because her mother did not trust her when it came to repairs, or because she was genuinely curious.

"The tiling is beautiful, Eva," her mother said. She'd stepped into the bathroom to get a better look. She brushed her fingers over the blue, green, and white tiles that Eva and Liv had found at a salvage yard and arranged into an arching series of waves along the back wall of the bathtub. "Where did you find it?"

Eva shifted uncomfortably. It wasn't that her parents were snobs, but they were the sort to look down their noses at creative uses of salvaged materials. Liv knew a guy who refurbished bathrooms and salvaged old materials. Eva had been willing to spend more, maybe even buy the tiles new, but it had worked out that he'd had just enough for them to do the bathroom. "You don't want to know, but it cost fifty bucks to do all of that."

276

"I'm impressed," Her mother said. "Were they on sale?"

"After a fashion, yes."

Eva's father stuck his head into the bathroom. "Anyone want bagels?" He glanced around at the bathroom. "This looks great."

"Thanks, Dad." Eva smiled at him.

They left the bathroom for the kitchen and ate in relative silence. It was punctuated with a few questions from her mother about what to do with the remainder of her grandmother's things that were still in the storage closet. "Mostly it's junk. I think you're okay to throw it out, Eva."

"Yes, but Eva did find those papers in there. Maybe we should do it together?" Eva's father chewed his bagel thoughtfully.

"I could just pull out the trash and leave the papers." Eva glanced between her parents. "I can tell the difference between important papers and junk, guys."

"I have no doubt that you can, Eva." Her mother's tone was clipped and cool. "But the point is that you have trouble letting go of anything, and it'll be faster if I'm here to help you do it." Eva exhaled. She knew what her mother was thinking: People like Eva could not be trusted to know how to let go, so how could her grandmother's junk be any different?

Eva bit back her reaction and chewed her bagel. It wasn't worth arguing with her mother about something that they would never agree on. Like the marks on her skin, these wounds were ones that Eva inflicted on herself a long time ago.

A few minutes later, Eva's father disappeared into the storage closet to collect a screwdriver and step stool. "Can you run down and turn off the breaker, Claire?" he asked as Eva's mother came back into the room.

Eva piled their plates into the sink and rinsed the cream cheese from the knife.

When the door closed, her father leaned against the door frame. "Salvage yard?" He wiggled his eyebrows suggestively.

Eva nodded. "Salvage yard."

He flashed her a thumbs up. "It saves us a buck, but probably best not to mention it to your mother."

"Wouldn't dream of it." Eva laughed. "I figured Gran would approve."

"The design is really something," Her father agreed. "Where did you get the inspiration?"

"I worked with Olivia." Eva followed him from the kitchen and into the living room. He took the light fixture from where they'd left it on the couch and started to fiddle with the plastic bag that contained the screws needed to hold it in place. "She's Mr. Schultz's assistant at the bookstore." Eva's cheeks felt heated. "She's, um, a bit of an artist."

"I can see that she is."

Eva moved to pick up the box of diaries from the coffee table. "Did you find anything out, about that?" he asked, pointing at the box.

Eva realized just how complicated the answer to that question really was. She could not just sit down and tell her parents all about the great secrets that she'd discovered. The light of the world was a completely different story. Could she even talk about that at all? Liv had said that she could only ever tell one person about the light of the world. Eva did not want to betray her confidence by sharing it with others. Still, there was no harm in telling a little bit of the story to her parents. She had been holding back until she was certain of everything that had happened to Catherine Monroe.

She knew now that there was no sense in waiting. Wren's fate was not the sort of tale that could ever be told. She could tell him most of the story. The light of the world could be left out, a little lie of omission. "Yeah, actually, I did." Eva picked up the box and set it on the stereo. "Gran had a really good friend or maybe a girlfriend, the diaries aren't that specific, and she went missing and was declared dead in the mid-'30s. From the sound of it, they were really close. We found a letter in a collection of documents from the girl—her name was Wren Monroe—to Gran that was never delivered. It was a goodbye."

Eva's dad stared down at the light fixture in his hands. There was something drawn about his worn features and a look of resignation that Eva hadn't been expecting.

"Did you know?"

He sighed deeply. "I'd always wondered if it was a long-lost love. I just never thought it'd be a girl." He let out a rueful laugh. "She always told me to hold onto your mom and never let her out of my sight when I was younger, but I used to think that that was just because she thought Claire would cheat on me or something."

It was funny to think about how much Eva's grandmother had disliked her mother when Eva's parents had started dating when they were two professionals working in the city. Eva's mother told absolutely hilarious stories about the strange rituals that the "crotchety old bat" would make her go through just to prove her worth as a potential romantic interest for her son. She'd always insisted that Eva's mother acted like a relic from another age entirely around her.

"Maybe it had to do more with love?" Eva suggested. "She saw how much you loved her and didn't want you to go through what she'd been through?"

"Christ, though, she disappeared?"

"If you read her diaries, it sounds as though she was pretty convinced Wren was murdered. She was the one who pushed the cops into investigating back in the day. They didn't do a great job, if the records we've found are at all accurate."

"A missing girl back then?" Eva's father shook his head. "I'm not surprised." He looked at the stepstool. "This isn't going to be high enough. Shoulda brought a step ladder."

"Yeah, because I'm sure that wouldn't have looked weird on Metro North." Eva reached out and touched the warm flannel of her father's shirt. "Are you really okay with this, Dad?"

"What's there to be upset about?"

"I just told you that at one point in her life, Gran was in love with another woman."

"That happened to a lot of people back then, Eva. It was conform or be ostracized. It isn't like today. She was just doing what she needed to do to survive. Even if it made her miserable." He pressed his big, warm hand against Eva's smaller palm. "Don't worry about me, Eva, okay? This is something I've had suspicions about for years. She was my mom, she still loved me. Her loving a woman when she was just a girl doesn't change that, okay?"

Eva nodded.

"All right, I need you to shine one of those nice flashlights you've got up at this light fixture. We'll take it down and your mom should be back up soon."

As if on cue, the power cut off.

Chapter 23

Bonds

EVA WAS GRATEFUL TO HER father for not reacting poorly to the story of her grandmother's adolescent love affair with another girl. He'd taken it in stride, or at least he'd seemed to, and Eva was happy that the rest of their visit had gone off without a hitch. There were no little tiffs with her mother and they got through the few projects they had to do together quickly.

The three of them sat down and made a list of what they thought the next few improvement projects on the apartment should be. Eva wasn't sure that she could tackle replacing the chipped polyurethane flooring in the kitchen by herself, so they were going to look into a contractor to do that, but painting the kitchen seemed to be the next major step in the apartment's journey.

After debating paint colors for close to an hour at the hardware store, they were unable to come to a decision and her parents' train would be arriving soon. They had to go all the way back to New Haven, so they were hoping to catch the express train out of Grand Central. Eva walked them down to the subway station.

"Seriously, Eva, I'm proud of you for figuring everything out," Eva's father said as he hugged her tight. His coat was bulky against the November chill. "Your Gran would be, too."

"Call me when you get in?" Eva asked.

Eva's mother kissed her cheek. "I promise we will."

They left in a hiss of hot subway air. Eva adjusted the scarf around her neck as she went back up the stairs to the street. She shivered despite the steam that rose from the subway vent beneath her feet. The bookstore was just up the road. Guilt gnawed at her. She wanted to apologize to Al for basically throwing him out of her apartment earlier that week. She checked her phone. It was late enough that Theo might have gone upstairs for the night. Maybe she wouldn't have to see him.

And Liv was sure to be there.

A small, happy smile drifted across Eva's face at the thought of Liv. The secret, the press of their hands together, and the brush of Liv's lips were promise enough. Eva loved the warm, content feeling that filled her every time she and Liv were close enough to touch each other.

Liv had gone back to work with Theo as though nothing were wrong. She never told Eva exactly what she'd said to Theo in order to excuse herself, but he was far too wrapped up in his own work to pay her much mind. Liv was in the process of making copies of every relevant document in the Talbot Collection as Kelvin at the Brooklyn Historical Society had asked for them back.

She didn't know how Liv could stand in the shadow of a man who was so obsessed with the light of the world. Eva felt ill at ease, knowing that if the truth ever were to come out, he could become incensed.

Liv shrugged off Eva's worries. "I don't think he'll be able to connect the dots back to me."

"Unless he catches you," Eva said dejectedly, but Liv just laughed. Her breath was hot on Eva's cheek. She was far too close, her eyes sparkling with mischief. "Pretty sure I can run faster than him." She winked at Eva and drew back. Her cheeks were flushed a gentle pink.

They both laughed then. Laughing was easiest. Anything else would have been too much, too complicated. Liv's fingers lingered on Eva's cheeks and the urge to whisper "kiss me," knowing that Liv would, was overwhelming. There were so many things that Eva could not say to Liv. Everything between them was growing more and more complicated by the day.

Eva stood before the bookshop window, her breath fogging on the glass. The faded sign creaked in the wind above her head. Eva could see Al leaning over his laptop. He was tapping the screen and smiling. Eva swallowed back her guilt and pulled the door open. The bell jingled, echoing in the dark store.

Al looked up, startled. His lips quirked up into a half-grin and Eva smiled back. His sweater sleeves were rolled up above his elbows and he had a Rangers hat perched almost precariously on top of his dreads. The chance to rib him for it was almost too good to pass up.

She stood in the stacks, not quite daring to go back to the workshop without Al as a shield. She ran her fingers down the spines of books that had become timeless, listening to him as he finished up with a phone call and powered down his laptop.

"Are you going to hide in the classics section all day?" Al asked. He was standing at the end of the aisle with his arms crossed over his chest. She wondered if he was mad at her, but his serious expression faded quickly into an easy grin.

Sticking her tongue out at him, she drifted back toward the front of the store. The place was mostly empty. They could be silly without having to pretend to be professional.

"Do you even watch hockey?" Eva asked.

Al pulled his hat from his head and stared at it for a second. "So *that's* what this team plays. I coulda sworn I'd heard of them before."

Al was ridiculous in so many ways. She grinned at him. "They do play in town, you know."

"Really?"

"For sure. Swear it on my mother."

"You don't even really like your mother, Eva."

Eva hummed. "Point. Fine, I swear it on Liv's honor as a researcher."

Al's lips drew into a thin line before relaxing. He ran a hand over his hair, fiddling with the locks and setting the one strand that was sticking straight up with the rest of them. He gestured with his head toward the back room. "What's up with her, by the way?" His voice was pitched low.

Not sure what to say, Eva swallowed nervously. "I don't know," she lied. She wasn't about to tell him Liv's secrets. She shifted uncomfortably from foot to foot, her feet scuffling against the aged grey-brown carpet. She was sick of the lies, sick of having to betray the bonds of friendship over and over again just to keep everyone safe.

Al scratched at his chin, where a day or two of beard was growing. "She's super quiet recently. Normally she's chatty as all get out, you know that as well as I do, but she's been mostly silent. Not even talking to Dad much. It's *weird*, Eva." He shook his head. "Real weird."

Eva bit the inside of her cheek to keep herself from spilling Liv's secrets. She shrugged in response to Al's exasperation. There was nothing that she could do about it and she was simply trying to get the point across as best she could. She wasn't the person to go to for an explanation on Liv, who could drive all coherent thought from Eva's mind effortlessly.

"How is she today?"

"A bit better." Al sighed. "It's just annoying to deal with that cryptic talk on a daily basis."

"Is your dad here?" Eva asked.

Al shook his head. "Nah, had to run some errands and take some stuff to the bank. Do you think that that's why she's a bit better today? Did they have a fight?"

Eva feigned ignorance. "I'm not sure."

"Well, she's back there if you want to see her." He indicated with his thumb. If this had been any other time, Eva would have felt drawn to Al, intrigued by him. She might even want to ask him out. This was the problem. She was cast into the same role with Liv that her grandmother had played for Wren. The whole situation was so frustrating. Eva didn't know what she wanted. She did want to see Liv, but she didn't know if she should so soon after Liv's revelation.

Al seemed on edge, and avoiding talking about Theo and Liv seemed like a good idea. She didn't want him to pick up on her discomfort and get upset, so she changed the subject. "My dad came in and installed a new light fixture in the hallway. My mom got it at an antique mall in some tiny booth in Bridgeport of all places. It's *hideous.*"

Al laughed. "I'll bet. Old people have the worst taste."

"Exactly. We have to paint the kitchen cabinets. I think I'm going to try to do that this Monday, or at least do the prep." Eva glanced down at the counter between them. She felt bad about asking him for help after running him off the other day. "I did tell Liv that I'd stop by, so I probably should go back and say hey."

He nodded his agreement. "Let me know if you want to borrow the sander again." He bit his lip and looked down a little guiltily. "Or if you want help in general."

Feeling just a little ashamed, Eva turned to go. "I will." She smiled over her shoulder at him and he nodded in response.

Preoccupied, Eva wandered toward the back of the bookshop. Off in the distance, she could hear the ancient furnace roaring beneath the floor. It was warm in the bookstore, but it wasn't toasty by any means. Theo skimped on the heating because the bookstore didn't make enough money to pay an exorbitant heating bill.

The door to the back room was half open. Liv was standing at the far end of the table, a book open before her and a pencil tucked behind her ear. Her face was drawn into a frown of concentration.

Eva easily slipped into the room unnoticed. She moved quietly to stand beside Liv and lean over her shoulder.

The book on the table was an anthology of anti-suffrage political cartoons from the turn of the century. The image depicted a group of obviously Victorian women sitting around a bar, smoking, drinking and reading the newspaper.

"It looks like a hopping party, doesn't it?" Liv asked, turning to look at Eva. She was so close... as close as Al had been, but Eva's heart was racing now.

"I wanted to sneak up on you," Eva replied. She frowned and Liv smiled playfully at her in response. "Spoilsport."

"I think you like it when I best you."

"Maybe." Eva leaned closer to read the caption of the cartoon. It mentioned the artist and little else. Liv shifted, warmth radiating off her body. Her hand rested on the small of Eva's back. Eva's ears and neck felt as if they were on fire, but she couldn't move. She couldn't ruin this moment. She was terrified to do anything. "I wanted to come by and apologize to Al. See you. Maybe try and talk to Theo again." she said.

Liv's fingers traced gentle patterns through Eva's jacket. Liv was quietly humming to herself as she leaned against Eva. The gentle vibration of her chest set Eva's heart aflutter.

"Why?" Liv asked.

"I don't know," Eva began. "I guess I wanted to try to find out more about why he's so obsessed with finding the light of the world, you know? I know he said that it was because of a story he heard as a child, but it can't be just that." She fiddled with the page, not quite willing to meet Liv's eyes as she turned around to get a better look at Eva. "There has to be more to it than just a childhood memory and a failed academic dream."

Liv sidestepped away from Eva and turned to meet her gaze evenly. "I don't know if there is," she replied. "And if there is, that you want to know the answer."

"I do," Eva said, nodding emphatically. "I have to know."

When Eva was much younger, she had asked her grandmother why some people didn't seem to care about others and why no one ever spoke up about injustice. A teacher in her elementary school turned a blind eye to the bullying of another kid and Eva was torn as to how to handle it. Her grandmother sat her down and looked her firmly in the eye. "If you are the only one who notices, you have to speak up," she told Eva. "Always. Because if no one else is noticing it, that person is invisible. That person who is being hurt has no one but you to speak up for them."

Eva always tried to be the person her grandmother expected her to be. She didn't know if getting to the bottom of the mystery of the diaries was what she'd had in mind for Eva. Maybe she should help Theo realize that he couldn't keep chasing a white whale and that the light of the world was just a fiction. Maybe that was the good she was supposed to do in her life.

Talking to Theo might help them both to come to some sort of an understanding that it was not the light of the world, but rather Eva's grandmother, who had brought them together.

"If that's what you want to do," Liv said. She looked off into the middle distance for a moment. Her eyes looked glazed and unfocused. Eva wet her lips. If Liv was going to be so close and not make a move, it would be up to Eva to cross that small distance between them.

Eva swallowed.

It shouldn't be this hard, and she knew it. She could just lean in and kiss her. Liv was close enough. She could take a chance and a leap of faith. Liv had kissed her once. Eva wanted her to do it again.

They were repeating the same pattern. She'd seen the story played out across the pages of her grandmother's diaries, but she didn't know if she could be as strong as her grandmother and let the future fall to chance. She did not want to become like her grandmother—trapped forever, mourning a lost love.

Liv let out a quiet breath and leaned forward to collect the book. Her warmth was gone in a flash. She crossed the room and put the book back onto a shelf on the far wall. She came back, grabbing her notes from the desk.

Eva raised an eyebrow. "More research?"

Liv's writing looked like dancing. It flowed beautifully across the page as she bent to add a few notes. Already the page was littered with details of early feminism and the pervading societal views of it. "There's *always* more research."

Eva laughed. There was no lie there.

Liv's blonde hair spilled over her shoulders and her cheeks flushed a little. "Your grandmother's story deserves to be told, Eva." Liv held out the pad. "This is what I've got so far."

Eva read greedily, following the loop and swirl of Liv's handwriting. Liv had documented the major events of 1925 from what they'd read in the diaries, carefully tracing a line of historical narrative through Eva's grandmother's almost banal comments on the newspapers she'd stolen from Judith-who-lives-upstairs. There were notes about Mrs. Talbot and her involvement in the suffrage movement up until the 19th Amendment was passed in 1920.

"I'm trying to figure out how to start." Liv trucked a strand of hair behind her ear. "I want to go out to Long Island and see if they have any information on the Monroe family beyond what we found in the online archive. If I can learn something of her family, I think I can tie them together..." She looked down, a warm flush across her cheeks. "I know that I should have told you that I'd started, but you've been avoiding the store since Theo said everything, and I really haven't had the chance."

"You could have come over again," Eva said, trying not to pout. She nudged Liv's shoulder with her own. "I wouldn't have minded."

Liv's hair had fallen back into her eyes. She looked so achingly beautiful that Eva was afraid if she touched her, she might break. *Now,* Eva's mind screamed. *Kiss her now.*

Eva leaned over, her fingers closing around Liv's shoulder. Liv let out a little, startled breath, but the smile that blossomed across her face was permission enough. Eva rose on her toes and pressed her lips to Liv's, sweet and chaste. The gentlest of kisses. Liv's fingers cupped Eva's face. Her fingertips were warm little jolts of pressure. She pulled away. Liv's eyes were half-closed, her lips a little pinker than usual from the kiss. Eva raised a hand to cup Liv's palm against her cheek. "Kiss me again," she whispered.

Their mouths crushed together; this was the kiss Eva wanted. Her fingers tangled in Liv's hair. Liv's teeth sank gently into Eva's lower lip. A quiet groan escaped Eva. She was smiling. Eva was smiling. Their foreheads bumped together.

This is surreal. She never thought that she'd find herself in a position like this again.

"I could go home with you now," Liv suggested.

Eva swallowed, wanting that as well. Still, the nagging feeling of guilt that she would be walking away from her chance to try and smooth things over with Theo in favor of kanoodling with Liv was hard to shake. She was already reaching for her jacket as she started to protest. "But Theo..." she started. She really did want to talk to him.

"Really, Eva?"

Eva leaned over and kissed her again, coat dangling from one hand. "I know, but I did want to speak to him."

"He went to the bank, he'll be a while. We can find lots of things to do with that while." Liv gathered her pad and pen, as well as a few printouts that littered the table. "Get your coat."

Eva shrugged on her jacket and pulled her scarf tightly around her neck. Her lips felt bruised, and she wanted to reach out and grab Liv's hand. She wanted to kiss her again.

Later, Eva told herself firmly. *You can kiss her all you want when you're back at home and there's no chance someone will walk in on you.*

She was half a step behind Liv as she bustled out of the back room, pulling on her battered army jacket and tucking her pad and papers into her messenger bag.

As they left the bookstore, Eva could feel Al's eyes on them. She turned to wave and he waved back. He took in Liv's mussed hair and flashed her a thumbs-up, his expression shifting, finally, into an approving smile. Eva shook her head. He was such a *boy*.

Outside, the temperature had dropped. It was silent. There were no words shared between them, just the sounds of the city and the howling wail of the wind. Eva inhaled deeply and let the wonderful feeling of calm wash over her. Liv was a solid presence next to her. Eva had no idea how far things were going to go when they returned to the apartment, but she didn't think she cared particularly. The intent was there, and she wanted Liv. She wanted to feel this contentment for as long as she possibly could. It was the happiest she'd felt in a long time.

It was late, and not many of Eva's neighbors were still awake. The apartment building loomed tall and dark against a charcoal sky. Eva buzzed them into the building. The four flights up felt daunting. Walk-ups had never bothered Eva as a child or now, but she somehow felt weary as she put one foot in front of the other.

On the fourth floor landing, Eva felt the nervous, anxious feeling of wrongness settle on her. It overrode her nervous anticipation of being with Liv. The door to her apartment wasn't quite closed. It didn't look right, as if it had been bashed in with something. She lunged forward, a curse on her lips.

Liv grabbed Eva's jacket to hold her back. "What if someone's in there?" she hissed.

Eva stopped short, her eyes wide with fear. She fumbled for her keys. When she was still in college, Eva's father had bought her an extendable baton that she kept in her purse. She rummaged for it and twisted it to full extension and inclined her head toward Liv.

Nodding, Liv reached out and grabbed Eva's hand. They inched slowly forward, pushing the door open and wincing as it creaked.

The apartment was dark, and Eva fumbled for the light switch. There didn't seem to be anyone in there. The apartment felt hollow, gutted. She held her baton as tightly as she could. Its solid foot and a half of steel was reassuring as Liv slipped away to check the bathroom.

Eva's heart was thudding in her chest as she saw the state of the living room. Boxes were tossed haphazardly on the floor and her grandmother's collection of 45s was spilled out. A few of the records were broken. In the middle of the floor was the box that had once held her grandmother's diaries. It was squashed, rendered completely unusable, and empty.

Chapter 24
The Missing Diaries

THE DIARIES WERE GONE.

Nothing else in the apartment was missing, save the diaries. Eva's laptop was still sitting on the coffee table undisturbed. Things were strewn about the floor, but Eva and Liv were quickly able to account for anything of value. The only real mess was in the corner of the living room where the stereo sat. It looked as though someone had pawed through the LP collection, dumping them out onto the floor before going for the diaries where Eva had left them when she and her dad installed the hallway light.

"It has to be him," Eva said angrily. "You said he was at the bank. It's nine-thirty on a Saturday night. How could we have been so stupid?" She picked up the empty box and clutched it to her chest. There was no other explanation. Eva knew that it was foolish to try to blame someone for this with no proof, but no one would care about the diaries other than Theo. It certainly wasn't her parents, and she'd been with Liv and Al all evening. They were the only other people who knew about the story contained within those pages, and the hints at the truth of the light of the world they protected.

The hollow feeling of that empty box consumed her. Eva felt as hollow as she had when she sank the razor into her skin. She saw the hospital room where her grandmother's life had slowly faded into nothingness as the heart monitor slowed to a final steady tone. This was her one connection, the only thing of her grandmother's that Eva wanted to preserve. Everything else had been purged and donated to places where it could be of use to those who were in need. This empty shell of an apartment she barely felt that she was living in and the diaries were all that was left.

The photograph of Wren and Mary lay on the floor. Someone had stepped on it. Eva picked it up. She was shaking with anger. Here was an image of a girl whose whole life shattered just after this was taken. There was nothing else left of her—only ashes and dust, and the memory of a promise broken.

"We have to go back to the bookshop," Liv said. She was inspecting a record. She spun it between her palms, checking it for damage before reaching for its sleeve. "He'll be there, and we have to confront him. It had to be him." They'd been so careful not to step on the records, but now her shoe grazed against one and Eva winced as she heard a crack.

Eva was sure it was Theo too, but it didn't make sense to not be absolutely certain. "What about those people that Wren wrote about in her letter—the seekers?"

Liv set the record down on the coffee table and turned to stare at Eva. Her blue eyes shone with unspoken emotion. "Has it not occurred to you yet, Eva?"

"Has what occurred to me?"

"That Theo is a seeker. He is one who seeks the light, and he seems far more driven than I would have given him credit for." She met Eva's surprised gaze with a steely expression. "We need to stop him before he tries to go down to the seal room."

Feeling about half a step out of the loop, Eva wrapped her arms around herself and surveyed the living room. It was so deliberate. So lazy and so obviously the work of someone singularly interested in one thing: the diaries. "Because he'd have knowledge now?"

Liv nodded, her expression grave. "All he needs is belief and the shadows will try to bring him into their fold. Even from beyond the seal, they have that power. We need to get there before he does." She grabbed Eva's hand and pulled her toward the door. Her palm was sweaty and Eva could see the fear in her eyes when they drew close together.

"Could he die?" Eva fumbled for her keys and thanked god that the lock in the door handle still worked, even if the deadbolt was busted. Their feet thudded down to the ground floor and they tumbled out into the night, Liv already stepping into the street with her hand raised.

A taxi driven by a Sikh man swerved out of traffic to stop before her and they bundled in, Liv telling the driver the bookshop's address. Eva slumped into the seat next to her and Liv sighed as she glanced out the window.

"He wouldn't die, I don't think," Liv said. Her hands were clenched into fists in her lap and her knee was bouncing up and down about a mile a minute. Eva tried not to stare at it. "I think that the fate he'd face would be worse than death. To be drawn into a void where shadows live, all based on a foolish belief... I can't imagine a worse fate."

"Al can help us find him."

"I know. I just hope we'll be able to catch him before he goes down there."

The driver of the cab said nothing, eyeing them both through his rear-view mirror and shaking his head as they fell into silence. Eva's hands were shaking and her breath was coming in uneven gasps. She felt like an idiot for not seeing this coming. It was bound to have happened. She should never have trusted a man who was so driven to find something like the light of the world.

She'd gone to Theo and had decided to stay with him because he reminded her so much of all the professors she had loved when she was still at college. He was as inspirational as any of them had been. He knew truths about the world that Eva had yet to discover. She was a fool, she knew that. She was too trusting, too gullible.

Liv's fingers found hers and squeezed encouragingly. Eva felt the warmth and the affection that she was only starting to realize was genuine and for her alone. She allowed it to seep into her skin, curl deep at the base of her spine, and calm her racing heart and ragged breath.

She couldn't play the same role as Mary had to Wren. She couldn't wake up one day to find Liv gone forever. She couldn't, but maybe she would have to because she didn't think she could stop herself. She just wanted to kiss Liv again.

Eva turned and looked at Liv as they clung to each other in the back of a cab that wouldn't go fast enough. They were doomed, and probably always had been.

The cab lurched to a stop and Eva fell back against the seat, blinking as they parked in the darkness outside the warm yellow windows of the bookshop's display windows. Light poured out into the night and Liv cursed quietly, handing the cabbie a ten and telling him to keep the change.

They clambered out of the cab into the freezing night.

"I want this, with you." Eva found herself saying. Liv's head tipped backward and she stared up at the second-floor windows. There were lights on, which Eva took to be a good sign. Maybe Theo was at home. Al would still be downstairs with the last customers of the day.

"Terrible timing is all," Liv said.

"We do have awful timing," Eva agreed. She stared up at the lit windows. Her mind felt hazy, and Liv was still too close for her to be able to think straight. "I've never actually been up there..." She'd never had the occasion and she felt guilty just barging in. "Think he's home?" The bell above the door rang and Al stuck his head out, a sweater wrapped around his shoulders. "You guys just missed Dad," he said. His expression was perplexed.

A cold, ringing sensation started to fill Eva's ears. She stepped away from Liv, and closer to Al so she could hear him over the wind. "What do you mean?"

"He came in, blew past me without even saying hello, got some stuff upstairs, and then locked himself in his workroom for a few minutes." Al shrugged and held the door open, ushering them into the shop. He stared into the back of the store. "I opened the door after about ten minutes to ask what was up and he was just *gone*. I think he went out the fire exit."

Liv let out a quiet curse. "Get your coat," she said, "And some boots and flashlights. We have to catch your dad before he goes down there."

"Goes where?" Al pulled his sweater over his head, his fingers wrapped around his shirtsleeves as they stuck awkwardly out through the arm holes, his head still not quite through the neck. His voice was muffled, but attentive.

Liv paced the small space in front of the battered old armchairs that dominated the front of the store beside the newspaper rack, her arms clasped behind her back. "Mary's diaries are gone; Eva's apartment was broken into."

Al's head popped out of the top of his sweater. "You think my dad took 'em?" His voice was hardly accusatory. For all that Al had struggled to tell her about his father, he had been honest about how prone to obsession the guy was. This was his white whale. This was the one thing that he was going to be completely and utterly unpredictable about.

Liv faltered, and Al hurried to reassure her. "Look," he added, stepping toward the door and flipping the open sign around to the closed side, spinning the lock closed. "I get that my dad's a bit nutty, but breaking into someone's apartment is a bit much, I think."

"No one else knows about the diaries, Al." Eva jammed her hands into her pockets. "Not unless they overheard me talking to my dad way back in August about them. I've emailed your dad about them a few times, and since then it's been just the four of us who really know what's going on with them." She didn't add that only two of them understood what was happening. "I wouldn't accuse him of anything, except for the fact that he's missing, as are the diaries."

"Where would he have gone?" Al frowned. "I mean, with the diaries."

Eva and Liv exchanged a searching glance.

"The cavern under Penn Station. Maybe. I don't know where else he could have gone," Liv said. "Look, there isn't much time, Al. We have to hurry if we want to get there before he does."

"Why does it matter if he gets there first? Not to mention, how the hell does he know about it in the first place? I thought we agreed never to tell him."

Eva's fingers tightened into a fist. Liv shot her a warning look. *Don't,* her entire demeanor seemed to scream. Liv had to handle this.

"Because if he gets there— Look, Al, there's no time to explain all this now. We'll do it on the way, okay?" Liv's expression was open and unguarded. Eva could see the desperation she barely kept in check. They had to *go.* They had no time to explain this stuff now.

Al seemed to consider this, before he turned on his heel and marched toward the back of the shop, beckoning for them to follow. He led them behind the half door partially concealed behind a bookshelf and up the narrow stairs that led to the upstairs apartment where he and Theo lived. Eva followed half a step behind him, Liv trailing behind her.

Over her shoulder, Eva saw Liv give the back room a cautious glance. Her fingers were warm on the small of Eva's back and her quick, tight-lipped smile when she caught Eva looking was reassuring. Maybe this would work out in the end.

The apartment upstairs was homey, if small. Books were crammed into bookshelves that lined the walls here as well. They were not new though; every one that Eva reached out to touch had worn covers and creased spines. She would have thought better of Theo, but it appeared that he read as he lived: brashly and without thought of consequence.

Al disappeared into the kitchen, which was hidden behind a half-wall with stools crammed under the counter. He was rummaging in drawers. Eva glanced over at Liv. "Have you ever been up here?"

Liv shook her head. Eva wondered what she was thinking about as she stood there her fingers clenched around the pendant at her neck and her eyes half-closed in concentration. They were going to have to tell Al because he was going to figure it out if they didn't.

They had to hurry.

"Got one!" Al flipped on a bright red flashlight with a white switch, the kind that you get for five bucks at a gas station. He directed the light in their direction and Eva could see that the beam was weak. "I don't know where all the batteries went," he said. "Dad probably used them in that light box."

"Or he took them with him," Liv guessed. She didn't even bother to look at Al as he brushed past her to get a jacket and his boots out of the closet. He slung a backpack over his shoulder, chucking what looked suspiciously like a first aid kit into it. Eva hoped that they wouldn't need something like that; she didn't want anyone to get hurt.

"Are you going to tell me what this is about?" Al asked as he took the stairs down to the bookstore three at a time. He hit a hidden switch on the wall and the place was drowned in darkness. Only the light in the front window was still illuminated.

Liv let her hand fall from her necklace and a small, startled gasp escaped Eva's lips. It was glowing brightly now, pushing light into the darkness of the bookstore. "The seal is threatened, we have to go."

Al almost blended into the blackness around them, his skin reflecting blue and purple in the light from the necklace. He leaned forward, his eyes bright and white in the darkness, his expression fearful. "What is that?" He stared at Liv's necklace with an almost reverent air.

Silence filled the room. Eva shifted uncomfortably and Liv stared down at the necklace for a long time, her hair blue-green against its light. When she eventually looked up, her expression was drawn and frightened. Eva was struck by how purely vulnerable Liv looked in that instant, her eyes wide and her body appearing to shake as she reached up to touch her fingers to Al's cheek.

"This is the light of the world." Liv's eyes fluttered half-shut and her expression steeled to grim determination. Eva was in awe of Liv. She was a force, able to push past any skeptic with the power of her belief. In a matter of seconds, she had taken Al's doubts and assuaged them, seguing perfectly into the terrible business of what they had to do next.

"That's it?" Al shook his head, his eyes still wide. "Seems like there was an awful lot of fuss over a glowing necklace."

Reaching down, Liv's hand closed around the necklace and she whispered a word that Eva did not recognize. The light between her fingers soon ebbed away to almost nothing. She tucked the necklace back under her shirt. "It's a lot more than that, Horral."

"I had somewhat figured, Olivia," Al retorted. He tugged on his backpack strap. "So my dad doesn't know…"

"He has some of the pieces, but not the whole picture," Liv replied. She glanced toward the door and then shifted half a step back and into Eva, their fingers touching and then hands clasping. "He knows who Catherine Monroe was and what her purpose in life was. And he'll go to the one place he should not go, with hopes of finding out more."

"That room…" Al breathed.

"Exactly," Liv said. She took a deep breath and related an abridged version of the story that she'd told Eva about what was sealed beneath the city. She told him of her fears for what his dad might do, and what might happen if the seal weakened. Al started to move for the door before she had even finished.

"The diaries never mentioned a seal." His voice was thin with anxiety.

Eva nodded. "Not in so many words, but I think it was implied that Wren at least told my grandmother a good deal of what was happening. I don't know. I just hope it's not too late." She stared down at her feet as Liv tugged them in the direction of the subway station. It was going to be a close thing, but Liv knew how to get down there faster.

"So… Mary was what, Wren's one?" Al asked, digging out his wallet for his Metro card. "Not that I don't believe you," he said, swiping it and pushing through the turnstile. "It's just that I really think my dad isn't the type to break down some sort of seal to a dark place where all the evil that was never in Pandora's Box in the first place is kept these days. It just… doesn't seem like him."

Liv sighed, her fingers ghosting away from Eva's as she followed Al through the turnstile. "As I said, I don't think he's got all the pieces. He might just think that the diaries have some sort of a clue that will come to him when he gets down there. I don't know. Either way, he's walking into a situation he doesn't understand and has no way to protect himself."

They stood huddled together on the platform. Eva hated that she could not hold Liv close and tell her that it would be okay. She seemed to be almost shaking.

"How closely are you connected to the seal?" Eva asked. She leaned in as the train arrived and screeched to a halt in front of them. Her lips brushed against Liv's ear and Liv froze. Her body was stock still as she turned slowly to face Eva. Her eyes were wide and Eva reached down and grabbed her hand, pulling her onto the train after Al.

Liv didn't answer her until they were three stops up, her forehead resting against Eva's shoulder and a handful of Eva's jacket clutched in her fist. Her breath was hot on Eva's neck and her eyes were unfocused. She finally articulated what Eva had suspected since Liv had revealed the truth to her.

"The seal and I are one," she said, and her face contorted with unimaginable pain. "And the shadows have found him."

Liv was silent for the most part during the ride into Penn Station, her breath coming in uneven gasps. Eva held her close as they sped toward their destination, and soon they were hurrying down the steps to the Long Island Rail Road track, same as before.

It was only when they reached the platform and dodged around the people milling about waiting for the train that Eva realized that the door was not there. The door that had so clearly been there the last time that they'd been in the station had completely vanished, and a smooth cream-colored wall was all they could see.

She let out a low curse and turned to Al, whose eyes were as wide as her own.

"Where the hell did the door go?" Al demanded, glancing down at Liv. Her hands were clasped around the necklace, and Eva could see the light emanating from between her clenched fingers.

She reached out as they grew level with where the door should have been, her fingers glowing with a blue-green light. "Take me to the seal," Liv murmured, as if she were attempting to coax a particularly stubborn child into doing her bidding.

Eva felt a terrible expulsion of hot, damp air around them, and suddenly there was nothing at all but a void of blackness that they tumbled forward into. Liv's fingers were glowing still, the necklace pulsing bright and pure between them.

Eva flung her arms outward into the darkness, reaching desperately forward to touch those glowing fingertips. They couldn't be separated or they would never find their way out of there. Her fingers closed around Liv's.

"I've got you!" Eva shouted over the rush of the air that engulfed them.

"I know."

The world fell into darkness.

Chapter 25

Out of Void

Eva was in the dark place again. Her eyes strained to see in the gloom. Everywhere she touched felt slimy. She was drenched in sweat and falling, falling.

Her mind was racing and the scream that escaped her lips felt real. It pierced through the dream, because this could only be a dream, and reverberated on and on.

"You seek the light of the world."

Christ. Not this again.

Eva shook her head. Her feet touched solid ground and she fell forward, her fingers squelching in sticky mud. "I don't."

The girl with no face stood before her, drawing a slow, rattling breath. "You seek the light of the world."

She wore a new face then, one of a girl with round cheeks and a kind smile.

"Wren," Eva breathed. Her chest ached. The air tasted foul with mold and decay. "Why are you haunting me? I do not seek what you are sworn to protect!"

"You seek the light of the world."

The third time the statement was made, it felt different. In the darkness, Eva could scarcely see her face. The truth burst forth and Eva scrambled to her feet. She took the apparition's hands and gazed into her blank expanse of skin that should have been her face. There was no emotion there; there was no face at all. "I seek to love its guardian, nothing more." She said it like a promise.

"You are out of sequence."

"Because Mary lived too long, Wren! She lived for over a hundred years missing you!"

The girl's brow drew down in concentration, and realization seemed to blossom across her face. Eva started to smile.

She started to speak once more, but no sound came out. Her breath felt forced from her body and she gasped, desperate to force air into her lungs. She couldn't speak, she couldn't breathe, she couldn't—

Eva opened her eyes. She was lying flat on her back, gasping for air. Water dripped onto her face and ran down into her eyes. She shook her head to clear it. Her mind felt fuzzy and achy from the dream in what felt like a quagmire.

It was pitch black, she had no idea where she was. *Where are the others?* Her mind started to race. It was as if bits of her were memory missing. Wherever this place was, it was damp and warm. It smelled of earth and mold just as in her dream. Everywhere there was water dripping.

Eva could not keep her breathing steady. With each drop of water, her heart raced faster and faster. Panic rose like a wave. She had to remain calm. If she didn't remain calm— She flailed wildly, trying to find something to grab hold of and orient herself. She had to touch something solid, she had to! There was no way to make her pulse slow. The anxiety that gripped her would not dissipate without something to reassure her that she was not trapped in a nothing space beyond the scope of time.

Had Liv done something to catapult them into the seal itself? Was this what that darkness she'd described felt like? There was no light here, no hope. Just darkness.

Oh god. Eva shook her head. She wasn't going to let herself go down that path. Didn't Liv say that beyond the seal was a place worse than death? She was going to go insane, trapped in the darkness. Her mind was racing, and the panicked thoughts came faster and faster. What had just happened? Where had Liv and Al gone? Where were they now?

Her eyes could not adjust to the black. All she could see were flecks of lights at the corner of her vision. They were the shock of the blackness that surrounded her, like when she squeezed her eyes tightly shut and then opened them quickly. There was no light anywhere.

Eva let out a shaky breath, and slowed her movements. She groped around in the darkness and felt a long leg and a boot. *Al, good.* Her hand brushed against the battered canvas of Liv's old army jacket. Thank god, they'd all landed in the same place.

How did we even get here?

Eva pulled her hands free from the muck and tried to shake off as much sludge as she could before she tried to rouse Liv. Liv was lying face down.

Worried that she might suffocate, Eva rolled her onto her side. She shook Liv's shoulder. "Liv," she hissed. "Liv, wake up."

Liv's necklace started to glow. The light stung Eva's eyes at first and she turned away. She didn't like the light from the necklace. It made her feel ill at ease.

Soon, her eyes adjusted to the dim light that Liv's necklace emanated. She refused to let her gaze linger on the glowing stone. Finally, she could see where they were. The low, sloping ceiling was familiar to her, as was the jagged rock face and the ancient smell of long abandonment. They were in a tunnel like the one that led down to the cavern. Eva peered into the darkness that edged the pool of light in which they sat, unable to gauge where they were in the tunnel. They could be anywhere along it. She hoped they were far enough away that the light would go unnoticed and not warn Theo.

"Oh thank god," she breathed. She dug her knee into the muck and wrapped her arms around Liv to turn her over the rest of the way onto her back.

Eva's fingers touched Liv's cheeks almost reverently. She was icy cold and did not stir. In that moment Eva did not care that they were trapped in a dark tunnel far beneath the city with no exit. All she cared about was Liv and making sure that she would wake up once more. She leaned forward and kissed her, mud and all, with all the emotion that she didn't dare express in words, her lips doing the talking that she didn't dare do herself.

Liv's lips were warm and soft, not chapped and chewed like Eva's own. She stirred, and returned the kiss with a passion that Eva had never felt in a kiss before. It felt like a homecoming, like a drink of water on a hot summer day. It was everything and anything that Eva had ever wanted. Eva didn't care that they were repeating the past or that they'd been repeating the past since the moment they'd met. This was inevitable, and all-encompassing in how romantic she felt the pain of that knowledge was. She didn't care until Liv was touching her cheeks and then her shoulders—pushing her away.

They parted and Eva stared at Liv with wide eyes. "Terrible timing?"

"Horrible," Liv agreed. "You should do it again. Just not right now."

"I can do that."

Liv looked around. She let out a low, disbelieving whistle at their location.

Behind them, Al sat up and shook water from his hair. It dripped down his cheeks and made his skin shine in the darkness.

He pulled his backpack from his shoulders and dug out his flashlight. Flicking it on, he sighed quietly. "Good, light." He frowned at the flashlight, turning its beam up toward his face. "Well, more light than Liv's glowing necklace, at any rate."

"Eh." Liv shrugged. "It can be plenty bright."

Al's expression was unreadable as he directed the light off to their left. "That way, right?" Despite his joking, Al was probably more concerned with his father, and Eva didn't blame him at all.

"How do you know where we are?"

"I don't." Al grinned at her. "Just a hunch."

"Not a bad one." Liv grinned at him.

The decision to start moving toward the cavern went unspoken between them. Al led the way, his flashlight trained on the ground. The floor was a rutted mess of pooling water, so there was no way to tell if anyone else had been down there.

The thought warmed Eva as they crept along. Maybe Theo hadn't made it this far yet. Maybe Liv's magical shortcut would give them a chance to head him off.

They grew quiet for a moment. Water dripped into the puddles like punctuation. Eva exhaled slowly as their feet squelched in the muck at their feet.

"How did you get us down here?" Al asked, trying to keep his voice low.

Eva turned to Liv, her head tilted to one side. There were rules about telling people. Liv couldn't tell Al the specifics about the light of the world, she'd already told Eva.

Is there something that will stop her from speaking? Eva wondered.

Liv shrugged. "Magic."

"O-kay... I'm looking for a more plausible answer than *that*." Al turned back to look at them. There wasn't one to be had, though. Eva was pretty sure that Al knew that there wasn't an explanation beyond what Liv had offered. She hoped he wouldn't push it. While she understood his confusion, she knew that Liv was being intentionally vague for a reason.

"We needed to get down here faster." Liv pushed past Al to lead the way down the tunnel. "I provided us a means to do that. If we can beat your dad..."

"Do you think we have?" Al asked.

"I have no idea. If I was going off of how I feel right now, I'd say no, though. The gem feels like it's on fire." Liv drew to a stop, Al nearly walking into her back. Eva was able to stop before she joined the collision as well. Al steadied Liv and she spoke, her voice barely a breath over the drip, drip, drip of water all around them. "The entrance to the seal room is right around the corner, so keep your voices down." Liv's voice was a low hiss. She clutched her necklace between shaking fingers, pulling it from around her neck. She mumbled something low.

Eva felt a warm glow wash over her. She looked down and was startled to find that her clothes were warm, dry and comfortable, as if they'd been in the dryer for an hour and she'd put them on while they were still warm. They were a little stiff and still caked with mud, but at least they weren't making squelching noises every time she moved.

"So... is this like a common thing? You're doing magic that totally shouldn't exist?" Al asked. His eyes were wide. "Because honestly, I'm not entirely sure that I'm not trippin'."

"I think you'd remember taking something if you were tripping," Liv said dryly. She glanced around before motioning for Al to lower his light to the floor.

A low hissing noise filled the air. At first, it was barely audible, but soon it grew in intensity to the point where it was almost deafening. It was coming from the direction of the seal room.

Swallowing, Eva tried to settle herself. She cast her eyes low and swallowed back her nervousness. She didn't want to know what they would find there. She was sure it would be unpleasant.

The magic around them filled the air with a strange pressure that caused pain to radiate from the center of Eva's forehead outward. It was an undefinable hurt that she could not escape. Nothing else could explain the humming, painful feeling.

When she looked at Al, she saw that he felt it, too. He was rubbing at his forehead distractedly and frowning. Eva tried to shake the pain away, but it would not dissipate.

How did Liv deal with this?

"Is it always like this?" Eva asked.

Liv turned to Eva, her expression closed off. "Yes and no. Sometimes you don't feel it all. Other times it is all-consuming."

"That's awful."

Liv nodded her agreement and Eva's heart sank. Liv had to deal with this feeling on a daily basis. Eva's heart ached for Liv, who was barely reacting to the feeling that was building around them. Ill will and terrible intent seemed to linger in the tunnel. She couldn't imagine what it would be like in the actual seal room.

Al trailed his flashlight on the ground before it slipped from his fingers, the beam swinging violently until the flashlight finally rolled to a stop against a stone on the tunnel floor. He clutched his ears and sank to his knees, his mouth open in a silent scream. No sound dared to escape his lips.

Eva took half a step forward before Liv grabbed her arm. She pulled Eva back to her side. They watched with fearful eyes as Al's fingers clawed at the sides of his head. Liv stepped protectively in front of Eva, her hand was still clutched around Eva's arm and her nails biting painfully into the tender skin at Eva's forearm. "Careful." Al's fingers were digging into his skull, as if he were trying to pull something from his head. "I don't know what's happening to him."

She wanted to go to Al; she couldn't leave him like that, full of pain. Eva tried to push Liv away, but Liv refused to move. Her jaw was hardened into a tight line of concentration. The light that emanated from the necklace was glowing at her fingertips too now. Through the tight grip Liv had on her arm, Eva's whole body felt as if it were abuzz with the power of the light of the world.

"Keep her safe," Liv mumbled. Her hand tightened around Eva's arm and Eva let out a small yelp of pain. Her body felt as if it were on fire. Liv looked terrified, staring at her with wide eyes.

She has no idea what she's doing. The thought was not comforting. At all.

"What's h-happening?" Eva's voice faltered as her body started to shake. She held her hands before her face, staring at her fingertips. They were glowing. The light emitted in a slow, warm pulse.

Liv's face contorted into a grimace of pain, and Eva felt a surge of fear and confusion well up within her. Liv was trying to talk; her mouth was working but no sound coming out. She reached forward, her fingers pulling from Eva's wrist to settle on her cheeks. They were the icy grip of death as she held Eva's attention.

A surge of memory hit Eva then, and she tried to pull away. This was like the girl with no face in her dreams. The girl with no face who'd tried to pull her skin from her forehead. Eva's breath came out in panicked gasps.

Her eyes met Liv's and the whole world seemed to dissolve away around them.

"You're like me." Liv's eyes were wide with wonder. "The light is reacting to you."

"What?" Eva still couldn't shake the fear. The fear that Liv was going to try to rip her face away was so great that she tried to pull away. "I'm not."

"You are, though!" Liv sounded jubilant. "It isn't hurting you."

"Is that what it's doing to Al?" Her voice was still shaky, but the pain had subsided. Liv's touch felt calming now. The power that radiated from her fingers didn't feel malevolent anymore. It had subsided into something manageable.

Eva didn't understand what was happening to her. She was so close to the light now that she wanted to reach out and grab it. She wanted to prove that she could hold it the way Liv could, her fingers glowing warm with golden light, ready to do its bidding. She wanted to prove that she could protect it. That she could protect Liv.

The light was driving the point home that they were repeating the past, repeating again and again into the future. This was who they were.

"That isn't this." Liv's voice was low and harsh as she gripped the necklace. Her fingers weren't glowing anymore. "And keep your voice down. We need to keep moving. I gotta let go of you, Eva, and you have to promise me that you're not going to freak out."

Eva's brow furrowed, "Why would it matter?"

"Just *promise*."

"Okay, okay." Eva nodded. "I promise." She wasn't entirely sure why Liv was telling her this until she stepped away and the contact was lost. The echoing emptiness filled her and felt as though it had grown ten sizes. It hurt so much even to do something as simple as suck in air to breathe. She grabbed at her chest through her shirt. Her fingers curled around the fabric, scrambling to close the gaping void she could not reach.

It *hurt*, and Liv wasn't doing anything to come back to her and help it to not hurt. She was standing away from Eva now, her fingers around the pendant and her lips moving silently. Liv's head was bowed and her demeanor was reverent, as if she were praying.

Al pulled his hands from his head and looked up. He was covered in mud and his skin glistening with sweat. He scrambled to his feet and stared between Eva and Liv. Eva had never seen his eyes so wild. The whites of his eyes were so prominent that he looked like a scared animal.

"What the hell!" he shouted. Liv crossed to him in three steps, her fingers clamping over his mouth. "Shut up," she hissed, "or they'll hear you."

He glared at her but was quiet when she stepped away from him.

"There are shadows here," Liv said cryptically. "They're watching, waiting. Just looking for an opening to steal into your mind and corrupt it."

Al scowled. "No, seriously, what the hell was that?"

"It was a shadow. You probably attracted one because of your dad." Liv touched Al's forehead, her eyes half closed and her fingertips glowing. Eva wondered if this was some sort of healing power that those who could touch the light could channel. "It's good we didn't land in the seal room, the light probably wouldn't have been able to chase it off you."

313

"Oh goodie, I have some sort of dark creature attached to me. Did I roll a two or something?" Al bent to pick up his flashlight.

"This is probably like rolling a one, actually."

Liv and Eva exchanged a long look, and Eva let her hands relax from the fists she'd unconsciously clenched them into. They were still shaking but not as badly as before. Fear gripped her still, and she didn't think she could shake that until they left this awful place.

Eva inclined her head in the direction of the seal room. "Is it going to get worse if we go in there?"

The silence stretched on for a long time. The three of them looked at each other uneasily before Liv shook her head. She looked defeated. Eva didn't think enough words in the English language existed to reassure her that it would be okay. There were no excuses, nothing that they could say or would say. Only the terrifying thought remained that nothing would ever be the same again once they stepped into that room.

"I don't know what will happen once we go in," Liv said.

They looked at each other, taking in Liv's doubt. They all knew, on some level, what lurked in the waiting darkness, with no need for further discussion of what was about to happen. They were three people against a force of evil awakened by the darkness in one man's heart.

Eva wished for a better explanation, but it seemed that the concept of the light of the world went back to a time when there weren't logical, scientific explanations for things. The seal room was different, filled with gods and magic and the great unknown that could only be explained by faith.

Eva had no faith. She'd never had faith like that.

"We should move." Liv said.

They crept silently down the corridor. Liv's fingers wrapped tightly around her necklace, holding it up to illuminate their path. Al's flashlight's battery died and he put it away wordlessly.

None of them dared speak.

The ground beneath their feet was nothing but squelching mud. Eva slipped a few times and lurched forward into Liv's back, her lips brushing hair and jacket. There was so much she wanted to say to Liv. She couldn't shake the feeling that she was going to end up somehow unable to say what she needed to. There was a foreboding ache in the pit of her stomach.

She kept her fingers wrapped around the belt of Liv's jacket and her eyes straight ahead, until Liv cut a sharp left through a side corridor and Eva stepped into a nightmare.

The seal room was bathed in an unnatural light that made stung Eva's eyes as she squinted up into it. The mural on the wall that had once struck Eva as being so beautiful was now crawling with something—she couldn't make out quite what. It looked as though the very rock was moving, shifting underneath, and changing like the surface of a lake disturbed by a stone skipped across it.

The smell of dirt and death was everywhere, like a cemetery at the height of summer; like her grandmother's gravesite. Eva clamped her hand over her mouth and tried not to choke on the air and the memories that overwhelmed her and forced her to hunch over, one hand on her knees, gasping for air.

Theo stood before the shifting rock. She could see him from the corner of her eye. He was right where he should not be. His head was tilted upward toward the ceiling and his arms were stretched out wide. Eva could see a great lurking blackness behind him.

A shadow…

She squinted into the blackness and forced herself to stand upright. Al's steadying presence was right beside her. She reached out, her fingers closing around his. She needed someone to keep her from running from the cavern in fear.

"I had wondered when you'd show up." There was something *off* about Theo's voice. It sounded as if it were coming from underwater, distorted and fuzzy. Almost like a multitude of voices speaking as one. Eva felt a surge of nausea streak through her. Her fingers dug into Al's hand.

Liv stepped into the center of the room, her footsteps sure and deliberate. She had put the necklace back on and it was glowing at her neck. She was looking up at the wall as well, refusing to give Theo the attention he seemed to demand. "The seal was threatened," she said. "Of course I would come."

Theo turned and stared at Liv with wild, unfocused eyes. His glasses were gone and their absence made his face look younger. "Do you know what this is?" His voice echoed high and clear through the roaring behind them. "This is *proof*."

And proof it was. It was proof of something truly amazing, something unique and powerful among all the things that Eva knew to be real and true in this life. She didn't know how to understand what she was seeing except in a metaphysical sense—a *magical* sense—and she was never the sort of person who dared question what she saw before her own eyes.

"It is a seal that cannot be broken," Liv replied, her hands held out wide. Theo took half a step toward her, and then another step. His eyes were wild and his lips were moving with words that did not seem to actually have any meaning. Liv held her ground, her gaze and voice steady. "I know you want to prove this place's existence, Theo, but you can't. This place has to remain a secret."

He shook his head violently, his fingers clawing at the sides of his face as he stumbled toward Liv. "I have to prove it to them! They laughed at me, Olivia! Did you know that? They laughed at me and told me that I was not worth the paper my thesis was written on! I can show them! I can prove them all wrong."

Liv shook her head, her fingers closing around the star of the light. "This was given to me by a young man who was facing his own doom, did you know that? Someone had come down here, someone had found this place as you have. He took one look at the seal on the wall and he stepped toward it and his heart became corrupted. Your heart's been corrupted, Theo. You came down here looking for proof and he saw it and took everything she left behind."

"Who are 'they'?"

"The shadows." Liv pointed, her finger tracing a glowing arc of pure, natural light. Eva watched it arc higher, the light dying out as it rose. It was as though Liv's power wasn't enough to hold back the surging seal, or she wasn't truly trying to stop it just yet. "They've found your heart full of belief in the light of the world, and they've latched onto that belief because it's your weakness."

"The light of the world is real. Can't you see that people need to know it exists?" Theo shook his head, his curly hair flying every which way as he tried to make his point clear. "People have to know this! This... this changes *everything*."

"It changes nothing," Liv replied. She took a step toward Theo, and then another. The light at her neck was glowing as it had that day in Eva's apartment, warm like the sun and as bright. It drowned out all the darkness in the room, pulling even the farthest shadows into the light of a midsummer day. Theo reached forward and grabbed for the necklace, his eyes almost bulging from his head as it just eluded his grasp.

"Why can't I touch it?" he demanded as Liv let her fingers close around his outstretched hand.

Eva could feel Al stiffen beside her. She could feel his breathing and she knew that he was scared. This was his father who was so clearly possessed by a force greater than himself, and there was nothing that Al could do to save him. All he could do was watch as Liv cradled Theo's hand within her own, pure light pouring from her hand onto his palm.

Al was shaking against Eva as they watched the light continue to travel up Theo's arm and shoulder. It arched high and he let out an almost inhuman shriek as it crossed his chest.

From the void behind Theo, a clawing, hand-like glob of pure darkness shot out and wrapped around Theo's leg. Liv stumbled forward, her grip on Theo not strong enough to hold him as he was yanked onto his stomach and slowly dragged backward toward the wall.

Behind her, Al let out a scream that turned Eva's blood to ice.

Chapter 26
The Great Seal

THE SEAL WALL MUTATED BEFORE their eyes. It was like something out of a horror movie, a great maw of darkness churning against an ever-changing rock face. Black tendrils of shadow roiled within the rock as they tried to tear free of their stony prison.

The inky tether holding Theo's leg twisted tighter. It shredded his pant leg to ribbons and cut into his flesh. He let out a howl of pain. His fingers scrabbled in the mud and left long, raking trails as he was pulled backward.

Eva's knees gave out under her. She fell forward, unable to keep her feet. Her heart hammered in her chest as she watched Theo's slow progress toward the seal. She couldn't move. It was as if she were rooted to the spot.

"Liv!" she shouted. "Liv, do something!"

Liv did not move. Her fingers clutched her necklace, the light barely showing through them in a warm red glow that pulsated slowly and steadily. She was a serene figure in a room that was devolving into chaos, her eyes squeezed shut in concentration.

"Damn it, Liv." Al shoved Eva roughly aside. She tipped sideways, off balance as he wrenched his hand from her grasp.

"Dad, hang on, I'm coming!" Al was half-running, half stumbling toward Liv and his father, his hands outstretched in desperation. Eva had never seen someone move so clumsily, and yet so desperately. She twisted, trying to regain her footing and run after him. She was too small to tackle him to the ground, but he couldn't go near Theo. Not now. He would get sucked in as well.

The shriek that escaped Eva's lips was inhuman, the cry of a girl desperate to save everyone she could. She pushed forward, her flat-bottomed shoes sliding unsteadily as she took first one step, and then a stumbling second. She lunged to grab Al and hold him back from the wall and from Theo. "Don't go any closer!" Her fingers tangled around the back of Al's jacket. She could feel how hot and how sweaty he was. How terrified. "It'll suck you in, it'll—"

"I have to—" Al started to pull away. "I have to get my dad!" His larger frame twisted around Eva's vice-like grip on his jacket. She held firm, digging her heels into the mud and refusing to let go.

"Al! No!" Eva felt her grip start to slip.

The necklace fell from Liv's hands. The room was bathed in light. Eva raised a hand to cover her eyes and staring up at the high ceiling of the cavern.

What did you do? Eva's thoughts were racing. *Oh my god, Liv, what did you do?* In her grip, Al fell still.

The seal quivered. The tendrils of shadow seemed to retreat with fear. They withdrew back into themselves as the rock face into which the seal was carved gave a great shudder. The roar that had filled the room died, leaving behind only the sounds from before—the city high above and the constant plink, plink, plink of water all around them.

Liv hurried forward and offered Theo her hand, squatting before him. "I can save you." She sounded desperate. It was an odd emotion on her. Liv was a proud person. She would never allow herself to be seen as desperate unless it was the only option left.

The light was glowing at her neck and it made her skin and hair look almost orange. Liv's entire body was radiating. "Please, Theo, let me save you."

The light was almost blinding. Eva could barely see anything at all. She was still holding onto Al. Eva knew that if he got too close, it would be his doom. Her eyes started to adjust to the sudden brightness and she was able, finally, to get a good look at Liv.

Eva's breath left her in a hushed gasp. It wasn't the light that was making Liv appear orange; her body glowed with a light that emanated from deep within her skin. What was happening to Liv? Why was she glowing?

The spiny tendrils of blackness had started to move once more, and eerie shadows danced across the great seal.

Liv was breathing heavily from the effort to keep the darkness at bay. "Please, Theo, let me save you," she said again.

The wall was pulsing faster and faster. The shadows were mutating now, licking at the corners of the light and pushing back against Liv, draining her. A trickle of sweat ran down Liv's nose and beaded before dripping to the floor. This was going to kill her.

"Liv!" Eva shouted. "Liv, look at the seal!"

Liv turned unseeing eyes upward and Eva let out a low, frightened breath. She looked like something out of Eva's nightmares. Her eyes were blank and light was pouring from her very skin. Eva struggled to stop Al from getting any closer. The wall was moving now, changing. Al couldn't go near it. He'd already proven himself susceptible to the void. Liv had better make her move quickly, or else all would be lost.

When Liv had told her of the nature of the evil behind the seal, Eva hadn't really believed her. All the evil of Pandora's

Box, trapped behind a seal created out of pure light that came from a fallen star—it seemed farfetched, impossible. Liv told Eva how the shadows had sought out those with good hearts and pure intent and preyed on them. They fed on the hearts that they took. Hearts that possessed a pure wish were the easiest to corrupt. With every true wish came a needle of doubt. It was the doubt more than anything else that the shadows preyed upon. Doubt fueled all fear, and fear was what the shadows needed to survive.

Theo was plagued by doubt. He doubted the light of the world his entire life and so had set out to prove its existence. Doubt was all Theo really had. He was a seeker. His soul was corrupted. But could Liv save him?

"What's happening?" Al shouted. Eva focused her attention on Theo and his desperate attempts to reach forward and grab Liv's hand. He lost his grip and went sliding back toward the seal once more. "Why isn't he taking her hand?"

"I don't know!" Eva's voice was barely above a whisper; it felt as though it had been stolen from her. She gasped in the moist, acrid-smelling air and tried again. This time her voice was strong. "She's trying, Al," she insisted, her voice rising in pitch. "She's doing all she can." Eva wanted to say that Theo was trying too, but she couldn't make that distinction. She wasn't sure that he could try. His hands were shaking and he was sliding backward even faster than before.

Al let out a strangled cry, and Eva had to wrap her arms around his waist to keep him from running forward. Her feet sank deeper in to the mud and she knew she could not hold Al back for long.

They slid forward as one.

From the necklace, half-buried in the mud where it had fallen, Liv had drawn what looked like a sword. Her face was a picture of grim determination. She was watching the wall and still trying to get to Theo, although she was careful not to go any closer than was necessary.

Eva and Al slipped forward again. Eva tried to hang on tighter. "Al, we can't go any closer!" she shouted. "It'll suck us in, too!"

Al didn't seem to hear her. Eva braced herself and hung on for dear life, her eyes latched on Liv. *Please. Please fix this.*

Transfixed, they both watched as Liv twisted and the blade of light in her hand sliced through the dark strands that wrapped around Theo's foot. Free of the arresting darkness, Theo's body sprang forward as if propelled out of a slingshot by the effort he was exerting to keep himself from being dragged into the void. He landed face down in the muck with a great "oof" and was still.

Liv stood over him protectively. Theo clambered to his feet and hurried away, glancing over his shoulder as Liv stood before the seal with determination etched in every line of her body. When she spoke, it was not in a tongue that Eva recognized. She saw the surprise clearly written on Theo's face.

Al pushed Eva off and hurried to help Theo to safety.

Eva was more cautious. She could see his hurt leg, and knew that she had to help him, but she could see the same blackness that had overtaken Al in the corridor settle over Theo, even as Al wrapped his arms around his father. She didn't like it; it felt like a trap. She slipped her way over to them and reached out to touch Theo's shoulder tentatively.

His eyes were wide and unfocused as he turned to stare at her. "You're just like her..." he whispered. His voice was hoarse and choked off in the darkness that surrounded them. "Just like Mary."

Of course, Eva thought bitterly. "Why couldn't you just leave it alone, Theo?" she asked.

"Because the world must know."

Al stiffened beside Eva. He loosened his grip on his father and took half a step back, concern clearly written across his face.

"I don't think anyone should know about this place, Dad," Al said quietly.

Liv's voice rose clear and true through the murky, moist air as she held the sword of light steady before her. "No one can know of this. This place was meant to be forgotten." She drew the sword of light downward and then upward at an angle that Eva soon recognized to be the first two lines of a pentagram starting at the earth point.

Her grandmother hadn't been religious, but she'd believed in something. When Eva looked at this wall and its monument to the power of darkness, it was testament enough that her grandmother was correct in many of her assumptions. Eva wondered if her grandmother had ever seen the wall light up like this—or if Wren had ever had the chance to tell her.

Theo's fingers wrapped tightly around Eva's shoulder and she let out a yelp. Liv's sword of light paused in its motion, somewhere between the line of air and the line of fire. Theo's sharp, dirty nails cut into the skin at her shoulder and forced Eva down to her knees, writhing in pain.

It hurts, oh god it hurts. Eva tried to pull away, her fingers wrenching at his arm. He wasn't letting go. His grip was an unrelenting manacle, and no matter how Eva turned, she could not escape. He was trying to get Liv's attention, Eva realized, as a haze of searing pain radiated down her arm and up across the back of her skull. He was trying to make her stop what she was doing. Since when had Eva become someone that a madman could hurt to get his way?

Al seemed frozen. His dull eyes were fixed forward and Eva's shouts for help fell on deaf ears. What had happened to him? Eva's breathing was coming in shorter and shorter gasps. Theo's laugh, usually so warm and full of life, sounded high and cold and unrelentingly cruel. Eva felt blood seep from where his nails cut clear through to the bone of her shoulder.

"Don't you see?" he demanded. His voice was thick with a malice that Eva did not understand. Was this the shadow talking? Or did Theo truly feel this way? "You will always repeat this cycle. You will never be happy, guardian."

Liv's shoulders stiffened, and through the blood and mud and slime, Eva could see that she was shaking. What had Theo said that had shaken her so? Eva wasn't entirely sure. All she could think of was the pain.

"She was not meant to know," Liv replied tersely. She drew the blade back through the pentagram of light that she'd drawn and held it steady. At the middle, a black pit of nothingness opened beneath her blade's touch. Eva couldn't see anything beyond the void. It was pulling them in, a great vacuum of darkness.

"Then you are an even greater fool than before, guardian! You were given a chance to start anew and you did nothing! There is one soul for you, guardian, and I am going to take her into the void with me!" Theo's laugh was almost caustic this time, burning through the ache that had settled over Eva's mind and lingered there. It made it impossible for Eva to focus on anything at all, and she hated it.

Liv turned then, her very eyes glowing with the power of the light of the world, and Eva's heart skipped a beat. She was a woman and a man, so many faces all at once over and over again. Every guardian across all of time stood before Eva. She could see the past, the present, and the future reaching out to do battle with the shadows.

"You will do no such thing," Liv hissed. She shifted forward and the sword of light flew past Eva and whipped back around like a boomerang, cutting through Theo's back and pulling with it a shadow creature that fought and clawed and desperately pushed back against the light. Its inky black fingers clawed at the beam of light. As it slammed into the wall, it reached out and wrapped itself around Theo's leg once more, tugging his feet out from under him and whipping him forward into the mud.

Eva fell forward, her hands landing in the slime and her shoulder a bloom of pain.

"Theo!" she shouted. Her right arm was practically useless, but she had to help him. She had to save him! She struggled to her feet. Her whole body was shaking. The exertion of the magic was taking its toll. She took a deep breath and lunged forward. She wrapped her hands around Theo's wrist and pulled against the blackness, desperate to keep Theo grounded here. She didn't care that he'd hurt her, or that her shoulder felt as though a hot iron had scrambled the muscles. She wasn't going to let anyone die. She couldn't.

Whatever spell had come over Al seemed to dissipate and he threw himself down beside Eva with his fingers wrapping around hers. Together they pulled as hard as they could.

Theo let out a pitiful cry. The shadow rose like a great wave, threatening to crash over them. It stared down at them, its face ever-changing. Through the inky film, Eva could see the wall mutating once again.

"The protection isn't going to hold," Liv shouted. The pentagram flickered. The shadows surged forward, but the protection held. The cavern filled with an inhuman cackle.

Eva looked at Al. "We have to do something."

"Let me have this man," the shadow hissed. "I want him. He is a worthy sacrifice to save yourself. Sacrifice him and let your soul roam free."

That could not happen. They had to close the seal and not allow it to consume another innocent. Far too many had already paid that ultimate price. Al's jaw was set and he nodded. There was no argument from him, and the silent conversation ended as they turned, almost as one, to stare at Liv. This was her call.

Eva's fingers slipped on Theo's wrist and she twisted, grabbing a handful of his jacket sleeve and tugging with all of her might. Her shoulder was screaming in protest, and she could feel the warm stickiness of blood. The light of the world had gone out for her grandmother so long ago. Was she prepared to lose it, too?

Theo looked up then, his eyes wide with fright. His fingers closed around Eva's wrist. Eva clasped her free hand over his and looked into the void behind them. The thread of a shadow that was still holding onto Theo suddenly let go.

All three tumbled backward and landed in a heap. Al hurriedly pulled them farther away from the void. The shadow crested over them once more, hissing menacingly at Liv before diving into the void. Liv's blade slammed through the rock of the seal. It cut into the very wall with a crash that reverberated through the cavern. The wall trembled, the sword embedded deep within it. It let out an unearthly shriek. Eva clapped her hands over her ears but that did little to drown out the wail.

The shadow slipped, inky and defeated, toward the sword at the center of the seal. It scrabbled at the edges of the light, unable to arrest its motion as it hurtled into the sword's path. It was like watching water go down a drain; the darkness was sucked in a spiral and away into nothingness. All the while, the shadow screamed.

Eva tried not to listen to the screams, but it was not just the shadow crying at its defeat. Sound bubbled out of her mouth, out of Al's mouth. Screaming, screaming for it all to end. Then, just as suddenly as the screams began, they stopped.

With a great gurgle, the last of the shadow slipped into the seal and the sword winked out of existence. Liv collapsed to her knees, her hair half falling into her face, panting heavily. She scooped the necklace from the mud. It hung by its chain from her clenched fist, glowing weakly. It pulsed once, twice, before it flickered out like a candle snuffed.

Light came streaming down from the grated gaps in the ceiling far above. The faint sounds of the city gave a feeling of normalcy to the eeriness around them. Eva was helping Theo to his feet when the light seemed to shift. It hit the wall and the seal exploded in an arch of red and white light. Black tendrils reached out and wrapped bodily around Theo. Eva tried to grab him but the force pulling him away was too sudden and too strong. He was slammed hard against the wall and slumped down to the foot of it, a thin trickle of blood seeping from his hairline.

"Dad!" Al shouted and ran to his side.

Eva sank to her knees. Her shoulder throbbed and her head ached. This didn't feel like winning. It felt empty and hollow.

"Are you all right?" Gentle fingers brushed against Eva's cheek. She looked up to see Liv, her hair wild and cheeks flushed with exertion. She settled beside Eva and gingerly pulled her close.

"No," Eva said. The world was growing cold and hazy. The pain in her body was intense. "I don't think I am."

Liv whispered, "I've got you." It was the last thing she heard.

Chapter 27
The Wish

THE LAST TIME EVA WAS in a hospital, her grandmother died. The time before that, she had very nearly died herself. She did not mix well with hospitals, especially when she was the patient.

She was unconscious when Liv brought her to the ER. She'd been out cold for nearly twenty-four hours, only to wake up and discover that her shoulder needed to be surgically repaired.

Her parents had apparently rushed to the hospital and had taken one look at her battered body and promptly panicked. The doctor had been convinced that surgery was the only way to correct the aching pain in Eva's shoulder, which she'd undergone three days ago. It was supposed to be a simple procedure, but she'd run a fever just before she was set to be released and they'd kept her overnight for observation.

One night had turned into two. Eva didn't even feel sick, but she was still "running hot" according to the doctor, so she was stuck.

What made matters even worse was that the staff subjected her to the usual battery of mental competency tests, and she answered their questions as best she could. Her rotator cuff was torn. She wasn't in any danger of hurting herself.

"I don't understand why you're asking me these questions," Eva said on the third day after her admission. She was potentially getting out today, provided her fever was gone. She was still a bit woozy from the pain killers and the antibiotics, but sharp enough to object to being treated like a ticking time bomb. "I'm not *at risk* or whatever." She raised her arm in its sling. She was covered in cuts and bruises and her body ached as it healed.

"Stop that." The nurse leveled her with a look that brooked no argument and Eva scowled and sat back on the bed. "You've done this before, Eva. We have to ask these questions."

"I'm not a drug addict. I got sad and overwhelmed. I went for an easy out. Years ago. Locking me up in a padded room isn't going to *fix my shoulder*."

Neither was hyperbole but hey, it was worth a try.

"Your shoulder is recovering nicely. The stitches will come out in about a week." The nurse shook her head. "Such a waste." She muttered, mostly to herself, as she swept from the room.

Eva was starting to go stir crazy. She didn't feel sick. She could recover at home. She wasn't sure how many times she could answer medically irrelevant questions before she started screaming at people.

She had no idea how she and Liv had gotten to the hospital in the first place, or what Liv had said to the doctors or her parents when they'd come.

Eva grunted with frustration and tried to get comfortable. The hospital's starched sheets crinkled beneath her. Her memories leading up to waking with her parents staring down at her, fraught with worry, were jumbled and hazy. She wanted to know what had happened after they pulled Theo away from the darkness and the seal closed once more, and Liv hadn't been particularly forthcoming with the details.

Liv came on the second day they'd lowered her painkillers and Eva had been woozy and half-asleep for most of the visit, slurring her words a little and annoyed that she was stuck in this room for at least another 24 hours for "observation." Her fever was down to 100 degrees, she thought she could go home, but the doctors and her parents disagreed. She had clung to Liv with her good arm and refused to let go until she knew what happened.

"I can't explain it." She didn't meet Eva's gaze. She was staring at the bandages on Eva's shoulder and the sling around her neck. A red tinge appeared on her cheeks.

"Why not?" Eva was sick of not getting the full truth from Liv. Every time she took what she thought was a step forward, there was another layer, another level of deception. Liv tried so hard to be honest, but there were moments when her truth spilled over into nothing more than omissions. The sword, the room under the city, Theo and the shadows, not to mention how they managed to end up at a hospital; Eva had questions about them all.

Liv looked pained. "Because I don't know, Eva," she said through clenched teeth. "All I do know is that one minute Al and I were trying to figure out how best to move two very hurt people and the next minute you and I were collapsed in a heap just outside the ER entrance. I filled out the forms and called your parents. I said that we'd been mugged. I don't know if they believed me though."

"Well, I guess we were mugged," Eva said. "After a fashion." A thought struck her. "You didn't leave Al and Theo down there did you?"

"No." Liv shook her head. "He called me just after they took you away. He ended up back in Penn Station with Theo.

They were in an ambulance and he didn't know where I was." She exhaled. "I don't know why I didn't bring everyone with me…"

"It's probably for the best; it makes the mugging story more believable." Eva replied.

"True."

"I'm glad he got to the hospital."

Liv smiled a sad smile. "Me too."

Eva reached out and touched Liv's hand. "He'll be okay. At least he's probably in bad enough shape to warrant a prolonged hospital stay. They've got me locked up in here because I'm running a teeny, tiny fever."

"Seriously?"

"This," Eva held up her arm to show the Band-Aid that covered the single stitch on the wound that stood red against the white scar at her wrist, "isn't helping my case. Mugging or no, it's a little suspicious. My parents freaked out and now I get to answer all of the awful psych evaluation questions."

"But it's your shoulder that's really messed up."

Eva looked down at her hands. "I think it's a burden I have to live with. I did it once and now no one trusts me not to try it again. I'm like the kid who cried wolf or something. My parents freak out when I *cry* sometimes. Once at suicide risk, always at suicide risk, I guess."

"That's awful." Liv reached out and squeezed Eva's good shoulder then dropped her hand away. "I'm sorry. I can't tell you any more about the cavern, I don't really know…" Liv's expression was distant. "I…" she started, "I think I made a wish."

Frowning, Eva reached forward with her good arm and tried to touch Liv. Her fingers fumbled, bumping against Liv's elbow and she moved, perhaps intentionally, just out of reach. Eva watched her jaw work as Liv wrestled with the truth of what had happened.

"A wish?" Eva echoed. "What would a wish do?"

There were so many questions that she could have asked instead of that one. They were finally starting to be honest with each other. Eva wanted to build on this openness.

Liv reached out and brushed her fingers against Eva's, and Eva's heart soared.

"The light has always had that power. We learn about it when we take on the guardianship and with it the memories of all the others. It's always possible to make things happen. That's how you close the seal. It works on a wish." Liv sat on the edge of the bed. Her shoulders were slumped forward and her eyes were half closed. "I just... there are certain things that you know when you find the light for the first time. There's a cycle of death and rebirth. Sometimes things line up, and sometimes they do not. We're not supposed to ask the light to grant our wishes. It's disrespectful to the position of guardian, as well as selfish. We're supposed to be above it."

"But you asked it to grant you a wish and it did?" Eva asked. Her head was fuzzy from the medication. She couldn't think straight. She was having trouble focusing on anything other than the sad look in Liv's eyes.

"I did. I wanted to help everyone and I didn't want anyone to die. Theo probably would have and I couldn't do that to Al. Or to you." She sighed, her cheeks puffing out as she blew out a small gust of air that made her bangs flutter like straw in the wind. "We wish for the ability to protect the seal, to know that the cycle will continue. We wish that there will be another guardian... those sorts of things. We don't wish to save people, ever. Just to continue the cycle."

"Is that why Wren left?" Eva asked. "Because she couldn't keep the light and my grandmother safe at the same time? Because she didn't want the cycle to continue?"

"Probably," Liv admitted. Her eyes raked over the bandages on Eva's shoulder. "I'm sorry that all this happened, Eva. I had no idea that you—"

The door opened and a nurse came in with a chart. Liv clammed up and lapsed into a stony silence while the nurse put Eva though the same battery of tests as before. After a few minutes, Liv was ushered out and told she could come back later.

Eva hadn't seen her since.

The memory of the conversation that they hadn't quite had was enough to drive Eva to obsession. She'd spent the rest of the week thinking about it. She sat back in her bed and folded her good arm over her chest. She wasn't going to play the incommunicado game with Liv. Her phone was on the bedside table and she leaned over to reach for it, her shoulder screaming in pain. Eva let out a low hiss of discomfort.

The nurse reappeared, looking friendlier than she had before. She must have seen Eva's contortion from the window. "Sweetie, I know that you're just itchin' to get out of here, but you gotta be careful with the stitches in your shoulder, okay?" she said, clicking her tongue over the way Eva was holding her arm. She crossed the room and pulled the phone from its charger, handing it to Eva. "Now stop it before you tear something."

"I'll stop when you stop asking me if I feel like dying," Eva grumbled.

"You know its protocol, Ms. Kessler." The nurse glanced at her watch. "Besides, you need to get dressed. Your friend from before is coming to pick you up."

"She is?" Eva frowned. "Wait, you're letting me go today?"

"Yes, didn't anyone tell you? That's why we had to ask you all those questions about you feelin' depressed."

The nurse rolled her eyes. "Your fever is low enough that you can recover at home. You'll just need to monitor your temperature carefully to make sure that it breaks completely. Doctors, I swear. They probably told your parents and didn't think to tell you."

Eva nodded her agreement. This whole day could become a textbook on poor communication.

It took the better part of five minutes of careful maneuvering to help Eva into her cardigan and put her sling back in place. The nurse draped Eva's jacket around her shoulders like a cape and let her get her pants herself. "I think she's supposed to be comin' with your dad."

A part of Eva wasn't sure that she would ever see Liv again after their conversation. Wren had done the same thing, cut and run after telling her grandmother the truth. How would Liv be any different?

"Oh," she said. "I had no idea." She was surprised her parents weren't pushing for her to stay longer.

The nurse gave her a long, searching look before sweeping out of the room as Eva tugged on her boots that her mother had bought her when her parents had come to visit. It had snowed here too, and the entire city was still a slushy mess. She couldn't believe no one had told her she was getting out today. She couldn't believe that Liv had met her *parents*. The thought made her stomach do an uncomfortable flip-flop. Would they like her? Would they think she was too odd for Eva? Would they approve of her interest in finding happiness after so many years of strife?

Was this even happiness?

There was a cough from the doorway. Eva looked up. Her hair fell into her eyes, but she could see her father through her bangs. He leaned against the door. "Why aren't you ready?" he asked, his tone was joking. "We're here to spring you from your sterile cage!"

"No one told me I was getting out today," Eva replied. She glared at him, but it felt weak. She couldn't ever stay mad at her father.

"Well, you are. I've got your friend Olivia with me, too." Her father bent before Eva and helped her to tie her bootlaces. "She was the one who called me after you got mugged. Do you remember any of that? Your mother's sorry that she couldn't come today. She's beside herself with worry and wanted me to tell you that." He touched the Band-Aid on her wrist.

Eva rolled her eyes. "Of course she is. I don't really even remember the mugging. Or this." Eva pulled her hand away from her father. "It must have been when I fell. I certainly didn't try anything like that on purpose…"

"It's a fair thing to worry about, Eva. And then with the fever." He paused, rubbing his chin. "I'm sorry that we had to keep you cooped up in here."

"I know, Dad," Eva answered. Liv's lie was not going to stand up much longer, but Eva wasn't sure she knew how to tell her father the truth. She got unsteadily to her feet and wrapped her father in a one-armed hug. "It was just a freak thing, though. I'll be right as rain in a few weeks."

He smiled down at her. He looked drawn and weary, and as exhausted as he had looked the day of her grandmother's funeral. Or at least she thought he did. "I'm glad you're all right, E," he said.

"Me too."

Eva caught sight of Liv leaning against the doorway and smiled fondly at her. She'd washed her army jacket, but some of the mud stains from their misadventure were still visible on the olive-green fabric.

"Ah, yes, Olivia." Her father caught sight of Liv and made a welcoming gesture. "From what she tells me, Eva, you've had quite the time discovering all my mom's secrets."

"Well, I told you most of the stuff already." Eva stopped speaking when she noticed the reusable grocery bag that Liv had slung over her shoulder. Inside, Eva could see a collection of little notebooks.

A smile spread across Eva's face. "But the story's so great that Liv's thinking about writing about it."

"You are?" Eva's father turned to Liv. "Really?"

"With your permission, of course. She was your mother." Liv nodded at Eva. "They were a wonderful read and I'm grateful for the opportunity to borrow them."

"Well, anytime," Eva's father answered.

Eva's eyes narrowed. She stepped away from her father and caught Liv's eye. She inclined her head toward the bag, but Liv just shook her head, mouthing, "Later." Eva decided that was good enough for her. "Hey," she said quietly.

"Hi," Liv replied, her cheeks flushing slightly.

She looked almost embarrassed to be there, and Eva couldn't help but smile. Maybe they were all right after all. It still felt new, awkward. Like it had been when they'd first met.

"Eva, did you want to just go back to your place for the time being?" Her father asked. He had his arm still protectively around Eva. "I have to go see the lawyers again later, but I can at least get you settled. Your mom would want me to do that."

"Okay." Eva stepped away from her father and closer to Liv. She held out her hand and Eva took it with her good hand.

"Well, then," Eva's father announced, "we should get going."

⌘

The apartment felt like an empty shell once Eva's father left for his one o'clock appointment. Liv sat on the edge of the couch, the canvas bag with the journals clutched in her lap as Eva stared at her from where she sat in her grandmother's favorite armchair.

The old clock that Eva's mother found at some antique mall ticked loudly and the sound of it echoed through the whole apartment. Finally, after close to ten minutes of silence, Eva shifted forward in her seat as best she could, and spoke. "So, was it you that I saw at my grandmother's funeral?"

"Yeah," Liv said dully. She still wasn't looking at Eva, her eyes fixed steadfastly on the small pile of broken 45s on the table. Eva didn't understand why she was being so quiet about everything.

"Why did you go?"

Liv did look at her then, her slate-blue eyes flashing dangerously in the bright, noon-time sun that streamed through the living room windows. "Why do you think, Eva?"

"I don't know," Eva replied testily. "Some misguided sense of duty to Catherine Monroe?"

Liv sighed then, running a hand through her hair and leaning back on the couch, her head tilted up to the ceiling. "You still don't get it, Eva."

"Then *tell* me, Liv!" Eva said, wincing as she moved her neck and pulled at her stitches. "How the hell am I going to know if you're not honest with me? You come in and out. You disappear for days. I'm terrified, absolutely terrified, that you're going to end up like Wren and just disappear."

And then they really would be repeating the past.

Eva refused to look away from Liv and Liv was trying very hard not to meet Eva's eyes, her attention seemingly on everything else in the room. Eva wasn't having it. Liv could be as stubborn as she wanted about this, but the truth had to be told. There was still something that had gone unspoken between them. At first, Eva thought it concerned the light of the world, but she instinctively knew it was more than that. She had to know what it was that Liv was unable, or unwilling, to tell her. There *had* to be more. Eva wasn't going to accept anything less than the full truth this time.

Liv tiredly blew her bangs from her eyes. Liv leaned forward, her elbows resting on the knees of her cropped jeans. Eva tried not to look at her brightly colored socks and oxfords. She tried not to look at Liv, with her face set in an expression of regret. "There is a cycle, of birth and rebirth. One is born when the other dies, and the light finds its way from guardian to guardian that way," Liv explained.

You are out of cycle. The words reechoed in Eva's mind.

Liv's entire body seemed to shake with exhaustion. The explanation, Eva knew, was not going to be enough, not unless she pushed Liv for answers. "You are... oddly, not supposed to be a part of it." Liv brushed her bangs from her eyes. "At all."

Eva didn't understand what Liv meant, but this was reminding her of the dreams she'd had about the faceless girl. She'd said Eva was out of cycle. What did that even mean? Why was that girl so dead-set on warning Eva off Liv and the light of the world?

"How do you mean?" she asked.

Liv crossed to stand before Eva, her hands hanging limply at her sides. She knelt down, steadying herself on the chair. "You are an anomaly in the pattern, Eva." She pressed her hands onto Eva's knee, her fingers warm and her smile intriguing and inviting. "The guardian has one soul across the whole of the cycle. I share with Catherine Monroe the same as I share with all the others before me. Guardians have their one person, the only one whom they can tell about the light of the world. That soul repeats the same cycle of death and birth, same as the guardian's." Liv smiled and tapped

Eva on her nose with her finger, her eyes twinkling with amusement. "You, my dear Eva, are an anomaly."

"Why?" Eva asked. She was still caught up on the feeling of warmth that came with Liv's confessing this to her.

"Because I was never supposed to fall for you, Eva." Liv bit her lip. "There is a matched set. A guardian and their one, they are the two sides of the same coin. In the eyes of the light, that one is the only person a guardian can love. Because Mary lived such a long life, I couldn't... well, fall in love. And the other guardians who came between me and Wren, they couldn't either." She shook her head, flustered.

Eva stared blankly at her, not really following.

Liv tried again, her fingers warm on Eva's forearm. "Eva, I went to your grandmother's funeral because she was the one who possessed the soul I was supposed to fall in love with. Guardians and their counterparts die together most of the time, murdered by seekers. Wren did everything in her power to keep Mary safe, and Mary lived a long life because of her sacrifice. Mary should have died with Wren and her soul should have been reborn, over and over as Wren's was. I don't think it was though. I knew as soon as I saw the um... the urn, there was this sense of finality about it. I don't know."

"So where's Mary's soul now?" Eva frowned.

Liv shrugged. "I suspect that in living so long, Mary broke the bond forever, leaving me free to fall in love as I choose. And I choose you. My anomaly. The one I was never supposed to fall in love with at all."

"You love me?" Eva faltered. She wasn't sure she was ready for that.

"I—I won't deny what this is. My fate was pre-determined, but everything's all out of whack now. Your grandmother lived long enough to throw off the cycle."

340

"Is that what that... thing was talking about?" Eva asked. She thought of the creature made out of shadow and blackness that had latched onto Theo and had taken over his mind. "I kept dreaming about a girl with no face telling me not to seek the light of the world because I was out of cycle."

"I'm not surprised." Liv pushed herself to her feet. She shoved her hands into her pockets and shrugged. "The guardian is not supposed to possess free will. I'm not supposed to be able to make a choice like that. Wait. The shadow said it, too?" When Eva nodded, she continued, "Ugh, I wasn't paying attention at all. Too busy trying to save Theo. But I'd assume so."

Eva blinked, realization dawning on her face. "So... there's like one person that the guardian can tell, and it shouldn't be me."

"But it is you. I was able to tell you," Liv pointed out. "Which shouldn't be possible, but it is." She looked at Eva sideways for a moment. "The shadow is a creature of habit. All the seekers are. When Theo found his way down there the first time, I'm sure his intent truly was to simply explore and maybe see if there was any proof of who Wren was and then get on with life. I don't think that he intended at the time to deceive us. But he had the belief, you know? That's all they need to latch onto someone."

"It's strange to think of Theo's belief as a bad thing," Eva said. She didn't understand why it was considered such a bad thing in the first place. Theo believed in the light of the world with every aspect of his being, as had Mary. He had never witnessed how terrible a power it truly was. Now, though, he knew better than most.

"The shadows got into him, and then he just... I don't know, they latched onto his belief and let it consume him. That's why he stole from you; he'd never do something like that normally, Eva."

"I know," Eva replied. She tried not to think of what Theo had looked like that morning before she'd left the hospital, lying still on a stark white hospital bed. They weren't sure if he would ever wake up. The damage to his head had been so severe.

Taking a deep breath, Eva tried to figure out how to ask the one question that she was afraid to ask. Was Liv was going to disappear someday like Wren had, leaving Eva to spend the rest of her life heartbroken because of it? She didn't want that fate, and she wouldn't accept it.

"Is there another soul for you?" she asked quietly. "Another person you could tell the truth to now that my Gran is dead?"

Liv sighed and nudged Eva's good arm off the arm of the chair. She perched on it, her back warm on Eva's shoulder. "Honestly? I don't know." She looked down at Eva then, her eyes strangely distant and unfocused. "The guardian is supposed to die when the seal is opened, Eva. I'm not supposed to be alive…"

Liv was supposed to have died? But she was here, warm against Eva. "Are all guardians supposed to?"

"Die on the seal? After a fashion, yes. Living long enough to see it open and the shadows threatening to jump into this world and surviving, is something of a novelty for us." Liv shrugged. "Before, we were never so lucky."

"Wren died that way."

"Yes," Liv replied shortly. "And the others who came before her and after her. A guardian is only as good as her ability to keep things safe and secret. I let a shadow out. I let it attack a person that I care a great deal for." She shook her head. "I failed at being a guardian." She held up the necklace, which glinted in the light that spilled from the windows.

Eva smiled. "I don't think you did, Liv."

"Why not?" Liv sighed. "I certainly mucked this up."

"No..." Eva started, reaching out and touching Liv's thigh. "I think you finally figured out something that generations of guardians before you didn't. You were able to save everyone. You weren't trapped in a cycle of love and loss. I guess because of me."

Liv shook her head, her expression darkening. "Theo's still in the hospital, you got hurt... I really screwed it up."

It would be easy to lie to Liv, to tell her that Theo would be okay in time. Eva didn't know that he would be, or that he'd ever be truly all right again. He'd seen things; he'd done things that no man should ever do to another person. Eva hated that he'd been the one to hurt her, and that Liv had been powerless to stop it.

"You're still the guardian, Liv," Eva said quietly. "And you saved us all. I'm sure that Al can't thank you enough for making sure that his dad got out of there alive. I know I can't, either."

Liv looked down at Eva's hand on her thigh and set her own on top of it. She hesitated for a moment before curling her fingers around Eva's. Her hand was hot and sweaty, and Eva wondered why she was nervous.

"Thank you," Liv said at length. She turned to look at Eva then, and her eyes were shining with everything that she didn't seem to be able to put into words. She leaned down, and pressed her lips gently to the top of Eva's head. Eva felt her cheeks redden as a warm feeling arched high across the bridge of her nose and across her temples. She pulled away, her fingers gripping Eva's fingers tightly. "I want to do this with you, Eva. I don't want to live for something that can never happen."

They truly knew what it meant to live in longing for love. Her grandmother had carried a terrible burden, and they'd found a way to give her peace at last. Pride filled Eva at their accomplishment. Perhaps now, in that cemetery out on the island, her grandmother would finally be able to rest.

"I'd like that too," Eva replied.

Liv slid off the arm of the chair and pressed her lips to Eva's. She was careful not to jostle her shoulder, and her lips were warm and tender. There was a smile in that kiss, and Eva knew she was smiling back at her. Liv tasted like cigarettes and mint gum, and Eva kissed her with all of her heart, rewriting what was set in stone.

Chapter 28
A New Beginning

THEO WOKE UP TWO WEEKS later, and he came home a week after that. Eva went over to help Al rearrange the bookstore's displays on a Monday morning in early December. Mr. Bertelli had cut her hours back until her shoulder was fully healed. He ostensibly did it so Eva would have time to go to physical therapy three days a week, but she could tell he was worried about her.

She liked the freedom the reduced hours offered her, but Eva also needed something to do. She spent her downtime researching city colleges. She wasn't sure that she wanted to go back, but she felt more ready to entertain the idea than she had been in years. Mary Oglesby had never had the opportunity to go to college, despite the extraordinary life she led. And Eva remembered her grandmother's quiet acceptance of her own decision to withdraw from college. She'd wanted Eva to get well above anything else.

She could go back to college for her grandmother's memory. She was in a good mental place now, and she was sure she would do better this time. The pride she knew her grandmother would have felt in her graduating was enough to make her want to finish her degree.

The days had turned bitterly cold. Eva stood shivering and stamping her feet as she waited to cross the street to get to the bookstore. The sky was a cold gray overhead, and the air smelled like snow despite the fact there was none forecast. The bitter cold cut deeply into her bones and made the still-healing wound on her shoulder ache.

Her feet hit the pavement in loud slaps and she winced. There was no one around to hear her disrupting the silence of the mid-morning. The side street was empty.

The bookstore door jangled open. Eva glanced around to see a handful of regulars in their usual spots on the overstuffed armchairs. The door to the back room stood open, and the gloom that usually permeated the far reaches of the shop was chased away by the brilliant early-December sunlight filtering in from the skylights beyond.

Al was leaning against the counter, his laptop open and ear buds trailing out of the headphone jack and up to his ears. He was moving his head along with the music, not really paying attention to Eva as she ambled up to the counter. She tugged her hat and scarf off, scowling as she felt the hair on her forehead lift upward in a burst of static electricity. Al glanced up then, all eyelashes and charmingly amused smile.

"Your hair is sticking up," he said, tugging his headphones from his ears. The thick beats of something that Eva didn't recognize could be heard before he hit the space bar on his laptop and they fell silent. He was editing photos again. The very idea of it seemed so absolutely boring and mundane after the excitement of their adventure. She leaned forward and peered over the top of the laptop.

The photos showed the clinical starkness of her hospital room. Liv was sitting by her bedside, her expression closed off and distant. "When did you take these?" Eva asked. She scooted around to the other side of the counter to get a better look.

They were powerfully evocative pictures, taken in black and white and filtered with high contrast. There were no real grays in these, but they didn't look to be intentionally shot to maximize white-black balance as some photographers tended to prefer. It was an interesting dichotomy.

"I took 'em right after we were allowed to see you in the hospital," Al explained. He opened a series of pictures that made Eva's heart ache.

She knew why Al had taken them. Eva's body lay in a hospital bed with tubes and wires running out of her like some sort of bizarre spider web. It must have been when she was out cold after the surgery. She looked so small and broken in the photograph. Liv was sitting at her bedside, her hand clutched around the blanket. Al had captured the desperation in Liv, and the anguish on her face was clear.

"She was really worried for you, yeah?"

"She was." Eva agreed. He still didn't know the full picture. He didn't know that this was Liv breaking the cycle. Liv was given a chance by the grace of Mary Kessler to *fix* what was wrong with the light of the world. Liv had stayed with Eva, her one. She didn't run the way past guardians had—the way Wren had. She stayed by Eva's side and waited for her because her parents weren't able to get home until after the surgery had been done.

Eva hated it. She hated everything about how sad Liv looked in this picture, how desperate she seemed sitting alone on that chair. She was doing something monumental. She should be happy, but Eva knew all good things taste bittersweet when they are tinged with loss.

"They're..." Eva didn't want to call them wonderful, because they weren't, not really. They were evocative and heartbreaking, powerful images of what they'd all been through together, but they were not wonderful. It wasn't the right word and Eva hated that she couldn't think of what the right one would be. "They're really good, Al."

He smiled kindly at her, as if he knew what she was trying to say but was strangely unable to. Eva liked that about him, how easygoing and friendly he was about things that she couldn't put into words. She knew that someday she would have to stop taking this for granted. For now, though, it seemed all right. A challenge for another, perhaps even a rainier day. "Thanks, E."

There was a quiet rustling of papers behind them and Liv appeared, a thick volume tucked under one arm and her legal pad held under her chin as she tried to balance three rolled maps in her free hand. Eva took half a step forward and caught the pad, holding it while Liv righted the papers.

"Hey," she said. She took the legal pad when Eva held it out to her and set it precariously on top of her maps.

"Hi," Eva replied.

She hadn't realized how much she missed Liv. The flicker of a smile at the corner of Liv's lips and the awkward way that she shuffled her feet while a blush blossomed across her high cheekbones was enough to make Eva very aware of how much time they'd been spending together lately.

It hadn't been a conscious decision that they would, either. After the conversation on the day that she'd come home from the hospital, Eva had told Liv that she hadn't wanted to rush things. It hadn't felt right to jump into any sort of a relationship after what they'd been through. They'd just kissed a little and that was nice and good and really rather excellent, if anyone was bothering to ask Eva. Those kisses had become more frequent, and the press of Liv against her was something that Eva never thought she'd miss, waking up in the morning in a cold bed alone.

Still, the long, lingering looks that they shared were getting ridiculous.

"You two are the worst," Al announced, folding his arms over his chest and scowling at the pair of them. "First it's angst central over how you can't ever be together, or whatever, now it's just awkwardly staring at each other whenever you get a sec." He made a grand sweeping gesture, as if to shoo them together. "Now, I feel it's my job to tell you to kiss, goddammit. Kiss all the time."

Eva grinned shyly at Liv who threw her head back, laughing long and loud and hard. "Been there," Liv began.

"Done that," Eva agreed.

They giggled.

Al, for his part, simply groaned loudly and slumped back down onto the stool behind the counter. "The worst..." he reiterated, fiddling with the power cord of his laptop.

It was easy to forget all that they'd been through together in this moment, but the wound still festered for Eva. She needed to speak to Theo to clear the air between them.

She waved to Al, promising to come back up to help him move the displays around later, and drifted toward the back room in Liv's shadow. They fell into step so seamlessly that it was odd for Eva to be half a step behind. She slipped into the office and tugged her coat from her shoulder gingerly. She slung it over her arm and stood there, not quite sure how to break the ice with Theo.

He was sitting at the table in the back room, empty boxes open before him and his glasses perched on his nose. He looked thin, far thinner than he'd been before their misadventure. The stay in the hospital had taken a great deal out of him. Al was worried that he'd never look healthy again.

They didn't know why he'd been unconscious for as long as he had, but they had been able to ascertain that he had little memory of what had happened down in the seal room. For that, at least, Eva was grateful. She didn't think that anyone should have to remember such a desperate struggle for his life. Now that she was closer to him, Eva could see how drawn and worn-out he looked. It was almost alarming how quickly the life had come out of him, and she took a hesitant step forward before he looked up. A smile blossomed across his face and he pushed his chair away. He moved slower, too, Eva could see, as he made his way around the table to clasp her gently on her good shoulder. It was all that she could do not to flinch away under his touch.

"I'm so sorry," he said quietly.

Eva looked away, biting at her lip. "I know," she replied. It wasn't all his fault, it couldn't be. There was so much more to what had happened than a simple man who had a fervent belief in something that, according to Eva's world view before meeting him, was not real. The light of the world hadn't been anything more than a tangential connection that she'd used to get his attention at first, and now it had changed her life forever.

Theo took Eva's hand when she offered it to him and led her over to sit on one of the chairs that surrounded the table. She sat and he settled into a chair opposite her, his hands resting on his knees. "Al has told me, for the most part, what happened down there." His brown eyes behind his glasses seemed almost comically large and Eva felt herself smile slowly. "And I truly am sorry, Eva. I had no idea that going down into that place would wreak such havoc on me."

"But why did you go down there without telling us that first time?" Eva asked. If only the four of them had gone down together, there was a good chance that nothing bad would have happened to any of them. The shadow would have been faced with three believers and a guardian to keep them safe. It seemed the perfect outcome, in retrospect.

Theo sighed, his shoulders slumping forward so that his sweater slipped off one shoulder. "I wasn't thinking clearly. I was looking at the truth, Eva. I saw it and I knew it was true—and then I knew no more." He let out a world-weary chuckle. "I guess that's what I get for trying to do everything on my own, though... possessed."

"Something like that," Liv said from the computer table. "But hey, you made it out okay."

Eva glanced over at Liv and she felt a smile tug at the corners of her lips. Liv was smiling to herself, her blonde hair spilling over her shoulders. She was tapping her pen against her notepad and very pointedly not looking at them. It was cute, to see Liv so at ease again. She belonged here, in this dusty room surrounded by books. This was where she could do the most good. Eva wasn't sure if she wanted to stay working at Mr. Bertelli's grocery store forever, but it was enough for the time being. She could spend her time with Liv, and Al, and help Theo out with his projects.

"I am truly sorry that I hurt your shoulder, Eva," Theo continued, resting his fingers gently on her knee for a moment to draw her attention back to him. "It wasn't exactly my finest moment."

She didn't know how to respond to that because somehow, "I'm sorry you got possessed by a centuries-old demon" didn't seem like the appropriate response. Eva bit the inside of her cheek and forced herself to smile pleasantly at Theo. "You got your answer, though."

"I did," he agreed.

They stared at each other for a long time before Theo straightened and leaned over to the table. He picked up a sheaf of papers and passed them over to Eva. "This is all that I found on your grandmother, Eva."

She flipped the pages over. They were covered in Theo's slanted handwriting, detailing everything that they'd found—a loose outline of the time that Mary had known Wren, right down to notes from the old cold case file that detailed the ineffective police search for Catherine Monroe after she'd disappeared. "Why didn't you show me this before?" Eva asked.

"Because I wanted to save it, you know?" Theo ran a tired hand over his face. "I know it was stupid, but I was convinced that there was something more to this than bad memories. My grandmother had a friend who used to tell us stories as a child. She helped a girl hide and the girl disappeared before her eyes. She always told me that was proof enough of the light of the world." He glanced toward Liv and then shrugged. "I figured that there had to be more to it."

"Once upon a time, there might have been," Eva agreed. "Thank you... for this." She wasn't entirely sure what to do with it.

"Liv's told me that she wants to write a book based on your grandmother's journals and some of the documents she found in the Talbot collection," Theo said tentatively. "I'd understand if you didn't want me to help her with it—"

Eva shook her head violently. The thought hadn't even occurred to her. She knew that Theo wouldn't go back down there, and she was pretty sure that Liv had told him exactly what he needed to know and nothing more than that. It would be enough, she reasoned, to simply keep him away from the place.

A few nights ago, Liv had told Eva that there was very little left down in the room beneath the city. The seal had been restored and when she'd made her way back there again, she had found nothing other than darkness. It was, Liv had explained, as it should be. There was nothing for a normal human down there, just rock and mud and memory. The people who would venture down there now would only be those who knew, and even then, Liv had pointed out, they'd never be able to touch the seal.

A wish was a wish, it seemed.

"I want you to help," she said quietly. Her fingers curled around the papers and she smiled brightly at Theo. "This can, I think, legitimize some of your own work."

He inclined his head, and Eva knew that it wasn't the light of the world, but it was close enough. This was the story of a young girl who'd fallen in love, and how her love had gone missing. "I suppose that it might be worth a second try."

Eva nodded, smiling warmly.

"And what about you?" Theo asked. "Are you going to go back to Bertelli's and leave us now?"

"Nah, I don't think you'll be rid of me just yet. I want to help too." Eva glanced over at Liv, who'd set her pad down and was leaning over the back of her chair, her chin resting on her palm, a fond smile playing at her lips. All she wanted to do was tell a story that had been told a thousand times before. This time it would be different, though, the cycle had been broken and the players cast anew.

"Next we'll get you back to school."

Eva shifted, uncomfortable that her secret perusal of college websites had been so easily detected. Theo smiled knowingly. "Maybe," she said.

Theo held out his hand and Eva shook it. There was something final about that moment, as Al called out to them from the front, a question about a book that only Theo would know the answer to. He let Eva's hand drop and stood up on his unsteady feet. Eva watched him go from the room, grumbling about how Al would never amount to anything if he didn't learn the trade.

The papers in Eva's hands were like a weight that kept her steady on the chair. She stared at them. He'd found all of this, all this research he hadn't mentioned until now. "Are you okay with him helping you?" she asked Liv. "And with me helping, too?"

Liv stepped up behind her and laid her hand on her back. It felt warm, lingering just long enough to reassure Eva that she wasn't pulling away.

"I'd like that," Liv replied. Her fingers trailed up to rest on Eva's good shoulder, squeezing gently, reassuringly. Eva reached up and took Liv's hand in her own. There was a future in this, and she knew it. It was definite and she couldn't wait.

"BOOK OF THE WEEK: TALBOT'S GIRLS — TALES OF THE 1920S"

James Hariden – In a debut historical work, Olivia Currance takes readers on a journey back to a time that is very different from our own. While the 1920s are idolized in popular culture, it was a time of great disparity between the haves and the have-nots of New York. Ms. Currance's book takes a critical look at the daily lives of the young women who came to live at the boarding house of one Mrs. Irene Talbot, a noted local suffragette. Through this very insightful window into the lives of these girls, Ms. Currance is able to string together a series of narratives that are eye-opening and page-turning.

I was able to sit down with Ms. Currance and discuss her book, as well as her motivations for writing it.

James Hariden: This is the sort of book that isn't oftentimes written, Ms. Currance. Why did you decide to write about the girls who live at Mrs. Talbot's home?

Olivia Currance: Precisely for that reason, James. There is so much focus on the young men of the 1920s that the women are lost in the shuffle after the 19th Amendment was passed, and they don't come back fully into the historical narrative until World War II.

JH: But why Mrs. Talbot's house? There are so many more like it in the city, some that are far more well-known than that.

OC: A friend of mine's grandmother is actually one of the central characters of this story. When she died, she left behind a series of diaries that detailed her life. My friend came to the bookstore where I work and asked for our help to get to know her grandmother better. The Brooklyn Historical Society was able to lend us the Talbot Collection, from which much of the research for this book was drawn, and through that we were able to piece together the bare bones of a story about what had happened to my friend's grandmother.

JH: So this all mostly started as a favor to a friend?

OC: Something like that, yeah. I hadn't intended to go out and write a book that would be so well-received, if you catch my meaning.

JH: Still, though, it's a wonderful insight into the lives of these young women. Can you tell us a little bit about the characters you've selected and why?

OC: Well, I had to include the story of my friend's grandmother because, honestly, it's one of the more interesting. She worked as a clerk for a lawyer in the city and was all of sixteen when she started. There's Evelynn, who worked selling women's hats and somehow was able to find herself designing them for all the baseball players' wives of the day. Edith, who is probably my favorite, is the most fascinating. She was a teacher who also taught English to the Chinese men who'd come to work in the city during the evenings. She was fluent in three different dialects of Chinese and could write it quite well for a woman who'd never been to China and had no Chinese ancestry at all. She eventually took a train across the country to San Francisco and got a job working for some Chinese businessmen who were investing in the city.

JH: How hard was it to track down some of this information??

OC: (Laughing) Well, James, if I'm honest with you, not as hard as you'd think. Women are usually pretty good about keeping journals and diaries. The hardest part was tracking down the families of some of these girls—a large number of them never married and didn't have children—to see if any papers or journals had been kept.

JH: Well, that's good to know.

OC: Seriously. I was happily surprised.

JH: You focus a great deal on the story of these two girls, Catherine and Mary. Can you tell us a bit about them?

OC: They really did become the focus of the story, didn't they?

JH: They did.

OC: Well, let's see. Mary kept a diary, which made it very easy to find a narrative to string this whole collection of research together. I chose to focus on her at first because I had such fantastic primary source, and from there I branched out to the other girls mentioned in Mary's diaries.

It's serendipitous, I know, but Mary meets this girl with whom she shares this intense connection, Wren—Catherine—on a train. In this day and age you might call it love. The diaries span about a year and really delve into the burgeoning romance between them, only to end in heartbreak. Mary's granddaughter wanted to know more about what had happened to Catherine because there was never any mention of her after that year in her grandmother's papers. That was the catalyst for my writing the book. We spent months researching, trying to figure out who "Wren" was and finally discovered her identity.

JH: I'll bet that was a kick.

OC: Oh, you have no idea.

JH: Are they the girls on the cover?

OC: Yes, I wanted to put them in the cover to give them a chance to be seen out in the world today— where no one will judge them for loving each other. It was a lot of hard work to find that photograph. It made sense.

JH: Well, your work has definitely paid off. The book is a fascinating read.

OC: Thank you.

Talbot's Girls is available online and at most major bookstores throughout the city. It is recommended for all readers and carries no specific content warnings. 8/10.

About Ellen Simpson

Ellen graduated from the University of Vermont in 2010, majoring in political science with an emphasis on media and its effects on society. She is the co-creator and social media editor for the popular webseries, Carmilla, now in its second season. She currently resides in North Carolina but is a Vermonter at heart.

CONNECT WITH ELLEN
Website: http://ellenannes.wix.com/site

Other Books from Ylva Publishing

www.ylva-publishing.com

The Return

Ana Matics

ISBN: 978-3-95533-234-1
Length: 300 pages (85,000 words)

Near Haven is like any other fishing village dotting the Maine coastline—a crusty remnant of an industry long gone, mired in sadness and longing.

Liza thought she'd gotten out, escaped on a basketball scholarship, but a series of bad decisions has her returning home after a decade. She struggles to accept her place in this small town, making amends to people she's wronged and rebuilding her life.

A Story of Now

Emily O'Beirne

ISBN: 978-3-95533-345-4
Length: 367 pages (128,000 words)

Nineteen-year-old Claire knows she needs a life. And new friends.

Too sassy for her own good, she doesn't make friends easily anymore. And she has no clue where to start on the whole life front. At first, Robbie and Mia seem the least likely people to help her find it. But in a turbulent time, Claire finds new friends, a new self, and, with the warm, brilliant Mia, a whole new set of feelings.

The Tea Machine

Gill McKnight

ISBN: 978-3-95533-432-1
Length: approx. 100,000 words

Spinster by choice, Millicent Aberly has managed to catapult herself from her lovely Victorian mews house into a strange future full of giant space squid, Roman empires, and a most annoying centurion to whom she owes her life.

Decanus Sangfroid was just doing her job rescuing the weird little scientist chick from a squid attack. Now she finds herself in London, 1862, and it's not a good fit.

Red Light

JD Glass

ISBN: 978-3-95533-519-9
Length: approx. 109,000 words

Victoria Scotts—Tori—supports her mom, is compared to her cousin, and has a family legend to live up to. She becomes an EMT in New York City and learns who's true, who's not, and who truly loves her. A deep betrayal leaves her questioning everything, especially herself.

Sometimes heroes need a hero of their own. Love, friendship, and loyalty, are tested and pour out like blood under the Red Light.

Coming from Ylva Publishing

www.ylva-publishing.com

Fragile

Eve Francis

College graduate Carly Rogers is forced to live back at home with her mother and sister until she finds a real job. Life isn't shaping up as expected, but meeting Ashley soon begins to change that. After many late night talks and the start of a book club, the two women begin a romance. When a past medical condition threatens Ashley, Carly wonders if their future together will always be this fragile.

Stowe Away

Blythe Rippon

Brilliant, awkward Samantha Latham couldn't wait to leave rural Stowe for an illustrious career in medicine. But when an unexpected call from a hospital forces Sam to move back home to care for her ailing mother, a life of boredom and isolation seems imminent—until a charming restaurant owner named Maria inspires Sam to rethink everything she knows about Stowe, success, and above all, love.

The Light of the World
© 2015 by Ellen Simpson

ISBN: 978-3-95533-507-6

Also available as e-book.

Published by Ylva Publishing, legal entity of Ylva Verlag, e.Kfr.

Ylva Verlag, e.Kfr.
Owner: Astrid Ohletz
Am Kirschgarten 2
65830 Kriftel
Germany

www.ylva-publishing.com

First edition: December 2015

Credits
Edited by Gill McKnight and Lisa Shaw
Cover Design & Print layout by Streetlight Graphics

CPSIA information can be obtained at www.ICGtesting.com
Printed in the USA
BVOW08s0830011215

429000BV00001B/14/P